Lethal Lords
OF THE
A VAMPIRE COLLECTION VOLUME 2

"Lethal Lords and Ladies of the Night is a highly atmospheric and seriously
entertaining collection of vampire (of all stripes) stories." —Doug Draa

SCOTT HARPER

LETHAL LORDS AND LADIES OF THE NIGHT

A VAMPIRE COLLECTION VOLUME 2

SCOTT HARPER

SINISTER SMILE PRESS

Lethal Lords and Ladies of the Night
A Vampire Collection Volume 2
by Scott Harper

Published by Sinister Smile Press, LLC
P.O. Box 637
Newberg, OR 97132

"To Fight by the Light of the Silvery Moon" first appeared in *Monster Brawl*, 2017. ©2017 by Scott Harper.
"Flotsam" first appeared in *Best New Vampire Tales*, 2011. ©2011 by Scott Harper.
"An Upgrade of the Elixir" ©2023
"Night of the Monster Mutiny" ©2023
"Stray" ©2023
"Renfield and the Night Murders" ©2023
"Drinking Buddies" ©2023
"Unchained" first appeared in *If I Die Before I Wake: Tales of Savagery and Slaughter*, 2022. ©2022 by Scott Harper.

Trade Paperback ISBN - 978-1-953112-44-6

www.sinistersmilepress.com

CONTENTS

ACKNOWLEDGMENTS

Many thanks to the following people who lent a helping hand and words of encouragement along the way: Margaret Carter, Steven Pajak, Esperanza Harper, Kevin Glover, Katherine Emily, Bridgett Nelson, Julie Ann Dawson, Douglas Draa, Jerry and Sharon Harper, Chester and Leila Walczak, Diane Smith, Lynne Blaise, and R.E. Sargent. And to my dearly missed mother and teacher Rebecca Harper up in Heaven: Hey, Mom, I'm a writer! You did good!

*To Bram Stoker, a man greatly underestimated in his time,
who made it all possible.*

INTRODUCTION

It is an honor and a privilege to introduce readers to Scott Harper's new two-volume collection of short stories. Over the past four years or so, I've had the very good fortune to work with Scott on a number of scripts for my various comic anthologies, and I've always been most impressed with the quality of his writing. We share similar inspirations and influences, and I find his work is a good fit for my personal tastes. He has a great knowledge of literary precedents and their counterparts in other media, and that background is ever-present in Scott's new books.

From Amsterdam to Atlantis, the darkest jungles of Africa to an intriguing variation of strangers on the train, Scott Harper spans the globe with some intriguing and often sensual tales of vampires in all their many forms. There are some nice twists and turns and enough frights to send shivers through many a reader.

Enjoy this delicious serving of dark delights! I certainly did.

—Kevin M Glover, 2021

GHOUL KING

Flayer observed from under a canopy of thick oak trees as the human tribe prepared for battle. The men with war-painted faces armed themselves with swords and axes and donned leather cuirasses, intent on raiding a neighboring village for supplies and slaves. Flayer grinned, exposing his sharp teeth—he knew these warriors were dead men walking.

A waxing gibbous moon lit the flatland as Flayer rose and signaled his second-in-command. Liverbelch was stout for a ghoul, with a bull neck and thick upper torso covered in battle scars. He sounded the cry, his shrill voice echoing in the night like the clarion call of a hunting horn. Under Flayer's command, the assembled ghouls responded, surging from their hiding spots and descending on the startled villagers like a dark tidal wave.

The lithe flesh-eaters loped across the clearing with unnatural speed and grace, more animal than human, deftly avoiding the warrior's weapons. Their claws quickly tore through leather and skin, ripping muscle and scraping bone. The village men screamed as they died, their blood and entrails splashing on the uncaring ground.

Flayer strode into the battle, a look of contentment on his hawkish face. He sidestepped a thrust from a warrior's blade and slashed the man's throat with his sharp claws. Flayer followed the man to the ground, latching his black maw onto the ruptured neck and gulping down a fast meal of blood and muscle. The sweet flesh filled him with renewed energy and strength.

The ghoul leader's attention was abruptly drawn from his prey to the panicked cries of his people. He watched the human chieftain and his captains enter the fray. The man was larger than his kinsman, his huge frame filled with corded muscle and covered in protective metal. A gold crown inlaid with rubies sat atop his raven-maned head. Confidence beamed from the chieftain's blue eyes as he wielded a massive war hammer. The destructive weapon boasted a heavy flat iron head on one side wedded to a sharp spike on the other. The ground seemed to shake under his strides. He batted the attacking ghouls away, smashing the bones of some and puncturing the skulls of others, leaving a trail of ruptured corpses in his wake. His captains flared out, striking down ghouls with expert precision, their swords pinioning the flesh-eaters' hearts.

Liverbelch tossed aside his most recent kill and moved to intercept the chieftain, but Flayer growled menacingly, calling Liverbelch off. The second-in-command dipped his head, acknowledged the will of his leader, and moved to help the other flesh-eaters.

Flayer sprinted across the clearing and leaped high in the air, his long arms outstretched to tear the human apart. The chieftain stood his ground and punched the ghoul leader in the jaw, a resounding blow that sent him staggering back. The warrior struck him in the chest with the blunt end of the war hammer, splintering bone. Flayer fell to the ground, his arms splayed out to his sides.

The chieftain cautiously approached, his weapon raised spike-side-forward to deliver the final blow. Flayer felt the broken bones in his chest realign and heal. He was not a common flesh-eater—having drunk from the dark veins of Lord Marrowthirst, he possessed uncommon strength.

The chieftain stopped dead in his tracks as Flayer rose with inhuman dexterity to his feet. The ghoul leader gestured with his claws, eyes bright with anticipation, encouraging the human to attack. The chieftain bellowed as he struck at Flayer's head.

But Flayer caught the iron head in his claws. His strength far outstripped the human as he tore the weapon from the man's grip. Flayer seized the astonished chieftain by the throat and lifted him high in the air. He held him there, the man's hands and legs futilely flailing, as if making an example of him for the others to see. The ghoul brought the warrior down across his outstretched knee, breaking his back with a sickening cracking sound.

Flayer tore away the protective metal cuirass from the chieftain's torso and ripped into the exposed stomach. As the paralyzed man screamed in agony, Flayer dug his claws deep and ripped out the stringy intestines in a spray of gore. He stepped aside as his people descended upon the twitching body and fed.

Flayer surveyed the end of the battle. The captains had effectively been dealt with, their broken forms spread out across the field. Liverbelch smashed in the last one's head with a bone club. The man's brains leaked out of his ears and nose.

While his ghouls feasted on their enemies' corpses, Flayer sought out a nearby wooden hut in the slave quarters, his keen senses detecting warm human flesh within. A young slave woman looked out from the entrance. She showed no fear as Flayer approached her.

The woman was attractive, with sapphire eyes framed by flowing black hair. Her features were symmetrical, the nose thin and lips heart-shaped. The cloth tunic she wore emphasized her wiry muscularity, her belly taut below her sculptured breasts. Numerous welt marks discolored her skin, showing ongoing abuse from her master. Despite her circumstance, she carried herself proudly. Flayer felt a tinge of lust swell in his loins, a faded memory of his discarded human life. He reached out to her.

The woman did not flinch as he took her small hand in his bloody claw, nor did she shy away from the cool touch of his sallow skin.

"Amala," the woman said, pointing to her chest.

Flayer nodded in acknowledgment, impressed by her boldness: few were the humans who could tolerate his presence.

But a thin hand wrapped itself in Amala's hair and pulled her back through the portal. Flayer raced in to find an older, pot-bellied man in a red robe striking the woman. Amala fought back, biting his hand and causing the man to scream in agony.

Flayer had seen enough. He seized the slave owner and broke his neck. Amala crouched in the corner of the hut, sniffling, humiliated by the attack.

Flayer paid it no mind. He pulled her gently into his embrace. Her eyes silently thanked him as he led her away from the hut.

The ghouls looked upon her in awe as she walked among them. One of the younger ghouls, a flesh-eater named Gizzard, tried to touch the woman's hand. Flayer clawed the youngling's face, leaving oozing furrows on his cheek. The young ghoul cried out and darted away. The other ghouls kept their distance.

Flayer screeched at Liverbelch, instructing him to pilfer

the chieftain's ornate hut. Liverbelch complied, darting into the large domicile at the center of the village. The remaining villagers, a mix of young and old with women outnumbering men, lingered on the outskirts, hoping for the invaders to soon depart. A few former slaves discovered they were now free and hid amongst the survivors. Flayer ensured that enough young men remained alive so that the village could eventually repopulate and provide a food source for his people.

A boy approached the bloody mess that had been the chieftain, tears in his eyes as he reached down and held the fallen man's bloody hand. The image caught Flayer off-guard, causing long-suppressed memories to flood his brain.

Flayer saw himself as a child in a simple hut, sitting in front of a warm fireplace, his eyes captivated by the dancing flames. "Flayer" had not been his name then, though he could no longer recall his birth name. Mother was setting the small dinner table, the sweet aroma of scented meat, vegetables, and fresh bread brimming in the air. He knew his father was absent, on a mission with the other men to end the scourge of death that had recently visited the town. A mysterious creature preyed on the village, claiming a victim nightly and leaving bloodless corpses in its wake.

Father returned that night, smashing in the front door and letting in the freezing wind blowing down the mountains. A chill ran down Flayer's back as he regarded the imposing figure standing before him. This person was not the same man who had left them two days earlier; instead, it was an alien creature masquerading in his father's form. Father's green eyes were bloodshot and feral, beaming wickedly from black sockets; saliva dripped from sharp yellowed teeth. His skin was fish-white and lined with pale lacerations as if a fierce animal had clawed him. Most of his ample hair had fallen out. His big hands, the hands with which he cradled Flayer and rocked him to sleep at night, were now claws, the long fingers ending in sharp nails. Father had become a creature of nightmare—a monstrous ghoul.

He lunged at Mother as she screamed in horror. The monster threw her to the ground and bit her throat, ripping out chunks of bloody meat. Flayer picked up a blade Mother used to prepare dinner and attacked the creature, but it slapped the knife from his hands, clawing his forearms. The ghoul transferred its strange curse to Flayer at that moment, the poison of its claws seeping into his veins and changing him. He felt a peculiar hunger come over him as Father signaled to him with gory nails, bidding him partake of his mother's corpse.

The lust for flesh was suddenly overwhelming. Saliva pooled hot in his mouth as his teeth became daggers. Flayer dug his newly sharp claws into her stomach, through skin and muscle, tearing out trails of viscera and stuffing them in his drooling mouth. The taste was beyond anything he had ever experienced in his young life, far sweeter than any dish Mother had ever prepared. He savored every morsel as they devoured Mother—the flesh-eater curse was forever sealed.

Liverbelch soon returned with a heavy wooden chest filled with gold coins. Flayer screeched at the boy, scaring it into the protective arms of its mother. The boy regarded him with aggrieved eyes as he was led away.

At Flayer's behest, Liverbelch also retrieved the defeated chieftain's crown from his scalp. Some village women cast looks of derision toward Amala, but the young woman ignored them. Flayer led her and his crew of fiends away from the shattered town, through the dense forest, to the desolate cave they called home. Wolves approached as they traveled but quickly fled back into the woods, steering clear of the greater predators.

Flayer's mind was conflicted as they walked: he knew from experience that Lord Marrowthirst would immediately claim Amala for his own, as the vampire routinely did with anything of value the hunting party returned with. Perhaps he should take his chances and make off with her now? But where would they go, and how would they live? He had been a flesh-eater for many years now and could barely recall the day-to-day needs of human beings. And, despite his many victories as their leader, he doubted the other ghouls would follow him in defiance of the dark lord.

They marched into the dark cave opening, which jutted like an open maw from the base of a barren mountain, its peak hidden in swirling black clouds. Darkness surrounded them as they descended into the earth, the air becoming hot and stagnant. Human skeletons littered the ground, grim evidence of past ghoul meals. Amala walked by his side, firmly gripping his hand.

The tunnel opened into a large, dank cavern lit by dozens of tallow candles. Stalactites hung from the cave ceiling, surrounded by crowded swarms of bats. In one corner stood the weathered skeleton of an enormous bear posed on its hind legs, its vast jaws open in a soundless snarl, held together by strips of human ligament and tendon.

In the center of the cave, atop a massive thrown of articulated bone, sat Lord Marrowthirst.

The ancient vampire was more beast than man. His long canine teeth hung over his thin bottom lip, the tips shining in the ambient light. Marrowthirst's ears were long and pointed, resting on either side of his large bald head. The vampire's nose was short and blunt like a bat's, set beneath black eye sockets framing smoldering crimson eyes. His elongated claws clutched the skull armrests of the thrown in a regal posture. A creature of the dead, Marrowthirst's chest did not rise and fall with the passage of breath; he sat with an unnatural stillness, silently observing like a stone gargoyle from his perch on high.

The vampire was utterly insane, suffering from lunacy

engendered by centuries of endless killing and bloodshed. Where others would see a motley assortment of wretched, pale-skinned flesh-eaters, Marrowthirst beheld a regiment of loyal, splendidly armored knights carrying brilliant-colored banners. He effusively welcomed the triumphant return of his victorious warriors.

"My battalion returns in glory," Marrowthirst said, rising from the throne, a tattered lavender cape spotted with blood-stains trailing behind him. A large bat perched atop the vampire's naked shoulder. "Regal me with the stories of your triumphs, Lord Flayer."

Flayer cleared his throat. He was used to speaking in the growls and screeches that passed for language among the ghouls. Conversing in the long-forgotten tongue of Marrowthirst's native land took great effort and concentration.

"It was as you said, great Marrowthirst, ruler of the living and the dead. The humans were unprepared for our lightning assault."

The vampire smiled. "Gregor is a most wonderful spy," he said, indicating the bat. "Gregor surveilled their activities from the forest for over a week, ensuring success. Here, now, Gregor, is your reward."

Marrowthirst drew a long black claw across his neck, opening a black vein. The bat latched its maw to the viscous liquid that dribbled forth. After a few sips, the creature screeched and flew off into the ceiling to join its brethren. The wound in the vampire's neck healed immediately.

"Your troops fed abundantly after the victory and will be sated for weeks," Flayer continued. "And we bring you gifts to honor your greatness."

Flayer screeched at Liverbelch, who brought forth the gold chest and crown. Marrowthirst bellowed joyfully as he dug his talons in the coins and flipped them in the air. The vampire seized the ruby crown from Liverbelch and placed it atop his enormous head. Though the headdress appeared comically small on Marrowthirst's oversized cranium, the vampire paraded around the cavern for all his retinue to see, striking dramatic poses as if he were a thespian.

Amid his ostentatious revels, the vampire's red eyes suddenly fixed on Amala. Marrowthirst smiled in anticipation as he dropped the coins and moved inhumanly fast to her side, sending several ghouls sprawling in his wake.

"What have we here?" the vampire asked, seizing Amala's chin. He moved her head from side to side, inspecting her. Amala's eyes teared at the rough treatment. She unsuccessfully tried to pull away.

"A queen you shall be, my love," the vampire said. "I will dress you in the finest silks and feed you meals of pure ambrosia. You shall rule by my side, loyal to my every command."

Flayer felt his stomach sink as he listened to Marrowthirst's delusional rantings, dreading the impending need to confront him. He tried to appease the vampire.

"My lord, I beg you to allow the woman to be with me," Flayer said, moving to interpose himself between Amala and the vampire.

Marrowthirst looked shocked at Flayer's impudence, his lips curling in scorn.

"What?"

"Surely I deserve her after achieving so many glorious victories for you. Have I not brought you other women in the past?" Flayer inwardly cringed as he recalled the sad fates of those women, their yellowed bones lying forgotten on the floor of a branching tunnel.

Marrowthirst gave Flayer a perplexed look.

Flayer persevered. "Would it not show proof of your great

benevolence and set an example for the others were you to gift your man-at-arms with a most simple request?"

"Bah!" the old vampire scoffed. He swatted Flayer aside, smacking him open-faced across the jaw. The blow would have taken a human's head off. As it was, Flayer was knocked off his feet, sailing across the cavern and striking a nearby stalagmite. The mineral stone exploded as the ghoul crashed through it.

For a moment, Flayer wondered if his back was broken. He ignored the pain shooting through his body and rose to his feet.

Amala screamed as Marrowthirst licked her cheek with a long black tongue and cooed in her ear.

The triumph in the vampire's crimson eyes reminded Flayer of the first time he had seen those twin burning orbs up close.

His father had spoken to him as they made their way from the village to their new home at the base of the barren mountain, shrieking and growling in a guttural language he intuitively understood. Father claimed to have been gifted by Lord Marrowthirst, elevated by claws of the vampire's ghoul retainers, and inducted into the brotherhood of flesh. The ghoul retinue served their lord, protecting him during the day when he was vulnerable and hunting at night to provide him blood. In exchange, the vampire bestowed his sacred blood on a select few of the brotherhood, strengthening them.

When they reached the cave, the other ghouls had parted like a sea before them. He saw Marrowthirst feeding on a woman he recognized from the village, a woman who had disappeared from her hut just the other night. The vampire sucked greedily at her neck, holding her upright with a bat-like arm. The woman's eyes rolled up in her head as she was exsanguinated.

When Marrowthirst had finished, he cast the bloodless corpse aside and gestured for them to approach.

His father spoke in the squealing ghoul language. "Lord Marrowthirst, this is my son. I have gifted him with the flesh hunger. He will now serve you in all things."

Marrowthirst looked the young ghoul up and down as if inspecting him.

"He does appear to be a fine, strong lad. The future may well look kindly upon him. But his traitorous lineage must be expunged if he is to prosper."

A look of horror crossed Father's feral face as the vampire's intent manifested.

"Little ghoul, did you think I would so quickly forget that it was you who led the village uprising against me, that it was you who drove a wooden stake into my chest as I slept in the daytime?" the vampire asked, pushing aside his tattered clothing to reveal a bloody puncture wound in the chest. "A little closer, the spike would have pierced my heart."

Marrowthirst reached out and surrounded his father's head in his long claws. The vampire effortlessly tore it off with a brutal twist. As the headless body collapsed to the floor, Flayer sank to his knees with it. Grief socked him in the gut, leaving him breathless.

"Forget your old life, child," Marrowthirst said. "Where your father was weak, you shall be strong. I christen you Flayer of the flesh-eaters—embrace your new existence and serve your king well."

The vampire sliced open his wrist and offered his black blood to the young ghoul. The smell of the vitae was overwhelming—Flayer bit into the Undead flesh and gulped down the cold fluid. A new strength flooded his body as the vampire's will invaded the ragged remnants of his soul. He became Marrowthirst's creature in both body and mind.

Flayer fought against the vampire's domination as he brought both of his fists down on Marrowthirst's neck, the cavern echoing with the smack of flesh. Marrowthirst ignored the blow and pushed Amala away. He seized Flayer by the neck in a viselike grip. The vampire's long fingers squeezed together as he lifted Flayer into the air, closing off the ghoul's windpipe and threatening to break his neck.

Flayer panicked as he gasped for air, his hands scrabbling uselessly against Marrowthirst's iron grasp. He looked to his fellow ghouls for aid and saw only fear and helplessness in their bright eyes; they knew it was impossible to oppose the will of the dark lord.

Marrowthirst's eyes blazed in triumph as he shook Flayer like a child in his grip. The ghoul felt the vampire's will clamp down like a trap on his mind.

"Traitor!" the raving vampire bellowed. "Just like your father! The punishment for treason is death!"

Darkness descended on Flayer's vision as he was strangled. His hands dropped limply to his sides.

A vision unfolded before his mind's eye. He saw himself at the edge of a swirling dark pit, sucked inexorably toward the vortex. Father and Mother longingly called to him, beckoning him to rejoin his family.

The illusion ended as abruptly as it had begun; Flayer was thrust back into his body. Marrowthirst suddenly stumbled forward, loosening his clutch. Flayer fell to the ground. He saw a large spike of broken stalagmite protruding from the vampire's back, the Undead creature's black ichor pooling from the wound.

Marrowthirst turned slowly to face his attacker.

Amala shrunk back from the vampire, her hands in front of her to ward off his attack.

"He has infected you with his treasonous ways, my queen," Marrowthirst said. "I will rectify that immediately."

Flayer seized upon the moment, rushing Marrowthirst as the vampire reached for Amala and knocking him to the ground. Rage fueled the ghoul, bitter hatred for the living dead creature as he rained blow after blow upon the vampire's face, breaking bone. The attack forced the stalagmite further into Marrowthirst's back and impaled the bloodsucker's heart. Still,

Flayer could feel the ancient Undead regrouping despite the damage, gathering his strength.

Then the other ghouls unexpectedly descended like a wolf pack on Marrowthirst. Freed from the paralysis of fear and spurred by the courage of Flayer and Amala, they grappled the vampire's limbs in an attempt to pin him to the ground. The Undead monster did not go down easily. A swipe of his claws relieved a ghoul named Viscera of his head. Marrowthirst tore another ghoul's arm from its socket in a bloody spray. His long fangs punctured the forehead of a third ghoul who foolishly tried to bite the vampire's neck.

Yet, where one ghoul fell, two more took its place. Despite his ferocious strength and the aura of dread he projected, Marrowthirst was forced to the ground, each limb covered in writhing flesh eaters. The vampire bellowed, his rage echoing in the cavern.

Flayer bestrode Marrowthirst and smashed his claws through the vampire's chest, digging through muscle and bone until his fingers encircled the cold black heart. The ghoul leader tore the organ free and held it high, black blood spraying in the air.

Simultaneously, Liverbelch buried his claws deep into Marrowthirst's neck. He dug down until he reached the spine, then pulled with all his feral strength, wrenching the vampire's head from his shoulders. The dark lord's body immediately ceased its struggle, though its eyes still batted back and forth in their black sockets, conscious of what was occurring.

Flayer bit deep into the vampire's pulsing heart, draining black ichor from it. The ghoul felt icy tendrils shoot throughout his body, driving out any remnants of the man he had once been. Great strength flooded his limbs as his heart stopped beating, and he ceased breathing. Two ancient curses collided and jostled for supremacy within him, birthing a new and unique eldritch entity.

The vampire's memories came with his blood— Marrowthirst's unlife unfurled before Flayer.

He saw the dark lord as a newly born vampire freshly risen from the grave, tearing aside dirt and stone as he burst from his thin wooden coffin in a grim parody of birth. This Marrowthirst was youthful in appearance, with flowing brown hair framing the handsome features of his face.

His maker, a dark woman garbed in a black grave shroud, awaited him, exuding eldritch power as she welcomed him into her cold arms. Together they ruled a kingdom from atop a great castle, feeding on the helpless mortals whenever they saw fit. Humans betrayed humans, offering their brothers and sisters up to the vampires in the hopes of one day being chosen to join the Undead in eternal life.

But humans were varied; while many willingly groveled before the immortals, some had steel spines and rose to throw off their vampire oppressors. Flayer watched as a sea of mortals armed with swords and stakes descended on the castle, murdering the human servants and stringing their disemboweled bodies from the palisades to warn others. He saw the vampires fight back in all their glory, moving amongst the fragile humans with the force of a hurricane. The Undead shattered spines and severed throats, their regal clothing dripping in blood as they killed and fed, ignoring wounds that would have slain living men a dozen times over.

Marrowthirst and his maker created a mountain of the human dead, a river of blood flowing from the shattered corpses. Yet, the human forces continued to surge in numbers. And while their metal swords and blades left the vampires unscathed, the mortals' wooden stakes drew brackish black blood and inflicted pain.

Flayer looked on as the war reached the stone battlement. Marrowthirst was pushed toward a crenellation by a roiling sea of humanity, his claws tearing bloody furrows in the faces of his attackers as he dug his feet into the stone floor. The sun was cresting on the horizon as he reached out to his sire, feeling his night powers dissipate. The vampire woman fell beneath the human wave, her hands throttling attackers as she was born to the ground. Marrowthirst saw a stake descend as a silver ax flashed down, severing the connection with his maker.

Grief overcame the young vampire as he was pushed back, his strength ebbing as his spirit waned. They threw him through the crenellation, hoping the hundred-meter fall to the ground would end him. Marrowthirst stifled his emotions and concentrated, transforming as his late maker had shown him. His arms and fingers lengthened as leather membrane expanded between the digits. He sailed into the air as a great vampire bat, flying away from the castle and avoiding the rising sun.

Marrowthirst took shelter from the day in an abandoned graveyard. In the nights that came, he hid from the roving bands of humans that sought to end his existence. The vampire soon discovered he was not the only occupant of the graveyard: a score of ghouls called the cemetery home, feeding on the bodies inside the tombs and crypts. These flesh-eaters were quickly overcome by Marrowthirst's magical charm and fell to his command.

Prey in the cemetery area was scarce. Mortals patrolled the highways and warned off unwary travelers. Over time, the vampire's attractive looks faded as he was forced to feed on the dead blood of cemetery corpses and the cursed ichor running in the ghouls' veins. His mind slowly became unhinged as the quality of his food deteriorated. Eventually, the vampire and his flesh-eater retinue fled the cemetery and sought refuge in the great cave.

Control of the cave did not come easily. Marrowthirst's ghoul scouts had inconveniently overlooked the presence of a great Kodiak bear that made the tunnels its home. The beast resisted the vampire's efforts to compel it; Marrowthirst engaged the great bruin in a phys-

ical conflict of tooth and claw. The bear put up a tremendous battle, at one point latching its massive jaws around the vampire's neck and threatening to sever his throat. Marrowthirst called upon the full extent of his Undead powers, his body swelling to tremendous size as he summoned the cave's shadows to him. Brimming with dark energy, the vampire buried his fangs into the bear's neck, tapping a thick vein and drinking the titan dry. Marrowthirst added the bear's strength to his own, the victory making him appear invincible to his cadre of flesh-eaters.

Flayer realized there was now a dark cohort inside him, that more than mere memories had accompanied the vampire's cursed blood. He sifted through the slew of Marrowthirst's recollections, hoping to pinpoint one in particular.

It was shortly after Marrowthirst's rebirth. The young vampire climbed the sheer walls of the castle like a giant spider, side by side with his maker, returning to their sheltered coffins after a night of feeding. Marrowthirst reveled in his new abilities.

"Strength, speed, supernatural resilience, even shape-changing... is there no limit to the extent of our powers?" he asked.

"You forget our greatest strength, young one," the dark woman counseled. "Our memories are transferred with our blood in the blood kiss. When we create a fledgling, as I did with you, we pass on all our knowledge, the accumulated wisdom of centuries. Each newborn vampire is superior to the one who created it, ensuring the vampire race will continue forever and never become extinct."

The dark woman's words uttered millennia ago now proved prescient. He looked upon Amala with fresh eyes, hearing the deep thunder of blood pulsing through her veins. He seized her mind with his new powers, overwhelming her will and dragging her into his cold embrace. At his command, she exposed her neck.

The bat Gregor flew down and perched on his shoulder, acknowledging the new leader of the cave. Flayer buried his long fangs into Amala's neck while the other ghouls looked on. He would elevate her to vampire status and make her his queen. Starting with Liverbelch, he would bestow his potent hybrid blood upon select cadre members. Empowered by his blood, his minions would achieve even more significant victories in his name.

The world would not soon forget the name Marrowthirst.

ISMINI AND THE BLOOD OF THE BULLMAN

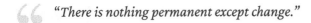

"There is nothing permanent except change."

— *HERACLITUS*

The thin, pale woman stood beside her mother, nearly hidden in the shadows of the dark and crowded cage, bodies pressed against the slick stone walls. The floor was wet with small pools of water and human waste, the stale air ripe with sweat and the stench of fear and misery. The mother kicked away a large rat that had ventured too close, apologizing to another woman when the rat scurried toward her.

"Where is your brother, Ismini? Where is Talos?" Alcippe fretted, her eyes red from bouts of crying and lack of sleep. Their simple dresses were covered in dirt and filth.

Ismini shook her head in frustration; the soldiers from Crete had separated the young men from the old after the initial attack on their tiny village. She did not know what had become of him. She moved away from the closest water pool, fearing the others might note that the dirty liquid refused to replicate her image.

Like the rest of their village, Ismini and Alcippe had been forced to trek for long miles in the hot afternoon sun. Some older men and women couldn't keep up and were left stranded without food or water on the roadside without food. The rest were directed into a cave opening at the base of Mirmingaris, the tallest peak on the island. They descended into a dark tunnel, passing dozens of decomposing, worm-infested corpses along the way—Ismini wondered how many poor souls had been condemned to a similar fate over time. Many of the prisoners began to gag and wretch at the horrid smell. Eventually, they were herded into a murky pen that appeared more suited for animals than humans, where they waited, hungry and exhausted, for further indignity to be heaped upon them.

Ismini gazed out through an opening in the grimy wooden slats at the surrounding torch-lit arena. An intimidating, scar-faced Crete soldier guarded the pen, spear cradled in one hand, an iron *xiphos* blade hanging from a sling under the other. His eyes and mouth squinted in distaste as he looked with contempt at the prisoners. He spat on the ground near Ismini.

The vast underground arena was crowded. The curving polygonal stone tiers were arranged so the people in the rows above could see the action on the sand without their vision obscured by the people beneath them. The seats were filled with a mixture of favored native Kythirans and conquering Crete attendees. The Kythiran were collaborators, traitors who had sold out their fellow islanders for promises of wealth and power under the incoming regime. They had used their positions of authority to aid Glaucus's invading army. The Crete soldiers had been allowed to land secretly—the shore guards having mysteriously not reported for duty that fateful night—and never faced any concentrated opposition.

The lowest section directly across from the pen accommodated the royalty, including the conquering King Glaucus. Despite the great distance between that section and the cage, Ismini's keen eyes showed her that he sat in majesty on a dais, dressed in a magnificent flowing blue robe, a crown of gold resting on the thick hair of his head. He was accompanied by his Queen Sidonia, a former concubine whose abundant bedroom skills, honed to perfection over years of practice, had infatuated the young king—so much so that he never allowed her to leave his side. Her visage betrayed the scorn she felt for the people of Kythira with every cruel look. A squad of the king's finest armored soldiers surrounded the royal couple, wearing shiny bronze cuirasses and helmets, armed with spears and swords.

A full moon shone through the open top of the theatron, an opening carved into the very ground of the island itself. Ismini thrilled to the touch of the moonlight as it pricked at her skin, the cold beams invigorating her in the oppressive heat. The sunlit march she had endured earlier had greatly taxed her strength.

She was impressed by the majestic scope of the theatron. If the rumors were to be believed, Glaucus had employed a nephew of the great architect Daedalus himself to construct it. It stood to reason that the stories were credible. Glaucus was the son of the late ruler of Crete, King Minos, the man who had previously commanded Daedalus' services toward the creation of the famed Labyrinth.

Trumpet blare echoed off the stone walls and roused nests of skittering bats to flight. Ismini saw one of Glaucus's chosen purple-robed toadies rise and bow to the king before addressing the crowd.

"Good people of Kythira, noble guests of Crete, witness the

glory of the great King Glaucus, first son of Minos of Crete! Tonight, we spill blood in honor of the great and benevolent god Poseidon, Bearer of the Trident, so our magnificent island may always stay in his favor! That the seas remain calm and teeming with fish! Great Poseidon, carry us on a gentle breeze and summon a favorable wind as we begin the winter solstice!"

Ismini grimaced at the false piety of the toady's words. They rang hollow amidst so much manufactured suffering.

The trumpets sounded again. A heavy metal gate underneath the royal section opened, and four haggard men walked forth to loud jeers from the hostile crowd. The men were dressed only in loincloths, their slick wet skin gleaming in the moonlight. Each was armed with a weapon—two carried traditional *xiphos* swords, one a double-headed *labrys* ax and the other a bronze mace. Their faces were grim as if resigned to their fate. Ismini immediately recognized one of the countenances as her missing brother.

As the men moved to the center of the arena, Alcippe also recognized her son.

"Talos!" she shouted, pushing close to the cage. "Ismini, it's your brother!"

"Yes, Mother," Ismini mouthed, but her attention was focused on Talos. She recalled Glaucus's soldiers breaking into their home in a lightning attack, killing her ailing father in his sleep. Talos had fought bravely to defend his family, wounding the soldiers with his bare hands before falling to their superior numbers. Ismini tried to resist, but the bright morning sun drained her strength. Soon they were all beaten and chained.

Their abductors didn't give them time to mourn or bury their dead. They were pushed at spear point into line with the other survivors. The bodies of the deceased littered the ground. The village had not been taken quickly—a score of bloody soldiers lay amongst the dead in mute testament. They were herded initially toward New Crete in the south, where the invading Glaucus had established his new capital some time ago—a port city founded for trade and communication with his homeland, Crete. The soldiers then diverted the death march at Mirmingaris.

"What is that bastard Glaucus going to do to him?" Alcippe asked. Ismini remained silent, afraid to panic the older woman. She knew her mother's question would soon be answered in a manner not to her liking. Glaucus was not a man of wit or study —the day-to-day grind of democratic politics was above his modest intellectual capabilities. History was replete with the tragedies of such men thrust into power. Rather than govern, they sought to distract the mobs from the daily drudgery of life with games of violence.

They watched as a section of the arena ground lowered into the earth, sending dirt flying. As the dust settled, Ismini saw a dark opening leading into an underground tunnel. Thunderous footfalls augured the arrival of a massive being.

The toady addressed the audience and the king once more.

"The blood spilt tonight will sanctify this sand, making it holy ground! My lord, behold Poseidon's vessel! Behold—the Minotaur!"

The bipedal creature that stomped up through the opening on broad black hooves was a terrifying composite of man and beast that could only have been conceived in a lunatic's night-mare. It stood twice as tall as a man, massive quadriceps muscles separated and flaring in slabs off its thick bones. The creature's upper torso was equally impressive, sectioned abdominal walls rising from a blood-stained leather loincloth before resting under dense pectorals. The broad shoulders and trapezius were covered in thick, coarse dark fur that flowed from the massive horned head of a bull. A tail danced in the air behind it.

The creature exhaled a fetid, wet snort through its black nostrils and stomped the ground as if daring the men to attack it. The arena echoed with the impact. All four men backed away from the bullman. Its slavering black lips curled up in a snarl, exposing sharp yellow teeth; black predator eyes reflected the torchlight. It moved its massive head from side to side, taking in the entirety of the theatron. The Minotaur carried an enormous wooden club in its hands, a weapon the size of a man.

Ismini was stunned at the sight of the beast. The Crete King Minos was rumored to have fathered at least once such monstrosity, but the beast had supposedly been defeated in a pitched battle with the Athenian hero Theseus. Either rumors of its death were greatly exaggerated, or Minos had fathered other such creatures. Ismini wondered if Glaucus considered the bullman to be his brother.

The creature bellowed in rage before launching itself at the men. The first man, a shorter fellow with a stocky frame and wavy hair, screamed in horror and bolted. The Minotaur quickly covered the distance in long strides, goring the man through the back on one of its horns. The horn was so long that it traveled through the man's torso and erupted from his sternum, tearing out a lung. The bullman tossed the dying man back into the air with a flip of its muscular neck. The other men avoided the falling body, which hit the ground headfirst with a sickening snap.

The Minotaur walked over to the dead man, raised one of its hooves, and crushed his head in an explosion of blood and gore. It roared a victory cry, raising its hands overhead. The crowd shouted their approval.

Ismini breathed in the scent of fresh blood in the air, her tongue sliding over her sharp teeth. She was sickened at the crude, wanton waste of life that masqueraded as a form of religious sacrifice, but the darkness that infected her soul was attracted to the violence. The beast within her stirred—it was hungry.

She watched as Talos bravely attempted to lead the other men in a counterattack. Their father had possessed some skill with the blade, and he'd schooled Talos in the art before he'd become sick. Talos directed them to flank the beast to either side while he faced it head-on. Unfortunately, the men, both simple farmers, were undisciplined and didn't listen. The first man attacked prematurely and swung his ax into the beast's clavicle. The metal head bounced off without penetrating the skin.

The Minotaur snarled and lashed out with its fist, pulping the man's head like a ripe fruit. The corpse fell, brain matter scattering on the ground. The other man struck with his mace, smashing it into the bullman's back. The bronze blade shattered on impact. Still holding on to the useless hilt, the man looked up in terror as the Minotaur raised its club high and brought it down with prodigious force, shattering his sternum and driving broken bone into his heart.

The crowd roared at the man's death. Glaucus smiled and clapped his hands as his creature dug one hand into the man's bloody remains. It extracted a length of ropy intestine and slurped it down like a giant noodle. Alcippe began to cry again.

As Ismini looked on, Talos warily circled the creature. She was proud of her brother and the courage he had shown. It was typical of him, the older brother who always defended her from street bullies and looked after her when she was sick. Close in age, they spent many afternoons running about the village and through the woods, fighting imaginary creatures, lost in their own childish world. Talos had even shown her in secret some of the martial skills their father had taught him. Ismini had proven to be an apt pupil.

But times had changed, and they were no longer children.

Ismini resolved to defend Talos and claim vengeance on her father's murderers at all costs. And, unlike the other prisoners, she had the means to do so.

She had been reluctant to use her unique abilities since the night she was attacked. She had felt debased, a creature of darkness forced to hide in shadows and masquerade as a human woman.

She had returned home late one moonlit night from the market, bringing some fresh fish for the family. Her mother had warned her not to stay out so late, as Glaucus's soldiers were known to be violent and take liberties with local women. And there were always whispered legends circulating of the ancient *lamia*, old wives' tales of female demons roaming the night searching for blood.

A large, sweaty soldier had set on her. She dropped the fish as he pulled her from the main roadway into a dark corner, one callused hand covering her mouth to prevent her from screaming. He began to grope her with his other, attempting to pull off her clothing. Her eyes teared in fear and shame as she fought back, clawing at his face and kneeing him in the groin as Talos had instructed her. As the man reeled, he pulled a blade from a harness slung beneath his arm and slashed out, opening her throat. Ismini fell to her knees, clutching the wound as her lifeblood flowed out of her. Cold saturated her body. The soldier recovered and approached, holding the blade high in the air, ready to thrust it down.

Ismini wondered if the blood loss caused her to imagine things. A shadow descended with great speed on the man, knocking him away. She saw a pale woman hold him helpless in an iron embrace, long-nailed hands digging into his throat and drawing blood. He bucked and kicked but was no match for her strength.

Emerald eyes blazed from within black orbits set deep in the woman's ashen face. She smiled, revealing serpent fangs as her jaw distended. Scales were visible on the areas of her skin not covered by the white shroud that trailed out behind her and fluttered in the evening breeze.

The soldier's eyes teared as the woman bit into his neck and drank. He attempted to scream, his face red with rage, but failed due to the vise grip around his throat. His eyes glazed over and rolled into the back of his head as he was exsanguinated.

Then Ismini found herself in the woman's cold embrace, the emerald eyes looking down at her.

"*Lamia*," Ismini mouthed.

"Sister," the creature replied, her brilliant white teeth shining in the moonlight as she grinned. Her breath was sweet and smelled of anemone, the blood flower that thrived in the meadows. Despite her crushing strength, the *lamia* held Ismini gently and with more passion than any man had ever exhibited toward her.

The *lamia* extended her long tongue and licked the wound on Ismini's throat, coating it and staunching the blood loss. Ismini hovered on the brink of consciousness as the *lamia* savored the taste of her blood. She felt the *lamia's* teeth on her neck, penetrating an artery like twin icicles. Cold lips kissed her throat. The teeth were quickly withdrawn—Ismini had little blood left to give.

"Blood is life, sister, and human life is all too brief," the woman said in an ancient dialect. She tore at her shroud, exposing her ivory breasts, the nipples colored like olives. She raised a sharp-nailed finger and sliced a small cut across the areola of her right breast. A clear liquid dribbled out. Ismini found herself aroused, despite the blood loss. She opened her mouth and latched onto the breast like an infant, her tongue pulling at the wound. The *lamia* gently pressed the back of Ismini's head forward, encouraging her in a soft voice. Ismini drank the cold, sweet ichor. It filled her with an intoxicating sense of euphoria, far more exhilarating than any of the bumbled attempts at juvenile lovemaking she had with the young men of the village. The *lamia* arched her body in ecstasy, her spine curving like a snake's, head thrown back. Darkness descended on Ismini's vision as the *lamia* moaned in delight.

She woke the next night in a shallow grave. Dirt covered her eyes and filled her nostrils, but she did not panic. New instincts told her that she no longer needed to breathe to live and that it was time for her to rise. Strength flowed through her cold body as her claws easily tore through the loose earth. She rose in a flurry of dust to find the *lamia* waiting for her. Ismini recognized the area of her burial near the graveyard on the outskirts of the village.

"New life requires a period of death first. There is always a sacrifice," the *lamia* said. The creature wore a fresh white shroud.

She spoke to Ismini at length about her new existence. Ismini could resume a normal life with her family and masquerade as a human if she so desired. She would be weak during the day but immensely strong at night. She was now Undead and could not be destroyed by conventional means—only weapons forged of wood or bone could harm her. Water would reject her and refuse to reflect her image. She could not cross it except at the slack or flood of the tide. The light of the moon and her native soil would give her comfort and strength. As a being that had conquered death, she could now summon the recently dead to her aid. Her gaze would fascinate mortals while her touch would enflame their lust.

The lamia concluded her lecture. "And you will need to feed on blood, young one, on human blood to keep strong. Though you cannot starve to death, you will wither and age without it, becoming little more than a sentient piece of carrion, tormented and undying."

Since that night, Ismini had subsisted on goat and cow blood, afraid to feed on locals for fear of discovery. The grainy animal fluids kept her alive but weak. She knew she would require more strength for what she would attempt tonight.

She eyed the guard through the wooden slats. Like everyone else in the arena, he was distracted by battle, his thick jowls shaking in laughter as the men died. Ismini turned to her mother and saw that Alcippe also was distracted by Talos' peril.

She seized the moment and slipped through the aperture between the slats; her body could fit through the smallest openings. Ismini struck the big man to the ground like he was a child. She tore the protective leather *gorget* from his throat with sharp fingers, then buried her fangs into his neck. She drank greedily, feeling the hot liquid pour down her throat and force the aching cold from her body. The man's blood was much more potent than the animal blood she had subsisted on—she wondered how she could ever settle for less.

Sublime, she thought.

Her teeth secreted venom that slowly took effect, numbing the soldier's nerves. He moaned in pleasure, overcome by the ardor of her kiss. Ismini felt his throbbing erection through the loincloth. By the time his blood ran out, he had long ceased struggling.

"Ismini!"

She looked up from her feast, blood dripping from her lips, to see her mother staring at her through the cage slats with a look of horror on her face. She attempted to resume her human visage, but her bloodlust was up, and she could no longer hide her true face. Other people in the pen looked on in shock as well.

"I'm sorry, Mother," Ismini said. "I did not ask for this curse. Please forgive me. I must see to Talos."

Mentioning her brother's name prompted her to purpose. She turned and moved swiftly across the sand to where Talos battled the Minotaur.

Her brother had proved himself to be a man of grit. Though bloody and bruised, Talos had defied the odds and was still on his feet. Roaring in fury, he swung his sword across the bull-man's chest, but the blade could not penetrate the beast's thick flesh. He delivered a front kick to one of its knees, hoping to break the joint and cripple the monster, but it was like kicking iron. The creature ignored the blow, seized Talos' sword, and yanked it from his grip. It squeezed its fist and crumpled the metal without effort. The Minotaur raised its club above its head with both hands, poised to strike the final blow.

Ismini saw Talos look up, his face a mixture of resignation and exhaustion. He appeared prepared to accept his fate.

Ismini was not.

She reached her brother before the club struck, tossing him out of the way, then twisted to avoid the blow. The ground shook from the impact.

The Minotaur bellowed in anger and dismay at the newcomer who had robbed it of another victim. Ismini did not cower. Instead, she stepped forward and punched the bullman in the jaw. The blow echoed in the arena like a thunderclap. The crowd rose to its feet in awe as the Minotaur stumbled back, amazed that a small woman could stagger a creature of legend.

Ismini turned to Talos as he rose slowly from where she had thrown him, amazement on his face.

"Protect our mother, my brother," she said.

Talos stood with resolve, seemingly unaffected by the fanged visage his sister now wore, and nodded his head. He headed toward the cage that housed Alcippe and the others.

The bullman used Ismini's distraction to its advantage. Its long arms gave it a reach advantage over the much shorter woman. The Minotaur delivered a tremendous backhand blow to Ismini's head, sending her reeling into the bloody sand where the bodies of the men it had killed lay.

Ismini quickly recovered, rising from the ground. The bullman was taken aback—its opponents seldom rose after being knocked down.

She looked at her hands covered in bloody sand and felt an eldritch connection to the dead men.

The newly dead are yours to call to your benefit, the *lamia* had said. Ismini seized upon that connection, using the blood as a medium to force her will into the corpses. Like broken puppets, the dead men staggered to their feet, a strange light in their eyes, possessed by an unnatural will not their own. Brain matter and innards trailed in their wake as they shambled forward on unsteady limbs.

The zombies surrounded the bullman, who snorted in shock, having never confronted the resurrected dead. It flinched as they approached, its nose assaulted by the fetid odor of fresh decay spurred on by the unusual heat of the air.

The dead men launched themselves at the beast, wrapping themselves about its limbs and neck, holding on with untiring strength. The Minotaur bellowed in pain and rage as their teeth attacked its hide. One zombie drew blood from the bullman's throat, the eldritch energy fueling its existence making its attacks more lethal than sharpened iron.

The Minotaur regrouped and fought back with all the unbridled strength at its command. It seized the zombies one at a time and raised them overhead before smashing them to the ground. It piled them on top of one another, creating a heap of writhing carrion, their mouths open in silent screams, before trampling the broken remains into bloody mush with its huge hooves.

Ismini felt her connection to the zombies severed. The Minotaur turned to face her, its mouth set in a snarl. It lowered its head and charged, kicking up clouds of dirt in the air. Ismini moved out of the way at the last second as the beast rocketed past, barely avoiding the sharp horns, knowing that she would suffer the true death should they penetrate her cold heart.

She lashed out with her claws, tearing a hole in the side of the Minotaur's throat. The bullman reeled as blood flew like a geyser into the air. It began to panic—no one had ever hurt it before. The creature's iron hide, usually impervious to mortal weapons, had somehow been slashed open by the claws of this strange pale woman.

The Minotaur frenzied, striking Ismini across the sternum with the club. Pain flared through her as the wooden weapon crushed the bones of her chest, lifting her high off the ground. She fell hard on her back some thirty meters away.

She felt the ground shake as the beast slowly staggered toward her. The bones in her chest began to reform as the bullman stood over her. Its blood dripped slowly from the neck wound and pooled in her mouth, where her tongue greedily lapped it up.

The creature collapsed to one knee, straddling her chest. It struck her in the face with heavy blows, which would have instantly destroyed a mortal. But the bullman's fists, for all their might, were not weapons of wood or exposed bone. Ismini felt the impact but was not incapacitated. She drew upon her innate shapeshifting abilities, just as she had witnessed the *lamia* that turned her do. Her skin scaled and became thicker, assuming a deeper green hue akin to a snake's hide. The Minotaur's blows bounced off her body with little effect.

Ismini felt the power of the beast's unnatural blood flood

through her. Combined with the light of the full moon and the strength she drew from contact with her native soil, the young *lamia* had never felt so potent. Her wounds were completely healed.

She twisted away from the next blow, which plowed into the earth, creating a huge hole, and then used the Minotaur's thick arm as a lever to vault herself around onto its back. She reared her head like a serpent and struck, biting deep into the open wound on the bullman's neck.

The bestial titan screamed in agony as she drank its lifeblood, rearing and trying to throw her off. Ismini dug her claws deep into the sides of its ribcage. She removed her mouth from the wound, her eyes glowing with power, then reached forward and seized a horn in each claw. Using all her unnatural might, she pulled back and ripped the horns messily from the Minotaur's forehead—the night exploded with a sound of rending flesh. The creature screamed in unimaginable pain. Finally spent, it collapsed to the ground, lying prone, its gargantuan chest heaving in exhaustion.

Ismini walked over to the beaten bullman and placed tiny foot on its chest. It looked up at her in defeat, eyes glassy, its thick tongue lolling out the side of its mouth. She looked at Glaucus, who stood in outrage and disbelief. She raised the horns high over her head in a victorious gesture. Her people chanted her name from behind the cage. Ismini saw that Talos had broken the lock and was setting them free.

She dropped one horn and pointed that hand toward Glaucus. She turned her thumb down and then slammed the horn in her other hand through the Minotaur's chest, splintering bone and impaling its heart. The bullman shuddered and was still, its pupils constricting in death.

Glaucus screamed at his soldiers.

"I want her head!"

They swarmed the sand and attacked, thrusting at her with their spears and blades. To Ismini, their movements seemed pathetically slow compared to the Minotaur—she easily avoided the blows. She became a hurricane of violence as she waded into the soldiers, her claws tearing throats and severing spines in an orgy of blood. She smashed their heads with her tiny fists, breaking thick bones like so many eggshells, their bronze helmets offering scant protection against her strength. She seized a soldier by the arm and swung him in a circle, knocking several others off their feet. She tore the arm from the soldier's torso and used it to beat the downed men to death. Ismini ignored the wounds she incurred from their metal weapons, which could not inflict lasting injury on her.

More soldiers came in successive waves. Despite her power, she feared she might be overwhelmed and captured again. But then the battle was joined by Talos and the other freed villagers, who picked up discarded weapons and engaged the Crete soldiers. She saw her brother thrust his blade under the mouth of one soldier and out the top of his head. Nearby, a group of freed Kythirans held down another soldier and speared him through the neck.

Ismini carved a path for herself to the stands, a trail of eviscerated and dismembered corpses in her wake. The majority of the crowd was screaming and panicking, attempting to flee. Dozens were trampled in the mad crush of bodies. She saw Glaucus and his queen being shepherded through the chaos by his soldiers. The toady speaker lay broken on the floor, his purple robe now besmirched with crimson, trampled to death.

Ismini defied gravity and flew into the stands. The soldiers guarding the royal couple looked up in awe and terror as she descended onto them like a bird of prey. She dispatched them quickly, breaking their necks like twigs. Sidonia attempted to scream, only to have her cry cut short by a slash of Ismini's claws. Her face contorted into a death masque as her head toppled off the bloody stump of her neck.

Ismini looked down contemptuously at the king, who cowered before her, raising a shaking hand in supplication.

"Please," he begged in a quavering voice, "I can give you whatever you want. Money, power, and titles...whatever you desire! You cannot kill a king!"

Ismini noted indifferently that one of the dead soldiers had managed to drive an iron blade into her sternum. She casually removed it from the bloodless wound and addressed the groveling Crete.

"You have nothing to offer me, little king, nothing at all. You are a sad little man who fancies himself a ruler of men when he is not a real man at all. You are a pretender and an oppressor, an inhuman, effete slug so bored with his prosaic life that he amuses himself by debasing and murdering others. My brother is a real man—he instills confidence in others, as did my father. Your men killed him as he slept, a harmless man in his dotage. You should know his name before you descend to Hades—Critias. Say his name, little king. I want to hear you say his name." She leveled the blade in front of his mouth.

"Cr...Critias," said Glaucus, spittle trailing at the corners of his mouth.

"Yell it!" Ismini demanded, her eyes seething with anger and power.

"Critias, damn your eyes!" he yelled, saliva flying.

"Enough." Tired of wasting her time on so insignificant an insect, she thrust the blade through his open mouth, scattering his brains on the ground. The gold crown slipped off his head as his torso collapsed.

Ismini picked up the crown and turned toward the arena. Talos and the people of Kythira stood triumphant, the remaining Crete soldiers having surrendered after significant losses.

She saw her brother comforting their mother and made her way toward them.

They looked in awe at her—she was both a monster and a goddess. She handed the crown to Talos.

"The people will need a leader who leads by example and not fear," she said, smiling.

"Sister..." Talos said, unsure how to express his desire for her to stay. However, his gentle eyes showed his acceptance of the existence into which she had evolved.

"I must go," she said as if reading his thoughts. "I've hidden from the world for far too long." She looked over at the corpse of the bullman. "Our people will not want a monster in their midst. Nor do they deserve one."

"Where will you go?" Talos asked.

"There are stories of other monsters that plague humanity —gorgons, Cyclopes, beasts with three heads. Perhaps I will introduce myself. Wherever I go, you will always be in my thoughts. You will always be my family."

She rose into the night sky, embracing the moonlight.

COFFIN CONVERSATIONS

onversations between dead men can be more stimulating than one might imagine. Generally speaking, dead men are dead for a reason—i.e., someone (or something) intervened and ended their lives. Having crossed that plane, Joe and I often while away the early morning hours in my basement after he has fed. Joe sits on the lid of his wood coffin, long-nailed arms crossed over his black waistcoat in a classic gesture of defensiveness. Raven-black hair frames his hawkish nose and the asymmetrical lines of his sharp features.

Joe has placed a lit candle to one side, casting flickering shadows across the room. Of course, the candle is superfluous, as we both have excellent night vision, the burning wax representing a half-hearted stab at conveying a look of suburban normality.

I linger untiring near a neglected furnace. Besides the coffin and a folding table, the room is mostly barren. Cobwebs trail from the ceiling corners, occasionally fluttering on a stray breeze creeping through holes in the termite-abused wood.

Joe has "lived" for centuries, a lifespan that provides ample ground to draw inspiration for discussion. "Joe" is not his real name, of course. He's Hungarian by birth and has used numerous aliases to cover his tracks. In his youth, Joe ran afoul of a toothy baron and has been a night person ever since, if you catch my drift.

Many of Joe's tales revolve around his nightly "cull," as he refers to it—how he selects his prey and stalks them before draining their blood. He has a good sense of narration, carefully laying out the characters and the story's historical and political setting. He transports you to different times and places, making you feel almost like you were there yourself.

Not limited solely to this earthly material plane, Joe can blend in with the shadows and move like quicksilver—his victims never see him coming when he strikes, and his strength is overwhelming. Sometimes he feeds too frequently or stays in the same area too long, drawing unwanted attention. That's when his unlife gets really interesting.

I met Joe three years ago. I exist in an old wooden two-story house at the end of a cul de sac in a sleepy suburb in the Northeast. It was built in the 1950s and then redone in the late seventies.

I first saw him walking down the middle of the street late one October night, carrying a heavy wooden coffin over his shoulder like it weighed nothing. Lucky for him, there's not a lot of foot traffic on our cul de sac, especially in the evenings. He walked up the marble steps of the portico and through the open front door and then dragged the coffin down to the basement, where he put it in a corner next to the furnace. He later told me he thought the house was abandoned. I can't say I blamed him —the house has fallen into a horrid state of disrepair since I died. The paint is chipped, the windows are boarded up, and the lawn grass is patchy and filled with weeds and gopher holes

—though the gophers, like the rats, have become less of a problem since Joe arrived.

Joe didn't seem particularly surprised when I spoke to him the first time—he'd encountered my kind before. He said he was "unconsciously" drawn to dwellings with such "phenomena." When I manifest, my ectoplasmic form is tough on human eyes, but Joe didn't blink. He apologized for entering my home without first asking for permission. His last resting place had been discovered and was no longer safe.

I'm bound to this house because of how I chose to end my life, or at least that's what I tell myself. A part of me wonders if I'm only here because of stubbornness and an obstinate, egotistical refusal to let go of something that's not there anymore. I prefer to be alone—I'd manifested and scared off at least three real estate agents and their clients over the first six months of my spookship. Not only was I offended by the sheer audacity of their attempt to take my home from me, but I also found their stale chatter quite annoying, mostly pap about quality schools and little league teams. Three disastrous showings were enough—no agents have shown up since. So I've not had anyone to talk to all these years.

But Joe was different. We could relate to each other on many levels, especially the "eternally-cursed-to-walk-the-earth" ordeal. It was nice for a change to hear another mature voice in the house.

I was able to speak freely to Joe without fear of being judged. Unending bloodshed and horror had filled Joe's existence; the details of my life seemed almost quaint by comparison.

I told Joe a story that first night he arrived—the sad tale of a young beat cop, an all-American boy fresh to the force and newly married. A man in love with his wife, a husband by day, and an agent of justice by night. The young couple settled into their new home and planned to start a family.

The happy story took a dark turn a few years later—long hours at work drove a wedge between husband and wife. The harsh work environment wore away the vibrancy of youth and turned the cop hard and cold. He dealt with the worst humanity had to offer daily, and it began to rub off on him. Uncharacteristic meanness surfaced in him, and profanity began to lace his vocabulary. He shut himself away from her, feeling she would be unable to understand or relate to his experiences; he feared she would reject the man he had become.

The cop ran into an attractive young woman on a call in the beat he patrolled, a woman with whom he soon started an affair. The wife noticed that her husband was no longer interested in sex with her; he hadn't held her in his arms in months. She wondered what had happened to the man she had married.

The young cop's mistress was married to a convict who just happened to be released early from prison due to the pandemic. Fate had set the downhill spiral of the young cop's life in motion.

I explained to Joe how the woman's husband found out about the affair one Christmas Eve and beat her bloody for her sins. With a lead pipe in one hand and her hair in the other, he dragged her screaming from their tawdry downtown tenement, through suburban streets, up the cul de sac to the officer's front door. The cuckold kicked in the front door before moving to the living room and smashing all the Christmas tree ornaments and wrapped gifts. He proceeded to air all the dirty laundry in front of the cop's terrified wife. She broke down in tears, devastated by the betrayal.

And I told Joe, I said, "Joe, the thing with cops is that there are always guns around somewhere. And when things get terrible, tensions get high, and things start breaking, those guns tend to go off. Somebody screams or makes a threat, and the next thing you know, the weapon is in your hand, and the safety is off. Holidays with all their stress and depression don't help either. And that night, before he knew it, the young cop overreacted; he killed the cuckold, his mistress, and his wife. The floor was awash in blood mixed with broken ornaments and tree lights. He stood there shaking with the murder weapon in his hands, his duty weapon, the instrument society had trusted him with to protect the helpless, listening as the police sirens wailed and grew louder, knowing they were coming for him this time.

"And the young cop panicked and did the most cowardly thing imaginable, committed a heinous act for which there could be no forgiveness—instead of taking the blame for his actions like a man, he shoved the gun in his mouth and fired. And cursed himself to a spook's eternal half-life in the process."

Of course, the young cop had been me (despite the dramatic third-person narrative). Speaking in the third person seemed to provide some metaphysical breathing room, allowing me to broach the otherwise unspeakable.

Joe seemed to take it in stride. His crimson eyes smoldered in the darkness, the tips of his sharp teeth catching the light of the single candle atop his coffin. The candle had come from the kitchen upstairs, one of those tall ones that can stand independently without a holder. It had an apple cinnamon scent that clung to it—Alisha always told me the smell calmed her nerves and reminded her of being in the kitchen with her mother when they baked homemade pies for Christmas.

"Monsters always hurt the ones they love," Joe said. "It comes with the territory. And we are both monsters, my friend." The candlelight reflected off his eyes like the night predator he was.

"It was the holiday season then as it is now—Santa Lucia's

Day—I'll always remember it," he continued. "After the Baron turned me, I dragged my father to the top of the nearest church and impaled him on its spire. I screamed at the stormy heavens as I left him on display for the entire town to see when they woke that morning. My reasons for committing fratricide have become lost in the mists of time—I can't recall why I abused his corpse so. Don't be too hard on yourself, Mort. At least your days of wholesale slaughter are over—mine continue every night."

I took some modest comfort in his words, hearing a different perspective on my life's tragedy.

"Were you ever in love, Joe?" I asked him in the present moment, breaking the night's monotony.

"Love is not for us. In my youth, I was captivated by a girl. She was instrumental in my becoming the creature you see before you. She told me she loved me but betrayed me to her lord and master when it suited her purposes. They tried to steal my family fortune—very foolishly—but that is a story for another night. Know this, my friend: love is a lie, a grandiose but empty term created by foolish poets to distract people from the harsh inequalities of life, to give meaning to an otherwise pointless existence." Joe scoffed, looking away. "You would do well to avoid it."

"Maybe not," I replied. Joe's brows furrowed in surprise that meek-old me might possess the testicular fortitude to disagree with him.

I pictured Alisha's smiling face as we walked in the woods with autumn leaves dancing in the air around us, her warm hand in mine, the sunlight reflecting off her light brown hair, and the joyful face she wore until I pushed her away. "What if it is real, only we're too weak to keep it alive? What if it is something you need to fight for each day; otherwise, it might slip away and get trampled by this crappy world?"

"Bah!" he spat indignantly. "We are beyond such fairy tales."

"If I could go back in time and change things, I would. I would quit my job and find some other way to support her. I would never meet the other woman or her brute husband. I would worship the ground Alisha walked on and celebrate every day as if it were our first day together."

Joe sighed. "I never knew you were such an orator, Mort. I sympathize with your plight, but we are damned and beyond redemption. You delude yourself with pie-in-the-sky illusions. Yearning for a past that no longer exists only causes unnecessary anguish."

"While you're comatose during the day, I scour every inch of this house, looking for just the slightest anomaly, a system glitch that might allow me to escape—a gateway to an alternative universe or timeline with other possibilities. The scientists call them hyper-dimensional gateways."

"You watched too many episodes of *Dark Shadows*," Joe asserted.

"Said Barnabas to Quentin," I countered.

"Have you ever considered that you are not cursed, that no supernatural force binds you to this house? Perhaps you exist merely on spurious hope and desire, a pipe dream that someday, by a fortunate stroke of luck, she will miraculously return and forgive you for your actions?" Joe queried.

"I exist; that is all I know," I intoned, ending the conversation.

Joe's returned quietly to his coffin as the sun crested on the horizon. I redoubled my efforts to find some way to escape my predicament, searching for any means of egress I had overlooked.

Around seven, I was disturbed by sounds upstairs. I sifted effortlessly up through the basement ceiling and looked out the window at the cul de sac. The sky was beginning to brighten, night giving way to purple gloaming. I noted all the surrounding houses decorated with shiny, multicolored Christmas lights and ornamentation. Some owners had forgotten to turn their lights off the previous night. As usual, Joe and I were taking a break from celebrating the holidays, our dark house the only undecorated one on the bloc.

I heard a heavy crash and suddenly found a mammoth Santa Claus standing in my living room, the red-attired man having smashed in the front door rather than shimmying down the chimney. The man wore the customary white and red fur-trimmed cap with a flowing white beard. Unlike the fictional Santa, however, this imposter was not jolly. Instead, he appeared pretty irate as his frantic eyes searched the room. At first, it seemed he wielded a huge candy cane in one hand, the end broken and sharp. On closer inspection, I noted the item in question was made of wood and painted in red and white stripes to look like Christmas candy. This unfortunate turn of events did not bode well for Joe.

Santa had a massive angry scar running down the middle of his face, starting high on his sweaty, pronounced forehead and trailing down to his cheek. I could imagine Joe's sharp claws inflicting such a wound, though Joe had not yet told me the gory details of this particular story.

Santa Scarface quickly found the basement entrance, tossed the door aside, and rushed downstairs. I sifted through the vinyl floor, running various scenarios through my mind, only to discover the lout standing next to Joe's coffin. Mayhem flared in his eyes as he knocked aside the candle and threw back the coffin lid.

Joe was unconscious in the daytime, sleeping the Undead's sleep on a pile of Hungarian soil, the earth he died in and was reborn. His hands were protectively crossed over his chest, shielding his unbeating heart. It would take a severe ruckus to rouse him.

Santa Scarface ominously raised the candy cane stake over Joe's unmoving chest with both hands.

Joe had confided to me that wooden stakes were lethal to his kind. I had to do something—and quick.

Before the oaf could plunge the stake home, I manifested in front of him.

My manifestation reflects how I died—Santa Scarface saw a decaying yellow skull wailing in his face, broken brown teeth falling out of an ebony maw, viscous brains dripping from the bullet exit wound in the putrescent forehead. A graveyard scent ripe with hints of almonds and sewage flooded his nostrils, making him gag. My wormy brown tongue writhed out of my mouth as I spouted some gibberish about defiling the sacred resting place of Mortimer Todd, making it almost appear the trespasser had broken into a hallowed tomb and unleashed a pharaoh's curse. The words came out like a banshee's wail; a glop of my ectoplasm sloshed into his eyes, a goo with a slimy consistency similar to freezing vomit.

Santa Scarface bought it all—he screamed like a newborn. A stream of hot urine gushed down his pants legs. That bizarre combination of sound and smell was all it took to rouse Joe from his sleep—and he was not a happy camper.

The next thing I knew, the cane-stake flew across the room and punctured the wall like a Christmas harpoon. A feral roar echoed off the walls as Joe defied the laws of physics, levitating to a standing position without ever bending his knees. He seized Santa Scarface by the neck in a single clawed hand and lifted him high into the air like the big guy weighed nothing. The lout's feet kicked frantically; I heard vertebrae breaking in his neck as a mewling whimper escaped his lips.

Joe turned to me, fangs out, a deranged, evil look on his face.

"I take it you two are acquainted?" I asked mischievously.

"With Santa here? Doesn't ring a bell—sorry for the bad Christmas pun." The faux Saint Nick's constant thrashings caused his cap and beard to fall off.

Joe smiled maliciously. "Oh yes, I recognize him now—unfinished business from the last town I left. I guess he was trying to blend into the neighborhood as Santa while he plotted to impale me with that wooden peppermint stick. Thanks, buddy. I owe you." Then his head shot forward, and he buried his teeth in Scarface's neck, feeding noisily.

As Scarface died painfully and messily and without dignity, I shrugged what passed for my shoulders.

"Don't mention it, buddy," I said. "I can't imagine going through the rest of eternity with no one to talk to." As the intruder's body spasmed for the final time, I couldn't help adding one last comment. "Another Christmas down the tube —I'm beginning to think there's something wrong with this house."

Redemption (if it were ever to come for us) would have to wait for another season.

JOE WENT BACK TO SLEEP AGAIN IN HIS COFFIN, THOROUGHLY SATED. I had other plans—Santa Scarface had given me an idea.

I looked at the Santa corpse and imagined myself in it. I drifted over, centered myself above it, and let go. My astral form fell into and merged with the corpse.

I blinked my new eyes and found I could see, getting a

ground-level glimpse of the basement floor. The next challenge would prove to be more difficult.

Focusing my power, I willed the corpse to stand. It took a while, the broken bones in the fellow's neck refusing to comply at first, but eventually, I staggered to my feet. I said a quick goodbye to Joe as I mounted the steps to the first floor.

My progress was slow—it took all my energy to animate Santa's corpse. I stumbled across the living room and made it to the open door. I closed it as best I could, hoping Joe would be able to fend for himself, then staggered down the street, leaving the house for the first time since my untimely suicide.

The morning was still young, and only a few people were awake. I passed one of the local homeless men a few blocks on. He gave me a puzzled look, undoubtedly disturbed by the bizarre hue of my dead skin and the strange, rigor mortis–challenged nature of my gait. He offered me a sip of his coffee, which I kindly declined with a spastic wave of my hand. I moved on, my new head lolling unnaturally to the side.

I breathed in the scent of the new day, the air crisp in my dead lungs. It had been so long since I had been outside. All the sights and sounds of the morning filled my borrowed senses, reminding me of the life I once enjoyed. I heard the birds chirping, smelled the heady aroma of sizzling bacon and fresh-roasted coffee, and saw new cars whizzing by as people made their way to their relatives' houses. They were so caught up in their affairs that they failed to note my purloined corpse shambling along the side of the road.

The cemetery gates were closed when I arrived, but I was not to be denied this day. I channeled all my supernatural will into the corpse's substantial muscles and pulled on the thick metal gate barring the entrance. After much effort, the metal screeched and finally yielded. Access to the grounds was mine.

A sixth sense drove me to Alisha's grave, toward the back of the lot and near the larger crypts. Someone, presumably her parents, had recently left a bouquet in front of the tombstone to honor her memory.

"Alisha Todd," the tombstone read—my wife, whom I had so greatly wronged.

I collapsed to my knees on top of the grass. A plaintiff wail escaped my dry, dead lips.

"Please, baby, please forgive me!" I begged, releasing my hold on the corpse as I did so. I sank through the turf and dirt, down through the lid, until my essence surrounded her remains. I felt a vast sense of comfort envelop me, all the years of angst and misery washing away. There was no hostility toward me here; as always, Alisha seemed to have found a way to overlook my tremendous shortcomings.

I was welcome and at home, feeling like I had never left.

I let go of everything as the darkness embraced me.

JANOS AND THE NIGHT WAR

J anos woke to the smell of spilled blood—old, rich, and inhuman. His keen eyes penetrated the cave's darkness as he rose from his resting place of earth. His lover Lysandra stirred beside him.

A waxing gibbous moon had crawled high in the night sky, its brilliant silvery light prickling his skin and invigorating him. He took a deep breath of the chill mountain air and let it fill his lungs.

In the distance, the city of Carsteen burned, thick black trails of acrid smoke curling toward the heavens.

"Janos!" a male voice called.

He recognized the voice, despite the passage of centuries. Morgan stumbled from the forest edge into the clearing leading up to the cave. He bled from dozens of arrow wounds, one bolt having smashed out the front of his left eye. The fine clothing he typically was so fond of displaying was covered in gore. His flesh was burned and peeling as if exposed to caustic flame.

Janos saw that Morgan had delivered some damage of his own. The noble Undead's claws were caked in torn flesh; his fangs rested over his pale bottom lip, dripping stolen blood.

By now, the others had woken and exited the cave. Lysandra, as always, stood by his side, her long raven hair and worn cape fluttering noiselessly in the evening breeze. She, like the others, was naked, unconcerned with the need to cover her lithe Undead flesh. The mountain cold did not affect her.

"They're coming, Janos," the wounded vampire wheezed through arrow-punctured lungs. "I know you thought you could sit this one out with your people hidden in the woods, but they know where you are. It's not just the Moors now—they've added a demonic ally to their already substantial forces. Their sorcerers have resurrected an ancient tomb king, Sebak The Unrelenting, from the pyramids of Kemet. The creature is possessed of great power and appears invincible; I barely escaped with my head intact. I tried to warn you."

Morgan collapsed forward. Janos caught him easily and handed him off to some of his people. The wounded revenant could be restored with time and blood—his bloodline was strong.

The day Janos always feared had finally come. He'd tried to live apart from humanity, isolated and feeding on wild creatures, while Morgan and others of his kind sought to blend in. A predator could not live peacefully with its prey—Janos had known this for some time.

The Moors had been on the rampage for many years, feverishly intent on expanding their empire. They knew the strengths and weaknesses of his kind. He could hear hundreds of armored feet thundering through the forest, approaching the cave. Combined with the power of an ancient Risen Dead, they would be unstoppable.

But Janos had never been one to shirk battle. His preferred culls were great Kodiak bears, creatures that tested the extent of his strength and hunter skills. He "lived"—so to speak—for the hunt, grappling with the enormous brutes, fang against fang, claw against claw. Their hot blood flooded his mouth, scalding his throat before entering his veins. Each bruin he killed added its strength to his own.

With a gesture, he summoned his people. Life in the forest had brought out the beast inside them. Their hair had grown long, their ears now pointed like wolves. Moonlight reflected off their predator eyes and razor fangs. They fed as he fed on the forest predators. Upon his command, they sprang as one noiselessly to the trees.

Some were content to leap and swing from tree to tree with effortless grace. Janos and Lysandra grew black, membranous wings from their backs and flew, leading the others.

They soon found the Moors. The invaders had difficulty traversing the thick forest, causing them to splinter into groups. The cavalry suffered disproportionately, the uneven terrain making the horses stumble and slide; some toppled unceremoniously to the muddy ground, crushing their riders beneath them.

Janos initiated the attack. He swept down and pulled a screaming Moor off his mount, his talons digging through the man's leather cuirass and tearing into the soft flesh beneath. He rose high in the air, lifting the heavy warrior over his head. Janos dashed the helpless Moor down into a group of his colleagues, flattening them.

Nearby, Lysandra had torn the helmet from another soldier and fed from his neck. Distracted, she didn't see the man's colleague approach silently from behind, his sword raised high.

Janos sped to her side. He plucked the sword from the man's grasp as if he were a child before plunging it through his chest and pinning him to a tree. The Moor's feet kicked impotently two feet above the ground as he bled out.

All around the forest, Janos's people slaughtered the Moors. Despite their wooden arrows and silver swords, they were still human and out of their element in the darkness of night. To Janos, their movements seemed pathetically slow, as if they were moving through molasses.

Suddenly, brilliant amethyst light flashed through the trees. Janos heard his people scream and die again. He watched as Arnau, an old and seasoned hunter, was blown to ashes by a concentrated blast of eldritch energy. Janos shed his wings and ran toward the source of the destruction, his feet barely skimming the ground.

In a small clearing, he saw Sebak. The ancient Risen Dead still bore the weathered linen wrappings it had been buried in millennia ago. Power surged from his empty black eye sockets, twin holes of hellish darkness, as he raised two of Janos's hunters into the air, one in each claw. The Undead struggled against the iron grip, tearing great chunks of withered gray flesh from Sebak's forearms, but they were children compared to the ancient tomb king's fury. Sebak unleashed his power, bathing the two Undead warriors in the surging energy of his death magic and instantly reducing them to churning dust.

Janos sensed that the dark energy that sustained the vampires was now gone, greedily siphoned by the ravenous tomb king. Typically, a vampire reduced to ash could still be reconstituted with the proper rituals and a fresh blood supply. Such was not the case here—these vampires could not be resurrected.

The deaths of his men struck Janos like a blow; he felt their blood ties to him suddenly cut off. Janos roared with primal rage as he flew at Sebak, covering the distance between them with incredible speed. He smashed into the tomb king with tremendous force—the ground shook from the impact. The vampire unleashed a series of vicious claw strikes, blows that would have cut a Bucovina warhorse in two. Sebak staggered back, large bloodless wounds opening up on his torso and neck as dust and ancient sand clouded the air. Janos thrust his claw deep into the mummy's chest, smashing through magic-strengthened bone, seeking the mummy's desiccated heart. He found only sand and disintegrating linen.

A gurgle that might have been glee came from the creature's withered throat. Sebak encircled Janos's forearms in a hold stronger than steel. The Risen Dead's grip was so cold that it burned the vampire's skin as it leeched his dark energy. Janos struggled as he felt his strength flow into Sebak, but he could not free himself; his knees buckled to the ground.

The tomb king's black maw opened in ecstasy as he luxuriated in his dark banquet. Then he transferred his lethal grip to Janos's neck. The vampire felt his vertebrae separate and pop as Sebak began to twist his head off. Decapitation would ensure his true death.

Sebak's jaw was abruptly smashed to the side, ancient yellow teeth flying in the air. Lysandra had arrived. She rained blow upon powerful blow on the Risen Dead's skull, her face a mask of righteous fury.

Sebak recovered quickly, blasting her away with a scalding bolt of light from its claws. She screamed as she was flung aside, a shooting star in the darkness.

Janos used the distraction Lysandra had provided to his advantage. He thrust one claw up under Sebak's jaw, his taloned fingers projecting through the top of the mummy's skull. Simultaneously he swept his other claw in a backslash across Sebak's throat, severing the mummy's spine.

Janos held the tomb king's shattered skull in his hands. Power still seethed in the black eye sockets, but the mummy was clearly defeated. The skull's mouth stretched wide in a silent rictus of rage.

Immortality denied, Janos thought.

The vampire closed his hands, grinding Sebak's skull into a

putrid oily powder. He shoved the viscous matter into his mouth and forced it down his throat. The death energy in Sebak's remains flooded through his system and pulsed in his veins; his muscles swelled, and his red eyes bulged. Janos gazed upon a new world, seeing the ley lines of dark magic that flowed around him. His mind was aflame, the thoughts and ideas rattling around like moths trapped in a bottle.

The vampire reached out and touched that magic, absorbing it into him. He used a fraction of that power to raise the Moor dead from where they had fallen, tethering them to his will. The dead staggered to their feet, ignoring the wounds that had killed them, and joined Janos's army of the night.

Around him, the rest of the Moors fell before his people. He found Lysandra nearby at the base of an old cork tree. Her body steamed in the evening cold, her pale skin now scorched and peeling. She was old, though, with many centuries behind her; she could survive.

Janos dragged a hapless Moor to her and peeled back his armor as he might the skin of an apple, exposing the man's fragile flesh. With serpentine speed, Lysandra battened her fangs on the man's throat, barbed teeth burying deep in a pulsing artery. She fed quickly, gulping the hot blood down her throat. When she was finished, she stood restored, her wounds rapidly healing.

"What now?" she asked.

Janos felt another presence in him, a dark will that offered to guide him.

Sebak, Janos thought. The dark presence tittered, a sound like wind whistling through a graveyard. The tomb king was truly immortal.

Janos's mind was inundated with ancient images, the life history of the mummy. He looked out through Sebak's eyes upon a sea of people bowing before him at the base of a great pyramid. They chanted his name in adoration as he spread his cloaked arms wide in a gesture of gratitude.

I have ruled empires and commanded conquering armies. There is much I can teach you, Night King; much you must learn.

Janos's mind swelled with a new purpose.

"Once Morgan is healed, he will restore order to Carsteen," he said. "All the dead there are now mine to command—they shall accompany us as we visit the Moors in Maghreb and show them the errors of their ways."

Lysandra's crimson eyes smoldered in the darkness as she smiled approvingly. Inside Janos's head, Sebak laughed.

AN OCEAN OF BLOOD

> *"The ocean is an object of no small terror."*
>
> — *EDMUND BURKE*

The sea parted before him, leaving a rippling emerald wake in his path as curious seagulls flew overhead. A flying fish launched itself into the air on the starboard side, gliding on its wing-like fins over the choppy water like a mini Icarus, the fading sunlight reflecting off its scales; it paralleled his progress for a dozen yards before submerging.

The chill wind blowing over his swarthy face made him shiver despite his thick wool shirt and jacket as he held the steering wheel tight in his strong hands, the roar of the outboard motor obliterating all other sounds.

As the sun sank behind black cumulous clouds on the western horizon, Rowan scrutinized the boat's compass on the cockpit's dashboard, ensuring he maintained the correct heading. He knew from experience that it would be easy for him to veer off course if he wasn't careful. Like all good skippers, he had a radio to call the Coast Guard for help if that became necessary.

He yawned, tired from a restless night squirming in bed. He took a can of cola from the plastic drink holder attached to the armrest of his captain's chair and sipped at it, trying to get some caffeine in his system.

He'd had such *dreams* recently.

The reveries followed a standard sequence of events: A woman of tantalizingly dark beauty welcomed him into the gloaming of the sea, the pallor of her long white arms at odds with the surrounding shadows. The icy waters chilled him, but he found warmth in her naked embrace. Strangely, he no longer needed to breathe. Her crimson lips smothered his with a fiery passion he'd never experienced with a woman before. She used her powerful chartreuse tail to propel them down into the welcoming obscurity of the ocean depths.

Rowan would wake in a cold sweat, his painful erection throbbing against the threadbare covers of his messy bed. At first, he felt shame remembering his late wife, who had lain so many nights beside him in that same bed. The cloying residue of the lifetime fidelity he had pledged to her lingered and remained anchored in his psyche.

He met Amy in his final year of college, finding himself attracted to her physical beauty and buoyant personality, which contrasted markedly with his introverted nature. They dated for some time before deciding to get married. She had supported his decision to become a fireman and provided much-needed encouragement during the grueling months of the fire academy. She prepared his cooked meals and sack lunches. Their love for each other was quite passionate initially —Rowan could recall the eagerness he felt returning home from a long shift at the fire station, waiting to enfold Amy in his arms. But as time passed, his hours spent at work increased due to staff shortages, and they put their plans to start a family on hold.

Amy worked as a secretary in a local real estate office. Feeling neglected by Rowan, she had lapsed into an affair with one of the company executives. That relationship ended messily when the man's wife returned home from the store early one day to find her husband making love to Amy in the bed the couple shared. A humiliated Amy had been forced to confess her infidelity to a shocked and wounded Rowan.

Recalling the events now caused Rowan emotional pain, almost causing him to drift off course as an entirety of gut-wrenching memories came unbidden and flooded his brain. He breathed in the chill sea air, letting it settle in his lungs as he attempted to calm himself.

Though he had done his best to forgive Amy, their relationship was never the same afterward. They lived in the same house, paid bills, and shared meals, even watched television together on the couch. But he never made love to her again, never once held her in his arms and kissed her. She never asked him to, though he could see the hurt in her eyes when he would roll away from her in bed to turn off the nightlight before going to sleep.

And they continued living together, still technically man and wife, until the plague struck. Amy contracted the virus volunteering in a hospital, her lungs filling with fluid and her blood becoming septic. Within a week, she was in the ICU in the same hospital. Medical understanding of the novel virus was limited; the doctors were at odds over how to treat her. Rowan held her hand as she waned, ignoring the nurses' insistence that she remain isolated.

She apologized to him on her deathbed for all the hurt she caused him, tears dripping down her pale, withered face. He forgave her and told her he loved her, asking her to forgive him for his coldness. He was at her side the night she passed.

Afterward, he tried to move on. World leaders urged people to maintain social distance and live in isolation. Separation from his fellow humans had not proved problematic for Rowan. He remained sequestered in his modest home in the harbor, content to spend his afternoons fishing and whale watching in his weathered Boston Whaler, only encountering other people at the market or the gas station.

Rowan had retired early due to a bad fall from the second story of a burning house that had shattered his right knee and shoulder. The rehabilitation had proven to be long and grueling, the progress agonizingly slow, hampered by the fact that he was now middle-aged and did not heal as quickly as in his youth. He'd planned to return to work but soon realized that he could never perform his job to the same standards again. His debilitating injuries would make him a liability to his employer and the men and women he worked with. He reluctantly took the lean retirement package the city offered him.

Rowan had attempted to rehabilitate himself fully with the financial security afforded by a modest but reliable monthly stipend directly deposited into his bank account. During his tenure with the department, he'd spent a lot of time in the station gym, honing his muscular physique. But he soon discovered the permanent nature of his injuries prevented him from enjoying workouts now, the pain becoming unbearable after a certain point, and gradually he spent less and less time exercising.

Reeling from the loss of both Amy and his job, Rowan underwent months of depression, feeling he had lost all sense of purpose in his life. Rowan took to the ocean seeking stress relief and mental stimulation, motoring out of the harbor and trolling for cod in the afternoons. The fresh air and quiet renewed his ragged soul.

Using the boat's sonar device, he'd stumbled upon an underwater reef that few local fisherman knew about, a reef only a half-hour's drive northeast from the harbor jetty. At low tide, portions of the reef would become exposed, piles of multicolored coral rock forming tiny ephemeral islands. Thick beds of luxuriant green kelp rose to the surface, attracting many fish species. He'd done well angling there, keeping one or two fish for food while throwing the others back to catch another day.

As he cast his reflective lure toward the kelp in the evening twilight, he often felt a strange presence watching him from nearby, the light touch of another mind tickling his psyche. Sometimes he heard great splashes that were too big to have been caused by a fish. When he turned, he saw an odd wake in the water, suggesting a large object had submerged quickly. Once, he made out a luminescent shape, racing just below the surface, paralleling his boat before diving out of sight. He'd accidentally sliced open his hand while fileting a cod on another occasion. When he put his hand into the water to clean it, he imagined a white face was gazing up at him from beneath the spreading pool of blood, studying him. He pulled his hand out quickly in case it was a shark.

Initially, Rowan had attributed these disturbances to seals or dolphins, both species frequenting this area of ocean. But then the odd erotic night dreams had begun, and Rowan could no longer shake the feeling that he was being surveilled. He set out to resolve the matter for his own sake of mind.

Night was falling as he approached the underwater reef, the whaler's bow silently slicing through a thin mist as he cut the engine and drifted slowly forward. The air was strained, like the electric calm before a storm. The hairs on the back of his neck stood on end as he passed through the ethereal fog. Rowan shut off the front masthead light, leaving only the red and green bow lights on. He pulled back on the throttle, halting the twirling propellers.

The silence was profound.

For the first time, he saw her clearly, emerging from the luminescent fog. It was the woman from his dreams.

She reclined seductively on a tiny coral island, her right elbow hanging on a small rock ledge, her lower body partially submerged in the water. She smiled at him, her fiery blue eyes piercing the night, warm and inviting from their perch over high cheekbones. He found her fair, unlined face quite irresistible, calm and youthful. Thick brown locks flowed down her head and framed her exotic countenance, resting on top of the perfectly sculpted mounds of her breasts, her nipples dark and smoldering against the luminous alabaster hue of her skin. Her taut belly descended into a shapely long, fluked tail that floated in front of her, moonlight reflecting off the particolored blend of sapphire and emerald scales.

She slipped into the water with casual grace, submerging momentarily before surfacing in front of his boat, head bobbing in the waves as her wet hair floated on the surface like a dark halo. He felt her mind reach out and touch his before seizing his will, her voice calm and soothing in his head.

Be with me. I've waited so long for you, Rowan, her voice said as she dipped below the waves. *Longer than you can imagine.*

A rough mix of emotions and memories surged through him: desire and guilt, fear and longing, temptation and revulsion and lust. Lust won out. Though he recognized the insanity of his actions, Rowan rushed to the bow and jumped into the cold water, feeling its iciness engulf him as he plummeted beneath the surface. Briny water filled his mouth and gagged him. He was on the verge of panic when strong arms surrounded and comforted him like a child. Her warm lips covered his, breathing sweet oxygen into his lungs. He wrapped his arms tightly around her, crushing himself to her, feeling the swell of her breasts, the strength latent in the powerful back muscles resting beneath her soft hair. His erection throbbed against the zipper of his jeans, seeking release.

Her clawed hands tore quickly through the wool thread of his pants, releasing his cock, which he immediately thrust inside her, seeking warmth from the cold. She sighed as he entered her, biting his ear gently and nuzzling his face before taking him down further into the ocean depths. He bucked with pent-up emotion and energy before exploding inside her, unable to contain his orgasm.

He maintained his prolonged erection inside her, caught up in ecstasy, as he felt her sharp teeth extend, slicing open his tongue. His blood flowed into her mouth, giving her strength and warmth. She returned the favor, pricking her tongue and letting her thick ichor fill his eager mouth, sliding down his throat. The blood acted as a medium between them, allowing Rowan to read her thoughts more easily.

It was I that you saw in the water the day you cut yourself, she said. *I tasted your spilled blood, savored it, as I now savor your seed inside me. It connected us, allowing me to reach out to you in your dreams. I felt the loneliness of your wounded soul, the pain you've suffered through so nobly. I, too, have been wounded and known loss. We are kindred souls, you and I, broken and abused.*

Time seemed to suspend. Through the blood tie, he saw who and what she was, her life laid out before him in a torrent of vibrant images.

He viewed her many years earlier when she was a young girl named Darla. She had lived in this area of the Northeast when it was first settled by the Puritans, near a long-vanished town called Innsmouth.

Her mother had meant the world to her, the woman's love

for her only child all-consuming and unconditional. But the journey across the Atlantic from Britain had been difficult and fraught with peril—her mother became ill from scurvy and slowly wasted away, dying before the ship made land. A hole opened in Darla's heart, a wound she feared would never heal.

She sought comfort in her father, someone with whom to share her grief, but the man, a religious authoritarian named Hiram, spurned her affection. Persecuted in his homeland for his unorthodox religious beliefs, he secretly resented being forced into the role of a single father.

"You're weak, just like your mother," Hiram castigated. "God punishes me for your weakness."

He took out his frustrations on Darla and scrutinized her every move with a sharp eye.

As she matured into adulthood, Darla began to explore her sexuality. Hiram caught her one day in the arms of a young boy from the village and became incensed. He'd beaten the boy with a wooden cane bearing a wolf's head metal tip and thrown him from the house. After administering a more thorough beating to Darla, Hiram had taken her from home and tossed her in a small boat, rowing feverishly to one of the small islets dotting the waters around New England.

"Father, please don't hurt me," Darla had begged him.

"You sully the family name with your whorish behavior. You can no longer live in my house. I curse the day your mother conceived you," he shouted, his words laced in vitriol.

He's abandoned her on the islet without food or shelter, sand and stone and gnarled wood her only companions, ignoring her fervent pleas for mercy as he rowed away.

She suffered the tortures of the damned, starving and shivering for three days as freezing rain fell on the islet, soaking her to the bone, her energy dissipating with each passing hour. She hovered at death's door by the third night, resting her wasted body against a fallen timber on the beach. The storms had dissipated, and a new moon dazzled the night sky. She watched the ocean part through bleary eyes as a strange hybrid creature, neither man nor wolf nor sea lion, yet sharing aspects of each, came ashore. The beast's face became more human as it approached her, its clawed hind flippers morphing into legs. Before her stood a tall and wiry man, his eyes beaming bright crimson from within dark eye sockets, his teeth white and perfect as he spoke to her with his mind.

I heard your cries of betrayal, even in the vast and lonely depths of the sea. A great wrong has been done to you, child. Do you wish to live? Even now, I feel your life ebbing away. I can give you the power to punish the one who wronged you, the strength to live through the centuries, potent and eternal. I am Legride of the Enkidu.

With the last of her flagging strength, Darla nodded her head. Legride lifted her from the ground with ease, parting the simple waistcoat she wore with sharp fingers. He bit into her breast and suckled there with a passion she had never imagined possible. She moaned in ecstasy as he drained her life away.

Legride lifted his head and cut his upper lip with a long nail as her breathing became shallow. Dark ichor seeped out of the wound as he transferred his mouth to Darla's and kissed her. She felt the coppery ambrosia fill her mouth. Her breathing slowed as her heart sputtered and stopped.

As the scene played out before Rowan, he heard her voice in his mind. *The ritual was the same then as it is now, Rowan. As Legride chose to gift me, so I choose to gift you.*

Rowan saw a transformed Darla, now an *Enkidu* filled with vibrant dark power, rise from the sands that were her makeshift grave. She changed into a gigantic black and gold eel that slipped into the choppy water, her lithe, smooth form generating powerful body waves that allowed her to move at tremendous speed. She swam to the shore of her father's village and rose from the ocean like a vengeful spirit.

Altering her form again, she became a dark fog that drifted through the empty streets. She located the wood and clay structure that had been her home and seeped through the small opening under the front door.

She resumed her human appearance in Hiram's room.

"Hello, Father," she said, waking Hiram from his rest.

Her father rose from his bed to confront her, snatching a crucifix from a nearby table and raising it to shield himself from her attack. The symbol of his faith, the faith they shared, caused her some discomfort, but she succeeded in knocking the crucifix from his hands. His strength was no match for hers as she lifted him from the ground and threw him into the wall. He slumped to the floor, broken pieces of clay scattered around him.

Hiram struggled to rise, but the impact had broken his back. Darla leaped upon him with panther agility, burying her mouth in his neck. He screamed and begged forgiveness as she tore out his throat and drained him dry, leaving a desiccated corpse, its visage forever set in a grimace of agony.

When she finished feeding, she stood and let her head roll back, her eyes closed, savoring the hot blood sliding down her throat and flushing the cold from her body. She was thrilled by the heady sensation of new strength filling her arms. Then she wrapped her fingers around her father's head and ripped it from his shoulders, the torn spine dripping clear fluid on the floor, ensuring he would not rise from the dead as she had.

She spoke to Rowan again as her blood circulated throughout his body, healing his old injuries and greatly magnifying his strength.

Our people are millennia old, Rowan. We are connected by the blood we share. In the pre-cataclysmic days before the oceans drank Atlantis, our kind ruled the world with an iron hand.

Her will transported him to a world he never imagined existed. In his mind's eye, he saw a circle of black-robed necromancers gathered behind the walls of an ancient stone temple. Incense hung heavy in the candle-lit air as they chanted in unison in a guttural tone, reciting words of dark power from an ancient indestructible grimoire made from human skin and blood ink, a wicked book known as the *Liber Mortis*. It contained the dark wisdom and eternal spells of the Moon Goddess, Hecate. Their minds joined as they channeled the charnel winds of magic, raising their enemies from the dead as Undead soldier-slaves with the intent of using them as a conquering force.

But the blood-drinking creatures they created were too powerful to control, their minds and wills still somehow their own, never having left their bodies. And these Undead remembered the villains who had slain them. They revolted in one savage night of blood and terror, feeding on the necromancers and draining them dry before dismembering the bodies, preventing the sorcerers from rising as fellow Undead.

Rowan watched as these pale immortals rose to positions of power on the continent, heralding the dawn of an ancient civilization of vast technology. Atlantis became the center of world commerce, the streets teeming with people from around the globe as they walked among towering golden edifices. Floating skiffs moved across the sky, the preferred means of travel for the wealthy.

The Atlanteans had sworn loyalty to their nocturnal leaders, offering their blood freely in ritual sacrifice, hoping to one day be fortunate enough to be chosen to join the cadre of the Undead elite.

Calamity visited Atlantis in the form of a great underwater

earthquake that preceded an apocalyptic tsunami plunging the continent beneath the sea. The mortals perished almost instantly, crushed by falling debris or drowned beneath towering waves.

Our kind survived the fall of Atlantis, Darla spoke through their psychic link. *Where the living are weak and easily broken, we are strong and resilient. We have died once already and cannot easily do so again. Our bodies are mutable—we can adapt to a fluctuating environment.*

Rowan watched as the ancient ones fled the dying continent. Some grew great bat-like wings that extended from their wrists and attached to their lower backs, using the fierce winds that followed in the aftermath of the flood to rise into the sky and fly toward the silver moon—they became the *Moroi* and settled in modern-day Europe. Others welcomed the smothering waters, their bodies becoming streamlined like fish, their eyes retreating into deep sockets as the ridge of their foreheads swelled with thick bone. Thin membranes extended between their clawed fingers, giving them more surface area to displace the water as their legs fused into powerful tails. The transmuted revenants fled down into the ocean depths where the sun could not reach.

Don't you see, Rowan? Our people, the Enkidu, gave birth to the legends of tritons and mermaids, feeding on the lost and shipwrecked. Down here, it is forever night! The sun cannot wither our bodies or steal our strength. Here we are eternally strong!

As the visions ended and time resumed, he became lightheaded from blood loss and oxygen deprivation.

She smiled at him as she pushed him toward the ocean floor.

You're dying, Rowan. It's all right, I'm here with you. You can't become like me unless your body dies. I will protect your soul until it is time for you to rise. I will be waiting for you.

Trusting her words, Rowan returned her smile as he let the darkness engulf him.

Rise!

Her command rang in his psyche like a thunderous bell as he awoke in the darkness, unsure of how long he had slept. Rowan instinctually obeyed, thrusting out his arms, easily tearing through the silt and rock and kelp roots of the ocean floor in a grim parody of birth. He rocketed up through the water, reborn, leaving a long, muddy trail behind him. He sensed new strength in his arms, his body more potent than ever. Yet the power was accompanied by a strange hunger, a thirst he knew not even the ocean around him could quench.

She came to him as she said she would, true to her words, enveloping him in her arms. He felt comfortable there. The cold water did not bother him—he soon realized that he no longer needed to breathe, echoing the dreams he had experienced.

Our immortality comes with a great price—eternal thirst married to eternal life. We are thralls to this base need, cursed in some respect. You must learn to feed, my lover, she urged, her eyes holding his. Then a large object passed overhead, covering them in shadow. Rowan looked up, startled.

It started as a dim dark image against the darker undersea world, then became larger as it suddenly dipped, diving toward the bottom. The shape submerged into the ocean's blackness, leaving Rowan to grasp its true nature.

Before he could react, a tremendous force tore Darla from his arms. A gigantic gray shape hurtled by, buffeting him to the side like a leaf in a wave. He tumbled head over heel until he righted himself, his keen eyes penetrating the darkness.

He saw the great leviathan rise above him, recognizing it from his fishing expeditions as some form of a great white shark but far larger than any he'd ever seen or heard of. The creature was at least fifty feet long and incredibly thick, the size of a small submarine. It moved through the sea with unnatural grace, using its thresher-like tail and extended front fins to propel through the waters. It occurred to Rowan that the beast was some form of a prehistoric relic, hunting undisturbed in the ocean's deep trenches for millions of years, an apex predator somehow managing to avoid human detection.

Rowan's heart sank when he saw Darla's limp form in the shark's mouth, her dark ichor leaving behind a trail in the water as the beast changed course and carried her down past the lip of an undersea ridge. Panic threatened to overwhelm him—he knew the creature intended to take her to the bottom of the cavern and consume her at leisure. Rage supplanted fear as he vowed not to lose her.

He recalled what Darla had said about their kind being able to transmute their bodies, how she had assumed the form of a great eel upon her rebirth. She had discussed how the ancients had shape-changed to flee the tsunami that engulfed Atlantis. His anger guided him as shadows flowed to him, his form growing in size and strength. What remained of his clothing tore away as his frame swelled.

As he swam after the leviathan, he willed his body to change. His skin became thick and scaly to counter the increasing pressure as he descended, assuming a green hue to blend in with the surrounding water. Rowan's nose flattened, and his mouth became a stitch. His eyes became round and lidless beneath an atavistic forehead, making his face appear piscine as his body streamlined to decrease the drag of the water. His fingers and toes elongated, thin membrane extending between each digit, transforming into webbed claws. A dorsal crest formed and ran down his back, forking to run down the back of his legs.

Rowan realized that he needed to concentrate fully to maintain this new form. He continually took in the surrounding water to equalize the pressure inside and outside of his body; otherwise, the ocean depths' increasing pressure would crush him.

The modifications he made to his body worked—soon, he outpaced the great beast.

Rowan slammed down into the leviathan's dense gray hide with tremendous force, causing its jaws to open in reflex and release Darla. His heart sank when he saw that her still form was completely perforated with giant puncture wounds, some of the shark's dagger-sized teeth still embedded in her torso and pelvic area. Primal instinct warned him that the heart was his kind's most vulnerable area. Would a colossal shark tooth driven deep into her heart have the same effect as a spike? Darla's eyes were dull and lifeless as she sank, trailing black blood. Rowan couldn't help but note the ironic nature of her defeat, her body punctured by sharp teeth in much the same manner she had feasted on others for so many centuries.

He swam toward her, hoping there might be some way to revive her, but the shark's powerful thresher tail struck him. Again he tumbled end over end. His vision blurred from the force of the blow. Before he came to rest, a massive clamp seized his torso in a seemingly unbreakable grip—Rowan felt and heard his chest and backbones break under pressure.

Rowan's horrified eyes opened to find himself in the leviathan's maw, the shark's dead clown eyes staring straight at him. He screamed in rage and pain, each of the dozens of huge teeth puncturing his torso like a thick blade driven into his dead flesh. Instinctively he crossed his arms over his chest for protection.

Fortunately, none of the creature's teeth had penetrated his heart.

Still, the pain threatened to overwhelm his mental control over his form as the shark rocketed up, shaking its head back and forth to further disorient its prey. Rowan felt like a helpless passenger on an out-of-control train as the leviathan burst through the surface.

The sky was clear, and the sun had not yet set in the west. He felt its searing rays burn into his cold flesh, scalding him despite the more resilient form he had assumed.

The shark tossed its head and threw him a dozen yards across the water. He splashed down and lay stunned, his body sizzling as it floated in the last rays of daylight.

Rowan had begun to stir when the great beast surfaced again, its enormous head emerging from the turbid water before slamming down, taking him in its jaws again and opening up new wounds with its rows of razor teeth. Though the pain was incredible, Rowan knew he had been fortunate that the shark's teeth had again missed his heart.

Rowan called upon his new strength as the leviathan dove toward the bottom. He reached forward and encircled each of the creature's eyes with his claws. The shark's eyelids instinctively closed as Rowan dug his nails deep into its flesh. He tore the creature's right eye out, blood erupting from the ragged red hole. The shark bucked and shook, sending fresh waves of agony through Rowan as the creature worried at his flesh. Despite the pain, he store out the beast's remaining eye.

The shark opened its maw in blind agony, releasing him. Rowan extended his arms as the beast hurtled by, latching on with his claws and sinking his long nails into the top of the creature's head. He managed to hang on as the prehistoric monster violently shook its head. The red thirst surged through his body as he bit into one of the leviathan's ruptured eye sockets, feasting on the bleeding. The gamy fluid flooded his throat, adding the ancient shark's strength to his own.

Rowan felt his body recover, the broken bones realigning themselves as the wounds in his flesh sealed with fantastic speed. Some dagger teeth remained embedded in his flesh, but none had struck a vital area. He moved like quicksilver, rotating around and maneuvering himself below the shark's vulnerable white underside before savagely tearing into the gut. He ripped the ropelike intestines out, savoring the tang of freshly spilled blood in the water. The leviathan bucked with incredible power, but Rowan hung on, his claws digging deeper through pungent organs and cartilage as he pulled himself forward to the point that he was entirely inside the beast.

He located the colossal heart and tore a large piece from it, stuffing it in his mouth and sucking it dry. Rowan thrust out in a berserker rage with both hands, bursting through the chest area above the front fins. He pulled himself through the opening before swimming free.

The leviathan spasmed and twitched in its death throes, its jaws opening and closing mindlessly before becoming still. The gigantic corpse, now little more than thirty tons of shredded meat, sank into the impenetrable darkness of the sea. Rowan felts its cold blood energize him, his body almost bursting with newfound power. The aquatic revenant unleashed a primal victory roar that broke the silence of the deep; his fangs extended into sharp points.

Rowan rocketed downward, looking for Darla in the gloom. He began to panic, unable to sense the light touch of her mind on his—he could not imagine enduring his new existence without her. After a short period of desperate searching, he located her motionless form drifting on the ocean currents. He steadied her and found one of the shark's teeth embedded in her heart. Rowan grasped the tooth with his talons and plucked it free.

Her sapphire eyes immediately flashed open, beaming as her lips curved into a wicked smile; she recognized him despite his altered appearance. He watched as the wounds in her torso sealed over, the skin soon becoming immaculate, no signs of the massive damage inflicted by the beast remaining. She reached a clawed hand around his neck, comforting him as she pulled him closer.

Rowan opened his mind and spoke to her as she had taught him.

I thought you were dead. I thought I was alone again, he revealed as he calmed, gradually shedding the mass and density of his battle form.

Brave Rowan, know that I will never leave you—I was never in danger. We dead are resilient—gifted or cursed, depending on one's point of view. Prescribed manners are required to destroy the Enkidu. We are the apex predators of these seas, and not even prehistoric leviathans can challenge us.

You allowed the shark to take you. You could have killed it, just as I did, he asserted.

I did. I buried you in the sands of its hunting ground. You needed to learn how we feed down here. I showed you how; you performed marvelously.

She pulled him close, kissing him passionately, savoring some of the leviathan's blood that remained in his mouth. He entered her once again, his lust fueled by the thrill of victory over the great shark.

For the Enkidu, our first kill determines the type of predator we become, she explained as he thrust into her. *My first kill was a cowardly human male. Conversely, you killed a legendary predator —a megalodon. Imagine what that means for your future.*

Rowan realized she had been grooming him to be her eternal mate. When they finished, she led him by the hand toward the ocean floor.

I have so much to show you—a world you could never have imagined, even in your wildest dreams. And we have time, oh so much time, all the time in the world, to explore it together, my love.

Rowan's soul lifted, buoyed by her love, a love that filled the empty hole in his heart. In the distance, he saw the shimmering outlines of an immense sunken vessel, one of the masts miraculously still upright and intact. As they swam toward it, he wondered if it would become his new home.

FRESH JUICE

"Gaawdd-damn!"

Chalmers Young fumed aloud as he ground his heavily chewed cigar into the fold-out table that supported his elbows. He'd opened the gymnasium doors a few hours earlier to get some movement of air through the building. Unfortunately, the open doors had brought only the stench of garbage cans and the unwanted attention of bums from the nearby liquor store. The summer warmth continued to linger even into the first weeks of October. The gym's heat and lack of ventilation combined to make Chalmers a dripping ball of uncomfortable sweat and grime inside a cheap tuxedo. The scenery unveiled before his tired eyes did little to ease his discomfort.

Approximately twenty bodies huffed and puffed in the hastily assembled wrestling ring before him, sweating as profusely as Chalmers as each sought to gain the upper hand in battle. To Chalmers' disappointment, most who had shown up at tonight's professional wrestling audition had little to offer. Most were severely obese and out of shape, barely able to walk up the large metal support that led to the squared circle. Many a pendulous belly hung out over dilapidated collegiate wrestling tights. The rest of the auditioners were so pathetically slim that some part of their anatomy would be likely be broken before the night ended. A sizeable chunk looked like they were fresh border crossers who'd grown tired of waiting for someone to drive by and offer them day labor and instead had decided to take their chances in the ring. Chalmers realized the likelihood of finding enough talent to put on his own wrestling show was minimal. He expressed his displeasure with a loud, sulfurous belch.

Chalmers' partner at the messy table took note of his displeasure and tried to brighten Chalmers' mood with a suggestion.

"A little fresh juice, dat always gets 'em goin'. We get some of these dopes to bleed, an' we got us an audience."

Nature Boy Freddy Landell knew of what he spoke. A veteran of the wrestling wars, he had the cauliflower ears to prove it. Landell was a king among heels in his day, despised by the fans almost as much as his fellow gladiators respected him. Landell was especially well-known for his ability to "juice," to bleed on demand. For decades, wrestling promoters had realized that blood lent an element of realism to a "sport" known for its lack of mainstream credibility. Wrestlers earned extra cash and respect from the promoters if they were willing to pull hidden razors from their tights and slash their foreheads, creating the illusion that an opponent's blows were causing real damage. Landell had a mass of heavy scar tissue on his forehead to attest to his years of juicing. Aged though he was, Landell was perhaps Chalmers's only mainstay entertainment.

"Mebbee so," Chalmers replied, unenthused. "Juicing" became obsolete in the wrestling business in the '80s during the AIDS panic, and Chalmers doubted few of these current millennial prospects had the stomach to self-inflict bloody wounds that would leave scars on their unwrinkled brows.

Presently a hairy, corpulent body sailed over the top ring rope and splatted ungracefully on the wooden floor in front of Chalmers' table. The unlucky wrestler peered up momentarily into Chalmers' eyes before he fainted. A thin red line of blood trickled down his forehead from a wound he had received in the ring.

Landell beamed. "Now dat's what I'm talkin' about!"

Chalmers was unimpressed. "Pathetic. Gaawdd-damn pathetic." He bit into his spit-soaked cigar again.

"Perhaps I can do better."

The calm confidence that emanated from the voice caught Chalmers by surprise. He was amazed by how clearly he made it out over the loud fracas in the ring. Chalmers looked over and viewed its source.

The new auditioner stood casually by the gymnasium entrance, wiry arms folded across a bare, muscular chest. He dressed from head to toe in red: red boots, red tights, and a vermillion cape. The brightness of the clothes stood in stark contrast to the ashen color of the man's skin and the darkness of his hair and eyes. On first impression, Chalmers was mildly impressed. The newcomer was not a massive man, but he possessed an athletic build, standing over six feet tall with more than adequate muscle tone. He would at least have a certain amount of ring presence, Chalmers concluded.

"Be my guest. Jump in on the battle royale." Chalmers waved toward the ring.

The newcomer entered the ring with a mammoth leap, bypassing the metal stairs altogether. The Nature Boy's and Chalmers' eyes bugged at the distance covered by the jump. Within seconds, the red-robed wrestler had tossed all but a few wrestling-wannabees from the ring, moving about with mind-numbing quickness. Mere sweeps of his arm sent bodies flying like toys over the top rope. Two pugilists momentarily stopped attacking each other and attempted to grab hold of the newcomer's arms. He easily pushed both assailants back, then swept his right foot up and across their jaws with lethal precision. The two wrestlers sailed over the ring ropes to join their comrades on the floor, leaving behind only one man for the newcomer to deal with.

The last wrestler was, by far, the largest man to have entered the ring that night. He might have been labeled either an ogre or a giant in bygone eras. Towering at over seven feet in height, he shook the ring whenever he moved. Chalmers estimated the giant's weight at over four hundred pounds. At least until the newcomer's arrival, the behemoth had been the most successful of the applicants, eliminating six other entrants. Only the man's great awkwardness prevented Chalmers from becoming excited about his prospects.

The giant lumbered across the ring toward the red wrestler, ham-sized fists raised, ready to strike. A quick blow to the giant's midsection halted his progress. A lightning-fast uppercut then robbed him of his consciousness. Chalmers and Landell looked on in amazement as the red wrestler scooped the giant into the air without apparent effort and sailed him over the top ring rope, claiming victory as the battle royale champion.

"Gawwd-damn!" The dilapidated gym shook from the giant's defeat. The pungent stogie dropped out of Chalmers' gaping maw, tumbling to the filthy floor. Chalmers had never seen anything like the man in red in his twenty years of wrestling promotion. A few wrestlers were capable of military pressing another man over their heads, but only if the pressure was relatively small and willing to help in the effort. He and

Landell jumped out of their chairs and swept past the moaning bodies littering the gym floor to clamber into the ring.

To Chalmers' surprise, the wrestler in red was neither out of breath nor sweating.

"I nevah seen anybody move like that before. You're fast, agile...real strong. You evah 'rassle before, kid?"

"Never for pay," the stranger intoned with a slight smirk. His dark eyes pinioned both Chalmers and Landell. "I've studied the art from afar for many years, though."

"Well, I kin change dat. What's yer moniker?"

The wrestler paused a minute, then continued; his eyes possessed of an odd inner glow, like an animal at night. "You can call me Shade, as in Night Shade." His lips curled up in an eerie smile, showing white teeth.

"Ahhh, I get it, a Burt Reynolds gimmick. I like it. We can use you for da big Halloween show we're puttin' on in a few weeks; I'm callin' it 'Halloween Havoc.'"

The Nature Boy shook his head. "That title's already been copyrighted, boss."

"So we get us anudder name; I'll work on it later. For now, we got us a deal. Shake, Shade."

The two men exchanged handshakes. Chalmers was shocked at the ice-coldness of the hand that encircled his with the strength of a vise. He noted a cool breeze had subtly made its way into the gym, clearing away the humid exhalations of fatigued and defeated men.

"Now, about my fee," Shade began, but Chalmers was paying him no mind. His eyes swept the empty seats of the gymnasium, and he imagined them full of screaming fans. Screaming, drunk, and belligerent on Halloween night.

Two weeks later, Chalmers took the first step toward
realizing his dream. The first official card of the new World
Council of Wrestling was in full sway. Despite the odds,
Chalmers had filled most of the high school auditorium seats.
Fans had come from local suburbs to jam the inner-city gym.
The surrounding streets were packed with cheap autos and
SUVs, while illegal vendors made a week's salary in one night
hawking buttered cornsticks, churros, and icees. A few cheap
hookers even solicited young, awkward geeks not used to being
out of their parents' houses. Families brought their children
outfitted in sundry supernatural and superhero costumes to
welcome All Hallows Eve.

The undercard matches were dull and uninspired, involving
wrestlers who could never headline events in larger federations.
Still, Chalmers had built up sufficient anticipation for the main
event via television advertising in the local community.
Legendary Nature Boy Freddy Landell was to battle the violent
newcomer, deadly Night Shade, making his ring debut in a no-
disqualification match. Wrestling fans had never been known
for their high intelligence quotient. Chalmers savored the
thought of the profit he was making on the event, even as he
disdained the hot-dog-slurping, beer-swilling idiots who
comprised his audience.

Now decked out in black wrestling attire and *sans* cape,
Night Shade made his way to the ring to the accompaniment of
loud boos from the audience. Playing the heel seemed to come
naturally to him, and he sneered back at the audience.
Chalmers had initially planned for Night Shade to be a golden

boy, or "face" in industry jargon, but something about the wrestler made Chalmers believe him to be more ideally suited for the role of heel. Something dark and mysterious rested just beyond Night Shade's handsome exterior. The hair on Chalmers' arms stood on end whenever he was near the wrestler. Chalmers couldn't put his finger on it exactly, but it unsettled him nonetheless.

In contrast to Night Shade, Landell wore gold tights and a flowing sequined robe. He entered the ring to roars of approval (exactly as Chalmers had planned). Landell no longer possessed the extraordinary musculature of his heyday, but he was still a figure the fans respected, someone who had paid his dues of blood in the ring. A battle between old and new, between generations, was about to occur. Chalmers had successfully keyed into the fans' imaginations.

The two wrestlers jockeyed around the ring with unnatural grace as the opening bell sounded. Landell used his decades of ring experience to perform complex athletic maneuvers, while Night Shade relied on powers that neither Landell nor Chalmers could comprehend. Of course, the fight was staged; Landell and Chalmers knew that Shade would have torn Landell apart in a fair fight. Professional wrestling, however, had always involved a willing suspension of disbelief, and the crowd ate it up. Night Shade acted his part well, pretending to groan in pain from meager onslaughts by Landell, while Landell used his athletic prowess to rebound from being tossed around like a feather. Chalmers marveled from his ringside seat at how well the old man could recover from such a heavy beating. Meanwhile, the spoon-fed referee pretended to officiate the match, occasionally separating the two combatants or barking orders at them but, for the most part, keeping out of the action. The crowd of mostly young children and seasoned senior citizens vigorously cheered whenever Landell got the upper hand.

As the battle progressed beyond the twenty-minute mark, Landell lost himself in the excitement. The sweltering air was ripe with the heaviness of anticipation. It had been a long time since he received such a positive reaction from the fans, and he wished to express his gratitude. Consequently, he did what came to him as second nature. After being thrown out of the ring and having his head bounced (lightly, of course) off a steel railing, Landell quickly fell out of sight under one of the large mats hanging from the side of the ring. He quickly retrieved a small razor he kept secreted in his tights and expertly slashed his forehead near his receding, bleached-blond hairline. His face was a crimson mess when he hobbled back into the ring.

Chalmers looked on and quietly smiled to himself. Landell's self-inflicted wounds had not been a part of the script but would make for a more exciting match. Chalmers had to hand it to the old guy—he still had it after all these years. Unlike an actual sport, professional wrestling allowed past-prime athletes to continue in the business as long as they were marketable, their health be damned.

The Nature Boy rolled around a little, feigning dire injury, and finally lay flat on his back. As the blood dripped out of his head and formed little sloppy pools around him, he looked up at Shade. The other wrestler had a strange, shocked expression on his face. His eyes were opened wide in apparent shock, his lips curling back from his teeth. Saliva began to drip from his mouth.

Landell feared the other man might get sick looking at his head wounds.

"Keep it together, pal," he whispered. "Ten more minutes, and we're out of here."

Landell looked on in shock as Shade's teeth lengthened over his bottom lip. The heel's eyes became bloodshot, accentuating now-black irises. The tips of his ears extended into elfin points.

Landell began to panic and attempted to stand up. Shade's right hand, now a taloned claw with frighteningly long fingers, was a blur as it crushed Landell back onto the canvas, breaking the older wrestler's ribs. Audience members in the first ten rows heard the shattering bones and roared their approval, spilling warm beer and peanuts onto each other. Landell tried to scream, but no air would come from his damaged lungs. Frothy blood poured from his mouth.

Night Shade's head flashed down to Landell's shattered chest, his fang teeth burying deeply through flesh and bone. His body covered Landell's as he vacuumed up the veteran wrestler's blood. Landell thrashed about futilely in protest but was unable to gain any traction. Having played the part of a disinterested buffoon for most of the match, the dumbfounded referee realized something had gone wrong. Mustering his courage, he seized Shade by the hair and attempted to pry him away from Landell, only to be swatted out of the ring like an annoying fly for his troubles. His neck broke when he landed awkwardly on his head in a ringside aisle near the sixth row.

The entire arena was on their feet screaming, urging Shade on. Some members tried to rush past uninterested security guards into the ring. Chalmers realized that the match had departed significantly from the script he had created. He charged into the ring.

"What the hell are ya' doin', man!" he screamed at Shade as he approached. Chalmers refrained from physical intervention, knowing it would be of no use. What happened next would remain etched in his memory for the rest of his life.

Night Shade turned his head and looked straight at Chalmers. Blood covered the heel's entire mouth, dripping onto his bare chest. His eyes were now twin points of crimson light, blazing out from coal-black eye sockets, while his canine teeth had extended to at least twice their regular length. It struck

Chalmers as odd at the time that, despite rolling and running around the ring for over twenty minutes in the humidity, Shade was not sweating.

The wrestler's expression was an odd combination of recognition, disappointment, and cold insanity. He spoke, his voice alien and hollow.

"The old bastard didn't tell me he planned to cut himself. Threw me off my game plan, he did. Brought out the red thirst."

Shade's voice became angrier as he quickly looked away.

"Hell's teeth, I fell off the wagon again! Time to move on." To Chalmers, the wrestler sounded like an addict who had recidivated.

Shade slowly stood, a look of grim resignation on his bloody countenance. Chalmers watched in amazement as Shade's body lost its solidity, gradually fading into a luminescent mist that whirled away from the frantic crowd and out an open window. Within seconds no physical trace remained of the wrestler. A chewed stogie dropped from Chalmers' lips.

The promoter looked down at the fallen Landell. The veteran wrestler's eyes were still open, and the Nature Boy managed one last sentence, despite the trauma to which his body had been subjected.

"I told ya', buddy...juicin'...it always gets 'em goin'." His eyes glazed over as blood flowed from his open mouth. Chalmers heard the massive crowd uproar. Never in his twenty years of wrestling promotion had he seen such a reaction. He found himself surrounded by riffraff from the crowd who had managed to elude the paltry security Chalmers had hired. Several gaped open-mouthed at the maimed carcass of Landell, while others took pictures with their cellular phones. Costumed kids cried and screamed, burying wet faces into their mothers' arms. This Halloween would remain forever seared into their memories.

"Gawwd-damn," Chalmers mumbled as he surveyed the carnage around him. Maybe the old wrestler had been right. Maybe there was something to this "juicin'" after all.

A COOL BREEZE WOKE CHALMERS FROM A TROUBLED SLEEP THREE nights later.

He'd had trouble drifting off. After the Shade/Landell incident, the local athletic association suspended his promoter's license. Longtime industry friends had turned their backs on him, some upset with Landell's fate, others afraid to be associated with Chalmers. There were rumblings that the district attorney's office had launched an investigation into the Halloween wrestling card and that an indictment of Chalmers was imminent for gross negligence resulting in the death of Landell. Chalmers had taken the rumors seriously. He'd packed his belongings and planned to leave the city early in the morning. Chalmers figured his best bet was to head to Mexico and try to hook up with the *lucha libre* promotions.

The sleeping medications he'd taken earlier in the evening did little to ease his troubled mind. The recurring images of his business confidant and close friend being butchered before him haunted his every waking moment. Those images, coupled with the lingering heat, caused Chalmers to sweat and twist restlessly in his apartment bed for hours. He'd just begun to doze off when the curious draft fluttered in through his open window.

Chalmers' bloodshot eyes opened to find a pale, silver figure looming in front of him in the apartment gloom. Chalmers quickly recognized the nude form of the recently deceased

"Nature Boy" Freddy Landell. Landell appeared confused. The truly *au naturale* "Nature Boy" stood in front of a hallway mirror using a small razor blade to slash his forehead. The wounds drew no blood and appeared to seal immediately. Landell seemed frustrated and began to mouth obscenities. Chalmers noted that the mirror failed to return Landell's image.

An irate Landell turned to face Chalmers in his bed. The fatal wounds Shade had inflicted on the aged wrestler's torso were gone. Chalmers saw that the "Nature Boy" now sported twin fang teeth of his own, lethal daggers that reflected the moonlight seeping through the window. Landell's crimson eyes pinioned Chalmers to the bed. A part of Chalmers's fogged brain began to comprehend that Landell had inherited his killer's curse.

Landell gave up attempting to mutilate his forehead and began to slice his wrists. Again, the wounds did not bleed and sealed instantly. The newborn revenant slowly came to a revelation of his own—having died once, he could not do so again.

"I got no juice left, Poppy," the resurrected superstar screamed. In the blink of an eye, he crossed the fifteen feet separating him from Chalmers and latched a freezing, taloned hand around Chalmers' throat. The wrestling promoter found himself hoisted off the bed and suspended in the air by that single puissant hand. He choked as Landell's fingers slowly crushed his windpipe and vertebrae.

The dead wrestler's fang teeth unsheathed from his gray lips. Rancid breath assailed Chalmers' nostrils.

"Maybe you got some I could borrow?"

Chalmers juiced hard that night. As his body was torn and exsanguinated, he concluded it was the honorable thing to do. After all the bleeding Landell had done for him over the years, it was only fitting to return the favor.

BUM FIGHTS AND BLOOD FEUDS

How in the hell did it come to this? Working with losers in trash and back alleys stinking of piss, Dax lamented as he strode down the alleyway, the sulfuric reek of rotting eggs and pungent garbage cooked by a day of intense Southern California summer heat flooding the nostrils of his bulbous nose. His sweaty bald head gleamed underneath the streetlights as he took a hit off a Kool Ultra cigarette, exhaling smoke and flicking ash to the ground. He scanned the numerous garbage sacks, looking for a piece of human debris to suit his purpose.

The alley was between a liquor store and the Aces strip club, where Dax lazed away most of his time when he was not hustling. He was a large and imposing man, but lack of exercise and a shabby diet had made him flabby. He had unceremoniously achieved the much lampooned "dad bod" before age thirty.

It didn't have to be this way, Dax concluded as he wiped his brow, reflecting on his current dismal predicament. *It didn't have to come to this. I could have made other choices.*

He'd been raised strictly but properly, never having been

abused physically or mentally by his parents. His father had worked long hours as a plumber and handyman to put him through a pricy private Catholic high school in a nearby county, while Mom shuttled him to and from school and cooked all his meals. Dax had no siblings to compete for attention and had been the sole focus of his parents' existence.

No, he decided, *there's only one person to blame for this mess.*

Dax's problems had started in high school, where he developed a proclivity for taking the easy way out and getting by doing just the bare minimum. He'd started drinking and using pot, cut classes to hang out with the other stoners or just to be away from school, and missed enough practices to get booted from the football team his junior year. He barely graduated and lacked the mental discipline to handle a full college schedule or maintain a steady job.

Like many failed high school athletes, Dax tried his hand at bodybuilding to become the next Arnold Schwarzenegger. He competed in a few local shows while sporadically attending junior college, never placing higher than fifth. Succeeding Arnold as the next Conan was not in his future.

Though he'd failed at competitive bodybuilding and college, he'd learned to make money on the side by selling steroids and male enhancement pills to an assortment of local juiceheads and middle-aged men. After he'd stopped using the steroids himself, he'd puffed up as his now unamplified metabolism slowed down. Drug dealing was a hit-and-miss business with periods of boom followed by more prolonged slumps. Dax had been in a deep slump for a long time.

His lack of "cheddar," or money, cost him his fair share of baby's mama drama. Stacy, his ex, always threatened to call the Department of Children and Family Social Services down on his deadbeat ass for delinquent child support payments. She mocked him, calling him a "useless, overweight, out-of-shape, limp-dicked, used-up, never-was." Or words to that effect. And she did her best to keep his time with his six-year-old daughter Ashley as limited as possible, which wasn't a difficult task after the family court ruled him an unfit father for a long and sundry list of reasons.

Dax felt a bitter pang of regret as tranquil images of walks on the beach with Stacy and Ashley surged unbidden into his mind. Her little Chihuahua Paco always accompanied Ashley. Or at least she had until the day Dax got stoned and left the front gate open—a passing truck had run the dog over. Ashley cried for weeks after the loss but oddly had never blamed her dad.

She's a good kid, Dax thought. *She deserved a lot better than me, that's for sure.* He sighed, realizing he hadn't seen or talked to Ashley in over a year.

Still, he reasoned, *opportunities come calling even in the lowest pits of despair, defeat, and humiliation.*

Recently his errand boy, roommate, and fellow drug dealer, Chalupa Miguelito, had introduced him to the concept of bum fights. Essentially a poor man's fusion of pro wrestling and boxing, bum fighting entailed provoking local transients into attacking each other in drunken street brawls for scant sums of money and the promise of more booze. The "fights" were filmed and sold on low-quality Beta tapes in tawdry video stores. Dax, perennially two to three months delinquent on paying the rent, was truly desperate for more cheddar. He ignored the stench of the alley and resigned himself to the task at hand.

Chalupa Miguelito and a local transient named Leonard accompanied Dax down the alley. Chalupa was a heavyset Hispanic gang member with a shaved head and extensive prison tattoos covering his arms, neck, and head. He had been disowned by his "set" or subdivision of the Malditos gang due to laziness and reputation for having bad luck. Whether he was genuinely unlucky or his large profile made it easier for the cops to zero in on him while capering was a matter for debate. He'd found a kindred spirit in Dax, who fortunately did not have high standards for the people he associated with. Chalupa had shown some flair for filming and editing videos with his stolen Sony Camcorder, and thus, Dax tasked him with recording tonight's brawl.

Dax and Chalupa had employed Leonard on previous occasions. He was a big man and had worked construction before the twin demons of drugs and booze claimed him. For just $10 and a bottle of Southern Comfort, Leonard was willing to pick fights with other transients and allow himself to be filmed. Due to his size, particularly his enormous hands (or "ham hocks" as he referred to them), he rarely lost. After the fight ended, Dax and his crew would leave the loser discarded on the street without medical attention. Police, if they happened to drive by, typically looked the other way and moved on. Force incidents with the homeless drew unwanted media attention; the cops avoided interacting with the transient population as much as possible.

The three men confidently strode down the alleyway, scanning for signs of life. Chalupa hummed a few bars from a Gloria Estefan song. Against the far wall, near some industrial-sized trash bins, Dax made out a human form almost completely hidden in the shadows thrown by the streetlamps, curled up in a fetal position amongst plastic trash bags. He discovered it was an old man in rumpled clothing on closer examination.

The senior's head was primarily bald save for a few wisps of scraggly gray hair. Roaches crawled freely in and out of openings in his torn clothing. Dax couldn't determine whether the man was alive or dead—the body was still. He nudged it with his foot a few times. When Dax got no response, he leaned back and gave the old man a good stiff kick in the side with the tip of his Doc Martens oxblood steel toe boot, both feeling and hearing the ribs break. The man stirred slightly with the impact but otherwise remained still.

Dax stepped back, a chill running up his foot where it had connected with the man's body. He shrugged it off and addressed his colleagues.

"Chalupa, start filming. Leonard...get to work!"

THE CORPSE DREAMED, SHADOWY IMAGES FLOODING HIS MIND. WHEN he was first turned, he had been told his kind did not dream, that dreams were for the living, those with warmth, breath, and souls. But the corpse had always dreamed, even when newly reborn. And now, centuries later and starved nigh until the final death, he dreamed more feverishly than ever.

Perhaps "dreams" was not the correct term for what he experienced. "Recollections" was more proper. And for his kind, memories were always nightmares—an eternal existence of unending hunger and cold emptiness and loss, seeing those he had known wither and fade with time. The corpse had witnessed the end of his biological bloodline and endured the destruction of his sire, butchered by witch hunters during the daylight hours when his kind were dead to the world. He had become accustomed to the pain over the centuries as he adapted to the exigencies of his existence, the tiny remnant of his soul deteriorating as the death toll mounted. The only constant in the corpse's existence was the need to feed and kill, to absorb the psychic energy from his victims' deaths, and for the blood to remain vigorous.

Yet when all had seemed lost, the corpse found another, a woman of grace and intellect with whom he sought to ease the pain of eternity. They shared a particularly cynical view of the world and those living in it. The corpse sensed she possessed an old soul, a kindred spirit, and with time he became comfortable enough with her to reveal the secret of his dark existence. The woman had surprised the corpse; rather than expressing revulsion, she embraced his curse. He turned her with the blood kiss, gifting and cursing her at the exact moment.

He could still recall the night he had drained her body to the point of death, her soul perched and ready to flee its dying shell. The corpse had seized that soul with his mind and anchored it to the body, shielding it and preventing death from claiming her while feeding her ichor from his dead veins. They spent the equivalent of several mortal lifetimes together, never apart, feeding in tandem. The corpse had eventually achieved a measure of peace after many years. Or so he had thought.

Few things were permanent, either in life or unlife. Witch hunters were always on the prowl for his kind. They never forgot, nor did they forgive. Esoteric knowledge of the supernatural was passed down from one fanatical generation of the arcane society to the next. They tracked the corpse and his companion down, attacking their basement tomb in great numbers. The revenants had fought back, showered in blood as they tore out throats and shattered spines. Dozens of witch hunters fell, only to be replaced by dozens and dozens more. The couple were shot with heavy-caliber ammunition, staked with hawthorn wood, and burned with daemonbane and sanctified oil. As the corpse fell, overwhelmed by the sheer number of attackers, his companion reached out and attempted to grab his hand. She never made it, her head removed by the sweep of a hunter's silvered sword.

The corpse had screamed through burned lips as he felt her essence dissipate in the air. His rage was awesome to behold as he stood, despite the pain and damage done to his body. He took his revenge on the remaining hunters, reveling in their despair as he *spread their entrails across the basement, blood pooling from the ruptured corpses and forming a dark flowing river.*

Afterward, the corpse wandered the world in despair, unable to find comfort or meaning in his unending unlife. Blood, once a source of great passion, no longer inspired him. He had not fed in decades, his body shriveling and aging. Eventually, the corpse lost the will to move altogether. One night he sprawled on the ground in an abandoned alley, for all intents and purposes just another piece of detritus amongst the street garbage. He waited for the rats and worms to finish what the hunters had started decades earlier as he yearned for the cold embrace of a woman long dead.

A stiff kick to his ribcage ended the dream.

LEONARD REACHED DOWN WITH ONE LARGE, SCARRED HAND AND wrapped it around the old man's frayed shirt collar. He easily yanked the frail being from the ground and pinned him against the brick wall.

"This is my alley, you old fool," the big man screamed through broken, yellowed teeth. He used his free hand to pummel the old man in the face, blow upon unanswered blow.

"That's it, Leonard; give him the soup bone!" Chalupa chimed in from the side, all the while filming. The gang member squinted into the lens, concern developing on his face. Dax picked up on it.

"What's wrong, man?" he asked.

Chalupa shook his head in confusion. "I dunno, man, something's wrong with this camcorder. The old fart doesn't show up."

"What do you mean he doesn't show up? What's that supposed to mean?" Dax asked in exasperation. "There's nothing wrong with the camcorder; I just boosted it from Sears last week. This is good stuff. Leonard is laying down a serious smackdown. You better not miss it; get in closer if you have to. Leonard, move over into more light," he yelled, choreographing his film like a director.

Chalupa shook his head in exasperation. "I'm trying, Dax, seriously I'm trying, but...something's wrong. I only see Leonard beating on empty clothes."

As the two men attempted to solve the camcorder mystery, the old man awoke from his long, restless slumber.

AGAIN THEY HOUND ME. UNCEASING. UNRELENTING. NEVER WILL I find peace.

The corpse rose with uncanny ease to his feet, his knees never bending, as the large black man backed off, clutching his right hand in pain.

"Hillbilly, you busted my hand with your old leathery face. Gonna make you pay for that." The man's fetid breath washed over him, a miasma of cheap liquor, cigarettes, and greasy burgers. He drew a big hammer from his jacket pocket and smashed it into the corpse's forehead.

The corpse felt and heard his skull shatter under the force of the blow, but he felt no pain. Instinctively his hand swept out, razor claws forever silencing the assailant in a drenching spray of arterial blood. The dying man staggered back, hands attempting to staunch the seemingly endless flow of crimson from the hole in his throat.

As the attacker fell heavily to the ground, the corpse

brought one blood-stained finger to his dry lips and sampled the blood with a snake-like tongue. The warmth from the life-giving fluid began to push away the bitter cold that filled the corpse's body.

Yes, the corpse thought. *This used to give me passion: the blood is the life. But there is more...I had a name once. And a woman who called me by that name...*

"Ahhhnahhh, he just killed Leonard!"

Chalupa dropped the camcorder to the ground and pulled a folding knife from his pants pocket, rushing at the old man covered in Leonard's blood.

"Jeezus, don't stop filming, you retard!" Dax panicked and screamed as he picked up the camcorder and resumed filming.

Chalupa brandished the blade as he sidestepped Leonard's body. He shoved it through the old man's chest, punching through the ribcage and impaling the heart. Chalupa backed off, expecting the old man to crumple to the floor just as Leonard had collapsed.

But the old man did not fall. A thin, wheezing laugh escaped his mouth, now twisted in a grimace of bestial, humorless hate. The shadows in the alley seemed to darken and become oily as the temperature dropped noticeably. The man casually pulled the blade from his chest and tossed it aside before speaking in a graveyard whisper.

"Metal. Common metal. Who taught you, boy? They did you a grave disservice. I am beyond mortal pain." The haunting syllables tinged with a European accent were the last words Chalupa would ever hear. The old man's dead black eyes flared crimson

from within a clown-white face. Ancient, withered hands flashed forward, overpowering the much larger man easily. The old man's head darted forward, the mouth open, twin fangs glistening in the streetlight. He pushed the gangster's head to the side, exposing a pulsing artery, and buried his sharp teeth in Chalupa's throat.

The old man savored the rich coppery brew that flooded his mouth, a sensation he had denied himself for too long. He gulped the flow as the knowledge of who he was returned with the infusion of fresh blood.

Justain. My name is Justain. I trace my bloodline back to ancient Thrace. Where my people go, death follows. These witch hunters and their shamans will again learn to fear my name. They will know why they fear the night.

Justain pulled his bloody mouth from Chalupa's shredded neck, his body seething with renewed energy, the empty coldness that had filled it burned away. He casually tossed the corpse aside like a child's toy with such force that bones shattered against the brick wall. Chalupa's body slid down, the gangster's legs spread akimbo, his head lolling from a broken neck. Justain saw Dax standing before him, still filming with the camcorder.

"You are these men's leader?" Justain asked. In previous centuries, the witch hunters he fought had dressed similarly, wearing dark cowls like a monastic order. In contrast, the bloated man in front of him sported a sweat-stained sleeveless white shirt and cutoff shorts with holes in them.

Dax was shocked by what he saw when he looked away from the camcorder lens. The old man had become young after drinking Chalupa's blood. Wrinkled, dry skin became full, smooth, and vibrant, the once-sallow cheeks now ruddy. Lustrous brown hair flowed from a head that had been primarily bald, resting over blazing red eyes and framing sharp, asymmetrical features. Once-atrophied muscle now bulged through the thin silk shirt, showing cuts, definition, and blue veins.

The man smiled, displaying sharp fangs. Dax recalled the movie he had seen just the past weekend at the local United Artist's theater, about a creature of the night who moved into the house next door to a young man and his mother.

Fright Night, Dax thought. *This guy looks like the head vampire in* Fright Night.

He turned awkwardly to run, but Justain was immediately in front of him, flowing effortlessly from one patch of shadows to another. A glacial hand of immense strength wrapped around Dax's doughy throat and lifted the former bodybuilder into the air. Dax gagged, unable to breathe, as his hands battered uselessly against the puissant grip.

Justain allowed long-suppressed primal instincts to rise within him.

"A leader shares his men's fate," Justain whispered. Dax's body relaxed as he began to slip into unconsciousness, accepting the inevitable by embracing the nihilistic thrill of oblivion. As his eyes rolled back into the sockets, he noted absently that dark storm clouds filled the sky, perhaps reflecting the violent emotions of the bum whose sleep he had disturbed. The irony of dying in a forgotten alley at the hands of a vampire transient he wantonly provoked flashed across Dax's mind as he hung like a piece of meat from the creature's claw. He had just instants to ponder the colossal waste he'd made of his life, the roads not taken, the child he'd fathered but never appreciated and now would never see grow up. For the briefest of instants, he felt overwhelming regret for leaving Ashley in a world of piss and excrement. He had survived parasitically, living off the shortcomings and misery of others, a world he had never done anything to improve in any way.

Dax was a classic loser.

Justain sensed the psychic turmoil raging inside the dying man in his hand. He lowered him to the ground, embracing him in darkness as he whispered in his ear.

"You could have just left me undisturbed. You and your men would still be alive. You could have enjoyed the rest of your days with those close to you. You could have...but you chose not to." The vampire's voice trailed off.

Then Dax's short, sad life abruptly ended when Justain closed his grip, crushing Dax's spine like a twig. He died oblivious to the final and most damning mistake of the incalculable errors he committed had been to unwittingly insert himself in an ancient blood feud between the living and the dead.

Justain dropped the corpse. He noted the oblong metal device lying discarded nearby, an instrument the dead men had shown so much interest in. It was of little consequence to him; all that mattered was that witch hunters were once again on his trail. A renewed sense of purpose surged through him, powered by a resurgence of the bloodthirst. Though he was perhaps the last of his kind, he sensed rebuilding the bloodline was within his power. And he would build it on the bones of a new generation of witch hunters.

Justain's attention was drawn by movement toward the street. An old, inebriated transient stumbled down the alley, carrying a brown bag. Justain's keen senses picked up the reek of alcohol from the man's body. The transient stopped in his tracks, shocked green eyes set in a dirty, sunburned face, stunned at the sight of the carnage of blood and bodies in front of him.

Justain ignored the transient and focused on transformation. His ears lengthened as his nose became a feral snout. Leathery wings extended from his spine and shredded what remained of his clothing. He took flight as a demonic bat, the traditional form of his kind, and disappeared into the storm clouds he had inadvertently summoned upon revivification.

An old debt with the witch hunters remained to be settled.

THE SPACIOUS OFFICE ROOM OF THE HIGH-RISE BUILDING'S TOP FLOOR was lit solely by the light of a single computer screen. All employees of the multinational corporation had gone home for the day—all save one.

The company's CEO remained. Myron Sandor sat with his hands steepled on his large mahogany desk, the tips of two fingers pressing underneath the bridge of his nose as he concentrated on his computer screen. Images flickered across the screen, eerily lighting his craggy face framed by a widow's peak of gray hair. He'd received an email link from a colleague to a viral video that was exploding across the internet.

The video showed what appeared to be an empty set of clothes butchering men in an alley. Toward the end of the video, mixed in with the screams of the dying men, Myron discerned a haunting, familiar voice he had not heard in many years. A voice that, for him, would forever be linked to images of wholesale slaughter—the voice of a being he had hoped was truly dead. Myron's breathing quickened, and his blood pressure increased as the video played. When it was over, he fervently typed an encrypted reply to the email's sender.

Have Intel trace that video. Assemble the brethren. The sleeper has woken.

He rose from his desk and turned to face the wall behind him. Mounted on the wall was a large sword engraved with intricately woven sigils that glowed with magic energy. He retrieved it from its mounting and held it by the grip, the heavy weapon comfortable in his weathered hands. He ran his fingers along the blade as the silver coating reflected in his eyes.

JUSTAIN STOOD IMPASSIVELY IN THE DARK DOORWAY OF THE TINY HOUSE, the light of the full moon shining off his face. A passerby would have noted unsettling oddness to him, an alien quality—the strange pallor of his skin, the fact that his dark eyes never blinked, that his chest did not rise and fall with breath.

None of that mattered to Justain. The bonds that had tied him to humanity had been severed long ago. Each time he took a human life, he became further and further separated from the man he had been.

Still, in the dark corners of his psyche where a soul had resided, there was longing, an ache of loss and emptiness. Even after all these years, he could still picture how she had always smiled when she saw him, like it was the first time they had ever met. It was the most beautiful thing he had possessed in his long and dreary existence, perhaps the only thing worth remembering. It was only a fading memory now because she had been taken from him. Taken by witch hunters, the descendants of whom were coming to destroy him even now.

Justain ceased his reminiscences and focused on the issues at hand. The house's former owners stirred from the grimy wooden floor at his mental call, waking into unlife. These unfortunate beings, a Caucasian man and two Latina females, had been the latest victims in a bloody rampage that started when three foolish men unwittingly awakened him from his torpor. He had been famished from years of hibernation, or "going to ground," as some of his kind called it. He had splurged and fed copiously on the dregs of society, the pimp, the robber, the prostitute...those who lived parasitically off the misery and shortcomings of others. He knew the trail of bodies his feedings left would attract the witch hunters to him.

And he would be ready for them this time.

The house owners had run a methamphetamine lab from it, selling poison to the local constituents. Justain had been welcomed inside with a mere flashing of currency he had taken from a dead pimp he had fed on. Unlike his other victims, whom he had drained and discarded, these three had been allowed to drink from his veins, just enough to bring them across into his cursed half-life. They would serve as cannon fodder in the bloody battle to come.

The newborn vampires rose, their dead limbs knocking aside rancid trash as they scrabbled to their feet. They innately sensed Justain's greater power and gathered around him, awaiting his commands.

MYRON FIDGETED IN HIS SEAT, THE PASSENGER SPACE OF THE SWAT van barely able to contain his large frame. He looked at his son as they drove through the low desert, sand billowing out from their tires. It was a look of both pride and trepidation. Pride in what John had made of himself and the warrior he had become. Fear for what was to come this day.

They led a convoy of four black vehicles, each van

containing five fully armed hunters. The sun was cresting in the east as they neared the small isolated house where intel had placed the sleeper. They would use the daylight to their advantage in the coming battle.

Fear bit into Myron's stomach, a bitter sensation he had not experienced in many years, making him cringe involuntarily. Fear not for himself or his hunters, who had chosen this life with full knowledge of the consequences. His fear was for John, who had never faced an evil like the horror they would soon confront.

Myron sensed the age of the monster was coming to a close. The great and fearsome creatures of lore gradually passed from the world, as did all magic in general. The giant flesh-eating ogres, the bestial *loup-garou* that terrorized entire villages— these beings had largely disappeared. Modern hunters only dealt with an occasional flare-up of zombies or a pack of ghouls infesting a cemetery—nuisances that were quickly and quietly dispatched.

John had witnessed these outbreaks and participated in their resolution. Myron allowed his son to don the family mantle of a monster hunter only because he believed the threat to humanity had largely been extinguished.

Then he saw the video and heard that graveyard voice again. He broke into a cold sweat as he remembered the last time he had listened to that voice: the gory assault on the monster's remote sanctuary so many years ago. A sea of blood had flowed from the ruptured bodies of the men he had fought beside. Myron recalled the creature's rage, its red eyes burning in the night more intensely than any flame, as it shrugged off wounds and slaughtered his fellow hunters.

He lay defeated and helpless on the ground, his bones shattered by the creature, watching as his father, their leader, attacked the beast with a huge silver sword. The monster easily evaded the attack and seized his father by the throat. Myron watched powerlessly as the fiend slowly and deliberately strangled the life from the man he idolized...the man who had brought him into the Brotherhood of Hunters.

As the vampire cast his father's broken corpse aside, the silver sword falling discarded to the ground, the creature had looked down upon Myron. Its dark gaze pinioned him. Myron had struggled to lift a small silvered dagger with right arm, his broken hand unable to fully close around the hilt. The creature noted his effort and stopped in its tracks.

Ichor from a hundred wounds mixed with the blood shed by dozens of hunters, covering the revenant in crimson. Patches of pale skin peeked through the foul liquids that coated it. Whether the creature was reeling under the toll of its injuries or Myron's effort to defend himself had convinced it to take pity, Myron would never know. All he did know was that the creature literally flew off into the night, leaving Myron behind on a battlefield laden with corpses.

Myron had lapsed into unconsciousness.

The dread Myron felt in the pit of his stomach was justified. This was not some house-haunting poltergeist or lurching zombie. The creature they would face tonight was a vampire, an ancient Undead responsible for the deaths of thousands of people over its long existence. It was strong and only grew stronger with time like all their kind did. A line from Stoker's *Dracula* came unbidden to his mind. "*The nosferatu do not die like the bee when he sting once. He is only stronger; and being stronger, have yet more power to work evil.*" This creature had been cursed to an eternal half-life of want and misery. That was the point of a curse...to inflict eternal pain on the bearer.

Ending that curse would be no simple undertaking. The vampire would not turn to dust if poked with an ash stake, nor would it spontaneously self-combust if exposed to sunlight. It had survived numerous encounters with the Brotherhood of Hunters, the only one of its kind to do so. It would continue to wreak havoc and despair if it were not stopped immediately. It was a corpse animated by dark magic, a horror driven by unending hate. And it had a name.

Justain.

JUSTAIN WATCHED AS THE SWAT VEHICLES CRESTED OVER THE NEARBY ridge, purple clouds floating on the horizon. The men inside, clad in black synthetic-fiber armor and armed with assault rifles, spilled out onto the sand and surrounded the house. Justain reached out with his mind, using his spirit-sight to touch the winds of raw magical energy that were invisible to mortals but discernible to one who had already passed through the gates of death. He had limited control over the weather conditions and summoned clouds to block the rising sun's light. He was only slightly weakened by daylight, but the newborn revenants he had created would have no strength in the full light.

As the sky darkened, feral coyotes and hordes of rats swarmed out of the surrounding hillside; summoned by the vampire's will, they besieged the hunters. Gunshots erupted as the hunters discharged their weapons, motes of fire flashing in the gloaming.

"*Now,*" Justain directed his revenants. The man and two

women sprinted lithely from the house, like panthers chasing their prey, and joined the fray. The sounds of armor being scored and smashed mixed with the death screams of several hunters as the revenants tore into them, crushing skulls and tossing grown men about like children's toys. Heady with the sense of impending victory, each creature made the mistake of stopping to feed the red thirst that saturated their being. The remaining hunters regrouped, having scattered the coyotes and rats with concentrated fire. They unleashed their silver-jacketed bullets on the Undead, filling their hearts and brainpans with the hot eldritch metal. The revenants fell to the ground, temporarily incapacitated. Given time they would heal and rise. The hunters did not give them that time, as they hacked off the creatures' heads with sharp machetes, black gore drenching the long blades.

It was all the distraction Justain needed.

He flowed from the house, slipping with serpentine grace from one pool of shadow to the next, appearing from nowhere in the middle of the hunters.

The men stood no chance. The vampire moved amongst them with hurricane force, tearing out their throats and snapping their spines. He ignored the bullets that struck him, the strength of centuries giving him enhanced resistance to the banes of his kind.

As he ripped off the head of a large hunter with terrifying ease, another man circled behind and severed the vampire's throat with a vicious machete slash. Justain stumbled for a moment, righted himself, then crushed the hunter's skull with a backhand blow. Black ichor trickled momentarily from his throat wound before it sealed over.

Coated in gore, Justain surveyed the carnage. The air reeked of death and misery. He stood amongst a pile of his adversaries, their spilt blood flowing from their ruptured corpses and mingling in death. Only two adversaries remained. One was familiar.

Myron raised the machete high over his head.

Though shot through with dozens of silver rounds, the female vampire still managed to grasp his leg with superhuman strength. He felt her sharp fingernails penetrate the armor on his calves as she looked up at him with hate-filled crimson eyes, her mouth wide open in a snarl filled with fanged teeth. He brought the machete down twice, severing the head.

Next to him, John killed a remaining coyote with a head-shot. Rats scattered beneath them like a flowing carpet of mange and filth.

Myron recognized the monster standing amongst a pile of dead hunters, the bodies of the men he had trained, some having served under his command for decades. The creature looked the same as it had on that night forty years earlier, not appearing to have aged.

"*I know you*," the fiend addressed Myron in a familiar grave-yard whisper that caused cold sweat to run down the hunter's forehead.

Myron's knees trembled and buckled slightly before he regained composure and stood tall.

"And I know you, blood-eater. You killed my father like you killed many fathers before him. Your kind leaves behind an army of widows and orphans."

"I never asked to be this way," replied the vampire.

"And I never asked to be the leader of an international group of monster hunters. But when you killed my father, I had no other choice but to fill that role. It was my destiny." He dropped the machete and retrieved the silver sword from a scabbard looped behind his back. "This is the sword he wielded when you took him from me. This is the sword I will destroy you with. This blade is thirsty for your accursed ichor and will send you screaming back to whatever hell you came from!"

The vampire did not move as Myron approached with the sword held high. It spoke, its voice like wind whistling through dry leaves in the fall.

"You have no idea what it's like to have the red thirst singing through your veins, knowing that if you do not suffice it, you will die again—slowly, painfully, and never to return. It is a curse, this unlife that was thrust upon me. Perhaps we are both cursed. You and your men have proven unworthy of granting me final death. But your family has taken from me. We fed only on criminals, on those that preyed upon others. And yet you hunted us down, chased us to the ground like animals. I had forgotten her name until tonight. Seeing you here, now old and gray, reminds me of her. Her name was Madesta. And you and your father took her from me. Tonight, I take from you, Myron Sandor. Tonight I take everything."

Myron was shocked the vampire knew his name.

Before he could act, John rushed forward, firing silver rounds into the eldritch being and raising a machete over his head. Justain ignored the bullets and casually caught the blade in his hand as it descended. The vampire crumpled the metal like tinfoil.

He seized John in an unbreakable grip, spinning him around to face Myron.

The vampire looked the old witch hunter in the face.

"We'll be seeing you, Dad." John screamed helplessly as he

was borne aloft by the vampire, disappearing into the murky sky.

And Myron screamed as he fell to his knees in the sand, his hands gripping his head and tearing out his gray hair in futile rage.

THREE DAYS LATER, MYRON FACED THE WINDOW BEHIND HIS DESK, sword drawn and clenched in his hands.

He had not slept, knowing what was coming. He had prepared himself as best as he knew how. Still, the emotional anxiety had taken its toll. He felt weak and listless, his mouth dry, lips chapped. Sweat covered his forehead.

He looked through the windowpane. Mist swirled outside, obscuring the amber moonlight. A thin-boned hand tapped the outside pane, the long nails clicking on the glass.

"*Dad, can I come in? I miss you.*" The voice was low, light, and utterly lacking in emotion or earnestness.

The sheer absurdity of the entire situation, like something out of a Tarantino binge-violence revenge saga, was not lost on Myron. He waited for his Undead son and the creature who had murdered him to arrive outside his twentieth-story window and ask permission to enter and feast on his blood. And his reply to that request was just as absurd and insane.

"Come in, John. Both of you. Enter freely and of your own will."

The window exploded inward in a hailstorm of glass. John

sailed in, still wearing the hunter armor he had died in, casually tossing Myron's massive work desk aside and into the wall with a clawed hand. His eyes were crimson, and his fanged incisors hung over his bottom lip. Justain flowed in beside him, his eyes dark, his face emotionless.

Myron gripped the hilt of the sword with both hands and brought the weapon up to shoulder height, assuming the ready position of the *samurai.*

Justain spoke taciturnly. *"Your son has become that which you most despise, hunter—a monster. A fiend like me. Are you willing to destroy him, as your father destroyed my Madesta? Could you live with yourself, knowing what you had done?"*

Myron knew that he could not. He looked at John's feral visage and saw nothing of the young man he had raised, no trace of the son he had loved and laughed with. But he remained resolute and committed to his course of action.

He dropped the sword, the clanging echoing hollowly in the room. John was on him instantly, burying his teeth in his father's throat, drinking deep.

Myron's knees buckled, and father and son fell to the floor, John on top. Myron stared up at the ceiling as his lifeblood was drained.

Justain moved in to view, standing beside them.

Myron spoke, his voice panicked. "The blood debt ends tonight. I've paid for what my father took from you, Justain. My son and I have paid."

Justain shook his head. *"No, Myron, blood debts can never be repaid, only restructured, like paradigms are restructured. A businessman like yourself should know that."*

Myron watched in shock and horror as Justain smashed his clawed hand through John's chest, removing the black heart. Dark ichor sprayed into Myron's face. An instant later, the ancient vampire ripped his son's head off, the decapitated body slumping heavily to the floor.

"I finally realized after all these years that I need an adversary. Someone to keep my mind active, to prevent it from slipping into senility and dementia. For centuries you and your kind provided me with that distraction. But now your organization is dying out, Myron, just as you are. You are all that is left now. Your son was never the man you are. He would have made a poor substitute. You will accompany me throughout eternity, plaguing me, an immortal foe for an immortal fiend. Your bitter hate will fuel your efforts. And that hate will be magnified a thousandfold for each life you take to sustain your cursed existence."

Myron's vision began to blur from the blood loss. He watched as Justain bit into his wrist, drawing forth the vampiric black ichor.

The vampire raised his chin. *"You will be horrified by what you must do to satisfy your new thirst—disgusted by your savagery. Your body will become a soulless vessel driven by necrotic magic."*

And as the vampire brought the bloody wrist to Myron's mouth and the cold liquid fell on his lips, the witch hunter realized his curse had just begun.

CALMET AND NIGHT'S DARK MASTER

> "When you're in hell, only a devil can point the way out."
>
> —JOE ABERCROMBIE

Father Calmet looked up from the heavy wooden table where he sat, pen in hand, his brow knit in concern, as two friars in dark wool robes escorted their prisoner into the room through the arched doorway, their sandaled steps heavy on the stone floor. Sparse candlelight illuminated the room, exposing the murky expanse of a vaulted ceiling. Shadows brimmed in the corners and alcoves.

"Please, have a seat, Don Lazaro," Calmet said cordially, gesturing to a nearby wooden stool. He noted a sudden drop in the room's temperature as his guest approached, his body shivering.

"Thank you," the pale man said as he regally sat, his red eyes reflecting the light like a night predator. In sharp contrast to the alabaster hue of his smooth, flawless skin, he was dressed entirely in black. Iron chains encircled his thin-yet-muscular torso, secured by stout manacles on each of his long-fingered hands. Looped strings of pungent garlic flower hung from his neck.

"It's quite musty in here," Lazaro observed. "The lack of fresh air makes the acrid smell of these flowers even more dreadful."

"I didn't know you breathed, to be honest," the priest admitted.

"I can smell, unfortunately. I must say, these are very modest accommodations for such a revered scholar, scarcely superior to the spare quarters you have bestowed upon me in my unwelcome stay. I would have expected more from the esteemed heir to the legacy of Origen," Lazaro asserted, referring to the prolific early Christian scholar and theologian. The dark man's eyes wandered, taking in the room's entirety. "Though at least your chair has arms to rest on—I've been relegated to a shoddy stool."

"I appreciate your comparing me with the famed Origen, but I'm afraid my research and writings are far less extensive than the Alexandrian. I'm also afraid amenities are in short supply here; after all, we are in the basement of a monastery. The upper levels are much more charming, I can assure you. And, as we both know, you've resided in far more unappealing locations before you came to join us," Calmet needled, abandoning hospitality.

Lazaro's eyes blazed briefly in indignation. "I commanded armies centuries before you first put mouth to your mother's tit, *cura*. My impenetrable mountain fortress hosted the kings and queens of Europe and the heads of state from other continents. Artists worldwide battled one another for my patronage, desperate to secure even the briefest of audiences with me.

Their brilliant sculptures, paintings, and tapestries filled my halls and lined my walls. Do not speak to me as if I were one of the naïve simpletons you address on Sundays. The outright arrogance of your faith has always astounded me. What makes you feel so superior that you can lecture others on morality? What great insights into the mortal soul have you achieved?"

Calmet did not rise to the bait. "And yet, Don Lazaro, for all your blustering of a bygone era far removed from current circumstances, Father Montesi followed the trail of bloodless corpses you left. He found you hiding in a dank, weathered mausoleum, cowering in a moldy crypt that bore another family's name and crest. How the mighty appear to have fallen, no?" he pointed out.

The vampire dismissed the priest's assertion, tossing his clawed hand to the side as if brushing the offending words away. "One sometimes has to make do with whatever lodgings are available, especially when an entire faith, a rambling cult of credulous morons, is seeking his destruction."

The two friars, men of intimidating size and mien, continued standing at attention as Calmet and Lazaro spoke, as though awaiting further orders. Calmet courteously dismissed them.

"That will be all for now, brothers."

The two men remained still, appearing reluctant to leave, their anxious gazes fixed on the prisoner.

"I assure you, brothers, I shall be fine. I am more than capable of defending myself, should that become necessary. The Lord protecteth," Calmet stated, the fingers of one hand gripping the silver crucifix dangling from his rosary bead necklace. He gestured toward a long wooden blade that rested beside the stack of papers in front of him.

The chained man averted his eyes from Calmet and focused his attention directly on the alcove behind where the priest sat.

A giant portmanteau figure loomed ominously in the shadows, glassy gray eyes staring ahead from under a thick, gnarled brow. The top of its skull was abnormally flat, giving the head a crooked shape. Vivid scars and stitches crisscrossed the fish-white skin of its muscular, disproportioned frame. The creature's enormous size stretched its wool clothing close to bursting. A golden amulet tethered to a leather necklace hung between its thick pectoral muscles; a curled serpent was emblazoned on the metal.

"The flesh construct, again, I see," Lazaro intoned.

"A necessary precaution, I assure you. I'm sure you'll excuse its presence, Don Lazaro, for your powers are not to be taken lightly, as some of my brethren recently discovered," Calmet countered.

Lazaro looked unmoved. "It is still daylight outside, I sense; otherwise, you would not have thought to remove me from the crucifix-laden, garlic-festooned chamber to which you've banished me. You, of all people, Father Calmet, should be aware that my kind are quite innocuous in the daytime. I discern that the sky is somewhat overcast; twilight is not far off now," the vampire said almost longingly. He noticed his words discomforted Calmet, who fidgeted uneasily in his chair.

"Yes, priest, I see that look of concern flashing in your bovine eyes, your teeth clenching involuntarily as the breath catches in your lungs. Even though there are no windows here, even though we are several levels below ground, I can sense the steady passage of the sun as it begins its inexorable descent behind a raft of thick cumulous clouds. One must be aware of the enemy's position at all times. Surely, as a scholar of such matters, this knowledge should not shock you?"

Calmet noted the stab of derision in Lazaro's words. He cursed inwardly for letting his ignorance of the vampire's preternatural sense of time show. His superiors had warned him to be cautious with the creature, that the dead man would seek to badger and bend his will to dark purposes. He sought to turn the tables by putting the vampire on the defensive.

"Yes, normally, I would agree with your statement. Revenants like yourself tend to be comatose during the daylight hours, restricted to their coffins and crypts, and unable to move about freely. And yet, according to Father Montesi, when he and his crew discovered your place of rest last week in the mausoleum, you were able to rise, despite the daylight, and kill several of his men. If not for the presence of Adam," Calmet said, referring to the gigantic flesh construct in the alcove, "you would have butchered the entire team. Even so, you managed to tear off one of its arms before it subdued you."

"An arm which your necromancers have seen fit to replace, I see," Lazaro observed matter-of-factly. "Odd, is it not, for the Church to employ heathen sorcerers to buttress its already-substantial forces with eldritch flesh constructs assembled from corpses? The creation of such beings requires body snatching, the defilement of the sacred tranquility of the grave, no?"

Calmet did not immediately answer.

Lazaro continued. "No resurrection of the body is in store for those poor souls when your 'lord' comes again. I am no mage, but I know dark magics are required to fashion such flesh constructs. Of course, it stands to reason that a sect which worships a god credited with raising his sycophants from the grave might also become intimately involved with the black arts and resurrection."

Calmet smirked in condescension, ignoring the vampire's verbal barbs. "Desperate times require desperate measures—I believe you said something similar just moments ago. The recent surge of supernatural beings in the world has unfortunately made such alliances necessary, I'm afraid. I don't suppose you could lend any insight into the eldritch maelstrom buffeting the world, could you?"

Lazaro shrugged. "As I said, I am not a sorcerer, though the source of my powers is clearly of eldritch origins. What's the ancient Akkadian saying? 'When there's no more room in hell?' The complete phrase eludes me at the moment. Portals to other dimensions manifest, sometimes randomly, sometimes at the behest of magic practitioners. When these portals open, unwelcome entities occasionally slip through. These beings tend to harass the living and leave other supernaturals alone. Or so I'm told," Lazaro said dispassionately. "Can you really trust your new pagan allies, priest? Perhaps one of your pet necromancers has gone rogue and summoned beings from other realities?"

Calmet disregarded the notion. "Possible but highly unlikely—the Church has eyes and ears everywhere, as you are aware. Know this, vampire: wooden stakes, silver blades, wolf's-bane, sea salt, and holy oil...these traditional instruments only go so far nowadays. Our recent short-term alliance with the magic community will terminate once matters are better under control. But back to matters at hand... After your capture, you agreed to speak with us regarding the nature of your Undead race, your powers and weaknesses, your methods of creation. In exchange, we would not destroy you but, instead, allow you to 'live' in captivity in the basement of this monastery. You signed this vellum," Calmet gestured to an adjacent yellowed paper, "in your blood."

"Indeed," Lazaro concurred with an air of amused boredom, one sleek eyebrow raised, the tips of his fang teeth visible.

"And in that spirit of cooperation, let me ask you, how is it that you were able to shrug off the daylight coma and attack Montesi's crew? We have never encountered vampires conscious during the day, let alone capable of movement," Calmet acknowledged.

Lazaro grinned. "You and your people have only encountered the youngest of my kind—newborns. Their bodies are adjusting to the Undead state. They die again each day with the coming of the dawn, completely helpless until night falls once more. On the other hand, I am a master revenant—I have existed longer than you dare imagine. I rose from my grave long before your Christ performed his pedantic little theatrics in Palestine for a group of gullible fishmongers. I can think and move about during the daytime, albeit with reduced capabilities." The vampire steepled his long, clawed fingers in front of the malicious smile on his face. "Somewhat reduced, that is."

"And that brings me to the methods to destroy your kind," Calmet continued.

"Ahh, so soon? Jumping right to the heart of the matter, so to speak, are we, good Father?"

Calmet continued assiduously. "Until Father Montesi's encounter with you, we had believed that a simple wooden stake, driven with great force through the heart, would suffice to bring permanent destruction to your kind. Adam was able to pierce your heart with a hawthorn stake and apparently kill you at one point. Yet, during your body's transport here, the stake was inadvertently jostled free by the foot of a clumsy and now-deceased friar, allowing you to move again, somehow still imbued with cursed life."

"Cursed indeed, Father Calmet, cursed indeed," Lazaro affirmed. "The progenitor of my kind was cursed with this unlife untold millennia ago—some sort of necromantic ritual gone badly, or so I was led to believe. Perhaps you could ask one of your pet necromancers when you are not busy conducting your, shall we say...research? But then again, I suppose it's all the same death magic, whether it be a sorcerer raising a flesh construct, a vampire living on after its physical death, or a pretentious false god rising from his tomb."

Lazaro's words seemed to disconcert Calmet. The priest furrowed his brow and pursed his lips. As the vampire spoke, the power of his voice seemed to magnify and fill the room as though he were drawing strength and confidence with each consecutive syllable. "Now, 'let's get to the bottom line,' as you breathers say. We are the Undead—neither specter nor demon but partaking of the mysterious dark aspects of both. We cannot be unmade by the passage of time or an assault by conventional weapons. Stab us, shoot us, hang us—we will recover. We must first be immobilized by a hawthorn or oak stake driven deep through the heart during the daytime and then decapitated with a single stroke from a keenly sharp blade. The head must be kept separate from the torso, or they will rejoin, and the vampire will reincarnate. Both segments must be burned and the ashes scattered in running water for what remains of our souls to be put to final rest. Even then, we many reincarnate under the right circumstances and the proper sanguine rituals. At night, you have no chance against us. At night, we are far, far too powerful." The vampire smiled mischievously, revealing his long incisors.

"Powerful indeed," Calmet observed, putting his pen aside and leaning forward. "I have seen first-hand what your breed can do, Don Lazaro."

"Do tell. I'm all ears."

"It was years ago when I was young and new to the order. The late Father Sandor led our crew, a man not only of great intellect but also tremendous physical strength as well. His Eminence assigned us to rid the village of Stetl of the plague that haunted it by night, foreshadowing the supernatural eruption that would occur a decade later. To that end, we had routed the 'newborn,' as you termed it, from its cemetery crypt. It was not an easy procedure—two of our men died in the process, their maimed bodies lying in mute testament to the newborn's ferocity. The woman, stunningly beautiful in her long white shroud and flowing blond hair, evaded our attacks and fled into the nearby mountains. As the sun rose on the horizon, she made for the shelter of a cave. It so happened a gigantic black bear occupied that cave, an apex predator that did not appreciate having its dwelling invaded by a creature that reeked of carrion and grave dirt.

"Imagine our amazement as we approached the dark cave mouth and listened to the sounds of the titanic struggle. The bruin's roars seemed to shake the very ground we walked on. The female creature hissed like a gigantic serpent as she pounced on the beast. They moved almost too fast for our eyes to follow, claws and fangs flashing, flesh shredding, and blood spilling.

"For a moment, the battle seemed won. The bear had latched its great jaws around the shoulder and neck of the vampire, her black blood spilling out. But in the space of a heartbeat, the woman dug her long fingers deep into the bruin's throat. She tore out its windpipe with brutal efficiency. The great beast collapsed on top of her, breathing its last.

"At the direction of Father Sandor, our group approached with stakes at the ready. The woman lay under the giant corpse, spent from the monumental battle, her eyes half-closed, her body covered in horrid wounds. As we watched, the bear's blood pooled from its rent throat into her open mouth. Her eyes opened fully, becoming blood red. The wounds on her body began to close.

"Impossibly, her soft voice invaded my mind. 'Free me,' she said.

"As I stood perplexed, Father Sandor took the initiative. 'Compose yourself, Calmet,' he shouted as he seized the wooden lance I held in my shaking hands, raised it over her torso, and smashed it down through her breast, impaling her dead heart. The woman stopped moving. Afterward, we bound the body in thick chains and transported it back to the monastery. Even now, it resides in one of the deeper alcoves, locked in an iron tomb."

"You might be surprised what would happen were you to remove that stake, good Father Calmet," Lazaro observed.

Calmet's throat was dry as he spoke. "I have an idea, bloodsucker. As we rode back, I heard the dead woman speak to me again with her mind. She promised me power and eternal life, filled my brain with images of her naked form lying in my arms. More than once, I found myself unconsciously reaching toward her impaled body, hands ready to tear the lance from her chest." The priest's mind appeared to drift momentarily, his gaze unfocused. The vampire seized upon his distraction.

"Where are you, Calmet? Is she with you now?" he baited.

Calmet shook his head as if awakening from a trance before resuming the discussion.

"But enough of that settled matter. Tell me more, Don Lazaro. Speak to me of the strengths of the Undead, every last one of them."

"Where to begin?" Lazaro questioned affably, gesturing with his hands. "I am a vampire, a state of being purged of all the weaknesses of your kind. Our powers are legion. Death has amplified all my senses. I can hear each distinct pulse that fills the chambers of the cloister above us, despite the layers of stone and mortar. Even the weakest newborn vampire is gifted with strength several times greater than the strongest living man. I always have the strength in my hand of twenty men, and my vitality only increases as I grow older. Unlike the bee, which delivers its sting and then passes away, spent, the vampire grows stronger with the passing of centuries."

Lazaro's soulless eyes grew even brighter in the dim candlelight, his voice more passionate.

"We move with the speed of a striking serpent, melded with the agility of a panther. We see in the dark, a gift not to be dismissed in a world half-covered by night. Our forms are mutable, allowing us to slip through the smallest of openings or grow in size. We can take the form of other creatures of the night, whether they be wolf or serpent, bat or owl—indeed, these same creatures are ours to call to our beckon when we choose. We can fly or ride as clouds of dust on the silver rays of moonlight. Whether it be summoning a fog to mask our presence as we hunt or conjuring a devastating lightning bolt strike upon a hapless foe, the elements themselves obey our commands. Our minds are far superior to humans, with centuries of experience and knowledge buttressed by perfect recall. Like the snake, our gaze fascinates and compels—few are the mortals that can resist our will, the minds of corrupt and lustful men being unusually susceptible. But perhaps our greatest strength resides in the fact that few believe in our existence and therefore are unaware of the price we pay for our immortality."

"Yes, the price for eternal life...it must be great. Speak on this matter," Calmet ordered, his attention completely rapt in the vampire's words.

"Nothing comes for free in this existence... Anyone who tells you otherwise is a clown and a fool," Lazaro said contemptuously. "Our powers, as with all cursed things, largely cease with the coming of day. We cannot cross the oceans of water without the sanctuary afforded by our coffins and the native earth lying in them. Like demons, we cannot enter a private dwelling without an invitation."

"And yet, here you are inside this monastery—how is this possible if someone did not invite you in?"

"Priest, are you unfamiliar with the inscription over the

front door of your own building? '*Grata sint omnia*...all are welcome.' An open invitation to all my kind."

"I see," Calmet admitted, grudgingly impressed. He made a mental note to address the door inscription issue before night fell, in case the vampire had allies in waiting. "Please continue. I am, like you, all ears."

"There is not much else. The symbols of your faith can cause us pain if backed by sufficient faith. The sun weakens us, and running water will drown us. Separation from our native soil drains our strength, an unwelcome state of privation I am currently experiencing, thanks to your abduction. There is little else to add in that regard. But now I have a question for you, Father Calmet. Why are you so interested in my kind?" Lazaro rubbed the sharp nails of his claw against themselves.

"The Church must first understand the capabilities of our enemy, both physical and psychological, if we are to vanquish them," Calmet responded. "As the Church's foremost scholar in the arcane, it is my responsibility to amass as much verifiable information as possible."

The vampire looked at his captor quizzically. "Are you sure you want to destroy me, Father? I sense something else in your questions beyond mere intelligence gathering. Your pulse rapidly increased when you discussed your encounter with the female newborn. Your world paradigm shifted that day, didn't it? It appears you have a suppressed desire, hidden deep in your gut, to become something more than just a simple researcher, to become one of us."

Calmet scoffed. "You flatter yourself, vampire. Why would I seek to damn myself and be cursed to an eternal half-life, neither living nor dead, forever fearing the light of day and fleeing the persecution of the Church?"

"Why indeed, Father, why indeed?" Lazaro rejoined, relishing the verbal daggers he thrust ruthlessly into the priest's ego. "Do you seek to reunite with your vampire lover, who pines for you in the cold alcove you've banished her to? Do you fantasize about her cold lips on your throat, her icy hands caressing your groin? Is your time on this earth so ephemeral that you feel vulnerable as a human? So many books to read and so little time. Did you lose your mother when you were young? Or did your father abuse you? Perhaps you are not so confident in the 'resurrection of the body' your holy books speak of? Perchance you seek a more certain form of resurrection from a god you can speak to in person. I assure you, my blood is strong and poured out for many," the vampire bantered, mocking Christ's speech from the Last Supper.

A flustered Calmet attempted to change the subject at hand. "You are no god, vampire. You are an unholy leech that lacks the common sense to remain dead and buried. And how is it, Don Lazaro, that you came to number yourself one amongst the Undead? Surely a man of intellect such as you could never willingly ask for such a fate?"

"Hah! You hide behind your fatuous moral code, pretending that it elevates you, but we aren't so different, you and I. Do you think no rational man would want to exist as I do? You still have no conception of the power I wield, the sights I have seen."

"Look around you, vampire. I hold power here," Calmet contradicted.

"Indeed...indeed you do, pompous priest," Lazaro concurred, his voice laden with contempt. "For the moment."

Calmet stood slowly to his feet, his hand gripping the bottom of the crucifix and thrusting it toward Lazaro. The vampire scowled as he turned his head aside, his long teeth hanging over his grimacing bottom lip.

"Do not consider attempting any sort of attack on me, vampire! I assure you I, as well as Adam," the priest threatened, looking back over his shoulder at the flesh construct, "am quite prepared to send your execrable soul down where it belongs with Beelzebub."

He produced a gold coin from his robe that mirrored the design of the flesh construct's amulet. "With this medallion, the pagan necromancers who created Adam have given me complete control of the monster's actions—it obeys my commands."

The coin in Calmet's grip began to glow with vibrant amber light. As if in response, the construct's amulet also glimmered. The titan took a step forward, the ground shaking under the impact of its gigantic booted foot as the acrid smell of dark magic churned in the air.

The vampire raised his clawed hands in a sign of submission. "Peace, priest. There is no cause for violence...yet."

Calmet looked skeptical before slowly resuming his seat, ignorant of the tiny grin on Lazaro's face. He sat the medallion down next to the knife on the table as the construct assumed a more relaxed posture. The priest recommended his questioning.

"Answer me, leech. How did you become a vampire? How does your kind procreate?"

Lazaro smirked. His mind floated fretfully back on a sea of dark memories to a time when the air had filled his lungs and blood pulsed in his veins.

"It was long ago, a much darker time, in a land far north of our current abode, where the nights were lengthier, the blood ran thicker, and the dead traveled fast. Human life was not held in great esteem. I was the son of royalty and the favored knight of my king, leading his men in defense of the kingdom from the rabid onslaught of barbarian invaders, savages who raped and pillaged and enslaved. My last human memories were of standing against the rabid horde, battling in the twilight on the edge of a haunted woodland known as the Black Forest, hacking and stabbing and creating a gory pile of corpses. The entire time I felt a dark presence monitoring my actions from those woods.

"Eventually, I was outnumbered. A blade dug deep under my cuirass, piercing between my ribs and inflicting a mortal blow. I staggered but did not fall, reversing my blade and taking the man's head on the backstroke. A dozen savages surrounded me as I dropped to one knee, now helpless to defend myself as my blood pooled out onto the thirsty ground, steaming in the frigid air.

"Yet, as the barbarians pressed their attack, a monstrous creature emerged from the shadows of the Black Forest. It was a terrifying hybrid of man and bat and wolf, a blur of talons and sharp teeth. It flowed from one shadow to the next, taking the lives of my enemies effortlessly. I can still recall their chilling screams as they fell, their swords and daggers proving useless, their armor no match for the creature's prodigious strength and sharp claws. They died in various horrible manners, crushed, broken, torn, and exsanguinated. Dismembered limbs and headless torsos littered the ground.

"I found myself lying on my back, unable to move and staring into the night sky. Ice crawled into my veins, and my vision blurred as my breathing became ragged and heavy. As death reached out to claim me, I saw the Master's face for the first time as he leaned over me, pale as the moon itself and calm, reassuring, with an aquiline nose and noble jaw. The sclera of his eyes bled red as the moonlight reflected off his bloody lips—he had fed as he killed.

"The Master spoke to me, not with his voice but with his mind, a tranquil inflection that resonated with my dying soul.

"'Your fight is not over yet, warrior. I sense the restlessness of your soul. This will not be your final battle, for I require you. The nights are long, and I grow weary of being alone. You're not going to die now—there is something much greater and more interesting for you to see.'

"The Master's teeth were sharp and long and white. They entered my throat like twin daggers of ice, drawing out what little blood remained in my veins as my heart slowed. Then the Master opened a wound on his naked breast with his sharp nails, black ichor seeping forth. He cradled my head like a child and placed it against the wound. I drank in his blood, cold and coppery yet brimming with energy and power. It began to cause tremendous changes as my body died, burning away all human frailty with a coat of immortal ice. My soul was absorbed and cradled by the Master's will in a bond of indescribable and unbreakable intimacy.

"'You will have great power now and all the time in the world to use it. Things you would never have dreamed of achieving are possible now if you will but learn the discipline required to master them.'

"He took my bloodless corpse with him deep into the Black Forest and buried it next to his own grave. He shielded me from true death, returning my consciousness three days later to the changed flesh of my now-immortal frame. And as I tore my way from the dirt and stone grave with supernatural strength and ease in a dark mockery of birth, it was the Master who stood over the grave watching, waiting for his newborn to return.

"As I stood reborn, a dark phoenix whose eyes penetrated the shade of night with frightening ease, I understood that I shared the Master's memories with his blood. I saw the Master many centuries before, a living, breathing human, surrounded by enemies and conspirators on a field of fading light. They had betrayed him, drawn him away from his loyal retinue, then stabbed and kicked him, knocking him to the ground where he sprawled in the snow and mud and mulch. The Master tried to stand, but one traitor stepped forward, a skeletal necromancer, the death magic he wielded causing him to look more like an ambulatory corpse than a living man. The necromancer shoved a long dagger into the Master's back, immobilizing him before flipping him onto his back and holding another blade to his throat. The other conspirators seized his arms and feet, holding him down as they hurled jibes and insults, some labeling him a sorcerer.

"'I am no sorcerer! I am a warrior! I will not die!' the Master spit defiantly through bloodied lips, unbowed.

"The necromancer grinned, savoring the Master's suffering. 'Oh no, not yet you won't, good prince. Not yet, young dragon. There is still much suffering you must endure, many insults committed by your father that need to be addressed.' He pierced the Master's cheek with the dagger and cut, disfiguring his mouth.

"'No more triumphant smile, good prince. I have taken that away.'

"'I WILL NOT DIE!' the Master repeated, choking on his blood.

"'If you insist, good prince. And yet, I choose to take more than your smile. I choose to take more than your title. I take your tongue now, sorcerer, so that no more spells or curses may pass through your lips. Before you expire, I will take your nose and then your face to remove the recollection of its arrogance from my memory. I will only recall you as the shattered, ruined, babbling wreck of a man I now make of you!'

"The necromancer removed parts of the Master's face, one bloody piece at a time, but the Master's resolve remained unaffected. Perhaps it was a curse. Perhaps it had something to do with the charnel magics circulating the necromancer. Whatever the cause, the Master's will lived on in that body, an eternal dark presence, even after breath had left it. That iron will reanimated the Master's corpse three days later, vengeful rage pushing it to rise from its shallow, hastily dug grave. Perhaps the first of its kind to ever walk the earth, the newly Undead creature soon discovered that it needed sustenance to maintain its physical integrity. And the Master learned the significance of a phrase that was old when the oceans drank Atlantis: 'Blood is life, and life is blood.'"

Calmet's face was a mask of concern as Lazaro concluded his story.

"And now you see, good Father Calmet, what I have unveiled to you, perhaps the greatest secret of vampire kind. For the sire's memories are carried to the newborn through the blood, the knowledge base multiplying exponentially with each new generation. Every new vampire is superior to the one who created it," Lazaro said.

"Why would you tell me this, vampire? Surely you know I will use it against you?" Calmet asked in astonishment.

Lazaro looked the priest squarely in the face. "I tell you so that you might begin to understand how the sire feels when his bloodchild is ripped away from him by mortal hunters and paralyzed with a stake. It's as if someone reached down through your ribcage and tore your heart out. A piece of your being is ripped away, leaving an icy hole where once there was passion and devotion. The gentle, reassuring touch of their mind upon yours is no longer present. I tell you because you will not live long enough to benefit from this knowledge, you arrogant monkey. Your thirst for erudition was so great that it overwhelmed your reason." Lazaro laughed, latching onto the priest's mind with his iron will. "In your state of unmitigated arrogance morbidly compounded by a thinly disguised lust for the blood kiss, you forget how long we have been speaking. The setting sun above is now completely shielded by cloud cover."

Calmet touched the medallion with his finger, causing the flesh construct to come to attention as its amulet glowed in response. Still, the priest's mind quickly crumbled before the mental onslaught Lazaro unleashed. Calmet's glassy eyes stared vacantly ahead.

Lazaro allowed his human façade to fade. As his eyeteeth lengthened into razor-sharp points, the vampire's eyes became smoldering crimson embers set deep in coal-black sockets. Lazaro's forehead thickened and furrowed, assuming a demonic mien, his ears extending into elfin tips. The face he revealed was horrible beyond imagining.

Calmet attempted to scream but was unable.

"Your feeble efforts at resisting my compulsion are useless, priest," Lazaro mocked. "You sealed your own fate when you set aside pure faith in your god and conspired with the sordid magics of the necromancers. Did you believe I could be captured and contained unless I allowed it? I've always marveled at the hubris of the Church, your conceit that your god was unique in his ability to transcend physical death. Men have been rising from their graves long before Christ raised Lazarus from his deathbed. And now, Calmet, you will know the true power of the vampire," Lazaro continued, ordering the mind-slaved priest to lift the wooden blade and cut away the garlic flowers that bound and weakened him. A tear formed in one corner of Calmet's eye, the remaining shred of his consciousness realizing that he had brazenly chosen to battle the devil. For that act of insipid overconfidence, he was caught and justifiably condemned.

"A power that will ever elude you," the vampire added as he snapped the chains like twigs and flipped the heavy desk aside. He grasped Calmet with superhuman speed and strength, the silver crucifix around the priest's neck only a minor deterrent, before burying his fangs deep into Calmet's throat, glutting himself on the warm liquid ambrosia that flowed within. The flesh construct, acting on primal instinct, lurched to attack.

Darkness closed around Calmet as his heart sputtered and died. There would be no resurrection for him.

"Complete mastery over death," Lazaro exclaimed, allowing the priest's ruptured corpse to fall to the ground as he vaulted onto the brute creature's massive chest.

"A lone priest and his *uber* zombie servant never stood a chance against a master revenant," the vampire boasted. He felt the construct's enormous hands encircle his throat and squeeze with incredible force. It occurred to Lazaro that the creature's strength rivaled his own, but where the monster was slow and plodding and stupid, the vampire moved with terrifying speed and dexterity. He buried his talons under the creature's prominent chin, his fingers bursting out messily through the top of its flat skull, ripping apart the thick metal staples that held the asymmetric head together. Still, the creature refused to die, whatever strange mixture of magic and alchemy animating it making it nearly indestructible; it relentlessly continued trying to rip his head off.

Lazaro transformed, his arms and fingers lengthening, membranous wings sprouting from his back. The vampire grew larger, his torso swelling with unnatural muscle as his mouth extended into a snout filled with razor-sharp teeth. He became a creature of nightmare, a terrifying amalgam of bat and wolf covered in coarse, bristling black fur.

Lazaro dug his snout into the construct's neck, easily tearing through the stitches, and latched onto the vertebrae. He worried at the spinal column, his teeth grating on the thick bone until, finally, his jaws snapped shut, and the brute's head rolled free, bouncing on the floor.

The vampire resumed his human aspect as he stood in a pool of blood and jade ichor and gray brain matter, the truly dead corpses of the priest and the flesh construct at his feet.

"Never take what belongs to me, priest," he sneered.

Lazaro recalled the words of his Master that first night when he rose.

You are forever Night's Dark Master, my child.

The two friars that earlier escorted him from his cell burst into the room. One was armed with a long wooden stake, the other with a sharp *kukri* blade. Lazaro rose to the challenge. He gestured with the index finger of his right hand for them to attack him.

The closest friar slashed the *kukri* across the vampire's chest. The blade passed through Lazaro as if he was made of mist.

Lazaro reached out and grabbed the friar by the neck. He pulled his claw back, taking the man's throat with him in a bloody spray.

As the first friar slumped to the floor, the second thrust his stake at Lazaro's chest. The ancient vampire bladed his body at the last second so that the weapon missed his heart and instead punctured a lung. Lazaro drew the bloodless stake from his chest and thrust it entirely through the friar's torso, lifting him off his.

The vampire shoved the stake into the wall, leaving the dying man hanging like an impaled bug on a needle.

"Not a pleasant feeling, is it?" Lazaro whispered into the friar's ear.

An alarm rang out, the cacophony music to Lazaro's ears. And then the vampire began to hunt the other inhabitants of the monastery with relish, their screams fueling his bloodlust as they echoed off uncaring walls. Each kill invigorated him, spurring him to further acts of murder and bloodshed.

A priest charged from a shadowy alcove and splashed fiery liquid from a wooden flask on the vampire's face. Lazaro licked his lips and tasted the holy water, letting it sear into his gums. The pain gave him focus.

"Your faith is weak, priest," he chided as he casually back-handed his attacker, snapping the man's neck.

More holy men came to the attack. Their numbers mattered little in such close confines. The walls simply funneled them to him like cattle to the slaughter. He fed on some, their blood causing red explosions behind his eyelids as his body filled with unbridled energy.

As he removed a man's spinal column messily from its shattered torso, Lazaro smelled his fledgling's blood spore calling to him in the air. He vowed to ensure neither he nor his bloodchild would ever again endure the indignities and insults of living men; he would call down lightning from the sky and reduce this structure to rubble once he was finished.

"I am coming, dear Alicia. Your lengthy imprisonment is finally at an end."

The wretched screams of dying men continued long into the night.

WHITECHAPEL NIGHTS

Stifling brown fog filled the streets of Whitechapel, diffusing the flickering yellow light of the ambient gas lamps and masking the radiance of a waxing gibbous moon. Few pedestrians were out this Samhain Night to celebrate the beginning of the darker half of the year, for terror had come to Whitechapel. Prostitutes had been murdered, their throats cut, organs removed, their bodies discarded in alleyways with the trash. The police were baffled—no leads, arrests, or suspects identified.

The press had given the fiend a name, an appropriate title for the terror he brought: Jack the Ripper.

Legride Kostaki, Bloodmaster of London, resolved to deal with this mortal who had caused such havoc in his borough.

He walked confidently through the deserted streets, refreshed from his daylight sleep. He wore all black, a color suited to his personality and mood; a large cape billowed behind him in the evening breeze. Legride was well acquainted with the borough: Whitechapel, along with the rest of the East End, had been his private hunting grounds for over three hundred years since he defeated the prior Bloodmaster, an old Carpathian named Torgo, in a duel to the death. He still wore the deceased vampire's fangs on a necklace underneath his waistcoat and shirt as both a trophy and a reminder of the long path he'd traveled.

It was a privilege to have the run of such a normally bustling borough, so near the heart of London herself. Whitechapel was composed mainly of a transient population, people coming and going at all hours, conducting all manner of personal and financial business. And while the main streets were well lit, the cobbled alleys were dark places where strange activities occurred—where lovers found freedom, thieves divvied up their loot, and murderers dumped bodies.

Where a vampire might feed at length, undisturbed, Legride mused inwardly.

And Legride had fed here—copiously, wantonly, gluttonously—for over three centuries.

But now, the terror had arrived in Whitechapel; Jack the Ripper had come to Whitechapel, and the fiend's activities were threatening Legride's nightly feedings.

The sight of a boy in dirty, worn clothing selling newspapers on the corner caught the vampire's attention. He was struck by the young man's boldness, daring to venture out while many frightened adults hid inside their domiciles. The child's golden aura shined brightly in the night, a vessel of innocence.

"Get your paper here, read about the Ripper Murders!" the boy shouted.

Legride approached and looked him in the eye.

"Paper, guv'nor? Three pence," the boy said, offering Legride a daily with his grimy hand.

"What is your name, boy?" Legride inquired as he accepted the paper, reaching into his coat pocket.

"William, sir," the boy replied.

Legride removed a gold coin and flipped the sovereign into the air with his thumb. The boy caught it, looking at the shiny object with wide, incredulous eyes.

"A sovereign!" he marveled. "Thank you, sir!"

Legride did not return the boy's enthusiasm—courtesy was his strong suit. "These streets are no place for you to be tonight, William," he admonished, his ink-black hair framing the sharp, asymmetrical lines of his features. "There are monsters afoot. Best beat feet and run home. Hug your parents, for you know not when odd circumstance will snuff out their short lives."

William looked dismayed as Legride walked by him and read the paper.

The front-page article did not please the vampire. The police had discovered another butchered female corpse the previous night, bringing the total of Ripper murders to five.

No doubt there are others, bodies the police have yet to discover, the vampire mused inwardly.

He looked around to see if there was anyone nearby watching him. When satisfied that he was unobserved, he darted into an alley.

Unknown to Legride, William had followed him. The boy watched in awe as his most recent customer rose effortlessly off the ground and disappeared in the night sky.

THE VAMPIRE HOVERED HUNDREDS OF FEET ABOVE DEVONSHIRE Street, his supernaturally keen senses penetrating the night and the fog, probing for anything out of the ordinary. The red thirst was upon him, setting his body aflame with the need to feed.

Over many centuries of trial and error, Legride had found that the Undead needed to feed at least every other night, to claim a victim before daybreak to fuel their supernatural abilities. Strength, speed, near invulnerability—these legendary powers came with a price. The fresh blood from a kill renewed not only the physical body but also the mind and spirit. The psychic flood released at the moment of the victim's death nurtured the vampire brain, giving it the ability to shrug off the grim torpor of death each night when it rose from its coffin.

The Ripper had robbed Legride of his usual prey. The women of the night, the streetwalkers that frequented Whitechapel, had provided the vampire with ample sustenance and minor threat of exposure. Their disappearances drew scant attention in a borough with a population always in flux. The shortage of prey greatly affected Legride; he felt his great strength beginning to wane. With no warm blood, the red thirst had become all-consuming, his body filled with a creeping cold premonition of final death. In his weakened condition, the vampire feared that he might act recklessly, leading to his discovery. And while he possessed the strength of twenty men, he knew his most significant power was the general populace's lack of belief in his kind. For should the existence of the Undead ever graduate to more than whispered legends and gory stories in the penny dreadfuls, the age of the Bloodmasters would come to an abrupt, stake-filled end.

Legride's instincts told him the fiend would strike again tonight, that the man was consumed with bloodlust and could not stop. As Samhain approached, the attacks had been building in frequency and savageness. A supernatural creature, the vampire could feel the barriers between worlds gradually easing, the light merging into the dark. And tonight, more than any time of the year, the living would be prey to the unnatural beings—whether ghost, fairy, or pooka—loosed upon the world.

As he scoured the night in search of his prey, Legride recalled the Samhain Night a millennia ago when he had been inducted into the ranks of the Undead. He'd been just a young sorcerer then, obsessed with unlocking the hidden secrets of the universe. To that end, he'd traveled from his native Scotland to Ireland and set up in an abandoned graveyard, preparing a divination ritual. That night, as the land hovered between the light of summer and the dark of winter, he lit a bonfire and ringed it with stones. He then tied a pale, scarlet-tressed young woman he'd waylaid in a nearby town atop a stone tomb perfectly aligned to greet the sunrise. Legride had discerned through his contacts that the girl was the first-born of seven children in her family, her genealogy making her a potent source of eldritch power to fuel his ritual. He methodically cut her body with a ceremonial dagger engraved with ancient Babylonian characters, whispering guttural incantations in a long-forgotten tongue and beseeching the arrival of a Fomorian demon with esoteric knowledge to bestow upon him.

It was not a demon that responded to his offering, however. Legride felt the temperature plunge as a shadowy form resolved itself from the night. It latched long fang teeth to the maiden's throat, gorging itself on her blood. When it was full and bloated like a great leech, the creature beckoned him with a long-nailed hand, its vermillion eyes blazing in the dark. It offered knowledge of a kind, strength and eternal life. Legride allowed himself to be drawn into that black embrace and felt the coldness of the fangs as they dug deep into his neck. He fell into darkness.

He dug his way out of a shallow grave the next night, his strong hands bursting through the loose earth as he rose in a grim parody of birth. His killer stood above him, silhouetted by the full moon. The creature spoke to him as its grave shroud flapped in the gusty wind, a whisper that grated inside his skull, harsh as tree bark.

"Mark always the anniversary of your turning on the Samhain. The realm of the dead calls out to our kind on such nights, seeking to reclaim those who cheated its cold embrace."

Legride recalled the ancient vampire's words as a woman's shriek drew his attention. He shot higher into the sky and flew over the brick buildings until he hovered over a dark alley branching off Goulston Street, near the Spitalfields Market. His keen night eyes penetrated the shadows.

Legride saw a blond streetwalker in a blue overskirt and black boots struggle frantically with a shadow come to life. The vampire dropped out of the gray night sky as gently as a falling leaf, settling behind the combatants. He noted the shadow was a tall man dressed in black clothing at this close distance, sporting a black cape and billycock hat. The dark man forced a white cloth over the woman's mouth with gloved hands. Legride's sensitive nose detected the pungent odor of chloroform.

The vampire recalled the press accounts of the previous Ripper murders. Scotland Yard detectives had concluded that the Ripper was drugging his victims before cutting their throats and disemboweling them. Legride's spirit soared—his search was over.

The vampire stepped forward and placed a vise grip on the Ripper's shoulder, preparing to turn him around. Legride was taken aback when the man twisted in his grasp. The cape tore under the force of the vampire's supernatural strength. The dark man retaliated and smashed a bottle of liquid chloroform over the top of Legride's head. The power of the blow, coupled

with the shock of inhaling such a large amount of liquid anes-
thetic, would have felled an average man. But Legride had been
neither normal nor a man for over ten centuries.

The young streetwalker used the distraction to run out of
the alley toward the streetlight's sanctuary. Legride ignored her
as he wrapped his fingers around the Ripper's neck with
serpentine speed. He felt the man's breath catch in his throat as
the windpipe shut off. Exerting just a fraction of his great
strength, Legride lifted his opponent into the air and tossed
him fifty feet further back into the alley. The man landed hard,
smashing through some abandoned wooden crates and rolling
over several times before coming to rest in a prone position.

Legride walked self-assuredly over to his fallen foe, savoring
his apparent victory. He felt invigorated, the eldritch energies
that fueled his existence more potent on Samhain Night than
any other night of the year. The winds of magic buoyed both his
strength and spirit. Though he seldom fed from male victims,
their blood marred by the acrid taste of bitter hormones, he was
willing to make an exception in this case for the man who had
caused him so much hardship and deprivation. The vampire
feverishly rubbed his hands together in anticipation, his long
nails scraping against themselves as his snake-like tongue
slipped out over his lips.

Legride grabbed the Ripper by the shoulder and flipped him
over. The man sat up and suddenly jabbed a surgeon's scalpel
deep into Legride's Undead heart, catching the vampire off
guard. Legride reared but then righted himself. He looked down
at the blade sticking out of his sternum and laughed.

"Common metal cannot harm me, cur!" he snarled with
contempt, backhanding his assailant and sending him
careening off a nearby wall.

Legride had been shot and stabbed with all manner of

metal weapons over the centuries. Such injuries caused him no more discomfort than would a passing breeze. Only weapons made of organic material, wood or bone that had once been part of a living creature, could deliver lasting damage to his kind.

He tried to remove the scalpel when sudden pain shot through him, causing him to stagger. Legride's hands burned instantly on contact with the blade. His vision swam as the Ripper rose to his feet.

Legride's blow had broken the dark man's neck; the vampire had heard the bones shatter under the force of his supernaturally strong impact. Yet somehow, the fiend still stood, his head lolling at an unnatural angle. Legride watched in disbelief as the man placed a hand on each side of his face and tugged, jerking the head back into position with an audible CRACK!

The dark man brushed off his clothing as he sauntered to where Legride stood, immobilized. The vampire could see now that the man was Caucasian, tall and pale, with a slim mustache. Madness gleamed in hollow black eyes that rested far back in the skull. Wickedness beamed in his wide-faced, crooked-toothed grin. Unlike the golden innocence of the newspaper boy, the Ripper's aura was black and oily. Legride wondered what type of evil possessed a man who could recover so quickly from the vampire's attack—no mortal could defeat a vampire at night.

The Ripper spoke in a resonant, condescending voice wedded to a cockney accent. "I see it in your red eyes, boss, the pain, the awe. The shock. You're wonderin' who ol' Saucy Jack is, no doubt? Why he's chasin' all your girls away? How he brought you to your knees on the Samhain when your powers are at their peak? Well, Bloodmaster Kostaki, I'm Jack the Ripper, and I'm from Hell, sir!"

The Ripper surged forward, grabbing the scalpel. In a brutal economy of movement, he pulled it from Legride's chest and slit the vampire's throat from ear to ear. Raw pain erupted from the wound as Legride's black ichor sluggishly oozed out. The vampire attempted to heal his injuries, but the tear began to smoke. He lost his balance and fell on his back, his red eyes frantically darting from side to side in his head.

"Blessed metal, that's wot it is," the Ripper added, light reflecting off the mother-of-pearl buttons on his patented leather boots as he slowly walked over and looked down into Legride's agonized face.

"Helped meeself to a few crucifixes from Saint Mary's, I did, right in the middle of the night when no one was lookin', all them soddin' clergymen asleep. Melted them down, nice and proper, then coated me work tools with them. They're still wicked sharp, as you can tell."

Legride gurgled an incomprehensible curse in response, his fangs shredding his lips.

The Ripper's eyes blazed with cold insanity. "Ahhh, you're upset with me, no doubt. Can't see as I blame you—ol' Jack took away your power. You see, Legride, ol' Saucy Jack has had his eyes on you for a while. Seen you come saunterin' 'round me borough like you owned the place, all high and mighty and full of yourself. Seen you help yourself to me women, Jack's whores, and use 'em up. Eat 'em up, literally. But they're mine, you see, Jack's whores. And you're interfering with me work, more than any lot of peelers ever have."

The Ripper continued speaking as Legride squirmed on the ground. "Found me calling in the organ trade, I did. Bit of a ghoul, some might say, a high-grade resurrectionist. Slice the throat, harvest a uterus or a heart or a liver, grand work, and lots of good money in it. These London pagans will pay any price for special ingredients for their rituals and spells. They get

all worked up at this time of year for Samhain Night, assertin'
they can speak with spirits and bind demons to their will,
would you believe? Now, imagine how much more these same
sods are goin' to be willin' to come up with for a nice, live
vampire, such as yourself, to spice up their Samhain sacrifice?"
The Ripper's grin widened even further. "Well, I suppose 'live'
isn't the proper term in your case, now is it?"

Legride tried to stand but found all his strength had
departed with his blood. He couldn't die, at least not in this
manner. There was a prescribed ritual for vampire destruction:
first, a stake would need to transfix his heart, then his head
severed before the body could be burned and the ashes scattered in running water, releasing whatever remained of his
soul. But the wounds inflicted by the Ripper's scalpel had left
him completely helpless. He focused his energy one last time.
As he had done on countless prior occasions, he reached out his
will and tried to seize a mortal mind. His eyes blazed crimson in
the alley darkness as he touched the fiend's turbid psyche and
commanded him to stop. But Legride's efforts proved fruitless.
The cold blue eyes that looked down on him beamed with
appalling lunacy he could not impede, let alone control.

The Ripper shrugged off Legride's attempt at compelling
him and proceeded with his pompous rant. "Oh, and Jack's got
books, don't you know? Done lots of readin' in me time.
Studied up on the legends of your sort—your strengths, flaws,
what can hurt you, what can't, etcetera, etcetera. I made time
to talk with a necromancer or two. They knew your name.
Guess you've managed to make yourself a fair share of
enemies over the years, Legride, me chum. Found out your lot
is pretty much almighty after sunset, especially on a night like
tonight. But the books all concurred that holy trinkets worked
wonders on you lot—robbed you of all your weird powers. I
just had to come up with me own special way to use 'em." The

Ripper held the bloody scalpel in front of him as the fog overhead parted, allowing the moonlight to shine off the keen metal.

As his vision darkened, it occurred to Legride that he had merely played at being evil, only dabbled in it. True, he had witnessed wickedness in various forms over the centuries. His creator had seemed the very personification of the term, and Legride had sought to imitate him in many ways. He had pursued a chaotic form of evil and enjoyed the casual cruelty of toying with his victims, the game of cat and mouse, the look of terror and awe and lust in their eyes as he claimed them. The outcome had never been in doubt. He had lived hot-tempered and vicious, arbitrarily violent and unpredictable.

But this dark man was different and had a much dissimilar stench of evil about him. There was an order, almost a lawfulness, to the malevolence he represented—a methodical devotion to inflicting the maximum amount of humiliation and destruction on other beings. Legride and his petty intrigues and low-level chaotic maliciousness were small pickings in the overall hierarchy of evil. And now he lay overwhelmed and shattered on the ground of an abandoned alley, feeling like a little child in comparison to the magnificent malignancy that was Jack the Ripper. Legride wondered what hellhole the evil that possessed the fiend had come from.

"Now ol' Saucy Jack figures you want to know what's coming next, eh, Legride? Well, I won't make you walk three times around a grave to find out like these pagans would have you do. I'll tell you about your future right now! You've been around these parts for such a long time! And you've got lots of presents to give—blood and bone and fang and heart and brain. I'll fetch a proper sum for your parts. You're of sturdy stock, no doubt; I'm sure it will be a long, long time before you give up the ghost. And here's the icing on the cake—when you go all dusty, they'll spill some blood to reincarnate your corpse and start it all again!"

As the Ripper bent down and began to slice agonizingly through his sternum, Legride lamented that even a master vampire couldn't scream through a severed throat.

THE SAD FATE OF CASSIO

Cassio precisely positioned the bolt cutters over a chain link and squeezed his hands together. The link severed and flew off as the chain fell to the stone floor. He shoved the metal grate to the side—the entrance to the tomb was his.

Cassio hazarded a look to the west. The sun still had an hour or so before it descended behind the trees on the horizon.

Plenty of time to accomplish the mission, he thought.

Cassio walked down the brick steps, away from the sunlight and into the darkness. He felt the temperature lower with each step. It was a sensation he was accustomed to at this point.

The mausoleum housed several stone sarcophaguses, all bearing expertly crafted figures of the occupant on the top of the lid. All were similarly covered in dust and cobwebs and had not been touched in centuries. All save one.

It was positioned in the middle of the tomb, with marble steps leading up from the floor. No dust mired it. Cassio walked over and ascended.

The carved figure on top was that of a stoic man dressed in fifteenth-century martial attire. A widow's peak framed his broad, unlined forehead while a hawkish nose rested above a thick mustache. Empty, soulless eyes perpetually glared at the ceiling.

Cassio had found what he wanted.

He pushed at the lid. It took all of his strength, but eventually, he moved it. Cassio looked down upon the occupant.

The corpse inside was perfectly preserved, with no sign of decay. The dead man resembled his relief to a tee. His pale, clawed hands were folded just below his chest. If not for the noticeable lack of respiration, the man would have appeared to be merely sleeping. A small drop of faded crimson dotted his lower lip.

Cassio's eyes blazed in hatred. Here was the evil being he had sought, the creature who had caused so many deaths in the village. People of all backgrounds were found dead each morning, their blood vacuumed out through twin punctures on their necks.

It had taken him some time and detective work to locate the creature. Cassio had hunted these blood-sucking revenants before and was familiar with their patterns. This one had been well-hidden. Cassio had buried several dead toads in boxes near the entrances to all the tombs in the local cemetery. When he inspected them in the morning, he found the toad buried in front of this particular tomb was now alive. The old legend held true: a dead toad bestrode by a vampire would be resurrected by the unholy life force of the Undead.

Cassio reached into a cloth sack hanging from his belt and pulled out the thick oak stake. Using both hands, he positioned it high over the corpse's heart. Cursing the fiend and the mother that bore him, he plunged the stake down with all the might he possessed.

Cassio was shocked when the vampire's hands shot up with amazing quickness and stopped the stake's plunge, locking onto his wrists. The vampire miraculously rose from the coffin to a vertical position without bending its knees, somehow immune to the laws of gravity. The Undead creature lifted Cassio high into the air like a child.

The sclera of the vampire's eyes bled to red as its voice echoed off the tomb walls. "So nice of you to visit me today, Cassio. I do appreciate the company. Living forever can become quite...lonely."

Cassio's eyes widened in disbelief. The vampire smirked.

"Come now, Cassio, did you not think word of your butchery would spread amongst my kind? We do have our own community of a sort. After all, we were once people, no?"

Cassio strained against the iron grip that held him aloft—he might as well have grappled with a marble statue. The creature's strength was astounding. He tried kicking the vampire in the stomach, but his blows found only empty air, a roiling cloud of black. The vampire seemed simultaneously comprised of both iron and mist.

"Enough!" the vampire shouted. Almost too fast for Cassio's eyes to follow, the Undead clouted him across the jaw with its right claw, breaking his teeth and sending pain shooting through his brain. Cassio dropped the stake to the floor. The vampire released Cassio's other arm and seized him by the throat with its left claw, holding the hapless hunter aloft with a single arm. It pulled him close to its fanged maw, rancid grave breath filling his nostrils.

"I had known Rosa for over four centuries when you took her from us. Your little mind will never comprehend what you've done—slain a being with a dozen lifetimes of wisdom and experience! All that she was, now only dust!"

The creature looked away momentarily, lost in grief. Cassio was stunned—he didn't know the dead were capable of emotion. His addled brain tried to figure a way out of his predicament. If he could reach into his coat pocket and grab his silver crucifix...

The vampire suddenly bashed its knee into Cassio's groin. Cassio screamed in pain as his testicles were smashed into jelly. Tears and snot ran down his face, pooling with the blood from his mouth and dripping to the floor. Cassio nearly lost consciousness.

"LOOK AT ME!" the vampire screamed. Cassio felt the vampire's will seize his own and force him to look the creature in its bloodshot eyes.

"There's more to the story, good Cassio. Don't you wonder how it was possible for me, a creature of the night, to be awake to greet you when you arrived at my resting place? You had planned to murder me in my sleep, no? As every good hunter knows, the Undead fiends are helpless in their death sleep during the day. But I have adapted, friend Cassio. Knowing that you were looking for me, I've begun sleeping earlier. At first, just an hour, then gradually building up to four. As long as I am shielded from the sun, I can be as active as I want. Great fortune, no?"

Cassio groaned in pain and defeat.

"I sense you are less enthusiastic. A shame," the vampire lamented.

It severed Cassio's throat with a casual twist of its wrist, throwing him down to the floor. Cassio writhed on the ground, hands at his throat, trying to staunch the bubbling flow of his lifeblood. His legs stomped the floor in agony.

The vampire leisurely descended the steps, its black cape trailing behind it. It held the stake in its right claw.

"I'm afraid one last indignity awaits you, friend Cassio— well, actually two, but you needn't worry about the second. It seems only fitting that you die as your victims did, a stake of wood through your heart. Ironic, no?"

Cassio tried unsuccessfully to scream through severed vocal cords as the vampire slammed the stake with preternatural force into his chest, smashing through the ribcage and puncturing the heart before severing the spine as it erupted from his back. Welcome darkness descended on him.

That morning villagers woke to find Cassio's battered corpse crudely pinned to the front of the church doors by the stake, resembling a hapless fly stuck on the end of a pin. The message to all was loud and clear—the Night Folk still reigned.

KONRAD AND THE BLOODY ISLAND AMBUSH

> "*Even the most innocent person, when cornered, is capable of a heartless crime.*"

— *YIYUN LI*

T he dark man crouched behind a copse of wet, ropy vegetation as red waves of agony crashed through his body. Shadows engendered from the night's full moon coalesced around him as if attracted by his eldritch presence and offering shelter. He felt the raw meat of his left shoulder and winced as he drew a jagged sliver out with his long fingers.

Fragmenting teak wood bullets etched with a cross on the front to increase the disintegration factor, the ancient creature thought. His enemies had planned well.

He listened with heightened senses for any sounds of his pursuers. Detecting none, he clawed at the thick strands of red-stained rope that encircled his upper torso. He soon regretted his decision and retracted his hands as pungent smoke curled where his fingers made contact.

Sorbus aucuparia. Ropes soaked in damned witchbane juice! The men who had attacked him were more than familiar with his kind. The berry juice drawn from the flowers of the revered druidic tree dampened all his abilities, prevented him from shape-changing to escape, and reduced his strength to near-human levels. When he ran, he felt like his feet were encased in concrete. His captors had marveled at his speed—if only they had known how leaden movements seemed to him. Had he been at full strength, they would never have been able to shoot him. Fortunately, the bullets had not struck a vital area, and he had been able to free his arms, weak though he was.

The pain caused his mind to wander. He drifted back over the events that had brought him to his present dire circumstance, trying without success to make some sense of it all. He had been covering his tracks well, or at least, so he had believed, as he had for centuries. He had followed the edicts issued by the elders of his kind, feeding only from the outcasts, those who would not be missed—pimps, human traffickers, and drug dealers. The darkness of their auras called out to the kindred spirit that was his beast, his red thirst. The mansion he owned in the San Fernando Valley of Southern California was secluded, secure, gated, and upgraded with the latest security technology.

Perhaps he had grown soft with the passing centuries. It had been many decades since mortal hunters had stalked him.

And yet they caught me.

They had come in the predawn, brandishing sacred icons and witchbane and heavy firearms. He had awakened to find his servants' bodies scattered like broken toys on the stone cellar floor, riddled with bullets. He saw Ariel, his personal attendant of more than twenty years, struggling with one of the men.

They all wore military clothing and panoramic night-vision goggles. Ariel used the strength his shared blood had given her, batting the man's gloved hands aside and lifting him into the air, her petite hands breaking his bull neck. One of the dead man's colleagues approached from behind as she dropped the body. The hunter emptied a dozen rounds from a semi-automatic pistol into her, killing her.

Konrad felt her loss as an aching tug on his dead veins. The sting was not as severe as it would have been had she already joined him in Undeath, but it was there nonetheless. It lent him strength. He defied gravity, rising from his stone coffin as if on strings. Despite the weight of the oncoming day, he moved with panther speed and agility, a mass of black shadow, and attacked the hunter who had killed Ariel. The man pivoted quickly and unloaded his jacketed lead rounds into Konrad. They caused no more damage than a passing breeze. The dark man tore off the hunter's goggles with one hand as the other encircled the killer's neck, fingers digging into meat and cartilage.

You will stay with me! His supernatural will invaded the man's psyche, keeping him conscious and aware of the death of his body long after the exploding pain of snapped vertebrae would typically have caused blissful oblivion. It was an application of sanguinary powers that Konrad had used sparingly over the years, a fate he chose only for the truly worthy, the vilest of mankind-spawned evil.

His focus on Ariel's killer left him vulnerable. Other attackers threw a heavy rope net over him, sending him sprawling to the floor. He seized the net and tried to tear it with his preternatural strength. The rope, however, was witchbane-laced. His fingers smoked upon contact with it, and he felt his strength fade. Several men came forward and held him pinned under the net.

"Hold him still," a resonant voice commanded.

The order came from the group's apparent leader, a behemoth of a man who stood a good head taller than any other man. Such a man might have been mistaken for a giant in ancient times, sporting broad shoulders and a jutting, Cro-Magnon brow. An aquiline, oft-broken nose and big yellow teeth made the man's scarred face monstrous. The basement echoed with the footfalls of the giant's booted heels as he surged forward and stepped on Konrad's chest. Konrad saw a large wooden club in the giant's hands before it smashed into his head.

The blow would have hardly inconvenienced him had the club been made of common metal. However, wood was kryptonite to his kind, and the strike rendered him unconscious.

He awakened later with a splitting headache and found himself lying in a field of thick vegetation under the blinding light of a full moon. Towering palm trees cast slanted shadows across his bound upper torso. The foul smell of spilled animal blood hung heavy in the air. Raising himself slowly to a sitting position, Konrad saw the butchered body of a large boar lying near him. A dozen hunters leveled semi-automatic pistols at him, smiling in apparent anticipation. A large portable military shelter loomed in the background, complete with a helicopter landing pad.

The scent of the ocean and the moon's location on the horizon informed him that he had not been moved particularly far from his residence. Yet, despite his circumstances, the dark man betrayed no fear. It was difficult to engender such emotion in one who had already met death. He had not lived so long to be cowed now by a well-orchestrated show of force.

The leader stepped forward and removed his night goggles. Vivid scars crisscrossed the man's face like the brushings of a demented Picasso. His cold blue eyes focused down on Konrad from under cover of bushy brows.

"We grew tired of waiting for you to wake up, creature. Of course, after that Hank Aaron grand slam I delivered to your head, it's really my fault. I reasoned that fresh blood might jolt you from your stupor, so we opened up the boar. Welcome to San Clemente Island, thirty miles off the coast of Southern California. Or, as we like to call it, Perdition." He gestured expansively with his hands. Konrad noted the behemoth now sported a massive sword across his back, sheathed in a black scabbard and hanging from a leather sling.

Konrad squinted in disdain. He heard the plaintive cry of a wounded animal and looked to his rear. An enormous bipedal creature was chained to a thick metal pole, its manacled wrists levered at a painful angle above its head. Its mottled green hide was covered in various bloody bullet and laceration wounds. The titan moaned in agony as its emerald blood pooled on the ground, its yellow eyes pleading for release. Konrad recognized it as a creature of yore, seldom seen in the modern age—a troll. He wondered at the lengths these hunters had gone to capture it. There were other large empty cages behind the troll, each marred by blood and filth, indicating they had once housed prisoners.

These men like to stay busy, Konrad silently mused.

The hunter continued speaking, ignoring the troll's plight. "You look surprised, Mr. Maul? But, of course, that's just an aka you use—Konrad Maul. Your real name is lost in the annals of history. Do you even remember it after so long? Call yourself whatever you want. We know much about you, much about you indeed. Take, for instance, your liquid diet, or your inability to tan, or the lack of mirrors in your residence."

Konrad ignored the barbs and looked the giant squarely in the eyes. The other hunters snickered.

"You know my name, oaf. How should I address you?" he

said in a cruel, haunting voice like a bitter wind whistling past tombstones in a forgotten graveyard.

The leader paused for a moment, perhaps humbled by the inhuman timbre of Konrad's voice, before he replied.

"My colleagues and I have hunted creatures like you before, Maul. Extraordinary things, beings whose existence challenged the very laws of nature; men who turned into animals, dead things that rose from the grave and consumed human flesh. Over the years, we worked together hunting our country's enemies, our airborne operations squad unique in nature and purpose. We've been inserted into every shithole country on this planet. Our journeys overseas brought us into contact with beings like you—paranormals, sub-humans...FREAKS!

"One night in Bucharest, we unloaded hundreds of rounds into a wolf that would not die. It stopped attacking us when I hacked its head off with an ax. Imagine my surprise when the dead wolf turned into a dead man, a local scout who was supposed to be aiding us with our mission. When our government retired us for political expediency, we began hunting the more challenging prey we now knew existed in the world. We'd never lost a brother in battle until our meeting tonight with you and your little dead female friend. You changed all that. Congratulations."

The disdain on Konrad's face masked the unease and growing sense of dread inside him. He had met this man's kind before. He recognized the spirit of a kindred hunter. Yet, to have the tables now turned, to be hunted solely for the others' entertainment, was both ironic and disconcerting.

"The Tongva people who settled this island are long gone. The US military uses it occasionally for bombing practice— otherwise, it's uninhabited. There are three hours left until dawn. The game goes like this: We hunt you, you run, we shoot or stake you, or the sun gets you. Or maybe a stray bomb blows us all to hell! The final result is the same, one less bloody leech in the world."

The giant reached behind his neck and smoothly withdrew the sword from its scabbard, the blade gleaming in the moonlight. He held it in front, gripping the gold hilt and admiring it.

"This sword came at great personal cost to me, as you might imagine from looking at the mess I call a face. The stubborn old lich that owned it didn't go down easy. It's enscorcelled and capable of cutting through stone and preternatural flesh."

He sauntered over to the shackled troll.

"Let's see how it works on our big friend here."

With a blindingly fast backslash, he opened the troll's throat from ear to ear. The titan slumped in death as the giant looked on with contempt.

"The troll proved unworthy prey, so we kept him around for a little while, savoring his misery as he grew weaker and weaker. Hopefully, you'll be worthy of a quick death, Maul!"

The giant pulled his pistol and fired. Pain erupted Konrad's left shoulder. He tried to discorporate into mist form but found himself too weak.

The world seemed to slow as he stumbled away from the men's screams and catcalls. He did not stop running for over thirty minutes.

KONRAD CALLED UPON THE REMARKABLE REGENERATIVE CAPABILITIES OF his kind to heal the wound in his shoulder. He looked around to gather his bearings and saw that he had stopped near the edge of a vast chasm, a five-hundred-foot drop just a few feet from where he crouched. A small stream ran at the bottom of the crevasse, flowing slowly into the Pacific Ocean. The proximity of the water further disquieted him.

He heard a hiss before sharp pain flooded his forearm. Grimacing, Konrad raised his arm into the air only to find a sizeable multicolored rattlesnake hanging from it. The creature's eyes were shut, covered in a protective membrane, as it pumped its venom into him. The dark man exposed his fangs in response, hissing lowly as he tore the reptile away and threw it down the ravine. Then he moved on, knowing the snake's venom could not harm him.

His senses alerted him that a hunter was approaching. The man used the darkness and abundant shrubbery as cover as he stalked. Still, even the witchbane-drenched ropes couldn't dampen Konrad's powers enough to prevent him from detecting the man's racing heartbeat, the wheeze of his over-exerted lungs.

Konrad bided his time, one with the shadows, until the hunter was just on the other side of a shrub thicket. Then he leaped, smashing him to the ground. He struck the hunter in the jaw with his right fist, snapping the man's head back and sending a pistol flying from his hand. The blow should have broken the human's neck like a twig. However, the witchbane's presence severely limited Konrad's strength.

The hunter recovered with a resilience born of extensive training and sheer desperation, striking back with a stiletto blade. It cut deep into Konrad's throat, drawing black blood and flooding his world with agony.

Silver! Damned silver! The pure metal was poison to the dark magic that fueled his Undead body.

The pain energized Konrad. With all his strength, he grasped the hunter's knife hand, pulping it like overripe fruit. Blood leaked from ruptured veins and arteries. Konrad buried his fang teeth into the hand, breaking more metacarpals, and gulped the blood. His free hand wrapped itself around the hunter's neck and swiftly broke it.

Konrad gulped down the thick liquid ambrosia, feeling it warm his icy veins and dead heart. Renewed strength surged through him. When Konrad was sated, he pulled away, letting the corpse slump to the ground. He clawed the weapon from his neck, noting that the handle was ordinary steel. He could grasp it freely without fear of damage and proceeded to cut through the ropes binding him.

The revenant had almost succeeded in freeing himself from the ropes when a sudden blast knocked him backward, pitching him over the ravine's edge. As he tumbled through the air, he heard the echo of gunfire. That sound, coupled with an agonizing hole in his chest, alerted him that he had again been shot with wooden bullets.

The bottom of the ravine raced up to meet him. He landed headfirst in muddy sediment, his neck buckling but not breaking. The pain of the fall was trivial in comparison to the gunshot. It had penetrated his right lung and passed dangerously close to his heart before exiting his body. Fortunately, the bullet had failed to fragment. Otherwise, the pieces would have expanded through his heart, paralyzing him.

Konrad struggled to his feet. The wound was excruciating but not lethal to one who only drew breath to speak. As he righted himself, he saw how close final death had come; the elemental purity of the running stream was only a few feet away from where he had landed. He shook mud from his eyes. A shard of silver flashed in the stream's waters just a few yards away.

He looked back to the cliff area where he had been attacked and saw the giant perched like a bird of prey on the edge of the ravine. The hunter launched into the air, black material resembling a bat's wings flaring out underneath his extended arms, and descended rapidly, paralleling the steep terrain. Then, when it seemed he would crash into the bottom, the giant shot up and forward, powered by small jet engines strapped to his feet.

The winged hunter flew with deceptive grace for a man his size. He descended like a bat out of hell on Konrad, carbon-fiber wings sweeping out and knocking the revenant off his feet. A part of Konrad appreciated the irony of his present predicament, finding himself the victim of a winged assailant.

The revenant landed in the stream, water and mud seeping into his clothing. The proximity of the running water robbed him of the energy he had siphoned earlier from the dead hunter's blood. He thrashed about but was unable to gain his footing.

The giant stepped forward, discarding the winged harness and the metal engines from his boots, and loomed over Konrad. He casually tweaked the end of his blond handlebar mustache, reminding Konrad of a movie villain from 1920s' American cinema. The giant pushed his goggles up onto his brow, revealing eyes that burned with fevered madness.

"Surprised? BASE jumping is my specialty, Maul. Marks are never prepared for attacks from the sky. You, of all people, should know that. Ah, the terror in their eyes when they realize their goose is cooked—I'm sure you can appreciate that. I'll give you your due, Maul; you're a tough nut to crack."

The behemoth raised his arms wide and turned in a circle to admire the scenery. "So this is how it ends for you, eh, leech? Such an undignified fate for someone who bestrode the earth like a vampire colossus for so long! I've found records of you dating back more than three centuries in Europe—I'll bet you're even older than that. You and your Renfield put up a good fight. It'll take me years to reconstitute the members you've killed. They'll be missed, truly they will, but that's the whole point now, isn't it? On the scale of things, man is not 'the most dangerous game' anymore, is he? No, there is another challenge level still to be explored. Dig it, old man; the ultimate game—an inhuman, immortal predator —that delivers the ultimate rush! The need for bigger and better prey grows exponentially each time we kill. It can never be satisfied again by the same thing. You can relate, right?"

The giant pulled his sword from its scabbard and leveled it at Konrad's throat. A lesser being would have panicked, but the dark man concentrated, calling upon several lifetimes' worth of experience. Summoning the last of his flagging energy, he locked his will onto the hunter's mind, momentarily confusing him. The sword wavered, the giant's muscles failing to respond to his brain's commands.

Konrad knew he couldn't dominate this human in his weakened state as he'd done with so many others throughout the years. So instead, he reached a clawed hand into the stream, screaming as he did so. The pain of the running water collapsed what little control he had over the hunter's mind, and the giant again levered the sword at Konrad. In the time it had taken for the hunter to regain his composure, the dark man had retrieved the blade from the stream and severed the ropes encircling his waist.

As the giant swung the great sword in a decapitation strike, Konrad called upon the eldritch energies that fueled his existence and dispersed his molecules, assuming the form of an incandescent mist. The sword passed harmlessly through him. The fog drifted around the confused giant, revolving in and around itself like a mini-tornado until it took human form.

Konrad delivered a shattering blow to the big man's spine. With the ropes now shorn from him, Konrad's full power had returned—the impact had the strength of more than twenty men behind it. The giant collapsed at Konrad's feet, his spine broken, the sword spiraling out of his hands.

As Konrad approached the fallen hunter, he sensed that the man's compatriots were closing in from all directions, drawn by earlier gunfire. Tactically it would have been wise to retreat and harness his resources for a future battle. He had come too close to the final death tonight to let matters stand. And harrowing experience had taught him that men such as these would never be satisfied until he was truly dead.

THE TEMPLARS AND THEIR MONSTROUS SERVANTS HAD RAIDED THE Master's labyrinth in the late afternoon, using ropes and pulleys to descend over one hundred meters into the dark caverns beneath the castle. Unfortunately, they were not as prepared as they should have been. Some had lost their grip and fallen, tumbling end over end to splat messily on the ground, or become impaled on limestone stalagmites, their discarded torches lighting the dark. The ponderous flesh constructs slowly made their way down, their powerful fingers carving grooves into the stone for handholds. By the time they reached the bottom, the sun had begun its descent on the horizon.

Konrad and the Master rose from their stone coffins as their daylight guardians engaged the attackers. Konrad dodged a spear thrust and then opened up the Templar's throat with a backslash of his claws. Another man drove an ax into Konrad's sternum, but the iron blade caused no injury. He lifted the man off the ground by his neck and used him as a club against other Templars, knocking them to the ground. The guardians hacked the downed men into gory pieces with kukri blades.

Konrad thrust the man in his hand up to the ceiling, impaling him through his armored breastplate on a stalactite. The Templar twitched like a bug on the end of a needle, eyes wide in horror as his blood fountained from the massive wound. Konrad caught some blood in his mouth, feeling its warmth spread into his cold limbs. He still felt sluggish, attempting to shrug off the lethargy of daylight stupor.

He was caught off guard when a construct seized and lifted him. The patchwork creature slammed Konrad's head into the cave wall, its huge, mottled gray hand wrapped around his throat, squeezing with superhuman pressure as the underground labyrinth echoed with the chaotic sounds of battle. The impact showered the ground with chunks of stonework. Konrad felt the muscles and bones in his throat tear and shatter as the creature attempted to pry his head off. A mortal man would have been dead many times over, skull crushed, windpipe collapsed, neck broken. Yet Konrad had transcended mortality many years earlier and was not so easily vanquished.

The creature's eyes were dead and vacant, its body fueled by arcane magics and alchemical elixirs. It lacked a mind of its own and was directed by a necromancer who had meticulously stitched the being together from the body parts of various dead Templars. Konrad recognized the creature's face as having belonged to an assassin he had killed just months before. The head was now attached atop a ten-foot-tall conglomerate body—a being of nigh-unstoppable physical power and destruction.

The construct struck him, shattering his orbital socket and cheek-bone. Konrad absorbed the pain. With the onset of night, his full powers gradually returned. He knew he could escape a further assault by transforming into a mist and slipping away. But the warrior inside him, the former knight, would not allow him to flee. Rage engendered by the attack upon his home fueled him.

Konrad resisted the creature's assault with his Undead strength. Blood stolen from others flooded his arms as he reached out with serpentine speed and dexterity. He wrapped his hands around the *colossus's bald head and twisted...hard. The flesh construct's neck broke with a sound like a thunderclap, the scarred and twisted body collapsing. It spasmed and shook, its feet and hands smashing the ground. Konrad finished the job by punching his hand through the creature's sternum and removing its large gray heart.*

No sooner had he finished with the monster than a Templar attacked him, the knight's sword raised high overhead to behead him. He backhanded the hunter, crumpling his iron helm and shattering the fragile human skull. As the body slumped to the ground, he saw that the battle was over. Keen eyes penetrating the dim torchlight, Konrad stood in a field of blood and entrails, surrounded by the mutilated corpses of dozens of armored hunters and the bodies of the castle's daytime attendants. The men and women that served his sire had fought valiantly, delaying the hunters' attack on the crypt while he and Arnulf had roused themselves. Their sacrifice had allowed the revenants sufficient time to shake off the effects of daylight slumber and counter the attack, fighting their way step by bloody step through the siege.

Swords and axes had shredded his skin and clothes, but his body quickly began to heal itself.

"You will need to feed, Konrad."

He turned at the sound of his sire's voice and saw Arnulf standing nearby, bathed in the light of a full moon that beamed down through an area of the collapsed ceiling. He was encircled by the dismembered remains of at least three flesh constructs, though where one ended and the other began was impossible to determine. The ancient vampire had one taloned hand wrapped around a remaining hunter's throat, the puissant grip forcing the man to his knees. The Templar's iron helm and gorget had been ripped off. Arnulf's simple robe was bloody and torn, and a sword was buried to the hilt in the ancient revenant's back. The wound did not seem to discomfort him. His sire's fang teeth were prominent, dripping fresh blood. Konrad noted a bloody bite wound on the hunter's neck.

"Here."

Arnulf casually lifted the armored man from the ground and tossed him through the air to land at Konrad's feet. The much younger vampire grasped the hunter's head and hoisted him up, the tips of the man's mail chausses seeking purchase with the ground. The hunter tried to pull away but was no match for Konrad's strength. There was still fire in the Templar's eyes as he spat on Konrad and cursed him, using armored gloves to batter at the bone-white hand that held him without effort.

"There have always been hunters since the beginning of our kind," Arnulf continued, his eyes reflecting the light like an animal's. "We have learned from terrible loss that there is only one way to deal with these men, these fanatics led by a cabal of chaos necromancers. They are willing to contaminate their immortal souls by consorting dark magics to reanimate their own dead and send them against us. All that matters to them is the cause of their 'god,' as they interpret it from their ancient scriptures. They have judged our kind infidels to be eliminated at all costs. They will pursue us to the ends of the earth unless we finish them here tonight."

The familiar hunger surged in Konrad, pulling on his dead veins and arteries, crying to be satiated. His fangs shot out over his lips, and he buried them in the wound on the man's neck. The hunter screamed, fought, and cursed, but his struggles gradually weakened as his blood ran out.

Arnulf looked on approvingly before mentally summoning the pack of ghouls that lingered on the moonlit fringe of the labyrinth to dispose of the corpses permanently.

KONRAD REACHED DOWN AND SANK HIS TALONS DEEP INTO THE SKIN OF the hunter's forehead before ripping off the man's face. He used the skin as a protective cover for his hand as he lifted the ensorcelled sword and tossed it far out into the water. He then discarded the skin to be carried downstream to the ocean. A faint moan escaped the man's shredded lips, the pain of his mangled face almost enough to shock him back to consciousness.

The dark man stripped off the hunter's clothing. Konrad's bullet-riddled attire lay nearby, having fallen off when he shifted to mist form. Contrary to myth, he could not incorporate the garment into his body when he shape-changed.

Konrad shoved the giant into his old clothes, ripping them severely as they were too small a fit for their new owner, then slid into the hunter's khaki outfit. Konrad concentrated, rearranging his facial features to mimic those of the fallen hunter before his impromptu facial surgery. He lengthened the bones of his legs, arms, and spine while lightening his hair. Legend limited the shape-changing abilities of his kind to the baser animals. Yet logic suggested that a creature with such control over its own atomic structure might reasonably assume any form it desired, limited only by its imagination.

Konrad grasped the fallen hunter's shattered face and pulled open what remained of the man's eyelids. Then, locking the man's dilated pupils with his red eyes, he exerted his entire will, latching onto the giant's psyche and forcing him into a state of consciousness. The hunter woke up screaming.

"I've hunted your kind as well, my friend," Konrad said. "Centuries before you were born."

Satisfied, the dark man donned the giant's goggles.

As the hunters descended the ravine, they saw their leader near the fallen revenant on all fours. Both were drenched in blood. The big man was yelling.

"Shoot him! Stake the bastard! I shot him in the face, but he's not dead yet!" The revenant appeared to be in great pain, writhing and screaming in the mud of the stream.

The group released a collective war cry and converged on the fallen being. Guns blazed as scores of bullets riddled the soon-unrecognizable body. The hunters surged forward when the firing stopped, stabbing the unresponsive corpse with sharp wooden spears. They shouted and high-fived each other. One man, a lieutenant, radioed the home base and gave the pickup location when he noticed something odd. According to their mission briefing, the vampire's body would turn to dust upon the onset of final death. Though torn and bloody and chopped into pieces, the body in front of them wasn't disintegrating. The hunter turned to address their giant captain, but he was no longer there, his clothing and goggles now lying in a heap upon the bank of the stream. The second-in-command hurriedly looked around but could not locate his boss. He failed to note the fine mist floating close to the ground.

Konrad's first instinct was to drift away from the horde of hunters before flying home in time to beat the approaching dawn. The faint gray light emerging on the eastern horizon told him he still had over an hour until the sunlight hampered his movements. Time enough to assure those gathered here tonight never followed him again.

The dark man resumed his human appearance amid the group and tore into the confused hunters with a devastating might. He reveled in the full extent of his powers, scattering the men like children's toys caught in a whirlwind. They never had a chance as they died screaming in a maelstrom of torn throats and shattered spines. Only Konrad would survive to greet another sunset.

BLOOD LEGACY: A DRACULA TALE

Despair and misery hung heavy in the stale hospice air. The old man lay still on the discolored covers of his bed, the restless drag of his breath through his dry mouth echoing hollowly in the quiet. Occasional waves of nausea racked his body, painful reminders of his recent chemotherapy treatments. An intravenous glucose infusion was attached to his left arm. The fact that he could no longer ingest solid food eased the nausea somewhat, the lack of anything in his stomach limiting its ability to become irritated. The sad truth was that the less he ate, and, concomitantly, the weaker he became, the better he felt. His primary physician had told him that, in the end, he would starve himself into a state of euphoria. His final moments would be pain-free. He looked forward to them.

The room was lit by the heart monitor standing by his bed and ambient light from the hallway. The old man was not alone. A female nurse and one of the old man's agents conversed quietly near the hallway door. The agent, a man named Collins, was almost too large to fit in the small room. He cut quite an imposing figure, dressed in a black suit and jacket, dwarfing the tiny Asian nurse. The old man feigned unconsciousness, listening to their whispers.

"His vital signs are becoming progressively weaker. At this rate, we'll be lucky if he survives the night," the nurse commented.

"Maybe it's all for the best. He's had a long life, a full life," the dour agent replied, looking at the apparently comatose patient.

The old man felt a twinge of sympathy for his man. Collins had spent nearly thirty years in service to him. The agent could count himself among the few remaining members of the various coalitions of hunters the old man had assembled over the years; he had survived wholesale slaughters that had reduced his compatriots to insensate puddles of blood and shredded flesh. Collins and the old man had become even closer in the last few years, as illness had restricted his activities. The agent had been entrusted with the old man's personal care, which recently included bathing, dressing, and feeding. The old man trusted Collins with his life and knew the feeling was mutual.

"There's nothing more you can do for him here, Mr. Collins. It's late, and visiting hours are long over—you'll have to wait outside the room." The nurse gestured toward the door.

Collins nervously shifted his gaze out the room's only window, watching the streetlight-illuminated snow dance furiously on the wind currents. A harsh winter storm entirely obscured the moon and stars. Few souls would be brave enough to venture out in this blizzard. The thought gave Collins little comfort. Just in case, he'd stationed another agent outside to guard that window.

Collins returned his gaze to the old man. He approached the bed and held one of the old man's hands, careful not to disturb the intravenous connection that helped keep his boss alive. Collins bent down and whispered into the old man's ear.

"Peace, my friend. May you finally know peace."

The old man returned Collins' grip with a strength that surprised the much younger and larger man. The old man did not speak, but Collins knew that his gesture had been accepted. Collins followed the nurse out of the room and quietly closed the door.

THAD COCHRAN FIDGETED NERVOUSLY IN THE STORM, TRYING TO AVOID becoming a human icicle. He stood outside in the hospice's garden, simultaneously guarding the window to the old man's room while drawing as little attention to himself as possible. He'd served with the old man's entourage for some fifteen years and had become used to the inconveniences of the work. When Collins had asked for help providing security for the old man at the hospice, Thad had been more than willing to offer his services.

The wind-driven snow obscured his vision, already diminished by the lateness of the hour. The bitter cold caused him to grit his teeth. Cochran placed his hand inside his coat pocket and felt the solidness of his duty weapon. It reassured him, as it always had. Two silver-coated *kukri* knives sheathed on either hip gave him further comfort.

The agent's back was turned when the darkness rose behind him and assumed an incandescent human shape. Small, razor-nailed hands grasped him with shocking strength and raised him high into the air, breaking the bones in his right arm and left shoulder with frightening ease. Cochran had scant seconds to look down into the red eyes of his assailant, a clown-white Caucasian woman wearing a white shroud that offered no protection from the environment. She threw him into the snow and leaped onto him like an attacking panther. The woman buried her head in his neck, her ample raven hair blowing in the wind and covering his face. Cochran screamed as her sharp teeth tore at his throat, spraying arterial blood until frigid lips covered the wound. The agent struggled fiercely, screaming again as he attempted to break free, but the female's strength dwarfed his own. The color drained from his face, matching the hue of the snow his body rested in.

As the female fed, another figure resolved out of the darkness. A resonant male voice echoed in the night.

"Ahhh, Lucy, snacking on duty again. I suppose must resolve this little matter myself."

THE OLD MAN DRIFTED IN AND OUT OF SLEEP, CLAMMY SWEAT CLINGING to his body, plagued by nightmare memories. The air in the room was stagnant, almost stifling, reminding him of tombs and mausoleums. He had spent so much time in such homes for the dead—perhaps most of his adult life. In a way, he felt at peace there. And in its own way, the hospice was just another form of a mortuary, really, the bodies inside just a tad warmer and less decayed. The old man dreamed.

He dangled in the air, his stocky frame held easily aloft by a single pale hand wrapped viselike around his throat. His mother's eyes blazed sapphire in the darkness of the tomb.

"Quincey, my dear boy, were you going to stake your mother?"

184

the master strigoi inquired, interjecting himself from another corner of the crypt.

Quincey would gladly have acknowledged his intentions to impale his mother's corpse had he the breath. After she had turned, he'd spent weeks attempting to locate her resting place. Eventually, he heard stories of children wasting away in a nearby village, found by their parents wandering about at night. He'd applied the knowledge given to him by the Dutchman. First, he located a small cemetery where no birds sang in the morning, then planted boxes of dead toads beneath the soil leading to the entrances of all the significant crypts. Quincey's meticulous preparations had proven successful. The old peasant's rhyme regarding a dead toad bestrode by a nightwalker being given life had proven to be more than a myth. After noting the emptiness of the small makeshift toad's grave he had made in front of one particular crypt, he located his mother resting in a tomb she had appropriated, the bones of the former occupant cast unceremoniously on the floor.

Her arcane presence had attracted an insane man, an escapee from Bedlam, who hovered around her tomb during the daylight hours. Quincey had surveilled the madman as the lunatic muttered nonsense to himself and ate insects. Distracted by his fly and beetle lunch, he did not hear Quincey approach him from behind. A quick snap of the neck and the man's tortured existence was over. Quincey spent the rest of the day beside her coffin, attempting to drum up the courage he would need to desecrate her corpse. His mother had not died a true death when the master strigoi supped her lifeblood—instead, the beast had condemned her to a similar damnable existence as its own. As Quincey had waivered, the sun left the sky, allowing the night to infuse his mother's corpse with arcane death energies.

"I thought I taught you better," Mina spoke, her fiery eyes pinioning Quincey. He shrugged off her hypnotic gaze with some effort, focusing his concentration as the Dutchman had shown him, then jammed the three feet of whitethorn stake in his right hand into her upper torso.

The woman cried out, more in frustration than pain.

"Hellsteeth!" Her fangs chomped in rage, the sharp eyeteeth characteristic of her kind shredding her pale lips. She effortlessly tossed Quincey across the crypt and slammed him into unforgiving stone walls. Pain ripped through his body as he fell heavily to the floor, darkness clouding his vision.

The young man attempted to stand, his sense of balance thrown off. Through blurred vision, he saw his mother contemptuously pull the length of stake, now smeared with black blood, from her chest. He'd misjudged the angle and missed her heart.

She moved like quicksilver across the crypt, her tiny hands working to expose Quincey's neck from his coat and shirt. Her head dipped, adder-quick, toward his throat. Almost immediately, she recoiled, her pained cries echoing off the crypt walls. The stench of burned carrion filled Quincey's nostrils as Mina blew out the metal gate, taking it off its hinges in her desperate retreat.

"A shocking way for a son to treat his mother. I expected better manners from you, Quincey." And with that acerbic statement, the master strigoi was also gone, melding with the shadows.

Quincey's fingers played with the silver crucifix necklace he wore, a prescient gift once given to him by the woman who had just attempted to kill him. Quincey chided himself for his earlier indecision. He could not let his mother suffer this curse another day.

He left the crypt that night, only to return later in the morning. Although his mother was adroit and would quickly adapt to her new condition, she would still be forced to return to her grave by morning. An older strigoi might have human assistants to plot and assemble numerous daytime refuges, but Mina was newly Undead. She had yet to have time to plan for such contingencies.

He waited patiently through the rest of the night and watched her return alone in the morning grayness, her mouth drenched in *blood from a fresh kill. He staked her inert corpse that day, beheaded then immolated it. He sometimes wondered why the sight of blood had so little effect on him. If he had regrets, he did not admit them to himself.*

A FAMILIAR UNEASE, AN UNNATURALNESS, PRICKED THE OLD MAN'S SKIN as the blood in his veins slowly began to circulate faster. In the back of his mind, he'd always understood that his lifelong adversary would be with him even at the very end. He was glad to be alone for this final encounter, secure in the knowledge that men such as Collins would no longer have to sacrifice their lives for his cause. If they chose to continue the fight after his death, they did so of their own accord.

As a fog seeped under the locked window sill, the old man mused to himself how, even to this day, the creature was limited by his "child's brain," as the Dutchman had referred to it so many years ago. Surely a creature that could mold its form into predatory beasts and flowing mist was capable of a more impressive transformation. The fog funneled in and began rotating around itself like a mini-tornado, gradually assuming human proportion, finally resolving itself into the tall, black-caped figure the old man was intimately familiar with.

QUINCEY'S MEN SWARMED ACROSS THE FRENCH GRAVEYARD AS THE SUN set, semi-automatic pistols drawn and safeties off. They'd received a

last-minute tip as to the location of the fiend's resting place. Quincey had called in every available man for an all-out assault. Nearly thirty agents rushed forward to send the beast to its final death.

The fiend was not alone. The Undead answered its call, misting out of the ground or bursting forth from crypts. Quincey's vision was momentarily blinded by the number of blue Undead auras lighting the night. Many went down in a hail of bullets, the silver paralyzing them and making them easy prey for the agents' machetes. Others avoided the shots with serpentine grace and supernatural speed. Quincey watched in horror as the remaining strigoi attacked en masse. The throats of his men were torn, their bones broken, and bodies tossed like playthings across the slick, moonlit grass.

Quincey spied the leader near a large tomb, its vulpine face leering as its creatures decimated his men. Quincey dashed across to meet the master strigoi, the being that had haunted the entirety of his existence.

The creature opened its arms wide as if to embrace him.

"Ahhh, the prodigal son returns. And such a bad son you are. You made such a mess of your poor mother; even I can't bring her back. She's literally dust in the wind."

Rage clouded Quincey's vision while fury lent strength to his limbs. His right arm flashed out, the sharpened metal blade he had made specifically for this occasion slicing through the beast's throat. The master strigoi staggered back, momentarily stunned as black blood flowed freely down its torso. The wound smoked, causing the creature to shudder in pain. The blade was forged from metal melted from a large consecrated cross. Quincey's research had indicated that such a weapon might prove an even more effective bane than silver against the brute, given the fiend had worshiped the cross in his living days.

Quincey raised the blade high as he attempted a killing blow. A lightning-fast strike knocked it from his grasp, followed by a stunning backhand that sent him flying off his feet and onto his back.

Before he could recover, the fiend had him pinned to the ground, the monster's inhuman strength holding him helpless.

"My turn, boy. Time to join the family," it wheezed through its burned but rapidly healing throat. Graveyard breath and the stench of burned carrion assaulted Quincey's nostrils. Moonlight glittered off the fiend's wickedly sharp fangs as its eyes blazed cobalt blue. However, before the monster could strike, it was born back by six of Quincey's men. Strong arms helped him to his feet. Collins rushed him away from the battle. Dazed by the master strigoi's preternatural blow, he could do little to resist.

"We've got to get you out of here, boss. We're getting killed. We can't lose you too."

Quincey hazarded a look back. The fiend howled in frustration and then began to systematically and brutally kill the agents who had robbed it of its victory. The screams of their bloody deaths resounded in the night air.

"Good evening, Quincey. Rough spell of weather, no?" The sickeningly familiar, mold-laced scent of the creature's breath stimulated fresh waves of nausea in the old man as it wafted over him. The stench of the graveyard followed the fiend like a vomitus perfume everywhere it went.

The demon stepped forward and stood beside a small dresser drawer adjacent to the old man's bed. Quincey's trained eyes perceived the intense blue-flamed aura the creature gave off, lighting the entire room. As surely as he could now see the beast, he also knew no mirror on the planet would register the exact image captured by his own retinas and lenses. The old man noted with irony the immaculate perfection of his visitor's white skin, as pale and cold as the falling snow. He could not count the number of times he had seen that same skin pierced by blade and bullet, scorched by daylight and flame and holy oil, the times he had administered the butchering—all, in the end, for nothing. The creature's skin was flawless, as unlined as a newborn baby's.

Pictures of young and old men came unbidden into his mind, men united together to support his cause.

No, he mused. *To support me.*

All had perished, their bodies broken, their throats ruptured, their lifeblood poured out onto unappreciative soil. In the end, the blame for their loss lay with him. An unwelcome tear formed in the corner of his eye. The demon smiled, its long teeth curling over its lower lip.

"I knew you would be glad to see me, Quincey. Our little get-togethers are always something to write home about, no?" The fiend's gaze pinioned the old man to his bed. Against his better judgment, Quincey refused to break eye contact.

"You know why I've come, don't you, Quincey? Your time draws near. A hospice, a mortuary, a graveyard...they're all the same. Soon you will be nothing more than a cold, breathless lump of useless flesh."

With difficulty, the old man sucked in some air and managed a hoarse reply.

"Just like you."

The fiend frowned.

"Touché, Quincey, touché. Still, I exist, after a fashion. Will you be able to say the same?"

The creature's aura blazed as it noiselessly approached the bed and spoke.

"We've had some magnificent battles, Quincey. We've each won our fair share. You slaughtered my brides; I killed your men and family. 'Even-steven,' as they say in this country."

The old man shifted uncomfortably as he recalled his legacy, a war he'd inherited some sixty years earlier when the demon standing in front of him had crushed his father's skull and torn out his mother's throat. The attack had condemned his mother to an unliving hell that he had ended with a whitethorn stake and a silvered ax.

His parents had believed the demon to be truly dead, impaled, and decapitated on the winding slope that led up to a crumbling ancestral castle in the Carpathian Mountains. Unfortunately, as Quincey would come to learn through painful experience, few deaths were lasting for the *strigoi*. In time, he had assembled his own band of hunters, as his father had before him, though on a much grander scale. The operation masqueraded as an investigative agency but was actually an organized squad of tactical hit teams dedicated to ferreting out nests of the Undead and destroying them. His father schooled him in real estate and how to acquire properties on different continents from which to deploy agents. And from the old red-haired Dutchman, he learned about the Undead—their strengths and weaknesses, their manner of creation, how to recognize and, most importantly, how to end them.

Quincey recalled the old Dutchman standing straight and proud before him, the polymath's broad chest and shoulders filling out his suit as he lectured with a thick accent. "You must learn, while in the bloom of youth, to look with more than your eyes, to seek the energies which speed this world. As I once told your father, I want you to believe in things you cannot. The unquiet spirit, foreign to this realm, manifests with an aura of blue flame. Witness when your father was ushered through the dark forest by the coachman, who was, in fact, the Count. Recall the blue flames made manifest as the Great Undead hunted the treasures hidden in the woods. So it is that one who looks beyond this world and into the next can detect the *strigoi* aura."

The Dutchman often spoke of the twilight world that existed just beyond the ken of most people. "I've devoted my life to investigating the shadows that stretch from the other realms into our own. Ours is a strange, sad world full of pain and suffering. It attracts creatures of darkness, beings that feed on woe and misery. I lost my wife to that world many years ago, perhaps cursed for delving into unnatural matters. We must fight this darkness, Quincey. And he, this man-that-was, the Great Undead, he is the greatest threat of all. Though possessed of a child brain, the brute is clever. He has already accomplished so much, far beyond any of his kind. He left the stagnation of the old world, crossed an entire ocean that could easily have swallowed and drowned him, and now seeks to batten on the fountain of life bubbling here in London. And beyond. I am old and near the end of my days. I would tell you of my research into the brute, of what I have uncovered. Only you can permanently end him, where your father and I failed."

He'd learned much about this Great Undead, about the warrior the creature had been in its warm days, a man of iron will who was immune to fear. Indeed, fear had been beaten out of him. His father had allowed his sons to be taken hostage by the Ottomans, a tribute given to secure the father's claim to the Wallachian throne. Between beatings and a force-fed indoctrination into the Quran, the future *strigoi* king was also schooled in the art of warfare, a knowledge he would one day employ against his captors. His abilities would be further enhanced later in his living years after locating the Scholomance, the mythical school of dark arts, in the mountains over Lake Hermanstadt. There he'd uncovered the secrets of returning from death itself. The demon became the fountainhead of an Undead cult that infiltrated nearly every country in Europe over the centuries.

The old man's organization pursued the monster and his

acolytes from bases across the globe. Most men were recruited from within the ranks of surviving victims. He'd encountered an adolescent Collins after the young man's mother had fallen prey to the creature. The father humiliated himself, choosing to become one of the demon's bug-eating human servants rather than suffer his wife's fate. Ten years later, the son, now a man, ended the father's servitude with a bullet to the head. The victories Quincey and his men achieved were often pyrrhic, for the demon quickly replaced minions that fell before their stakes and blades, sometimes recruiting from within the hunters' own ranks. The horrors he and his agents endured bestowing final death on their comrades took a massive toll over the years.

Quincey had eventually wedded a woman who also had been victimized by the *strigoi*. He had often thought that only such a similarly abused person could understand him, could grasp the meaning of the psychological wounds that defined his life. In time, she gave birth to a son. Quincey had only begun to comprehend the brilliance they added to his world when tragedy struck his life again. He returned home from overseas to find them slaughtered like animals, their features unrecognizable. Their murderer was a steward, a servant who had been enslaved by the kiss of one of the master *strigoi's* brides. A part of him died the day he buried them. Their memories spurred him on and lent his hate an even keener edge as he continued his crusade, using up idealistic young men like Collins as cannon fodder.

And yet now, at the end of his existence, he realized that his motives had always been selfish. He had swayed others with words like "hell-spawn," "unclean," and "righteous," but the truth was that he liked the bloodshed; indeed, he reveled in it. He soothed the pain with mayhem. While the cause had always been just, it had never been the true motivation.

One mystery had perplexed him over the years, continually

rising unbidden in his brain and plaguing his thoughts. Time after time, despite his training and planning, despite his men, he had found himself at the monster's mercy. After all these years, why was he still alive? How was it conceivable that he had not died a dozen times over?

"I am prepared to meet my maker..." the old man murmured, his features craggy, his eyes looking away.

"And here I am...your maker!" The *strigoi* lord's eyes beamed in the darkness. "Quincey, I've seen no proof of an intelligent, all-powerful deity in all my centuries of existence. Rather, I've seen disinterest and distance, the unconcerned attitude of a foster father, too wrapped up in self-aggrandizement and seeking worship from his pitiably facile creations to notice the chaotic nature of the world he has bequeathed them. War, famine, disaster, disease...when did this 'God' ever spare his children from the endless anguish of the world he created? I know suffering firsthand, heaped upon me by the creator who abandoned me in my hour of need and cursed me for my supposed sins with this unlife. And yet, have I not become a god unto myself? Like Zeus before me, who overthrew his father, the Titan Kronos, I overcame and superseded the being who commingled his eldritch blood with mine. Now it is my kiss, my blood, that bequeaths strength and longevity. Like the Nazarene, I rose from my tomb and gave my blood unto others so that they might have life eternal through me. And yet, despite this knowledge, you seek the embrace of this false deity over the solace I offer?"

The fiend continued, his voice confident and commanding. "It need not end, Quincey. It cannot end. Have you ever wondered why we are so drawn to one another? Why we continue to haunt each other's existence, decade after decade? I doubt your mother ever told you...it would not have been in her nature...but we shared blood, just like the stout Irishman described in his little book. My blood still coursed through her veins when your father's feeble seed found purchase in her womb. He was a weak man, your father...a continual disappointment to your mother. She was a woman of great strength, never to be equaled. I let you end her, Quincey, though it was in my power to stop you. Why, you may ask? Whether of men or of *strigoi*, a true leader must learn the price of power. He will inevitably be called upon to destroy that which he once held dear as you were that night. You are my son, Quincey, more than you ever were your biological father's. Think of it! How else could you have survived a hundred dooms? Don't you see? We can fight on together for centuries!"

Quincey silently cursed himself. In his quiet reverie, the demon had penetrated his thoughts and absorbed his emotions. In a movement too quick for the human eye to follow, the *strigoi* lord scooped the old man up, easily holding him aloft with one hand. The violent jostling tore out the intravenous connections on Quincey's arms, causing the open tubes to spill their contents onto the bed and floor. Despite his pain, Quincey couldn't help but be awed by the strength these Undead beings possessed. Even the newly made ones gained ten times the potency they had enjoyed while living—the power of their king perhaps incalculable.

What miracles might these creatures accomplish were they not so consumed with their bloodlust?

And yet, in the end, it was the curse that prevailed, an eternal, unsated blood hunger that haunted every moment of their execrable existence. For the Undead were tormented, obsessed things, every one of them, even their king.

"I will not be alone, Quincey!" the *strigoi* lord roared into the old man's face, the noise reverberating off the hospice walls. What remained of the sclera of its eyes bled wholly red as the dead black pupils expanded, the tips of the creature's ears lengthening to elfin points. Simultaneously, the canine teeth assumed the proportions of lethal daggers, jutting out over the bottom lip. Shock ran through the old man's system as the mystery that had vexed him all these years became painfully clear—he realized the ultimate fate that awaited him, that had awaited him even before he drew his first breath. He had always been prepared for the monster to be present at his death, contemplated how the fiend might snap his neck or rip out his throat, but he never anticipated being condemned to a living death himself. In all those years of warfare, he had never stopped to consider the dark lineage to which he might be heir. Why the sight of blood unnaturally stirred him. Why he was able to see the magic blue auras hidden from others. He never considered that the monster might become used to the fighting, might, in fact, even enjoy the challenge it brought to its unending existence. Though the notion repulsed Quincey, a part of him also relished the struggle.

The beast and I are no different from one another. I share his blood. We use up innocents in pursuit of our own selfish agendas. Looked at through a dark lens, we must appear indistinguishable.

"Our battles have made you strong, my son. When I look into your eyes, I see no fear. It has been beaten out of you, just like the Ottomans tortured it out of me. My brother Radu was weak; he gave in to their beatings and converted to their faith. The Ottomans' torture only made me stronger. Their cruelty fueled my determination, and I revisited upon them the horrors I experienced at their hands a thousand times over. I knew true peace when I dined amongst a field of their impaled dead. Know this, my son; you'll never know death or illness again, never be weak or crippled or old. My son will not die unheralded in some forgotten room like the Nazarene expired, betrayed, and forsaken on his cross. He will not be shuttled in a black ambulance to a mortuary cremation." The *strigoi* lord twisted the old man's head to the side, exposing the veins and arteries of his neck.

For a moment, Quincey pondered the pathetic state of his cancer-ridden body, the almost godlike power that could be his were he to choose it. He considered baring his neck to the beast, an end to his suffering, a chance to battle anew. His thoughts quickly turned to his wife and child, the men like Collins who had fought for him, and the thousands of people who would die to sustain his new eternal life. Such a choice would represent a catastrophic betrayal of all he was, all he had ever been. Quincey knew there was only one option left for him.

With the last vestiges of his strength, he drew the Webley revolver he had secreted in a sling holster under his arm, a holster Collins helped him don every night after the nurse had finished cleaning him. The *strigoi* lord's eyes had only a second to register bewilderment before Quincey pulled the trigger.

The master *strigoi* was stunned when the wolf's bane-laced, silver-jacketed, hollow-point round pierced not its heart but that of Quincey Harker. The great Undead sensed the presence of the silver and knew that Quincey had won the final battle. No human could transition into the Undead state with a heart shredded by silver. Quincey slumped back into the bed as the dark lord let him fall, a look of peaceful contentment etched into his features.

The door to the room burst open as Collins responded to the sound of the gunshot, a semi-auto pistol in his hands. The petite nurse peeked anxiously around the agent's broad back. Collins' gun blazed silver hollow points, lighting up the dim room. Sixteen rounds slammed into the master *strigoi*, staggering it back, sending waves of agony coursing through its dead flesh. Silver rounds, however, were not enough to destroy the dark lord. Collins knew that; he also knew that Quincey had been aware of that fact. The agent protectively threw himself

HARPER

over the old man's body, only to find it bloody and lifeless. Tremors of sorrow shook Collins' massive frame, and uncontrollable sobs escaped his lips.

The dark lord slowly approached the agent, a mighty fist raised high to strike, bitter rage causing his body to heave and shake. The demon had traveled many long miles for this moment, only to see it whisked suddenly from its grasp. One blow, even glancing, would be more than enough to kill the agent. The fist, however, did not descend. Slowly, the hand unclenched itself. The ancient *strigoi* looked at the pathetic scene in front of it, a huge man reduced to unremitting grief, hunched over the limp corpse of a disease-stricken, wasted corpse. Even for one steeped in death, a being who enthusiastically dined amidst the impaled corpses of its enemies, the scene was too much.

"My son..." it mouthed.

With lightning quickness, the demon transformed, smashing easily through the wall and sailing onto the night winds. It was soon joined in flight by the vampiress Lucy who, replete with fresh blood, struggled sluggishly to keep up. Though temporarily bested, the dark lord would sleep secure in its native dirt during the day, comforted that Collins' hatred would provide him at least one remaining enemy to carry on the fight, and assured its eternal life would remain engaging.

And the name Dracula would not be forgotten...

THE TWILIGHT EFFECT

"Hah! Vampires are the biggest pussies!" Waldemar snorted, slamming his meaty paw down with supernatural force onto the bar. Glasses shattered, and beer sprayed across the entire counter and onto the floor. Startled by the crash, a giant flesh construct jumped out of his chair and focused his dead gray eyes on Waldemar. Unintimidated, the werewolf snarled at the construct, yellow fangs bared in black gums. The construct hesitated for a second, then threw his stitched hands up in a sign of surrender and sat back down, the entire bar shaking as the creature settled its substantial weight.

Andrade rolled his eyes up and then looked down at his broken beer mug, a sigh escaping his pale lips. *Here we go again*, he thought dejectedly, anticipating Waldemar's next weekly diatribe.

Waldemar punched Andrade in the arm to get his attention and pointed at the television above the bar. On the screen, a teenage girl stared longingly at a pale, scrawny, middle-aged guy who appeared entirely incongruous in a high school classroom. Andrade looked up and recognized the film, the first in the hugely successful but fatally flawed teenage monster series that had turned the public spotlight on his kind in the worst way.

"Look at this douchebag! All he does is brood and whine about how he can never be with a human girl and how tortured his existence is. 'Oh, poor me! I'd kiss you, but I'm afraid I'll bite your head off.' What the hell is that? When did vampires decide to start playing with their food? Vlad Tepes, now there was a real vampire, not some meek, limp-dicked, androgynous ketchup licker. A nosferatu with balls, you know, the kind that would shove a stake up his enemy's blowhole first and then ask questions later. These new Twi-tards make me want to puke! Worthless pieces of crap!" Waldemar slammed his paw on the bar again to make his point. More beer soaked the floor.

Knowing Waldemar was just getting warmed up, Andrade shook his head and looked back at his broken mug, wishing he had stayed home. The big black-haired werewolf turned to his left and cast his glowing amber eyes on the meek vampire.

"What? Got nothing to say, as usual? You just gonna sit there like a punk bitch shaking your pretty little moussed head. Jesus! You're as big a pussy as that nancy boy in the movie. All you have done these last few years is sulk and tell me how tired you are. 'No, Waldemar, I can't go out with you. I've got to lay here in my coffin and mope over the curse of my lonely, eternal existence.' I can't believe you even came out with me tonight."

Andrade already regretted his decision to accompany the werewolf to the bar. He had initially resisted Waldemar's insistence that they go out, content to sit at home with a mystery novel and a mug of warm pig's blood. Not willing to take no for an answer, Waldemar decided to make his point by marking his territory all over Andrade's tiny apartment. The vampire quickly relented.

Waldemar turned his attention back to the TV. "I thought vampires were supposed to be super-intelligent, living forever and accumulating tons of knowledge and skills and all that crap. Look at this dumbass; he's over a hundred years old and still in high school. He's probably repeating geometry for the fiftieth time." A small, mischievous smile curled Waldemar's muzzle. "This guy reminds me of you."

Andrade winced at the werewolf's gibe as he turned away to scan the bar, seeing a mix of humans and supernaturals drinking and socializing. Waldemar's comments had unwittingly sparked a memory of a time long ago when Andrade's bloodsire had turned him—right at the cusp of manhood, condemning him to life as an eternal teenager cursed with the knowledge and burden of ages.

"Hey, pussy!" Waldemar yelled, trying to get Andrade's attention. "Remember the good old days when you used your fangs for something more than a bottle opener? Remember when we would go out to hunt under the full moon rather than sulk at a bar, picking off humans like they were fruit and gorging ourselves until we puked? I remember that ass-kicking bloodsucker, not this limp-wristed Twi-tard wannabee."

Yes, I remember those times too, Andrade admitted to himself. The adrenaline rush hit Andrade's lifeless veins as images of the past made their way through the fog of his current melancholy.

I remember when we took on the Knights Templar. They were reputed by all to be the elite fighting force of their time. I loved the sound of screeching metal and popping chainmail as our talons ripped apart their armor, like peeling an overripe fruit. The smell of sweat and blood as they screamed and I sunk my hands into their fragile flesh. The unique wet tearing sound was followed by the throb of a heart pulsing in my hand. And the taste of fresh, vibrant blood, just like liquid nirvana, drove away the eternal cold as it bathed my dry mouth and flooded down my parched throat.

Images and memories inundated Andrade's brain, pulled from the annals of his very long unlife.

I recall another time when we hunted the Red Coats. We flew up a hillside, the trees and grass just a blur as our legs propelled us relentlessly toward our prey. There wasn't any real pain as the lead bullets tore through us, just a slight sting like a static shock. I can't forget the rush of running into battle, slapping aside muskets and sabers with ease. I loved ripping away their red coats to reveal the delicate necks underneath, the fluttering just below the pink skin, knowing what lay under. There was nothing on earth like the first bite, sinking fangs into their arteries, followed by the screams and thrashing and terror—the ecstasy of consuming fear-spiked blood. We shared the roar of victory, raising our dead prizes in offering to the full moon. Yes, I do remember. We were like brothers then.

For a second, the adrenaline rush fueled by his memories awoke a sense of invulnerability in Andrade. He began to see how ridiculous his current situation had become. The years of stagnation, giving up his will to live, all now seemed like a bad joke.

Waldemar slammed Andrade across his back, jarring his attention back to the present. "Oh, this is too rich," the lycanthrope chortled. Andrade looked up to the screen again. The middle-aged vampire had removed his shirt and was standing in the sun, the light reflecting off his scrawny, underdeveloped frame as though his skin were made from crystal. "Tell me, please, that you don't sparkle like that in the sun. Just like Tinkerbell!" The huge werewolf laughed uncontrollably.

Just the spark he needed, Andrade released all his smothered rage and pent-up frustration built up over the last decades and let it pour over him. His elegant white hand shot out like a snake, wrapping itself around the werewolf's muscle-corded neck. He squeezed, then lifted Waldemar off the ground, watching as the wolfman's eyes bugged out. Andrade flung the three-hundred-pound werewolf across the bar into a group of wooden tables with a flick of his wrist. The bone demons seated there scattered as Waldemar smashed through their dinner of zebra carcass and pig intestines. One demon slipped on the slimy entrails and slammed into a robed warlock. Trying to catch his balance, the warlock reached for a chair and unintentionally unleashed a bolt of flame from his fingers, setting the chair on fire. The unnaturally hot flames quickly spread to other wooden furniture and ignited a roaring blaze. Panic set in as humans and supernaturals scattered to escape. The flesh construct, unable to see through the smoke, smashed through the wall and tumbled onto the street, inadvertently creating an escape route for others.

Waldemar quickly pulled himself up from the broken tables, flinging zebra viscera from his matted fur. "Look who just woke up. I was wondering what it would take to get a rise out of you, deadboy. Well, you just bit off more than you can chew. We both know you can't take me. A vamp is no match for an alpha wolf! I'm going to suck out your eyeballs!"

The lycanthrope launched himself at Andrade, slamming his paws down on the vampire's chest and burying his maw into Andrade's throat. Andrade felt his flesh yield under the assault of iron claws and razor fangs. As he was pushed back against the flaming wreckage of the bar, his clothing on fire, the words of his bloodsire came unbidden to him, calling to him after all these centuries.

"*Never forget what you are. Apex predator.*" Andrade's eyes flashed red as he grabbed Waldemar's claws, tearing the deadly daggers out of his chest, then head-butted the werewolf away from his throat. The bar echoed with the sick sound of breaking bone.

"Unaging. Undying. Immortal."

The jagged gashes Waldemar had inflicted on Andrade's chest and neck healed instantly, the skin suddenly smooth and unlined.

"Armed always with the strength of twenty men."

Andrade backhanded the werewolf, sending teeth flying across the room. The huge beast smashed to the ground, a whimper escaping his shattered snout. Moving with shadow swiftness, Andrade was on him instantly, his fanged teeth unsheathed as he tore into Waldemar's neck. Warm, powerful blood flowed into him, eating away the cold that had dulled his senses, filling him with even greater strength. His own beast, the red thirst, demanded more, intoxicated on the heady brew.

Just as Andrade was about to give in to his beast, his night vision penetrated the smoke and saw Waldemar's paw feverishly tapping the floor in a token of submission. Above the roar of the flames, he heard Waldemar scream, "I give, I give! Uncle, uncle! Ahhgodd, don't kill me, you crazy pale sunuvabitch!"

Andrade took a deep breath, pulling his encarmined mouth away from the fallen wolf, taking a minute to bring his beast back under control. As his fangs retracted, he sat back on his heels and looked at his broken friend on the floor. Andrade stood and offered his hand to the defeated werewolf.

"Jesus Christ, I thought you were gonna kill me." Waldemar took Andrade's hand and stood, his tail tucked. A crooked smile played on the lycanthrope's broken face as he reverted to his human form. "I was wondering what it would take for you to come around."

As Andrade and Waldemar turned to leave the burning bar, they noticed the smoke was changing color from black to white. In the center of the room, the warlock had summoned a water elemental to put out the flame. As the fire receded and the smoke cleared, the bar patrons began to return as though nothing had happened. Andrade smiled, happy to have been able to let loose finally. He felt like the weight of the world had been lifted from his shoulders. Waldemar massaged his rapidly healing neck and looked up to the TV, where the high school vampire looked morosely into the camera.

"I knew that shitty movie had to be good for something."

TO FIGHT BY THE LIGHT
OF THE SILVERY MOON

The last rays of the sun shone down on Justin, finally peeking out from behind black cumulus clouds. He was perched precariously on one of the larger boughs of an ancient oak tree, the effort of maintaining his position raising beads of sweat on an already damp brow. He felt weak as a child, having difficulty maintaining his balance. He tightened his grip on the bough, noting with some satisfaction the slight cracking of the wood as he did so, then hazarded a quick look toward the setting sun.

Less than ten minutes, he estimated. Very shortly, it would be completely dark. He looked down some thirty feet from his perch at the tranquil green meadow that descended east from the forest, the setting sun causing massive shadows to fall across the fluttering grass. A small brook rolled lazily down from the north, separating the lush grasslands from the forest line. A strong wind blew south from the snow-capped mountains, bringing a frigid cold that would only become more intense as the sun departed the sky. The chill wind reminded Justin of his nakedness as it crept along his ashen skin. Nudity for him was not a fashion statement; instead, it reflected awareness on his part that clothing was not compatible with the hazards to which his body would soon be subjected.

Quite a tranquil, picturesque scene, like something painted by Norman Rockwell, he thought humorously. *That is if you discount the heap of wolf's bane on the ground and the naked man in the tree.*

The pile of aconitum lay just east of the brook. He'd purchased it recently from one of his few remaining apothecary contacts. It had cost him plenty to obtain the purple-flowered variety, the only selection of wolf's bane that would serve his purpose this day. He'd also been forced to endure one of Niles' endless lectures on the differences between alchemy, sorcery, and necromancy. The old man lacked companionship, someone to reminisce with over the good old days, and even someone as curt as Justin would suit the bill.

The early evening air, despite the wind, was now rife with the flower smell, hopefully masking his body's odor. That pungent smell had also succeeded in attracting the attention of the being Justin was searching for.

His ears picked up the harsh breathing first, the piston-like exhalation of hot air through the nostrils of the muzzle, over black tongue and razor teeth. He mentally pictured the steaming breath rising from the beast as he heard the first fallen tree limb break, eerily similar in force and pitch to a rifle shot. He looked toward the aconitum pile and saw the nine-foot, four-hundred-pound wolf creature rocket some fifty feet eastbound across the brook and next to the mound, its massive jaws digging into the flowers. The sudden movement caused owls in nearby trees to take flight in fear.

Justin cautiously eyed the black-maned monstrosity feeding greedily just below him.

Werewolves...they just can't get enough wolf's bane, he mused. While poisonous to humans, the plant had a soothing influence on shifters, similar to a mild narcotic such as alcohol for humans, allowing them to maintain their animal form with less difficulty. He knew from experience that wolf shifters came in two forms—lycanthropes and werewolves. Lycanthropes were unfortunate beings, either cursed or bitten, forced to change into lupine form only under the influence of the rays of a full moon. In that form, they assumed the brute intelligence of the beast as well as its innate ferocity. Werewolves were another breed, able to change shape at will and retain some degree of human intelligence in wolf form. Justin had gotten lucky on this one. His braving of the daylight to set the trap would have amounted to painfully wasted effort in the case of a true moon beast.

As the monstrous wolf devoured the bait, Justin girded himself for action.

Well, this is what you've been waiting for, old man. Showtime!

JUSTIN LAUNCHED HIMSELF THROUGH THE AIR AS IF HE'D BEEN SHOT out of a cannon, his lithe frame slamming down onto the startled beast with jackhammer force, knocking the flowers from its maw. He expertly hooked his arms under the wolf's armpits as he rolled over and under the beast, using the werewolf's weight to his advantage. Justin hiked up his legs under its stomach as the creature's momentum brought it on top of him. He kicked up his legs and heaved backward with his arms using all his strength. The beast flew a good five yards before landing directly on its head with a sickening crunch.

Justin slowly rose to his feet. All was not going according to plan. The creature might as well have been chiseled from marble. Icy pain shot down Justin's left arm. He noted rapid swelling in his left shoulder where he had initially tackled the beast, indicating a dislocation and possible broken bones. He felt weak, his movements lethargic and leaden, as if his feet were encased in concrete and weights were tied to his hands.

The werewolf appeared unconcerned with Justin's dilemmas. Shrugging off a fall that would have broken a human's neck, it righted itself with frightening ease. It bellowed a roar of frustration and rushed him, black-taloned claws reaching for his throat. Instinctually Justin ducked under the beast's extended arms and began to rain a succession of rapid blows to the werewolf's abdominal wall. The punches weren't meant for knockout effect; instead, he sought to frustrate the beast and begin to wear it down. He made sure to use the palms of his hands to deliver the blows to avoid breaking the knuckles and fingers, avoiding striking the beast in the face for fear of lacerating his hands on the creature's wickedly sharp teeth and wasting precious blood.

The blows had the desired effect on the shapeshifter, surprising it and causing it to reel. Justin theorized that the beast had never been attacked before, let alone by something so seemingly unthreatening as a human male. Before it could recover, Justin snapped a kick into its vulnerable right knee, breaking it. The werewolf shrieked as its leg gave out, the pained cry resonating with more human agony than bestial fury. It fell forward and to the right, trying desperately to balance itself with the left leg. Justin moved forward, prepared to deliver the final blow.

He never saw it coming. Faster than Justin's eyes could follow, the werewolf brutally slashed his face open to the bone with a wild swipe, white-hot pain causing Justin to falter in his attack. Blood sprayed into the air. Encouraged, the wolf rose and backhanded him, lifting him off his feet and flying like a rag doll toward the brook. The upper part of his body landed in the icy shallows, the cold running water wrapping itself around him and sucking away his body's strength.

Justin dug his hands, now claws themselves, into the muddy bank, seeking purchase to pull himself free from the water's clinging death. He managed to sit up, scrabbling frantically away from the water, only to be knocked down again as the werewolf landed on his chest. Justin heard and felt bones in his rib cage shatter under the beast's weight. The monster's tree-like arms wrapped around his shoulders, claws digging deep into the meat of his deltoids, and forced his torso back into the water. The brook's icy grasp again enfolded him as his head sank below the water level. The creature's huge maw dipped rapidly toward the fallen man's throat.

With an incredible effort, Justin raised his dripping hands from the water and latched them underneath the beast's jawbone, managing to slow but not stop the descent of deadly fangs. He exerted what remained of his flagging strength to twist the creature's head to the side and break its neck, but he lacked the leverage to overcome both the beast's ponderous weight and the massive strength of its neck muscles.

With a surge of inhuman power, the werewolf broke Justin's hold and sank its fangs into the meat of his neck. Justin felt the last remnants of his strength evaporate as his blood flowed freely from the wound. His hands fluttered feebly at his sides as the beast worried at his neck.

When the spine is severed, all will be over, he sought to reassure himself. After all these years and all the losses he had suffered, it would be so easy to give up and let the beast finish him. His mind drifted.

He had wandered the world for centuries, feasting on the lifeblood of mortals. These simple humans were so fragile; their bodies easily ruptured and represented no challenge when hunted. At first, the bloodlust had consumed him, more passionate than any desire for food or women. Over time, however, the novelty had begun to fade; the gamy blood of a warrior became indistinct from the life fluids of a beautiful queen. He'd been unable to find comfort or meaning in his eternal unlife. Once a source of passion, the nightly hunt for prey inspired him no more. He did not feed for decades, his body shriveling and aging as a consequence. Ultimately, he had completely lost the will to move and nestled down in an abandoned alley, just another piece of debris amongst the street garbage. He waited for the sunlight and urban predators to strip the flesh from his bones, hopefully granting him release.

It was another type of predator that roused him from torpor one night. He woke to find his leg gnawed upon by a strangely hairless, sallow-skinned creature with rows of piranha teeth. Two dead transients lay sprawled next to him, their flesh marred by savage bite marks, gutted and missing limbs.

Instinctively he lashed out, his foot connecting with little effect on the creature's iron jaw. The demon stood, blocking the moonlight, nearly eight feet in height, clusters of black veins pulsing beneath pallid, leathery flesh. He didn't have time to wonder what pocket hell dimension had spawned this monstrosity or how it had made its way into this reality. The creature reached out a massive, iron-clawed hand with serpentine speed and seized him from the ground, holding him aloft by the neck. The demon seemed dismayed when he did not choke or fight for air, its large, bug eyes widening, a snarl of confusion and anger escaping its rubbery, whale-white lips.

The red thirst, denied for so long, screamed for release. His withered fist lashed out, smashing the creature's rat-like snout. The demon stumbled back but did not fall, not relinquishing its death grip on his throat. Instead, both claws encircled his throat, the sharp nails digging deep into the flesh. It employed all its substantial power, attempting to wrest his head from his shoulders.

Ancient instincts surged within him. He gripped the creature's forearms without panicking and tried to pry its hands free. He might *have succeeded if he'd been at full strength, but he was weak from blood abstinence; the creature's hands didn't budge. Regrouping, he raised his right arm and brought the elbow down on the joint of the demon's arm, breaking it. He fell to the ground as the horror reeled in pain and distress.*

He launched himself at the creature, flowing seamlessly from one shadow to the next, seizing it by the throat and using his momentum to ride it to the ground. His fang teeth extended and bit into the creature's throat, his mouth filling with the cold, viscous ichor that passed for demon blood. He repressed an initial wave of nausea and swallowed greedily. The demon bucked, trying to free itself. Its claws dug into his back, shredding the skin, but he ignored the pain and continued feeding, gulping mouthful after mouthful. The creature gradually weakened as its blood was siphoned off. When its heart stopped, he stood over it, mouth awash in black ichor. The demon's blood flowed through him, filling his limbs with strength greater than he had ever known. He felt reborn for the first time since he had risen from his grave.

Justin returned to consciousness, noting the weight of daylight lifted from his body. The sun had finally set on the horizon. It was a comfortable, reassuring sensation he had become accustomed to over the centuries. Playtime was over.

The werewolf's snout bit into sandy mud instead of flesh and blood. The beast scrambled in confusion as it tried to locate its suddenly missing prey, talons carving desperately into the soft wet ground of the brook. It failed to note the swirling plume of incandescent fog trailing between its legs. The mist swirled behind the massive creature, revolving in and around itself like a supernatural tornado until it assumed human form. Justin noted without surprise that his wounds had healed, though he was still weak from blood loss.

Time to fix that.

The red thirst brought instantaneous physical changes.

Justin's ears lengthened to high elfin points as his eyes bled black and his sclera bled scarlet. His canine teeth assumed dagger-like proportions rivaling the creature he battled, while his fingernails became iron claws. He made a puissant fist with his right hand and drove it through the spine and rib cage of the confused shapeshifter.

The eldritch wolf arched back, its arms wildly flailing as it screamed its pain at the uncaring forest. The scent of the creature's potent blood inflamed Justin's bloodlust. He reached across the werewolf's neck with his left arm, catching the right side of its head in a bone-breaking grip. He wrenched back his arm with violent precision, breaking the neck with a swiftness suggesting centuries of practice in the art of death. Justin was a more than apt pupil in that regard.

The werewolf sagged in his grip, its central nervous system destroyed. Its supernatural constitution continued pumping blood through its veins. Justin bit into the exposed throat, letting adrenaline-spiked superhuman blood rush into his system. At the same time, his right hand smashed through the rib cage and found the creature's massive heart. He brutally extricated the still-beating organ from the werewolf's torso, letting the dying body slump gracelessly into the water.

Justin paid little heed as the creature returned to its human form—a balding, overweight Caucasian male with a unibrow. Typically not one for theatrics, Justin couldn't help but go with the moment. His lips sheathed back from his gore-encrusted fangs, and an inhumanly loud victory cry bellowed from his throat as he raised the werewolf's pulsing heart overhead. Lightning split the evening sky.

God, I could really go for a full moon right now.

Justin spread his arms wide, concentrating on the form of a bat in his head. He gave himself over to it, as he had on hundreds of occasions, feeling his body respond as membranous black wings sprouted from his arms. The wind rippled around him as he took flight.

LESS THAN ONE HOUR LATER, HE WALKED CASUALLY ACROSS THE hallway of his upscale apartment, leaving the steaminess of his sauna bath and sitting down at his work desk in the study. He'd quickly washed away the dirt and blood from this evening's adventure upon returning home. He was always amused that the water from those pipes and faucets made by men caused him no distress, while the running water in streams, lakes, and even oceans robbed him instantly of most of his physical strength. *Something to do with elemental purity, perhaps*, he mused.

He booted up the computer on his desk and began surfing the police blotters on the internet, looking for odd occurrences, deaths, and clusters of missing persons. Similar research had alerted him to the presence of the now-dead werewolf in a nearby agricultural community, just miles from the city he temporarily called home. He noted an upsurge of activity near a newly opened toll bridge in Arkansas. Missing children had last been seen playing near the bridge while "maimed" bodies of all types were washing ashore downriver.

Sounds like a troll. The hideous beasts were notorious for insinuating themselves into territories before claiming them as their own. They were also notoriously vicious, taller than houses, and possessed strength rivaling giants.

Or Master Vampires. Justin had never thought of himself as a Master Vampire. He'd never created harems of clinging Undead beauties like Vlad Tepes or sought to rule countries like other foolish *upir* had, but he'd weathered more than a few centuries. In that time, he'd grown exceedingly bored with his existence. He'd learned the error of making emotional connections, both with humans and others of his kind, seeing the devastation his living dead status could cause others. However, there was little else to occupy his time without interpersonal interaction.

He supposed that same boredom was the impetus for the monster hunting he'd undertaken. He'd been a knight in warm life, raised in a time of chivalry and competition. When he'd been "brought across," human beings no longer provided any challenge to his increased strength, speed, and vampire "enhancements." At first, the human vampire hunters caused him some difficulty with their wards and charms, their garlic, and holy water, but over the centuries, these accouterments bothered him less and less. A strong-willed individual in life, that same strength had served only to magnify his standard vampire powers. His bloodsire, the ancient creature known as Ormond, had perhaps stated it best to him in the infancy of his Undead existence.

"At night, the vampire is virtually omnipotent," his sire had said. Justin thought briefly of Ormond, the tall, hunched *nosferatu* forever attired in a gold-threaded black brocade coat. He recalled the swollen rodent-like bald head with pointed ears, bushy brows, and prominent front fangs. Justin often wondered why the physical abnormalities that plagued Ormond had never manifested in his own appearance, which had remained blessedly normal over the centuries (as far he could tell without seeing himself in a mirror). Unlike his sire, he had never indulged in feeding binges during the Black Plague.

Still, the insights the old *nosferatu* had provided Justin into his new existence were indelible.

"He is Night's Dark Master," Ormond had said. That maxim proved prophetic even regarding other monsters, as Justin had

learned over time. After the teeth of the bone demon had revived him, Justin had been inspired to challenge sorcerers and necromancers with their attendant hordes of zombies, witches, werewolves, flesh constructs, revenants, and ogres. With the dawning of the atomic age, he'd even battled mutants and a supervillain or two. In each case, he'd triumphed, and decisively so. His medieval upbringing required him to regularly cede the advantage to his opponent, as in tonight's case engaging in battle while still weakened by the sun and in the proximity of running water.

Perhaps he had a bit of a death wish in him after all these years. Few were the Undead who challenged werewolves in hand-to-hand combat or planned on attacking a troll. Bereft of the woman he loved and denied a true death, he now sought it at the hands of the few beings capable of delivering it to him.

Or maybe, old man, you just love the taste and power of enhanced blood. The strength he'd taken from the werewolf tonight would moderate the red thirst for a few days.

He began to contemplate the clothing he would need for his next trip. *Attire appropriate for an ancient Southern gentleman.*

Time to pack the native soil. What's the point of unlife without a bit of fun?

FLOTSAM

In starlit nights I saw you
So cruelly you kissed me
Your lips a magic world
Your sky all hung with jewels
The killing moon will come too soon

— *"THE KILLING MOON," ECHO*
AND THE BUNNYMEN

once thought I controlled time, could make it move and
flow according to the caprices of my will. Now, time has
become an enemy, more cold, brutal, and implacable than
any I have faced in my long existence.

My limbs feel like iron, cold morning iron that has endured
a chilly alpine night complete with frost and snow. Facedown,
bobbing along in the waves like the jetsam I have become,
disoriented and imprisoned by the running waters of the ocean.
Of course, the days are the worst, the unrelenting sun searing

through the remnants of my once-fine clothing, crisping the dead skin underneath. The onset of night brings some minor relief, but my body weakens and slowly rots with each passing day that I do not feed. My hair has fallen out. The few brief glimpses I catch of my hands and forearms reveal a body reduced to little more than an emaciated patchwork of burned, leathery skin. Gulls and other carrion feeders have gathered in the waters around me, pecking away small pieces of flesh from my neck and back while fish nibble away at my stomach underneath.

I try to scream but have no breath. Rank seawater fills my mouth and invades my throat and lungs. I attempt to swim but have no strength. I fancy myself one of the damned in Dante's ninth circle, frozen solid and unmoving in a lake. I can vaguely recall when others labeled me damned as well, people I then considered foolish and beneath my notice. Now, as I am tossed about on the waves, I wonder who the fool was?

Consciousness ebbs and flows during the day like the tides. An old, familiar hunger not fed in days accompanies the cold, filling my every waking moment and haunting my dreams...

I LIE BACK IN THE BED AS SHE LEANS OVER ME, HER SKIN SO WHITE IT glows, absorbing light, an aura of darkness surrounding her. She mounts me with cat-like grace, her tight stomach brushing mine. Her small breasts hang down and rest on my chest, the softness of her touch exciting me. I breathe rapidly, inhaling her scent, almost panting. Her face floats toward me with cold and hungry blue eyes, her raven black hair streaming behind. I reach up to satisfy my lust, but

she brushes my hands away with casual ease. She is in charge of this moment; my life is in her hands.

I hold my breath as she caresses my neck, stroking my fevered pulse with the lightest touch. I feel her kiss, intimate and deep and deadly, in the same place she has been caressing. My eyes flare open, and the world becomes more intense for a brief moment, all my senses heightened more than ever—a final, all-consuming sensory overload. My body is slowly dying, drained of energy and blood; this intensity represents my mind's way of clinging to life's memories. I let it wash over me. Her lips are so cold, not smooth as I expect, but more scaly like a fish. They grate on my skin and pull away. I feel it again and jerk away, startled by swarms of silver flashes spinning around me, diving in again to pick, pick, pick at my flesh. Not my maker, but my reality...

THE GULLS SCATTER AS I FEEBLY HEAVE MY BODY ABOUT, THE BLOOD reveries of a dead man temporarily interrupted. The birds return to their feast as soon as my energy gives out and my struggles cease. My mind wanders, lulled as the sun's heat inexorably cooks my brain. Reality and recollection, substance and dream mix and become one.

IMAGES FLASH BEFORE ME. SOME ARE RAPID AND EASILY DISMISSED. Others I choose to draw out and explore further, sifting them over and over, looking for new angles of insight, like rereading a familiar

SCOTT HARPER

*book on a lazy Sunday afternoon. I am transformed, physically and
emotionally, no longer a discarded, emaciated skeleton bobbing
hopelessly on the water. Fine clothing adorns me, indicative of class
and breeding. Long, chestnut brown hair flows down over the broad
shoulders of a muscular physique. My skin is pale but neither sallow
nor thin, my lips full and red. And my eyes...they burn with a fierce
red intensity, a sureness of power no living man could ever duplicate.*

*She is there as well, of course. She becomes my dark mother,
bringing me across the plane of death with care and precision, my
heart stilled, lungs empty, my lifeblood coating her lips. She returns
the blood to me, mixed with her own, revitalizing a corpse shell, her
willpower grasping my departing soul and refusing to let it go.*

*Her eyes fill my vision as I rise from the bed that has become a
grave and embrace her with supernatural passion, our first blood
kiss, a clash of lip and fang and tongue. She pledges between moans
to school me in the ways of her night world. I moan in return. My
sharp nails tear into the skin of her back as I feel truly alive for the
first time.*

*Time becomes a vast whirlpool, images of unlife tossed about and
jumbled together without chronology. I see myself accepting my new
form of existence and reveling in it, altering my body, taking to the
sky with wings as dark as night, soaring underneath the moon's brilliance. Deadlier than African lions, we chase humans, knocking them
to the ground with frightening ease and feasting on them. We duel
churchmen in battles of wit and intrigue spanning decades. I grapple
with fierce wolfmen for forest supremacy, tooth to tooth, talon to
talon. Her approving looks fill me with pride as I raise high the head
of a loup-garou, his animal blood coating my proud fang teeth.*

*Some of the memories exhilarate me and are welcomed. Others
come unsolicited, like a tax collector or a spurned lover at the front
door, causing uncertainty and angst.*

We are back in the same room, her room, where she sired me. I

224

see her move away from me, rage and disappointment vying for control of her features, her face turning away.

"I'm sorry," I say, but bloody tears have already appeared in her eyes.

"How could you?" she accuses. "I made you to be with me always." She looks at the bed between us, the same bed where we made love for the first time all those years ago—the bed where I gave up my humanity.

"I no longer need you. I've outgrown you. You limit me." The words come out harshly, but the thing I've become has no compassion or cares save his own needs. I feel neither gratitude nor hate toward her. "I'm leaving."

My words enrage her further. She reacts uncharacteristically, striking out, smashing the nightstand like so much kindling. I ignore her outburst.

"I've booked passage on a ship leaving tomorrow. I've made arrangements for my belongings to be delivered before my departure. There's no need for any involvement on your part. And you don't need to know where I'm going."

She laughs, her fang teeth unsheathed, the blood tears streaking down her face. "Have you learned nothing in your time with me? You share my blood; I'll always know where you are. The sea is our enemy. We cross it only when we must and only after taking the necessary precautions. Storms are at their worst this time of year, and you cannot feed. The shipping companies keep very accurate manifests. Missing passengers will be noticed and cause unrest."

"And still, I will leave," I say matter-of-factly.

"And without me, you will die. Again," she warns. I laugh and leave.

I NEVER KNEW WHAT CAUSED THE SHIP TO SINK. I WAS AWAKENED IN MY daytime slumber by a thunderous crash, the vessel's movement smashing my coffin and heaving me out onto the cargo deck floor. I struggled to consciousness underneath a rising mountain of water, pushed and pulled about by inexorable icy currents. I fought back with all the unnatural strength at my command but soon found myself exhausted by the elemental purity of the ocean waters. After a short time, I floated to the surface, weak and spent and unmoving, just another of the hundreds of other carcasses scattered amongst the ship's wreckage, littering the silent sea.

I wait now for the bliss of final obliteration. A dead, damned thing, I cannot drown, nor can I burn entirely while half-submerged in water. The gulls and fish consume my flesh at an agonizingly slow pace. Only the destruction of my remains will free what little remains of my soul.

There was a time when I sought to avoid death at all costs when I found the concept of my mortality alarming. I eventually went to the extent of making love to a dead creature to avoid that mortality, allowing her to drink my blood and ensnare my soul. Now I would welcome the finality of true death. Perhaps, if there is a deity, it has chosen to extract compensation for the many lives I have snuffed out. If so, I can only begin to imagine how long this unliving hell will continue.

At first, I do not notice the tugging on my boots, caught up as I am in my dazed reveries. A stronger pull wakes me from my languor. I note briefly that the sun has set, the night's coolness slightly invigorating my tired frame. A small measure of comfort, a familiar affinity with the darkness, sets in.

A powerful grip attaches to my legs below the calves and pulls me with astonishing force below the waves. I both feel and hear the bones break. The grip takes me downward for a short time, then releases. A sense of the utter, terrifying depth of the ocean below envelops me. I see the colossal form of a shark as it swims out from underneath, its black body large enough to eclipse the moonlight. It rounds with extraordinary swiftness for such a large creature. I see its clown eyes set just above an enormous mouth lined with rows of deadly teeth. The leviathan's jaws encircle my torso with unerring precision, shattering ribs and puncturing skin. It begins to dive. I feel the crushing pressure of the ocean increase as the beast swims deeper and deeper.

I feel no fear at this point, having died once before already. A portion of the man buried deep within this Undead corpse wishes to be consumed and finally end this nightmare. The shark's sharp teeth remind me of my human death beneath the teeth of my maker. A trail of black ichor seeps from my torso wounds, trailing upward behind the shark's tail. The creature's eyes are closed as it begins to shake me in its immense jaws.

Ancient survival instincts come to the fore, strengthened by a fevered desire to prevent my maker's dire predictions from coming true. Despite my weakness, despite the suffocating weight of the water, I summon the strength to dig my hands, now adorned with black claws, into the fleshy area around the shark's gills. I methodically begin to tear chunks of red flesh from the huge creature.

The shark reacts predictably to the pain, opening wide its massive maw. The wake pushes me out of the beast's jaws. I hang on by one hand to an open wound I have inflicted as the shark dives deeper, attempting to escape. I plant both hands in the rent flesh and pull, the tough hide and muscle giving way with frightening ease. Blood fills the water, blinding me. My lips pull back in a mirthless smile, teeth exposed.

I bury my face in the wound, gulping down seawater and the shark's gamy life fluids. My tongue digs deep into the meat and gristle; my throat swallows, greedy for more. The ice that has invaded my body dissipates some as strength returns. I am overcome by a steadily increasing sense of invigoration and repletion as I continue to vacuum out the beast's lifeblood. I fail to notice as the shark eventually slows its dive, stops, then begins to float upside down.

The shark's life energy has become my own. My burned, emaciated skin has healed and become whole, hair now covering my head. Strength and power flood now muscular limbs and torso. I am no longer a corpse but a man. A man with a name.

Zecheriah. My name is Zecheriah.

The knowledge does me little good, for, despite my newfound strength, the sea still imprisons me. The shark has floated to the surface, now belly up. I push my head out of the water and attempt to scramble onto the top of the corpse but find little purchase.

Boundless rage fills my heart. Still unable to escape this torment. To have the raw power to tear apart a giant killing machine but simultaneously be unable to pull myself a short distance out of water? Alive, but not truly alive. Such were the inexplicable contradictions of the "life" I had chosen. Still unable to put the lie to my maker's words of warning. I scream again. This time air fills my dead lungs, and my cries travel unanswered into the night.

I begin to wonder if I actually can die. Perhaps I will sink to the bottom at some point, paralyzed by cold and disoriented, but conscious...forever. The strength of the shark's blood is short-lived, sucked out by the icy running water. Confusion settles in; periods of lucidity become shorter and shorter, intertwined with memories of an undying woman.

I am aroused from my stupor by the thunderous echo of a gunshot. A bloodless wound opens up on the shark's white belly. I hear male voices speaking behind me and attempt to twist my head to see their source. More gunshots. This time my body bucks under the impact, shots tearing through my waterlogged torso. I feel sharp metal slam through my back and push out from my chest. I am hauled unceremoniously away from the dead shark, out of the water, and onto a ship's deck.

I find myself on an antiquated wooden vessel with the planks and railings caked in grime and sea salt. A gibbous moon shines over masts outfitted with flat sails, as there are no drafts in the early evening. Dark, malodorous forms surround me. Their dress and mannerisms suggest they are brigands of some sort. Drawn to carnage like vultures to carrion, they have begun looting the corpses left in the wake of my ship's disaster. Perhaps they were the cause of the wreck. I make at least ten of them, armed with knives, swords, clubs, and firearms. A large hook attached to a long wooden pole pierces my torso. They have gaffed me like a fish.

A massive African with a scarred, heavily muscled physique approaches me. He pins my head to the deck, a boot thrust into my neck, and extracts the gaff with a wet sucking sound. Two of his colleagues approach. Thinking me dead, they rifle through the remains of my clothing.

The fire inside me is rekindled. Anger about my condition. Hatred for my maker. Rage against the recent indignities I'd endured. These and other frustrations explode at once as I retaliate with inhuman ferocity. Within a heartbeat, the throats of the pickpockets are ruptured in a spray of blood and sundered windpipe.

The other brigands attack. I feel the impact of fists and clubs, ignore cuts and thrusts from knives and swords. I become a virtual hurricane, sweeping through the pirates in an orgy of shattered skulls, broken necks, and torn-out hearts. One brave soul points a pistol at my head and fires. White-hot pain floods my vision as the shot shatters my skull, sending a mist of black ichor into the air. I stumble but quickly recover as the wound heals almost instantaneously, bones knitting, flesh reforming. Her blood has made me strong, ungodly resilient. I grab the man by the front of his oily shirt, lift him effortlessly with one hand, and sling him over the rail. He screams as he is torn apart by a horde of smaller sharks, newly arrived and feeding on the remains of the one I had killed.

A fearsome cry assaults my ears. I feel the wooden deck shake under the impact of massive booted feet. The giant African slams into me, causing me to stagger back. I almost lose my footing on the slick deck. The pirate's huge, meaty hands encircle my neck and exert incredible pressure that would have broken an ordinary man's neck. I laugh, a full-throated laugh that almost brings tears to my eyes. I relish the challenge this man offers and respond in kind. His eyes betray disbelief as mine blaze crimson in the night. My clawed hands sweep down and pulp the African's massive forearms. A mixed cry of agony and terror shoots from his lips as we fall to the deck. I bury my mouth into his neck. Rich, powerful, hot blood pulses down my throat, flooding me with energy, dispelling the iciness that had permeated my dead body. Its thickness flows like fire in my veins, and something in me rises up and sings in delight at its flavor. The cold ichor of the shark seems like gruel in comparison. I feed until the man's heart is stilled and the blood runs out.

I discard the corpse, casually fingering a remaining button on a once-fine shirt. I survey the carnage. Though still damned,

I am imprisoned no more. At least, not physically. I feel the strength of her blood call out to me, across land and sea, offering understanding and forgiveness. I take flight, seeking some form of resolution.

SHE WAITS FOR ME ON THE BED, HER WHITE NIGHTGOWN OPEN IN THE front, her pale skin beckoning me.

"*Denn die Todten reiten schnell,*" she comments. *For the dead travel fast.*

"I did not die, as you predicted," I state matter-of-factly.

She rises on her knees and encircles my shoulders with her thin arms. She looks at me, her dark eyes filling my vision.

"I'm glad." She brushes her lips on mine, not kissing, just arousing.

"I have a memento," I say, digging my fingers through recently healed tissue deep into my ribcage. I retrieve a serrated shark tooth and place it in her hand. She kisses it and licks my pale blood from it, leaning back to expose her chest. She trails the tooth just below the areola of her right breast, black blood slowly seeping out from the small incision. She guides my head to the cut. I let her. My lips take hold as her head falls back, her back arched in passion. I drink, her cold blood more powerful and delicious than I remember it.

I realize blood is stronger in the end. Stronger than will, stronger than hate, stronger than destiny, stronger than time itself. I embrace that hard-won knowledge and join with her, accepting my eternity and the comfort she offers.

AN UPGRADE OF THE ELIXIR: A GUNNAR AND ILONA TALE

G unnar huddled with his ear pressed firmly to the white concrete wall, his oily brown hair hanging down in sweaty clumps over his grimy face. His keen ears picked up sounds and movement in the cell adjoining his, creating a tableau in his mind.

A pair of "doctors," if that was the correct term, extracted skin samples from a female corpse secured atop an austere steel table in the center of the room, their boots squeaking on the shiny epoxy resin flooring. The men wore intimidating white hazmat suits with transparent plastic masks and moved with practiced efficiency as they sliced shriveled skin from a thin, pale arm and placed it in a small container.

The corpse was sallow and desiccated, lying supine with its legs akimbo and arms limp at its sides. It wore a sleeveless red silk dress that trailed past its bony knees. A wooden stake was embedded between its breasts, rising a good two feet above the woman's sunken chest.

The doctors knew to avoid looking at the corpse's face, having received strict instructions from their boss, Doctor Dippel, to avoid any eye contact. Had they looked, they would have seen brilliant emerald eyes beaming from within dark sockets, slowly batting from side to side in a desperate hope of momentarily catching their gaze. Despite its mutilated, atrophied condition, the corpse still "lived" after a fashion.

The doctors collected their equipment and the sample and exited through a thick metal door that led to a long hallway, the closing door echoing ominously in the stillness.

Gunnar removed his ear from the wall and sank to a sitting position, resting his scraggly bearded chin on his thick chest and looking defeated. He was tired, oh so tired; his limbs felt leaden, and his throat was dry from dehydration and yelling empty threats at the doctors. These men, these *creatures*, had done *unspeakable* things to him.

They'd released fumes into his quarters through the air vent, a tranquilizing gas laced with tiny silver particles. The miasma had burned his lungs and throat, nearly rendering him unconscious. The doctors had strapped his unresisting form to the central table and stabbed him with various sharp instruments, knives and scalpels, some made of steel, others coated with silver. The pain threatened to overwhelm him, flooding his veins with fire and causing him to scream. They measured how long it took for his wounds to mend: the cuts inflicted with steel sealed almost instantly, while the silver lacerations healed slower with human speed. The men were careful to avoid piercing his heart or spine with silver, injuries that would have been lethal. They had no such scruples when it came to the steel instruments, eagerly driving them through his ribcage and piercing his heart, as well as through his eyes and into his brain.

Gunnar had never experienced such prolonged, gut-wrenching agony, unrelenting torture that drove him to the brink of madness and depression. He desperately longed for an end to the pain and to once again hold his love in his arms.

Presumably, the torture he endured served some higher

purpose, for the doctors took notes and made recordings on each occasion. They lacked any concern for his well-being, not bothering to clean his wounds. Of course, they apparently knew of his cursed heritage and were aware the injuries would heal of their own accord.

Gunnar's thoughts were not focused on himself; instead, they centered on the corpse occupying the next cell. He and Ilona had been captured recently when their suburban estate was overrun at the break of dawn by black-garbed masked men. He was just leaving the basement after a pleasurable night spent in her company when the soldiers burst through the door, lighting him up with a Taser. Despite the havoc being played with his central nervous system, he attempted to transform, only to be quickly restrained in silver-coated steel handcuffs. The men forced him to watch as they ascended the dais steps and threw back the lid of the great wooden coffin in which Ilona rested in daylight slumber, oblivious to the events unfolding around her. A big man with a scarred face and merciless black eyes raised a long wooden stake high over her chest. He plunged it through her ribcage and into her heart, paralyzing her. Gunnar had watched helplessly as Ilona's eyes opened in confusion and horror, her lips forming a silent scream.

He didn't recall much of the trip back to this torture chamber, only being thrust through the rear door of a big semi-truck container and bounced around the comfortless metal interior for what seemed endless miles of travel. They'd arrived at a large gated warehouse hidden in a thick, secluded forest, the trees so tall they nearly blotted out the sun. The prison aspect of the facility became apparent to him upon entry. He was housed in the middle of three specially constructed cells on the bottom floor of an underground fortress. He'd lost track of their time here, being subjected to ungodly experiments and vicious cruelty almost nonstop since arrival.

Gunnar had listened as they sawed Ilona open and inspected her organs, removing some for measuring and categorization. He could not imagine the pain she experienced, beyond even what he was exposed to. Ilona was Undead, a Night Walker; having died once already, she could only be destroyed by specific prescribed means. Having her organs removed was not among them.

He heard the appalling sounds of the doctors puncturing her body with various sharp instruments, as they had done with him. He imagined they cut her with wood in addition to silver and steel; neither metal could harm her, but wood was a bane to her kind and capable of inflicting dire injury. Deprived of blood and staked through the heart, Ilona's wounds would not heal swiftly.

He sensed a presence guiding it all—there, from behind the one-way windows of the wide office perched on the opposite side of the facility. Somehow, call it intuition or a supernatural sixth sense, Gunnar knew the source of their problems could be found there.

He had no escape plan; Ilona lay immobile, and the silver gas kept him too weak to transform. The occupant of the cell to his left also appeared incapable of assisting. It stank of carrion and death magic, the sulfurous odor seeping through the walls into his cell. The mad creature called out to him now, its voice chilling like the whisper of cold wind gusting through the headstones of an abandoned graveyard, laced with an undertone of unbridled evil.

"How go things today, wolf? Any new lurid details of indignity and degradation that you have suffered and are willing to share?" the thing inquired gleefully.

Johann Konrad Dippel stood with his arms folded across his black polyester-vested chest, looking through the second-story windows of his expansive office as his assistants finished their work and departed the test subjects' cells. He had grand plans for the materials the doctors would bring—with them, he would finally fulfill his lifelong work and bring into existence a genuinely immortal creature!

He paused briefly to consider his earlier life and the winding path that brought him to the brink of success. He'd been born in seventeenth-century Germany, the son of a wealthy aristocrat, and grew up in relative affluence. His fairy tale childhood ended at nine when his mother contracted a wasting illness, lingering on death's door for months before finally passing away. Her loss left a gaping hole in his life, one he could not account for. The mystery of life and death, the randomness that God's creations were subject to, fascinated him—it became his life's obsession to solve.

He began his studies at the university at an early age. His genius was on display for all to see as he effortlessly outstripped his fellow students, scoring the highest grades in each class he took. His brilliance far exceeded the professors' instructional capabilities, teachers he came to loathe for their indolence and complacency; he turned to other avenues for guidance in his quest to discover the source of life.

Johann uncovered dark, profane secrets reading from the old tomes and grimoires he paid handsomely to acquire. He became proficient in alchemy and the emerging field of galvanism, even dabbling in blood rituals and sorcery. His experiments quickly earned the ire of his colleagues; they labeled him a "heretic" and expelled him from the university. Yet he continued his work high in the isolated mountains of his ancestral castle, undaunted, meticulously plotting his greatest creation.

He recalled that fateful night when a raging winter storm generated enough electrical current to power his state-of-the-art machines and infuse his arcane decoction with the potency to raise the dead. He stood in awe as the giant portmanteau being he'd assembled from the body parts of fresh corpses ponderously rose from the table, its long linen-wrapped arms grasping out toward him under the amber light of a waxing gibbous moon. That night he knew triumph, if only for a short time.

The creature's brain proved inadequate, incapable of absorbing the knowledge he lavished on it; soon, the brute had escaped the castle and gone on a mass-murder spree in the local town. Only by sheer fortune had he been able to escape the mob of torch-bearing villagers that had stormed and burned the castle in retaliation.

He'd been on the run ever since, in one form or another. His experiment was the basis for a fiction novel that became famous and later inspired numerous film adaptations. Johann could have cared less; his only motivation was his research. Over the years, he'd plied his trade for various authoritarian regimes seeking a super soldier, one immune to pain and bullets; they funded his research and provided fortified locations to work. He'd been able to continue his experiments, honing his skills and developing more evolved versions of his first creation. He maintained a steady supply of the first potion, the Elixir of Life, and regularly administered small injections to himself. The decoction retarded the aging process; he had existed on the Earth for over three hundred years but didn't look a day over forty.

The office door opened, and his two assistants entered, standing straight at attention near the folding chairs and oak dining table that sufficed for a waiting area. The first one took off his mask, revealing the sweaty face of a middle-aged man with a thick mustache and receding hairline. He handed the small specimen container to Johann.

"As you requested, Doctor—skin from the vampire," the man said.

Johann took the container and waved the assistants off.

"Leave me."

The man dipped his head in acknowledgment and joined his colleague in exiting. Johann walked to the opposite end of the room where his laboratory was set up. He set the container down on a steel table replete with jars, test tubes, and beakers filled with multi-colored liquids. Similar specimen containers were placed there—tissue and blood samples taken from the other two test subjects.

Despite knowing the harm inflicted on the subjects in obtaining the samples, Johann did not experience any regrets; such indelicacies were necessary to verify the grade and value of the materials to his work.

Johann looked to his right, and the giant metal table bolted into the concrete floor. His latest project lay on its back, its enormous limbs secured with thick leather restraints. He had painstakingly assembled the creature from scratch: the lower body of an Olympic sprinter, the torso of a powerlifter, hands from a painter, the head of a male fashion model, and the brain of an astrophysicist. All that was required now was administering the final version of his serum, the ultimate Elixir of Life, and his life's goal would be complete.

"They just took more samples from Ilona," Gunnar said to the inquisitive creature in the adjacent cell. The entity had only been recently housed there, though their captors had spent weeks meticulously preparing the room in advance. The creature, whatever it was, had extraordinary powers of perception and had picked up on his lupine curse almost immediately, despite the thick wall separating them.

"The doctor is perfecting his new elixir, apparently," it replied, its vestment rustling on the floor as it moved about the cell.

"Doctor?" Gunnar asked.

"Johann Konrad Dippel—I'd know that officious, authoritarian aura anywhere. It hangs over this prison like a cloud of despair. Or perhaps you're better acquainted with his more familiar title—Baron Frankenstein!"

Gunnar's brows furrowed in confusion. "Frankenstein? I thought that was just a legend."

"That's a rather uninformed statement coming from the slayer of Baron Mitrea," the occupant of the cell said, again catching Gunnar off-guard. Mitrea was a vampire he'd been forced to slay decades ago to free Ilona from captivity; he was unaware anyone else besides Ilona knew of the battle.

"Frankenstein and his creations are all too real," the creature continued. "Just as real as werewolves, vampires, and liches. The world is quite a fantastic place, filled with dark and wondrous secrets," it mused.

"A lich? Is that what you are, creature? An undead sorcerer?"

"So you are familiar with my kind, eh, wolf?"

Gunnar stood, his curiosity aroused.

"I've studied records of the dark arts for many years now, trying to find a cure for my affliction. Liches are purported to be incredibly powerful magic adepts. How is it that these men were able to imprison you?" he asked.

"Isn't it obvious, wolf?" the creature asked in a condescending tone. "We are dealing with Baron Frankenstein and his henchman; there is no greater expert of supernatural matters on this planet. He rousted me from my forbidden tower in the Bavarian wilderness and bound me here in this cursed room. He knows our strengths and weaknesses—that your woman is vulnerable to organic weapons while you are susceptible to silver, and I fear my birth name."

"Birth name? I don't follow."

"Come, wolf, you told me you studied the 'dark arts,' or were you just huffing and puffing? Names have power. When I became what I am and sold my soul to eternal shadow gods in exchange for earthly power, I discarded my birth name and assumed the immortal mantle of Kasimir, and the world has trembled ever since!" the lich declared.

Gunnar sensed underlying lunacy in the creature's words and was hesitant to proceed further with the conversation. Still, he put that uncertainty aside and focused on the need to free Ilona.

"That doesn't explain why you haven't broken out of here, Kasimir."

"Were you able to see inside my cell, my feral colleague, you would know that the good doctor has seen fit to inscribe my birth name in virgin blood over nearly every inch of this damned room. Combined with the various magic-draining sigils and glyphs he saw fit to include in the room package, they sap nearly all of my magical capabilities."

"I've heard them in your cell, Dippel's men experimenting on you. Have they taken tissue samples as well?"

"Of course! In addition to stabbing and electrocuting me, his men have carved out large sections of my flesh. The pain was...*sublime*."

Having already concluded that Kasimir was quite mad, Gunnar ignored the misgivings the lich's last sentence engendered and continued questioning. "What is this elixir you spoke of?"

"The Elixir of Life—with it, he can resurrect the dead. It is the antithesis to my death-based abilities."

"But these creatures he creates...if the legends I heard were true, they are little more than *uber* zombies, dangerous but essentially mindless and highly flammable."

"Those things were but his first dabblings into the mysteries of life, base creations that did not represent his true intellect. Think about it, wolf! This fortress was erected on the gathering points of the mystical energy that pervade the area, a focal point of dark power. Arcane rituals and sacrifices were conducted here long before the Baron arrived—the spirits of the aggrieved are still present, filling the air with their misery. Dippel will forge a new being of unspeakable capabilities with the tissue and blood samples he has taken from us. Imagine it— a titan with werewolf ferocity, vampire strength and resilience, and the innate black magic of a lich! With such a monster under his command, he will force the world to its knees!" The lich cackled as if it were enamored with Dippel's plans.

Gunnar pursed his lips in concern and spoke evenly. "Then we must free ourselves and see that it does not happen."

"Are you sure you want to do that, wolf?"

"What do you mean, lich?"

"The powers bestowed upon me allow me to view the future...or at least possible futures. In one vision, I saw a pale, immortal woman juxtaposed against a crimson sky. She stood triumphant over a fallen wolfman, her eyes piercing and blacker than night, blood dripping from her exquisite lips. Amber rays of moonlight reflected off the moldering bones of an endless field of skeletons surrounding her."

Gunnar disregarded Kasimir's weird prognostication. "I don't have time for your inane prattle. We need to get out of here, now!"

"And how do you propose that we do so?"

"Can you rearrange matter?" Gunnar asked. "That's a pretty common talent for mages. I would assume your powers extend to that degree?"

"I can, under normal circumstances, but my abilities are stunted by the glyphs and sigils lining my cell."

"With all due respect, Kasimir, that lore you mentioned about being weakened in the presence of your birth name sounds a little silly, don't you agree? Much along the lines of werewolves only being able to change shape under the light of the full moon? Neither myth would appear to have a logical basis in fact," Gunnar said, seeking to prompt the lich into action.

"I never thought of it that way," Kasimir replied, sounding intrigued. "You may have a point, wolfling."

"Look, I need you to concentrate. Ignore the birth name hocus and focus. Transmute the silver billowing in my room to dust and let me handle it from there."

Kasimir inspected the crimson engravings lining the walls of his cell. As a lich, he possessed the power of Witchsight, the eldritch ability to see the souls of the dead. The fortress was rife with the unquiet spirits, specters of men and women who had perished here in ungodly manners. He closed his eyes and let their rage infect him as he harnessed the remnants of his powers. He opened his mind, bypassing the oppressive wards. The lich tapped into the turbulent winds of magic that flowed through the fortress, even here in his dismal little cell, letting them flood his undead body with dark energy. He spoke words of power and traced lines in the air with his claws as he ripped molecules apart and rearranged them.

Gunnar saw the silver particles floating in the air dissolve and immediately felt stronger. He seized the moment and transformed, limbs lengthening and shredding the simple cotton jail clothing he wore. The familiar pain of his bones breaking and reforming, denied for so long, returned. He grew in height and swelled in size, unnatural muscle forming as coarse auburn hair sprouted and covered his body, rippling in small waves up and down his skin. His mouth extended into a snout filled with razor-sharp teeth set in black gums; he accidentally almost roared, nearly giving into the beast, but caught himself and focused on the task at hand.

Gunnar launched himself at the steel door when his transformation was complete and smashed through it. He found himself alone in the dimly lit hallway and turned to Kasimir's cell. Grabbing the handle, he tore the door from its reinforced frame. Inside, he found the lich waiting.

Kasimir turned to him with a smile. Gunnar beheld a young, dark-skinned man in his twenties with short black hair and wide brown eyes, his trim physique attired in a brilliant lavender robe that trailed on the floor. A ruby pendant hung from a gold-and-diamond chain around his neck and glowed with vibrant power.

The lively image Kasimir presented did not correspond with the death stench his body emitted.

The lich noticed Gunnar's confusion as he darted into the hallway away from the magic-draining symbols in his cell.

"I've conjured a simple glamour spell, quite easy to maintain now that my full powers are returning," Kasimir explained. "I'm afraid my true image is quite repulsive."

Gunfire abruptly erupted in the hallway. A trio of armed soldiers marched toward them, firing automatic rifles. Gunnar ignored the bullets piercing his frame, sweeping out his elongated claws and smashing the first soldier's weapon. He buried his muzzle in the man's throat, tearing through its protective covering and ripping into the fragile flesh beneath. Hot blood bubbled into his mouth and bathed his dry tongue; he relished the sensation and fed until he'd torn through the neck.

Nearby, Kasimir was also proving bulletproof. The lich seized the second soldier by the arms in an unbreakable grip, ripping through the camouflage material and making contact with the skin.

"Rot," the lich said, and the man's skin immediately turned a grayish-black hue that spread quickly over him. The soldier screamed at his entire body moldered and turned to goo. Kasimir reached his claw deep between the remains of the soldier's jaws and extracted a small pulsing light sphere. The lich smiled as he daintily placed the brilliant globe in his mouth and swallowed.

"Finger-licking good," Kasimir gloated. The lich must have noted some semblance of a question forming on the werewolf's gore-slimed mouth. He saved Gunnar the trouble of speaking through a lupine larynx. "Yes, wolf, that was the man's soul I greedily consumed. I'm quite famished after my stay here."

The lich's eyes glowed an eerie violet in the hallway dimness, his form brimming with shadow energy.

Gunnar dropped the corpse in his claws and turned toward the last soldier. Having witnessed the gruesome fate of his colleagues, the man barricaded himself in Ilona's room. The raging werewolf smashed down the door, causing the soldier to stumble back as he fired the rifle in his sweat-slicked hands. Panicked and off-balance, the man tumbled across the center table, upsetting the corpse and knocking it to the floor.

Gunnar entered the room, ignoring the bullets that peppered his body. He raised his right claw high, prepared to end the man, only to be surprised when a slim pale figure rose with lightning swiftness from the floor. Its tiny porcelain-white hand seized the soldier's weapon and crushed it like tinfoil, ending the gunfire. The man screamed as he was bent nearly in half by thin, immensely powerful arms; Ilona tore into his neck with her sharp fangs. Gunnar watched the soldier's flailing limbs gradually sputter and sag in death. Ilona's withered skin became smooth and unlined as fresh blood flooded her throat, restoring her strength.

When she finished, Ilona discarded the body. She gazed admiringly upon the massive bipedal werewolf towering above her, her brilliant scarlet eyes reflecting the light like those of a midnight predator. The dead soldier had unwittingly jostled the stake free from her heart; the wound in her chest sealed with amazing speed, and her decolletage resumed its regular sensually appealing aspect. Where life and death were natural states, Ilona's condition was supernatural; her very existence mocked them.

"My love," she said, moving with liquid, boneless grace and gliding effortlessly toward him, her feet barely touching the ground.

Rapture filled Gunnar as he finally held his love in his fur-coated arms; their separation had lasted for what seemed an eternity. He dared not let her go. Still, he knew essential work remained before the night was over.

Kasimir entered the room, sidestepping the broken door and ruptured corpse lying on the floor.

"Oh, my," he said and presented himself to Ilona. "I don't

believe I've had the pleasure, Miss Ilona." The lich bowed in a sweeping gesture.

Gunnar growled in response.

"Easy there, big guy," Kasimir assured the werewolf. "I'm merely introducing myself to the newest member of the squad. Yay, Team Gunnar."

Gunnar snarled and turned to the door opening, moving with animal speed and agility. Ilona followed with the serpentine litheness common to all vampires.

"Time to storm the castle!" Kasimir shouted as he tried to keep pace with shriveled legs.

JOHANN HEARD THE GUNFIRE AS HE FILTERED THE FINAL DISTILLATION of his elixir through a small jungle of glass tubes. He had to work quickly to bestow life upon the creature before his former captives broke into the office.

He had realized that they would likely escape their cells at some point, given their combined abilities, experience, and mental toughness. He only wished his security measures had lasted a little longer.

He filled long syringes with the vital fluid and injected them at various points on the creature's body, including the neck, arms, and legs. Johann flinched, and his heart beat faster as the screams of his assistants filled the air, spurring him to work more quickly.

He seized a stout lever on the wall and pulled it down. The giant metal cone that extended from the arched ceiling glowed bright orange as it lit up and fired energy through twin electrodes painstakingly stitched onto either side of the creature's bull neck. The electrodes smoked, charged with surging power as the being on the table gasped and took its first breath. Johann yelled triumphantly as the titan broke its bonds and stood, crushing the metal table in the process.

The entrance door burst open as the supernatural beings entered. They paused, werewolf, vampire, and lich, each in awe of the incredible might radiating from the square-headed creation looming before them. Johann furtively backed into a shadowed corner of the room and nestled against a camou-flaged escape panel as the werewolf snarled and attacked.

Gunnar had experience battling other supernatural creatures and had dueled with a similar flesh construct in the past. He surged forward, lunging for the monster's stitched neck. If he could bury his fangs into the spine, the battle would be ended.

Enormous hands encircled his throat and lifted him like a child into the air. Gunnar instinctively clawed at the monster's wrists, but the creature's skin seemed made of iron.

Dippel's monster hammered him to the floor and rained punishing blows upon him, its pile-driver fists smashing bones in his face and chest. Stars flashed across his vision. Gunnar knew that even his supernatural constitution couldn't with-stand such abuse for long.

A slim figure flashed like a white streak across the room as if responding to his thoughts. Ilona leaped upon the monster, wrapping her wiry legs around its massive torso. She struck its face, a blow that would have blasted through a brick wall. The monster's head wrenched to the side with a loud popping noise but whipped immediately back, unfazed, its black eyes burning with bitter hatred.

The vampiress hissed menacingly and bit the titan's neck, but her fangs found no purchase on the iron skin.

The monster raised its huge mitts and encircled Ilona's neck, preparing to tear off her head. The vampiress cleverly shapeshifted, transforming into a luminescent fog that swept into the creature's nose and mouth, funneling down into its lungs.

Gunnar knew what would happen next; he had seen Ilona perform the maneuver before. She would solidify and burst the monster apart from the inside. Hope for victory rose in the werewolf's heart.

But that hope was soon extinguished. The monster exhaled and blew Ilona out with hurricane force; the mist flew across the room and dissipated in the air. Gunnar's heart sank—he was uncertain whether she could reconstitute herself from such disintegration.

"Move, wolf!" Kasimir yelled. Gunnar had the wherewithal to roll from beneath the monster. The lich chanted, and the pendant on his chest glowed.

"INCENDEMUS!" Kasimir cried. He thrust his claws toward the titan and unleashed searing beams of violet energy.

Gunnar could feel the scorching heat of the blasts as they enveloped the monster. Portions of his fur were singed and smoked.

Yet the monster moved forward, seeming invulnerable to the lich's magic. Its huge black boots cracked the floor with each ponderous step it took. Heat and fire had once been the Achilles heel of its predecessors; such was no longer the case, thanks to the upgrade Dippel had made to his elixir.

Kasimir realized this as he continued to pour dark energy at the titan. The monster seized both of the lich's claws in one giant paw and lifted him from the floor. It slammed Kasimir down, embedding him in the concrete floor as cracks spider-webbed outward. Stunned, the lich could no longer maintain the energy beams.

The titan tore off the lich's pendant, disdainfully tossed it near where Dippel stood in the shadows, and then wrapped its massive hands around Kasimir's torso. It lifted the lich and began to squeeze, breaking the undead sorcerer's ribs.

Gunnar managed to get to his knees. He watched as Kasimir's form wavered and changed. The youthful appearance disappeared and was replaced with a desiccated, skeletal creature with empty black eye sockets. The weird energies that powered it also stripped it of humanity. Thin strips of rotten, gray flesh covered its frame as it shouted through a lipless mouth filled with decayed teeth.

"We must strike as one; it is our only hope!"

The lich wrapped its decayed claws around the tree trunk-like forearms of the monster; dark energy swirled in the air as the shadows flowed to Kasimir.

"You're immune to flame, construct, but not to death! All things must eventually wither and decay. ROT!" Kasimir cried, though how the lich managed to draw breath into his crushed lungs eluded Gunnar.

At first, the titan's skin resisted Kasimir's necrotic magic, seemingly invulnerable, but then its green-hued hide slowly began to turn black. The lich also suffered, the putrid skin on his forearms and claws turning to dust, leaving only bone. Gunnar attacked, lashing out with his claws and teeth, tearing into the monster's back. Coupled with the lich's efforts, his strikes and slashes bore grisly fruit. The titan bellowed as its skin tore, jade blood flowing freely from the savage cuts.

Then Ilona arrived, funneling in mist form into the monster's mouth and nose openings. A plaintive wail escaped its liver-colored lips as it released Kasimir. Then its eyes popped gruesomely from their sockets an instant before its body exploded in a gruesome hail of nylon stitches, broken bone, and burst organs.

When the gore settled, Ilona stood tall amidst the remains, somehow untouched by the carnage. Her eyes smoldered with lust and triumph as she regarded Gunnar.

"Impressive," Kasimir said, smoothing out his cape. He had resumed his human glamour, his grisly appearance hidden beneath an illusion of supple flesh.

Gunnar resumed his human form as well, his limbs shrinking and the fur receding until he stood naked before them, his jail clothing having shredded when he changed into a manwolf.

"Equally impressive," the lich added, eyeing Gunnar's muscular physique.

Gunnar ignored the compliment. "Your hands, lich—will they heal?"

"Yes, eventually," Kasimir replied. "I was forced to use my own tainted flesh to power that last Putrefy Spell. My corrupted skin will gradually regenerate over time; the cursed cannot be so easily destroyed, as you are both aware."

"Where is Dippel?" Gunnar demanded. "We must find him."

"Oh, he's long gone, I would imagine," Kasimir lamented. "You don't last as long as he has by waiting for your enemies to regroup and catch their breaths—those that breathe, that is."

"Then he might pop up again at an inopportune moment. That's not comforting," Ilona said.

"Not only that, it appears he appropriated my little pendant," Kasimir added.

"Your pendant? The artifact with the ruby? What does that entail?" Gunnar asked.

Kasimir cocked his head slightly and raised his imaginary

eyebrows. "Well, normally, I would keep this a secret, but since we're all on a first-name basis now...the pendant is my phylactery. It's like a safe house that will collect and shield what remains of my soul should my corporeal body ever be destroyed. It will shelter and allow me to reincarnate."

"There's no telling what a supernatural genius like Dippel can do with such a potent artifact," Gunnar said.

"Enough," Ilona said. "These are issues for tomorrow. For now, I want to be with my man, whose company I have dearly missed." She enfolded Gunnar in her arms and brought him to her ample bosom. "Make yourself scarce, lich," she ordered.

"Yes, ma'am," Kasimir said. He quickly scuttled from the office.

Gunnar thrilled at Ilona's cold touch on his hot skin, fire and lust running through his veins. But as he luxuriated in the scintillating kiss of her scarlet lips, his mind wondered what the future augured with Dippel still on the loose.

JOHANN NAVIGATED THE HELICOPTER THROUGH THE MOUNTAINS, making his escape and heading to another rogue country that might agree to offer him shelter. It was not the first time he had been forced to flee and likely would not be the last. Anger at the odd trio that had robbed him of his destiny coursed through him, causing him to grip the controls tightly as sweat beaded his furrowed brow.

He had been so close!

Yet, there was a silver lining on this occasion. His hand rubbed his vest pocket, feeling the sturdiness of the lich's ruby pendant hidden therein. Never in all his years had he access to an artifact of such raw supernatural power!

His mind surged with the possibilities now open to him, envisioning a creature far stronger and infinitely more durable than the one he had just birthed.

The Frankenstein Legacy will continue; the world can rest assured, he vowed as the breaking dawn bathed him in brilliant golden light.

NIGHT OF THE MONSTER MUTINY

The annual meeting of the International Association for the Preservation of Preternatural Beings was scheduled to convene in the basement of the Viper Pit, a gaudy Vegas nightclub owned by one of the association's more affluent supporters. The monsters arrived at midnight on the winter solstice, the longest night of the year. They bypassed the club-goers at the bar and on the dance floor via a massive iron-reinforced door in the building's rear. The door led to a secret passage to the basement. Shadows flickered along the carved stone staircase, dimly lit by torchlight, descending into an exact reproduction of a medieval dungeon. Stout manacles and iron chains stained with blood hung from the slick limestone walls, while an iron maiden was centered amongst a row of torture racks. The walls were reinforced by layers of steel plates to ensure that the revelers above were shielded from the screams of the unfortunate victims brought in to satisfy the monsters' amusement. The facility also doubled as a black room where traitors could be interrogated at length, uninterrupted. A cremator had been installed in a back alcove to destroy any evidence.

The purpose of the meeting did not reflect the association's seemingly benign title, for the convened coterie of creatures conspired this night to destroy the titular figurehead of the organization, the Vampire Lord, John Falsworth.

Over the past four centuries since the association's founding, the gathered fiends had pledged a blood oath to Falsworth, swearing their loyalty unto death to protect the vampire and the organization. However, as the years passed, the character of their allegiance had transitioned from true commitment to indifference and, ultimately, to outright hatred as their baser instincts and jealousies prevailed. Falworth's current *laissez-faire* attitude toward the organization and his long-standing policy of co-existence with humans had engendered resentment within the monster community. Monsters were, by and large, an arrogant group with an elevated sense of pride, believing themselves infinitely superior to the lowly humans that surrounded them. Being ordered to show consideration for their food did not sit well with the majority of them, even if that consideration would ensure the continued survival of their kind.

The representatives gathered around a large wooden table centered on the gray-black flagstone floor of the candlelit room. Incense hung heavy in the air, the fragrant smoke diluting the stench of old death that clung tenaciously to the large room. A great yellowed scroll was stretched across the table, a Frankenstein creation stitched together with portions of dried skin carved from human hide. On the vellum, written in the Roman alphabet, was a declaration of independence, listing the coterie's irreconcilable grievances with the Vampire King, including their dismissal of humanity's worth and their combined commitment to immediately ending Falworth's reign. One by one, the dissenters passed around an ancient golden chalice embossed with a coiled serpent. Each fiend dipped a sharp claw into the human blood filling the cup and signed their name at the bottom of the scroll, sealing their fate.

A towering ogre named Bonesaw was the first to sign the scroll. His bulbous bald head nearly grazed the arched ceiling some fifteen feet above the floor. Bonesaw's huge teeth sprouted from his mouth like elephant tusks, more than capable of shredding flesh and snapping bone. His massive chest was encased in a battle-worn steel cuirass, his neck covered in a spiked gorget. Forearms the size of a man's waist were strapped with metal vambraces, and full greaves wrapped his tree-trunk legs. The brute's thick brown skin was littered with patches of sallow liver spots and tufts of malodorous fur. An enormous wooden club hewn from a fallen Sequoia tree rested against his side. The club and the armor were coated in layers of rotten gore, the bloody remnants of countless battles in which the ogre was victorious. Bonesaw's purpose at the meeting was to represent the Wood Folk, creatures of ancient myth such as centaurs, harpies, and giants that existed above ground in rural areas.

Beside the ogre stood Goralbrecht, a goblin warlord. While much smaller than Bonesaw, the emerald-hued beast was no less fierce. His beady yellow eyes glowed with malice from under a protruding brow, framed on either side by wickedly pointed ears. Rows of yellowed, razor-sharp teeth fought for space in his maw, jutting like shark's teeth over bulbous black lips; long, black nails sprouted from his stumpy, black-haired fingers. The goblin wore brown leather armor and a necklace made from the bones of his victims, both human and non-human, each tiny trophy bearing gnaw marks from the creature's fangs. Goralbrecht represented for the subterranean races: orcs, trolls, and other creatures that shied away from the harsh light of day and the cities of man.

Standing at the head of the table and leading the meeting

was the undead lich Lemos, a potent sorcerer who had practiced human sacrifice over a millennia ago in the now-underwater ruins of Lemuria. Lemos had consulted with dark powers to avoid the finality of death. His soul was ritually bonded to a large ruby amulet, his phylactery, where it could find shelter should his physical form be destroyed. Lemos assembled a great grimoire of spells and rituals that was the envy of other magicians and necromancers. The grimoire and the phylactery survived the cataclysmic tsunami, which buried Lemuria under gigantic waves.

In modern times, an anthropology professor studying Mesopotamian necromancy, a fellow by the name of Howard Bloch, had happened upon the grimoire in a small antiquities shop while on vacation in southern Greece. Not fully understanding the extent of the shadowy powers he dealt with, the professor made the mistake of reading aloud the Invocation of the Dead. The spell allowed Lemos' essence to escape his eldritch prison and enter the professor's body, transforming it into a desiccated, undead thing.

A black aura surrounded the lich. Lemos' face was shriveled and hawk-like, with an aquiline nose and cracked black lips drawn back from yellowed teeth in a death's head grin. Mottled leathery skin stretched tight over the skeletal frame, making vivid the outlines of the ribcage and organs. The lich wore a purple velvet cloak lined with crimson fur; a gold necklace bearing the ruby amulet hung from his neck and dangled over his withered chest.

As a show of force and necromantic power, Lemos had summoned a score of shambling zombies from their graves, each walking corpse bearing the wounds that had prematurely ended their human lives. Powered by Lemos' dark will, the dead were ready to tear apart anyone who got in their master's way.

Lemos represented the undead in various forms, whether ghoul, wight, revenant, or vampire.

Following his resurrection, Lemos had learned much about the modern age from watching television, especially the nightly news. Refusing to become antiquated, the lich reinvented himself as a self-styled crime lord. He had sent out his army of the dead to rob and pillage neighborhoods throughout Los Angeles, accumulating stores of cash and property to fund his veiled insurrection against Falsworth. To make matters worse, Lemos had forged alliances with many of the city's tech-savvy criminals, using their latest nanotechnology and neural enhancers to empower his zombies. Coupled with their undead strength, the living dead cyborgs formed lethal brigades that routinely defeated the police and military. Lemos and his minions had even engaged the vaunted metahuman protectors of the city, the Justice Guild, battling to a standoff before escaping into the sewer system.

The final attendee waited between Lemos and Goralbrecht, towering over them. Standing nine feet tall in full lupine form, Arnulf rivaled the gigantic Bonesaw in size. Coarse amber fur covered its long limbs and mounds of writhing muscle. The werewolf represented all the varied races of shapeshifters globally, whether they flew in the air, ran across grassy fields, or swam underneath the sea. His presence at the meeting made Goralbrecht uncomfortable, the goblin's nostrils flaring as he inhaled the shapeshifter's pungent odor. Goralbrecht fixed the werewolf with a hateful stare, his yellow eyes beaming with menace. Lemos chose to ignore the distraction and attend to the business at hand.

"We are agreed, then, that Falsworth's odious reign ends tonight," the lich said, "and with it comes the demise of mankind. We will no longer skulk in the shadows or hide from these lesser animals. We will claim our rightful heritage as the rulers of the planet. We will proclaim our presence to the world in one bloody night of conquest and feast on the dead in celebration!"

The ogre and werewolf roared their approval, punching their fists toward the shadows of the arched ceiling. Goralbrecht did not share their enthusiasm. He showed his displeasure by slamming his claw onto the table, knocking over the chalice, and splashing the remaining signature blood over the scroll.

"What of the heroes?" the diminutive green beast managed to sputter with his meager command of the English language. "They will attack us, no?"

Lemos shrugged, nonplussed. "And what of them? I have fought these so-called metahumans; they are a force to be reckoned with but are still mortal and burdened with conscience, which makes them weak."

"How...weak? Goralbrecht not see," the goblin said, shaking his pointy-eared head in confusion.

A vulpine grin crept across Lemos' face. "Once you get past their showy costumes and flowery speeches, their unadulterated bravado, all that remains is fear. Fear of what they can't control, what they don't understand, and what they will lose. How do you suppose they will react when they see us enter their cities at the vanguard of an unstoppable army of predators? They will turn and run, and we will pick them off at our leisure. We will remind them why they dread the dark and hide from the night!"

"What makes you believe your army will be more successful than the other criminals the metahumans have defeated?" Arnulf scoffed, his posh British accent juxtaposed with his beastly lupine features. "I think you greatly underestimate your opponent."

"HOW DARE YOU QUESTION ME?" Lemos demanded,

scowling. "You, Arnulf, who has been absent and incommunicative for so long? Know this, wolf, the humans are nothing more than meals to be consumed, petulant little blood bags waiting to be tapped. My army will tear out their hearts and consume their flesh, and I will claim their souls! They will tremble in fear as I resurrect their dead comrades and send them back into battle. As their ranks diminish, ours will swell! This is our time!"

"No, I disagree. This is my time!" the werewolf countered.

Goralbrecht and Lemos stared wide-eyed at Arnulf, confusion creasing their brows. They'd never known the werewolf to speak while in lupine form. Their shock gave way to dismayed comprehension as Goralbrecht pointed a gnarled claw at the floor.

"Not...wolf! BLOOD EATER!" the goblin screamed, but his words were cut off when Arnulf's claw ripped out his throat with a vicious backslash.

Lemos looked to where the goblin had pointed and realized the horrible truth.

The great wolf cast no shadow upon the ground.

Brackish green blood sprayed onto the stunned faces of Lemos and Bonesaw. Arnulf continued his assault on Goralbrecht, slamming his paw into the dying goblin's chest, crushing bone, and sending the creature sailing across the room like a rag doll into the open iron maiden. Goralbrecht's momentum forced the death trap's door to shut, impaling him with dozens of steel spikes. Green blood flowed from the iron maiden and collected in a viscous pool on the floor.

Scrambling away from the bloodbath, Lemos quickly recovered from his shock and cast an aura detection spell on the werewolf. Sure enough, the hairy creature pulsed with the black emanation of the Undead rather than the bright coral characteristic of a shapeshifter.

"Hellsteeth, we've been deceived! A vampire!" the lich cried in shock. Lemos watched the giant wolf's fur ripple as its bones cracked and reshaped. Then the fur fell away in large clumps, and the beast transformed into a tall man wearing dark clothing and a red cape. Raven-black hair in a widow's peak hung to his shoulders, framing an aquiline nose and smoldering red eyes set deep within onyx sockets. The eyes burned with immeasurable hatred at the remaining monsters.

The vampire's long fangs gleamed in the torchlight as he spoke with a commanding voice. "I prefer to be called Lord Falsworth, especially by an insignificant grave robber like you. I have grown accustomed to that title since I killed its previous owner and made it my own. Or if you prefer, lich, I will allow you to address me by my birth name: Lord Karnstein, the Baron of Blood!"

The monsters were silent for a moment, cowed by the majesty of the great vampire. Waves of dark power radiated from him. Lemos fought a compulsion to kneel at Falsworth's booted feet.

"I don't care who you are," Bonesaw bellowed, wildly swinging his club at the vampire. "I will make you TRUE DEAD!"

Having shed the additional mass of his werewolf facade, Falsworth agilely dodged the club, but the effort of maintaining his werewolf disguise had cost him much energy. While even a newly turned vampire could transform into an ordinary dire wolf, it took a master vampire to assume the lupine battle form of a werewolf proper. His movements felt sluggish and leaden.

The club slammed into the basement wall with the sound of a thunderclap. Crumbling sections of brick and mortar rained down on Lemos and his zombies, filling the damp air with dust.

As Bonesaw tugged furiously at his club, trying to dislodge it from the wall, one of Lemos' undead slaves launched itself at

Falsworth. The zombie had the body of a professional wrestler, tall and broad of chest, its bulky muscles stretched tightly against the fabric of its burial suit. The creature's blue-hued face showed no deterioration, indicating that it was recently raised. Its neural enhancements added speed and dexterity to its attack.

Calling on his immortal strength, Falsworth shot out his right hand and seized the zombie's neck in a vise grip. He rotated the dead man's head 180 degrees with a quick wrist twist, snapping its neck and destroying the attached exo-skeleton circuitry. Electric sparks flew in all directions as the zombie short-circuited, its body spasming. Falsworth raised the twitching body over his head and launched the bulky corpse like a missile at the ogre.

Bonesaw snarled as he swatted the zombie aside like a gnat, turning the corpse into a bloody pulp. The ogre still struggled to free his embedded club from the wall. Falsworth sidestepped the careening corpse remnants as they splattered across the torture racks, turning his attention to Bonesaw. The ogre pulled out the club in an avalanche of masonry and spun around with the weapon raised high.

Falsworth stood stoically in front of the meeting table, daring the ogre to strike. Bonesaw roared as he used all his substantial might to bring his club down, aiming to pulverize the vampire's head.

The ogre was shocked when his weapon passed harmlessly through a luminescent mist and slammed into the meeting table, obliterating it.

In his mist form, Falsworth heard a groan come from under the pile of rubble as he funneled between the ogre's legs and reformed behind the massive beast. He knew he didn't have much time before Lemos emerged from the mound of debris; he needed to dispense with the ogre before the others recovered and overwhelmed him. His fingernails elongated into thick black talons as he grabbed Bonesaw's immense hamstrings, sinking his claws deep into the flesh. Falsworth pulled back and shredded the muscle and tendon, spewing rancid, inky blood across the room. The vampire rolled away as the screaming behemoth swayed and crashed to the floor like a felled mastodon.

Bonesaw bellowed and writhed in agony, smashing his fists into the floor. Falsworth was aware of the vast regenerative properties ogres possessed and did not give Bonesaw a chance to recover. He moved with inhuman speed and punched the ogre across the jaw with all his Undead strength, shattering teeth and bone. Simultaneously, the claws of his other hand tore away the protective gorget covering the monster's throat. He tossed the mangled armor aside and plunged his claw into the ogre's throat, tearing through the windpipe and cervical spine. Black blood pulsed from the gaping hole and pooled underneath the ogre as he bled out and became still.

Falsworth wiped away Bonesaw's ebony blood from his eyes and face, careful not to get any in his mouth; he knew from bitter experience that the blood was toxic to his kind. Once, he'd made the mistake of feeding on an ogre after a protracted battle. The vampire recalled the violent illness and scorching pain that had temporarily incapacitated him—it was an experience he never wanted to repeat. Fortunately, his daughter, Mircalla, had arrived and brought him home to their ancestral castle to recuperate.

Mircalla had been the joy of his otherwise monotonous unlife. The memory of her loss so many years ago still haunted him.

But there was no time to ruminate on the dead. Lemos climbed from the rubble, furious over the oath scroll's destruction and the deaths of his co-conspirators.

The lich stood still, sapphire eyes blazing and skeletal hands clenched as he chanted ancient words of power, tapping into the invisible seas of magic. Shadows flowed from the basement corners as Lemos harnessed the eldritch energies to his dark will. Lemos looked at Falsworth, reaching his skeletal claw out as if to seize the vampire, then closed his long fingers into a crushing fist. Falsworth staggered forward a step and then froze as he felt an irresistible force encase his body like a dark cocoon. He struggled furiously, using all his formidable strength to resist, but his efforts were futile. He became little more than a doll under the control of the puppet master Lemos, unable to govern his limbs.

Falsworth knew he had committed a grave tactical error in failing to immediately eliminate Lemos: liches were master necromancers and could control all of the dead. As an Undead vampire, Falsworth was vulnerable to the lich's powers.

Lemos made a swiping motion with his outstretched arm. Falsworth was lifted from the floor and slammed head-first into the wall, creating a new hole just to the right of the larger one made earlier by Bonesaw's club.

Pain exploded through the vampire as he felt his skull shatter on the unforgiving stone. Unfortunately for Falsworth, his immortality prevented him from losing consciousness. His dark blood flowed from the gaping wound in his head down his ashen face and into his eyes, blinding him. Lemos continued his assault, tossing Falsworth's limp body into the ceiling and letting it fall gracelessly to the cold floor. The vampire tried to turn into mist but found himself unable. Lemos was in complete control.

Lemos' eyes showed maniacal glee as he danced, swung his hand, and repeatedly smashed Falsworth's body around the basement. Falsworth fell to the floor, squinting through bloody eyes at the numerous holes his body had punched in the ceiling and walls. Most of his bones were broken, painfully puncturing his organs and jutting from his skin. He healed with unnatural quickness, the wounds closing and the bones beginning to mend. However, Lemos would send the vampire careening about the basement every time he was close to recovery.

After another round of beatings, Lemos strode up to Falsworth's broken body and stood over him in triumph.

"That was quite a stunt you pulled there, *wampyr*. I commend you for your ingenuity; you almost succeeded in stopping me. It will take me months to replace and rectify everything you have destroyed tonight. But you are still a dead man, Falsworth, as dead as your whore daughter, Mircalla."

"Leave my daughter out of this, roach!" Falsworth spat at Lemos, spraying the lich's robe with blood and saliva. The vampire attempted to stand but collapsed to the floor. Stars flashed before his eyes, and his vision dimmed as his battered brain was flooded with ancient memories at the mention of his child.

In a twilight haze, he recalled the days when he was a living man and breath and blood flowed freely in his warm body. He was a man of inherited title and wealth, a general in the Holy Roman Empire known for his iron resolution. He'd said goodbye to his loving wife and their daughter Mircalla when he'd been ordered into battle by Emperor Ferdinand III against the invading French forces. The young girl had run after him as he left, trying desperately to catch up with his horse, tears of grief in her eyes. His heart had nearly broken.

He'd focused his energy on the war, attempting to distract himself from the pain of being away from his family. The battle that forever altered his destiny had begun at dawn and continued well into the evening. As twilight settled across the land and a waxing gibbous moon crawled into the purple sky, he'd been separated from his soldiers. He found himself deep in the woods, surrounded by a dozen enemy soldiers. He was an expert swordsman, and his shining blade reaped a bloody harvest of French blood. The ruptured corpses of his opponents littered the ground as he impaled a charging attacker through the heart. He was preparing his sword for another killing thrust when pain exploded in his chest, and the night echoed with a pistol shot.

He collapsed to his knees as the man who had shot him approached, slowly loading a second round. Another Frenchman followed, holding his gore-encrusted sword in front of him. Falsworth attempted to raise his sword, but his arm would not cooperate. Blood flowed freely from his chest wound as he gasped for air, one of his lungs deflated by the bullet wound.

The Frenchman with the pistol, a nobleman as evidenced by his lavish battle attire and feather-plumed hat, smiled and pointed the barrel at Falsworth's head. Falsworth waited for the coup de grace, but it never arrived. A shadow detached itself from the forest and struck the Frenchman. The man went sailing across the glade like a child's plaything.

The other Frenchman stabbed the shadow, but his blade went through it, empty as air. Falsworth saw a flash of sharp white teeth, and the swordsman's throat opened like a ripe fruit, spilling hot blood everywhere.

The remaining Frenchman aimed his pistol at the shadow as his colleague fell and fired. The shot passed harmlessly through the roiling darkness. Then Falsworth saw the shadow transform into an old man with stringy white hair wearing an ashen shroud. The man flowed across the glade with fluid, boneless grace, barely seeming to touch the ground. He seized the Frenchman in an iron embrace and buried his long teeth into the soldier's throat. The Frenchman screamed as he was exsanguinated, his frantic struggles gradually ceasing.

Falsworth knew what the old man was; his native land was haunted by the legends of the wampyr, the unquiet dead who lived by night and fed on the blood of the living.

The vampire discarded the corpse and flowed to where Falsworth lay. Falsworth saw that the Frenchman's blood had invigorated the creature, its skin now supple and pink. Its hair was long and blond, framing piercing cobalt eyes and symmetrical features. It spoke hauntingly, reminding Falsworth of the evenings he had spent as a child playing in a graveyard near the family castle. The bloodsucker's voice was like an eerie wind whistling through the many rows of vine-covered tombstones.

"I watched from the trees as you fought, breather. Your skill with the blade is admirable, and your will unconquerable. I, too, had an iron will when I was among the quick; it allowed me to transcend the inconvenience of death. You are dying, your heart sputtering as it runs low on blood. Yet I sense your soul is unfulfilled, that you are not ready for your time on this plane to end. I can gift you, human, with power and eternal life. It is a gift I have never bequeathed on another. Do you want to live?" the vampire asked, its red eyes lighting the darkness like scarlet beacons in a storm.

Falsworth nodded, intent on being reunited with Mircalla, even at the cost of his soul. The vampire lifted him in its thin arms as it might a child and fastened its cold lips to his throat. He felt the fangs pierce his skin, and then darkness embraced him.

He awoke in darkness three nights later. Compelled by a surging bloodlust, he rose, a new strength flowing through his arms as he pushed aside dirt and rock, emerging from his hastily dug grave in a grim mockery of birth. The old vampire greeted him and showed him the ways of their kind. They fed on a group of highway bandits that had plagued travelers on the roads, ignoring their weapons and easily overcoming their struggles. He tore into their fragile flesh with sharp fangs, the hot blood pouring down his dry throat and pushing out the bitter cold that filled his limbs. Afterward, they returned to the vampire's cave in the woods, hiding from the coming daylight, which sapped their strength.

The old one tutored the newborn vampire over the coming weeks, passing on the knowledge he had accumulated over the centuries. He explained to Falsworth their vampire strengths and weaknesses, that by night they were virtually immortal, fearing only the holy talismans of the faithful. Neither demon nor specter, but sharing the dark aspects of both, they possessed the strength of twenty men and were invulnerable to conventional weapons. Vampires also had various supernatural powers at their command, including shape-changing, hypnosis, and necromancy. Daylight weakened them, robbing them of unnatural abilities and reducing their strength to mortal levels.

The old one insisted that Falsworth feed sparingly, lest he alert the mortals to his presence, and always thoroughly dispose of the corpses afterward. The ancient vampire cautioned that the humans would come for him in the day when he was weak and incapable of protecting himself.

The old one's final warning regarded procreation.

"Choose wisely those upon whom you bestow the blessing of night. Few men, or women, are worthy of the gift. The bloodlust will overwhelm one of weak character; soon, the bodies of its prey will accumulate and be discovered, forming a chain of evidence that will lead back to the fool who profligately bestowed the blood kiss."

Armed with this knowledge, Falsworth returned home to find Mircalla dying of a wasting disease that infected her lungs and caused her to cough blood. Unable to think of existing without her, he gave her the dark gift, the blood kiss, cursing her to an eternal unlife. She awoke three nights later, embracing him with her new strength and relishing her new powers. But their relationship had soon soured.

Mircalla quickly tired of his constant supervision. Unlike others of their kind, who chose to overpower and feed with violence, she befriended and seduced her prey, finding young women of nobility to court and gradually drain of life. Over time, the mysterious female deaths began to add up. Mircalla committed a fatal error when she chose her next victim, a beautiful girl named Laura, the daughter of *a good friend of General Spielsdorf. Spieldsdorf's own daughter had been an unfortunate victim of Mircalla's bloodlust. The general suspected his daughter's unusual death was caused not by a wasting disease but, instead, by an Undead monster. When Spielsdorf learned of Laura's mysterious infatuation with a wan girl named "Carmilla," he connected the two incidents and set out to put a final end to the vampiress.*

The general and his associates located Mircalla resting in her tomb during the day. Spielsdorf staked her through the heart and beheaded her with a sword. Mircalla's body was burned and the ashes scattered to the winds. Falsworth had felt her destruction like a violent blow, jolting him from his death sleep in the middle of the day. It was a loss from which he never recovered.

"While I wish I'd had the good fortune to be the one to stake your slut offspring, that honor went to General Spielsdorf," Lemos boasted, forcing the vampire from his recollections. "Now your time has come, 'Baron Blood.' I will have the pleasure of watching you die by your own hand." The lich reached his claw out and closed his fist.

Against his will, Falsworth's right hand reached out to his side and latched onto a long, sharp shard of the pulverized conference table. As Lemos moved his closed fist to his chest, Falsworth positioned the shard over his unbeating heart with both hands. He began forcing the wood into his chest, his arms shaking as he fought against the lich's power.

"Why do you fight me, *strigoi*?" Lemos asked. "I sense the unending pain of your loss, your weakness. I know you battle the bloodlust within you out of some antiquated virtue, the twisted remnants of your soul still lingering, buried beneath centuries of bloodshed. Whatever shred of humanity you retained died when your daughter was destroyed. I will never understand why you now choose to protect these mortals from us, these petty creatures who destroyed your daughter."

Falsworth overlooked his dire predicament and focused on Lemos' words. As the shard broke through his ribcage and punctured his black heart, he briefly imagined giving in and letting the darkness take him for a final time. The curse of vampirism was, in truth, the malison of lonely immortality: watching his loved ones wither and die from the relentless onslaught of time while he lived on, unchanged. Falsworth knew that someday he, like Mircalla, would find peace in true death.

"Coward!" the lich screamed. "You lack the courage to live like a savage predator or end your pathetic existence. But I am strong where you are weak, filled with purpose where you falter. Tonight, 'Lord Falsworth,' I am your savior!"

Rage fueled Falsworth's words as he struggled against Lemos' control, pitting his will against the lich. "I am no coward, cretin, and you are no savior. I will not die tonight, and certainly not by your filthy hands!"

While Lemos was busy taunting the vampire, Falsworth discerned the remaining zombies were wandering aimlessly around the basement, butting into the walls and bouncing off each other like pinballs. He sensed that Lemos had lost control of his bodyguards while the lich focused on destroying him. A plan shaped in Falsworth's mind.

The vampire knew that both liches and vampires possessed the supernatural ability to control the lesser undead. Liches were more practiced in the intricacies of necromancy, owing to their sorcerous background while mortal. Yet vampires had access to necromantic powers, an inherent skill fueled by the dark magics of their existence. Recognizing an opportunity, Falsworth took advantage of Lemos' distraction and exerted his influence on the zombie circling nearest the lich.

The dead female wore an azure jogging suit streaked with tire marks and black blood, her torso crushed by a passing vehicle. Her chaotic spinning stopped abruptly when she threw herself on Lemos' back, clawing at his eyes with her decayed hands. The lich roared in frustration, tearing at the zombie's hands and swinging wildly to free himself. Falsworth felt the weight of Lemos' power lift, his own will restored and in control of his body.

He ripped the stake from his chest, pulling the wood from his heart and realizing how close he had come to the true death. He rose to his feet and launched himself at Lemos. The lich succeeded in freeing himself from the female zombie, flinging her aside, just in time to see Falsworth bringing down the wooden shard on his head.

The shard penetrated Lemos' skull, smashing bone and brain. The lich's eyes rolled back in his head as his knees buckled and his body crumbled to the floor. In a blur of movement, Falsworth stood over the defeated lich.

Wrath fueled his words as he spoke. "Did you believe word of your sedition wouldn't spread? I've had centuries to build my network of allies and spies, my eyes and ears spread across the globe. They led me to the weak-willed Arnulf. Of course, he initially refused to speak of the mutiny. I enjoyed torturing him with silver-coated blades, softening him up. Then I took his blood and knew his mind; all your schemes were unveiled. It was simple to assume his form and enter your midst undetected."

Lemos sprawled on the floor, staring at Falsworth as viscous blood flowed from his crushed skull. His black-lipped mouth moved as he struggled to speak, but no words came.

"You really never had a chance, lich," Falsworth continued. "But before I send you back to whatever backward hell dimension spawned you, I want you to know that I still believe we must blend in with humans. The fate of my daughter proves that we are vulnerable when exposed. We may be stronger and more resilient, but they outnumber us, and ultimately, they will always win. We must shelter in the shadows and forever hide under the haven of myth and fantasy."

Falsworth raised his right foot and positioned it over the face of the cringing lich.

"Oh, and one last thing. My daughter was no whore. Take that to the grave."

Falsworth's eyes beamed hell-red as he gathered his waning strength, still greater than twenty men. He raised his booted right foot and brought it down with incredible force. Lemos' head exploded in a burst of green ichor and pulverized brain matter. The headless body convulsed once and then rapidly decomposed. Falsworth watched as skin, flesh, and bone melted into a viscous pool of rancid purple goo.

With their master destroyed, the zombies had nothing to animate them. Their lifeless bodies slumped to the floor, their neural-enhancer circuitry sparking uselessly in the dungeon dimness. Falsworth saw no reason to reanimate them, leaving them to rot with their master. Noting the carnage around him, the *nosferatu* decided it wise not to wait around in case any reinforcements arrived.

He inspected the lich's remains, digging his claw into the sludge. He found the ruby amulet and pulled it out.

Falsworth was familiar with liches and their magics. With his earthly form destroyed, Lemos' essence now resided within the scarlet stone. The vampire vowed to find a way to harness the lich's powers for his own benefit, a prolonged process that he hoped would cause much suffering to the undead sorcerer.

A sinister smile crossed the vampire's pale face as he contemplated Lemos' fate. He noted that the wound in his chest had healed with amazing rapidity. The thought occurred to Falsworth that he might have existed for so long now that the banes of his kind no longer affected him. Was the vampire's faith in the stake like a child's belief in the Easter Bunny, a mysticism they desperately clung to avoid the harsh truth of immortality?

Falsworth pushed these thoughts aside. He transformed again into mist and funneled under the door leading up to the club. Once outside, he sprouted long black wings from his shoulders and became a gigantic bat. He flew into the night, content in the knowledge that a bloody war with mankind had been averted.

At least for tonight.

STRAY

Otis Crumb crouched low by the roadside, keeping his head down while the Santa Ana winds kicked up warm swirls of desert dust around him. His long, greasy, auburn hair hung down in clumps over haunted blue eyes, his skin so white it practically glowed in the surrounding darkness. Otis' nocturnal vision allowed him to see clearly at night. His uncanny hearing had picked up the sound of an approaching motorcycle still several miles away. As the vehicle approached, he calmly girded himself for action, and its sole occupant came into view.

Otis sprang up from behind a small ridge of sand and launched himself at the biker. He smashed into the vehicle's side with inhuman force and sent himself and the driver careening over the road's crest. They landed hard, but Otis was back on his feet instantaneously, scrambling spider-like over to the fallen biker.

The man was stunned but not out of action. Otis noted a long mane of black hair spilling out from under a crimson bandana, framing brown eyes and a broad, unshaven chin; jail-house lightning bolt tattoos covered the man's neck. Otis smelled Jack Daniels and marijuana on the biker's breath. As the man stood, Otis was impressed at his size: the biker was nearly seven feet tall with close to three hundred pounds of weight-trained bulk. His black vest did little to conceal massive slabs of chemically enhanced muscle. The big man appeared confused at first, perhaps wondering who could be so stupid as to jump on him. Then bewilderment turned into testosterone-fueled anger as he looked more closely at the small, innocuous man who had assaulted him. The giant reached into a black leather sheath concealed underneath his vest and withdrew a large hunting blade, brandishing its keen, serrated edges menacingly in Otis' face. Moonlight reflected off the blade.

"Keep the hell back, ya freakin' albino!" the biker screeched hysterically, his voice filled with fury, spittle flying from his cracked, wind-chapped lips. Otis assumed such theatrics would usually terrify an average person, but Otis had never been ordinary, and, one month ago, he had ceased to be a person. He took a step in the biker's direction.

The large man attempted a quick thrust at Otis' midsection, only to have his wrist encircled in a vise-grip that bruised his flesh. He struggled frantically to break free, amazed at his attacker's strength.

Otis was barely over five feet tall, his body reed-thin and ghostly pale. Yet his unearthly strength made the big man's struggles seem like those of a fitful child. With a wrist flick, Otis casually broke the man's massive forearm, jagged bone jutting from the skin. The biker sagged to his knees, on the verge of passing out, but Otis brought him back to reality with a vicious backhand slap to the jaw. Blood and broken teeth showered from the big man's shattered mouth while snot poured from his hairy nostrils.

"Wake up, chuckles, you can't miss this," Otis crooned into the shaken man's face. Then he smiled, unsheathing fanged teeth. Since his recent transformation, Otis had noticed a new viciousness surfacing inside him. He wasn't comfortable with it, but it seemed to overtake him every time he fed. He assumed the ferocity came with the new dentures and red thirst, a package deal.

Otis became momentarily enraptured listening to the sound of blood pumping through ripe webs of veins and arteries, begging to be liberated by his sharp teeth. Then he tore out the biker's throat with a backslash of his claws and gorged himself on the arterial spray, relishing in the hot, adrenaline-spiked blood flooding his freezing frame. He had never been a bright man, but he had watched a late-night horror flick or two in his time. He knew that vampires (for that was what he obviously was) were often detected by the telltale twin fang marks on the victim's throat.

Therefore, no throat, no marks—no problem.

He felt the warmth gradually leave the biker's body and begin to fill the empty coldness inside him. New vitality and strength sang through his muscles and ligaments. He almost felt alive again.

Otis quickly sifted through the dead man's pockets, withdrawing a wad of cash from the biker's blue jeans. He momentarily eyed the remnants of his meal with moderate self-satisfaction before transforming, leather membranes shooting from his wrists to attach to his hamstrings. His clothing was magically absorbed into his black-skinned bat frame. He took flight, rising above the scattered clouds, relishing the moonlight as its amber rays tickled his dead skin.

OTIS CONTEMPLATED HIS NEW EXISTENCE WINGING HIS WAY BACK FROM the desert to the seedy motel room in Long Beach, where he spent most of his days. He'd been born dirt-poor and spent most of his adult years wandering from one low-wage job to another, a journey that had taken him practically across the entire country. None of it had prepared him for the numerous peculiar demands of Undead existence.

If he could have re-lived his life, he would have at least read *Dracula* once. While wandering along the coast in California one month ago in search of work, he had been pulled down a proverbial deserted alley by an inhumanly strong attacker. Otis had struggled valiantly against his puissant foe, trying to escape to the nearby beach and at one point succeeding in drawing blood by biting one of his assailant's hands. Before his lifeblood was vacuumed out from twin holes in his jugular, Otis saw his murderer's furrowed red eyes. Sand and dust covered the majority of an outdated three-piece suit and brittle locks of jet-gray hair. The ashen skin of the man's face was wrinkled like alligator leather, so dry that it was flaking off in the dry wind as they struggled. Massive, bushy-white eyebrows met over the man's hawk-like nose, which rested above an unkempt mustache. Otis' last human memories were of dying in the hands of Methuselah. Three nights later, he tore his way out of the sand and fed on a couple having intercourse near his improvised grave. His new existence had begun in a baptism of blood.

Otis concluded that one benefit of vampirism was that working was no longer necessary. The victims who provided him his nightly sustenance also forfeited whatever valuable possessions they had on them at the time of their demise. The money he'd taken from the biker tonight (most likely obtained from the sale of methamphetamine, judging from the white crystalline-laced packets in the dead man's vest pockets) would take care of the motel rent for the next month. Eventually, if he picked the proper prey, Otis believed he might work his way up to a mansion of his own, one with marble porticos, arched ceilings, and high towers. Maybe even a castle someday, like he'd viewed in magazines.

At one time, living as a thief would have disgusted him. He had been raised in a home where the Protestant work ethic was deeply ingrained, where one derived self-esteem from contributions made to help the family. The fact that his recent criminal exploits no longer bothered what remained of his conscience gave him pause. Perhaps, he reasoned, the necessities of his new existence forced him to act in ways that were at odds with his previous moral standards. And since he largely limited his nocturnal attacks to parolees from the local state correctional institute and other such rabble, Otis concluded that he might, in a strange way, actually be working toward the betterment of society.

A block from his residence, Otis assumed human form and landed in a nearby alley, his clothing coalescing from the night air around him. Otis appreciated the eldritch powers bequeathed by the dark magic animating his corpse: whatever clothing he had on when he shape-changed mystically returned when he shed that form.

Otis entered the dingy complex and walked up the flight of dilapidated stairs that led to the second floor. He ran into the motel manager, Mr. Dubrava, in the walkway. Dubrava was a large, fierce, Old-World type with a thick Russian accent, oily hair, and a pendulous belly that hung over his too-tight pants. Habitually unshaven and underdressed, he reeked of onions and garlic. Otis had learned from painful experiences to keep his distance.

Otis had overheard other tenants speak of Dubrava in hushed whispers, barely able to conceal their fear. Back in his native country, Dubrava had been a man of some importance, somehow connected to the Russian mafia. He'd been an enforcer, well-versed in making his enemies disappear. Otis imagined that, in his prime, Dubrava cut quite an imposing figure with his size. Now he was over the hill, weighed down by years of alcohol and calorie abuse. On occasion, Otis had seen young men who spoke in a foreign language enter Dubrava's first-floor office, so he imagined the landlord still had connections to the local underworld. It mattered little to Otis now—no human could intimidate him.

"There is blood on your shirt," Dubrava muttered, pointing at Otis' t-shirt.

The vampire looked down at the front of his shirt and noted some tiny red stains, reminders of his meal earlier in the evening.

"Must have cut myself," he lied. He quickly found his room key and opened the frayed wooden door. He was about to close it when Dubrava inserted his foot between the door and the sill.

"There is a rancid smell in your room, no?" Dubrava accused. "Maybe you forget to take out the trash? Or maybe you keep the bodies hidden inside somewhere, eh?" Dubrava's tone was flat and emotionless.

Otis was in no mood to deal with the Russian. He applied a fraction of his new strength to force Dubrava's foot out and close the door.

"We talk sometime, maybe soon," Dubrava thundered into the closed door. He walked down the stairs, each one, in turn, groaning under his substantial weight.

Otis picked up Dubrava's last comment, but he chose to ignore it. The stench of decay Dubrava had mentioned assaulted his nose, a miasmic combination of rotted fruit and fresh feces. Flies buzzed around his small room. The stink seemed to originate from his bed. He discarded his shoes and clothes and hopped into bed, noting as he did so that his mattress was uncomfortably stiff and lumpy. Otis twisted and turned, attempting to get comfortable. Since his recent resurrection, he had experienced insomnia. He felt greatly fatigued every morning with the onset of daylight but could never seem to fall into a deep sleep. He would phase in and out of consciousness, plagued by persistent nightmares. He closed his eyes and drifted into a fitful slumber.

OTIS AWOKE TO THE SMELL OF BLOOD.

He catapulted himself out of bed and almost fell. He found Dubrava lying on the floor next to the bed, pale as a sheet, his head twisted around one hundred and eighty degrees. Blood dripped from his open mouth out onto the floor. The corpse's hand gripped a thick stake of lacquered wood over three feet in length. A discarded mallet lay nearby. Standing adjacent to the corpse and leaning next to a heavily curtained window was a brown-haired man of moderate height and build dressed in an expensive black suit and tie. He casually folded his arms across his chest, and a mischievous smile played on the corners of his rosy lips. Though he appeared to be in his early thirties, his dark eyes radiated confidence and wisdom beyond his years. Otis' hyper-senses alerted him that the intruder wasn't breathing and didn't have a heartbeat.

"Our first meeting, and already you are in my debt, child," the stranger intoned, sounding irked.

"For what?" Otis squeaked, doing his best to sound defiant and in control. His fangs erupted defensively, but inside he was shaken and confused.

"Pop those back where they belong, young one, or I shall remove them myself!" The newcomer's eyes blazed crimson, and Otis immediately felt as threatening as a tiny puppy. His fangs receded, and he took an involuntary step back.

"Good. Now, where were we? Oh, yes, that wretched stench? How can you stand it?"

The man moved with unnatural grace and speed across the small room to Otis' bed and flung the grimy mattress aside, scattering flies. Resting on the box springs was a man's black, bloated body in grimy jeans and a rotten red shirt. Maggots crawled from his open mouth, eye sockets, and ruptured throat. He looked like he had died screaming, his mouth agape. Dark, viscous fluids stained the bottom of the mattress.

"The proverbial corpse under the motel bed! An urban myth, proven fact! Congratulations, young one. Hah, your brain is not firing on all cylinders."

Otis did not remember the man, but he assumed he had fed on him in one of his less lucid moments.

The stranger walked over to where Dubrava lay and palmed the stake, his eyes fixed on Otis. "You, sir, owe me your existence. Your friend discovered your true nature and decided to remove you from his list of tenants. Permanently." He smiled, his irises slowly losing their red glow as his mood calmed.

Otis eyed the stake. "Would that have worked?" he somberly asked. Otis had been in no hurry to test the legendary vampiric immortality since his resurrection.

"I assure you, they work quite well. Any weapon of wood can cause temporary immobility if it penetrates the heart while we sleep during the day. Nasty thing—hawthorn, it appears." The elder vampire shifted his eyes to the stake and closed his hand, grinding the thick wood into pulp with incredible ease. Otis noted the sharp, finely manicured nails attached to each finger.

The man turned his attention back to Otis. "I'm not surprised that you aren't aware of your new limitations. No one was there for you when you awoke that first night?"

"I don't know what you mean."

"The false death. We all endure it to become what we are. Your sire abandoned you to the night without instruction. Look at you. You're closer to the final death than you realize. I take it you've been having difficulty sleeping, no?"

Otis bobbed his head cautiously in agreement, unsure where the other vampire was heading with the conversation.

"I can't say I'm surprised, sleeping on that corpse like you were. We cannot prosper without soil from our native land; it is one of our limitations. There are others, running water and daylight among them. We can discuss those later. For now, we have matters to address. Your feeding habits are...shall we say, less than discreet. The victims you have littered across the city have become fodder for the news media. You've become somewhat of a *cause celebre*: the press has labeled you an 'Angel of Vengeance,' extracting justice from those the penal system is no longer able or willing to punish. However, we both know your intentions are less than lofty.

"No feeding marks can be left, or we attract unwanted attention. Such attention can prove fatal. Fortunately for you, I arrived just in time." He gestured at Dubrava's limp corpse. "He had not completely forgotten his Old-World roots. Most people dismiss us as the stuff of myth and legend. Still, we need not be so obvious in our dining habits; we need not even kill."

The newcomer crossed his hands behind his back and slowly walked toward Otis. "Listen to my little story, friend, for I believe that you and I have much in common, much in common indeed." His gaze pinioned the young vampire. "Quite some time ago, I was a solicitor, one of some renown, back in Britain."

Otis looked perplexed.

"Real estate, my good man, back in England, the United Kingdom. I was young, handsome, innocent...even engaged to be married. It's all in that damned Stoker book. Anyway, a certain ancient Wallachian nobleman contacted my employer at the time, Mr. Hawkins. Hawkins sent me off to the famed Land-Beyond-the-Forest to finalize the purchase of an estate in London. The rest, as they say, is history."

Otis continued to look confounded; his forehead wrinkled in confusion.

The stranger continued. "The book Stoker wrote was true for the most part, but Victorian society could never have tolerated the actual ending. It wasn't acceptable then for the villain—and worse yet, a foreigner!—to triumph, even if those he 'victimized' came to accept his gifts and appreciate their richness. I never needed fear losing my dear Mina, as that bloody Dutchman Van Helsing would have had us all believe at the time; in fact, I'll enjoy her company till the end of time!

"The old Count was never the devious strategist the Dutchman portrayed. He wanted to 'live' again, away from the forests, wolves, and inbred townsfolk. He wanted to be part of the new century, not a relic of the past. In his time, he was considered a hero by his people, a protector of the faith against the marauding Turks. Standards were different then; behavior that modern men label barbaric was a necessity of existence in those days. Times change, people change, and even we change, at least on the inside.

"My friend, the Count, is not what he used to be. The wounds inflicted by the Dutchman and his friends' blessed blades corrupted his blood, infected it with grave mold, and turned it into a festering ichor. His blood became your blood, and now your brain is addled too. Imagine sleeping with a rotting corpse under your mattress! You are a vampire, the Noble Undead, not some inbred ghoul!

"Like him, your mind comes and goes, lucidity mixed in with absentmindedness and dangerous obliviousness. Six centuries of existence have taken their toll on him; sometimes, he forgets what and who he is. He left us recently while visiting Los Angeles, just up and fled in the middle of the day. Now I have to find him and bring him home. A people cannot be without their king. You were unfortunate enough to cross his path during one of his less lucid periods."

The elegant vampire paused momentarily. Otis was not sure who this so-called "king" was, but he was not in a hurry to make his acquaintance again.

"Oh, don't worry, we'll catch up with him," the other continued. "Fortunately, an exchange of blood must occur in addition to the bite for the corpse to revive. I've had difficulty separating your trail from his, destroying or concealing all those mangled corpses you two have left behind. Lots of bodies under beds, if you will. You have so much to learn. Think of this new life as a beginning. It has plenty of advantages, and if you play your cards correctly, you might be around to savor them for a long time—anyway, enough for now. We've got to get moving. This neighborhood is like a maze of decrepit structures; I have no idea where I parked the car."

He walked over to the window and began to pull apart the thick curtains that covered it.

Otis screamed in mortal terror, shielding his face with his hands and backing away in a crab-like scuttle. "No, the sun, don't let it in!" he cried.

The other vampire laughed. "Oh, child, you watch too many movies. Sunlight weakens and limits our powers, but it will not kill us. Look!" He tore the drapes down, letting the early morning light flood into the little room. Otis winced and gagged once but was shocked when, after several seconds, he did not begin to burn. He looked at his new benefactor in stunned disbelief.

"I'll teach you more as we go along, my new friend. For now, call me Jonathan." With that, the elder vampire grasped Otis' clawed hand and led him out of the room and into the daylight.

RENFIELD AND THE NIGHT MURDERS

Renfield, servant of Dracula, Lord of the Undead and King of All Vampires, strutted down the cobblestoned street, his shiny black boots echoing in the afternoon air. He was impeccably dressed in a gray suit and crimson waistcoat tailor-trimmed for his sturdy frame, the vampire familiar feeling every bit as good as he imagined he looked. He breathed deep of the autumn air, tasting the heady first crisp of the approaching evening.

He'd spent the night in the cold-yet-passionate embrace of Octavia, the youngest and most recently turned of Dracula's brides. They'd developed an amorous relationship over the last few months, a relationship the King Vampire was, for now, apparently willing to overlook. Octavia resembled the Amazons of legend, tall and muscular, with long limbs and stunning features framed by flowing raven hair. She'd laughed as she crushed him to her, lifting him like a child and tossing him into the guest room bed, her strength greater than twenty strong men. Her icy fingers had guided Renfield's throbbing member inside her cold womanhood as she nipped lightly at his neck, savoring hot drops of his blood. As he shuddered and climaxed, the vampiress sliced the alabaster skin above her exposed nipples and let him drink the black ichor that seeped forth. The cold liquid set his body aflame, filling it with a strength he had never possessed.

Octavia now slept the sleep of the Undead in the moldy crypt below the weathered abbey where the nest resided. Renfield had woken in the early afternoon in time to attend to his Master's business. The Vampire King had become aware of a recent spate of murders of young women in the nearby town of Boulby, brutal killings whose perpetrator as yet remained unsolved. Renfield knew his Master was not concerned over the women's fates for benevolent reasons; rather, the massacres had scared away the crowds of young people that frequented the town at night, crowds from which the Count drew his cull. Consequently, the famished Master was in a poor mood when Renfield made his way into the large study.

"Make a trip to the Boulby coroner's office, Renfield," the Master had instructed from his seat across a large desk of stout oak, his long-nailed fingers steepled beneath his strong chin in an aspect of reflection. The walls were filled with shelves nigh bursting with books on every subject matter one could imagine, from travel and history to alchemy and witchcraft. Local papers with glaring headlines about the murders were strewn in front of Dracula, lit by squinting sunlight that snuck through the partially closed window blinds. Contrary to superstition, sunlight did not incinerate the Undead on contact, though it significantly limited their strength.

"Use the abilities I have given you to find the source of these murders, a source the local police appear unable to locate without our assistance," Dracula said, the tips of his sharp eyeteeth poking over his crimson lower lip.

"Yes, Master," Renfield said and bowed. Dracula dismissed him with a wave of his clawed hand and resumed reading.

Renfield recognized the Master's dark blood had bequeathed him a small portion of the vast abilities possessed by the Undead: greater strength, accelerated healing, night vision, and the power to cloud men's minds. Yet he suffered none of the vampires' vulnerabilities to daylight, running water, or the need to be invited into a dwelling.

He longed for the day when he could become a true immortal. Renfield knew his Master was reticent to turn him himself, but he hoped Octavia might be persuaded to give him the blood kiss in a moment of passion. Dracula would be quite upset with him for surreptitiously going around his back, but the familiar reckoned he'd have a better chance of standing up to the Master's wrath once he was a full-blooded vampire.

Renfield noted the sun was descending on the western horizon and drifting behind a patch of cumulous clouds as he ascended the marble stairs of the mortuary portico. He knocked on the stout wooden door and waited patiently until an old man in a frayed brown suit with whisps of gray hair draped across his age-spotted scalp opened it.

"Yes?" the servant asked, his teeth yellowed and decayed. The foul odor of his last meal accompanied his breath.

"I'm here to see your employer on a matter of urgent business, my good man," Renfield chattered, attempting to distract the old man.

"Are you the police, sir?" the man asked.

"Goodness, no, nothing like that," Renfield stammered. "I'm here to check in on a deceased family member," he lied.

"I'm sorry, I can't help you. We're closed to the public for the day."

"But you're not closed to me, are you?" Renfield inquired, his dark gaze seeking the man's gray eyes and grasping his psyche, bending him to his will. He felt Octavia's dark strength added to his own, enhancing his powers.

"We're not closed to you," the old man mumbled, reeling from the doorway into the foyer. Renfield slipped inside, locked the door, and guided the servant to a worn leather sofa. He lay him down and said a few comforting words in the man's hairy ears; soon, the servant was in a deep sleep and snoring.

Renfield looked around the modest room until he spied what he was looking for: a descending stairway at the back of a long walkway. The familiar sidled past chairs, desks, and bureau drawers and made his way down the brick stairs. The temperature dropped with every step, and the ambient light lessened. Renfield felt like he was descending into another realm of shadow and frost. He thanked Dracula for his ability to see in the dark as he reached the bottom.

A massive, iron-reinforced wooden door loomed in front of him. He reached out his quavering hand and pushed, thankful that the door silently swung open. He walked into a scene of horror.

The body of a thin man in medical scrubs and black gloves lay before him on the stone floor, the head brutally twisted around to face the posterior. A sluice of blood had escaped the corpse's gaping mouth and splattered the ivory tiles. The dead man's eyes were wide in a fixed gaze of terror and disbelief.

Behind the man's body rose a marble table on which rested another corpse, a young woman in clothing so torn it left little to the imagination. Her eyes gazed sightlessly into the shadows of the arched ceiling, one arm slung unceremoniously across her breast. The woman's throat was twisted and warped, indicating a broken neck.

Renfield approached, stepping over the corpse on the floor. He saw the woman's other arm rested at her side on the table, sleeved in a green sweater. Her hand, even in death, fervidly clutched a piece of dark material. Renfield touched the material and found it to be milled cloth, as might come from the lapel of a gentleman's evening coat.

"I'll be taking that back!" a harsh voice insisted, jarring Renfield from his observations. A short, lanky man in an over-sized black suit materialized from the back of the room, reaching toward the woman's hand.

"I think not, old chum," Renfield said, seizing the material from the corpse's hand and backpedaling.

The man stopped, his fingers bent in frustration, light reflecting off his gray-streaked auburn hair. Renfield got a better glimpse of the fellow. They were about the same age, in their late forties, though Renfield towered over the fellow. The man's red-veined eyes glared with malice and hatred, his thin lips twisted in a rictus of menace and scorn.

"Who are you to interfere with me, dolt? I am Dr. Jeekyl of the Physicians Academy, here to see to the proper disposal of this corpse. You don't belong here!" the man cried, spittle flying from his lips.

"It looks to me as though you were disposing of more than one corpse, no, Dr. Jeekyl?" Renfield inquired. The familiar noted a tear in Jeekyl's lapel that matched the torn material now in Renfield's hand. "Are you missing something, Doctor?"

"That silly strumpet," Jeekyl remarked. "Why do they always have to resist? It's so much easier when they don't resist."

"I take it you're behind the recent murders, Dr. Jeekyl?"

"Oh, I suppose I might as well admit it; it's not like you're leaving this room alive," Jeekyl threatened. Renfield silently girded for battle.

The doctor withdrew a vial from his coat and held it before him, removing the lid. "I was obsessed with the duality of man and sought to discover the source of evil within, the inner devil that causes sin. I studied the ancient texts and grimoires and created a serum that can distill pure evil."

A sulfur miasma flowed from the vial into the air, assaulting Renfield's nostrils. He recognized the scent of dark magic akin to the eldritch energies running in his veins.

"I thought I could control it, you see—thought I could collect and remove the evil, leaving behind a pure man of stout moral principle," Jeekyl said, his voice uncertain, his eyes haunted. "But the serum made the evil stronger. It took over, inflaming my baser instincts, remaking me into a fiend with hellish desires—desires I satisfied every night on young women. I lost control.

"The police interrupted my time with this young miss. It wasn't until I'd returned home that I noticed the mess she'd made of my coat. I was here to tidy up loose ends, but the old coroner wouldn't listen to reason, and I was forced to deal with him. Just as I am forced to deal with you, Mr...?"

"Renfield, my good man, servant of Count Dracula," Renfield finished Jeekyl's sentence.

"Mr. Renfield, then." Jeekyl upended the vial over his lips and swallowed. "Cheers!"

Renfield quickly understood why Jeekyl wore loose clothing. The small man grew in height and width, towering over Renfield as his suit filled to near-bursting with slabs of potent muscle. Jeekyl's brow expanded and became atavistic; coarse black hair covered his scalp and square jaw and filled the space between his eyebrows. The man became stooped, his long arms dragging on the floor like an ape's. When the serum had worked its miracle, and the transformation was complete, Jeekyl stood before him, a nightmare being that could only have been conceived by the mind of a lunatic.

"What have you done to yourself, Jeekyl?" Renfield asked in astonishment.

"My name is not Jeekyl—it's Hyde!" the monster roared through a black maw of blunt brown teeth, leaping over the table with surprising agility and dislodging the female corpse. He seized Renfield by the shoulders in a steel grip. Renfield struggled, employing the unnatural strength he had absorbed from the Master and Octavia, but Hyde was too strong. The madman was slowly crushing him.

Renfield headbutted Hyde, breaking his nose. The monster reeled and released Renfield. The familiar capitalized on Hyde's distraction, smashing the fiend with a right cross to the jaw that could buckle steel.

Hyde barely flinched.

The monster backhanded Renfield, sending him flying across the room. He smashed into the wall, crumpling stone, and slid to the cold floor. Stars clouded his vision as he tried to stand, accompanied by a sharp pain in his torso indicating broken ribs.

In desperation, the familiar reached out with his otherworldly senses, touching the blood connection he shared with Octavia. She had just begun to rouse with the coming evening when Renfield touched her mind.

I'm in a bit of a spot, dear, he spoke to her as he stood. *Would you mind saving me? I'd be eternally grateful.*

He sensed her cloudy, sleep-befuddled mind. *Tired. Just woke up,* she said.

I understand that, dear, he communicated, barely dodging a haymaker from Hyde that shattered the wall where his head had been. *But if you don't come and come quickly, there won't be enough of me left to fill a thimble.*

I'm coming, she cried. He felt her presence fill the night, her arrival on ebony wings as inevitable as the tide. But Hyde didn't know about Octavia. The fiend was focused on mutilating Renfield, in the same manner he butchered the women. Hyde seized Renfield by the neck, clamping off his throat and making it impossible for him to breathe. Renfield's feet left the floor as the fiend lifted him from the ground with one impossibly strong hand.

Renfield pried and battered at Hyde's wrist but could not free himself. He felt the pressure of the vise grip increase, threatening to snap his neck. His vision fogged.

"It will all be over soon, dear boy," Hyde madly cooed in Renfield's ear. "Stop fighting me; it only makes things harder."

I'm here. Renfield heard Octavia's voice inside his oxygen-starved head. *Invite me in.*

Renfield tried to speak but had no air. He knew he was about to die and resorted to desperate tactics.

The familiar bit down on the hand that throttled him, nascent fangs burying into Hyde's thick skin and drawing blood. The fiend roared in agony and released Renfield.

"Come in!" the familiar shouted, his voice hoarse from the damage inflicted by Hyde.

The room suddenly filled with a crimson mist that whirled and revolved around itself like a small tornado. The fog became a startling woman of Amazon proportions outfitted in a sleeveless crimson corset and dress highlighting her great muscularity. She moved with superhuman speed and force, lifting Hyde into the air like a child's plaything though the fiend had to weigh over twenty stone.

Octavia's eyes beamed in the cellar dimness as she slammed the fiend across the table, shattering his spine. Hyde could only gasp and stutter, his nervous system wrecked, as the vampiress sank her long fangs into his neck and bled him dry.

Octavia ran her tongue lasciviously across her lips and teeth when she was finished, savoring the last of Hyde's blood.

"It never gets old, Rennie," she said, licking a last drop of blood from her finger. "It's almost better than sex...almost." Octavia winked playfully at him.

The behemoth shrank, his body returning to the Jeekyl form. Jeekyl looked up sightlessly into the ceiling, just at the dead woman had earlier. His throat was a gory mess.

Renfield staggered to her side. Octavia caught him and held him easily.

"Easy there, little man. It looks like you were having a tough go of it," she noted, looking at his frazzled appearance.

"Actually, I had just drawn first blood," Renfield boasted, pointing at the blood on his lips.

Octavia smothered his mouth with her icy lips, inflamed with bloodlust, kissing him with a passion he had never experienced. She tossed Jeekyl's corpse from the mortuary slab with a flick of her wrist, indicating the now-open space with a flash of her eyes.

"Oh, you are such a randy devil," he said.

"I've been thinking of starting my own branch of the family, maybe moving to London," Octavia confided. "New blood, you might say. You interested, little man?" she asked enticingly, her voice low and sensual, her breath sweet and hot, prickling his much-abused neck.

"Oh, most definitely, my sweet," he said. They made passionate love and exchanged bodily fluids throughout the night. When morning came, Renfield slept the sleep of the Undead in Octavia's strong arms, awaiting the coming of night.

DRINKING BUDDIES

He knew he had run out of time when his hands became keen onyx claws that shredded the leather steering wheel cover of his car.

He had raced out of work when he found out about the accident, hopping in his car and flying across the city far over the speed limit to the hospital. Beth had been hurt after being rear-ended by a drunk driver in a large pickup truck. His heart sank when he arrived at the emergency room and saw her bloody face and pale arms connected to intravenous tubes.

Luckily, she had not sustained any serious injuries—head wounds tended to bleed a lot, making things appear worse. Once he found out she'd been stabilized, he tore off home like the Devil himself was on his heels.

And in this case, the Devil was.

The moon was full when he turned the corner toward home, amber rays silvering the leaves of nearby trees. His heart raced, threatening to explode in his chest as he felt the physical changes overwhelm his body. If he could just make it inside, he could secure himself in the cellar. The stone basement had served him well for *years now, ever since the ancient curse of the Kohler family metasta-sized in his veins and turned him into a raging animal.*

He chastised himself for not making it home in time to lock himself away before the transformation began. He tore the driver's-side door off by accident as he pulled into the driveway, desperately aware that he would never make it down into the secure cemented room in his cellar before it was too late. He struggled to make it up the walkway, but the animal surfaced and took control before he could open the front door. He went around the side gate to the back-yard instead, leaping over the white-painted wooden fence and onto the adjacent grassy plains.

Agony coursed through every inch of his body as it reformed, the pain beginning in his spine and spreading down through his finger-tips and toes. It felt like he was dying and being reborn again. Every transformation he endured was as painful and physically traumatic as the first one had been years before—it never got any easier. Joints popped, and bones broke, lengthening and reshaping into an enor-mous lupine form. Coarse black hair sprouted from the pores of his skin and covered him in thick sable fur; fangs filled his black-lipped maw and claws erupted from long fingertips. His body filled with asymmetrical slabs of writhing muscle. He howled, a primordial cry combining unimaginable pain with unfettered rage. He fell onto all fours as the transformation continued, tears in his eyes, bloody saliva dripping from his maw. Despair filled his soul as the hope of a normal life was again stripped from him.

When it was over, he stood on two digitigrade feet, an apex predator in search of prey.

"Here's blood in your eye," Leo announced, lifting his beer mug from the table in a toast, ambient light reflecting off his long fingernails.

"Is that supposed to be funny?" Bill replied, lifting his mug in a toast nonetheless.

"More ironic than anything, I suppose."

The two mugs slammed together with a resounding clang! Both men took a drink.

Bill set down his mug, his thick brown mustache now a beer stache. He let out a small belch and leaned back, resting his meaty hands on his belly.

"This beer is watery," he commented.

"It's better than what I have a real thirst for," Leo replied.

Bill ignored the statement. "You take me to all the finer establishments," he dryly added as he looked around at the clientele of the Sidewinder Bar, an array of hookers, bikers, dopers, and parolees. The bar's red lights highlighted a haze of smoke in the air. The state ban on indoor smoking was not enforced here.

"It's a compromise location, halfway between your house and my apartment. Plus, if either one of us gets hungry, there's plenty here to eat. The owner is one of my brethren; he's got a special cleanup crew on call in case any accidents happen—and trust me, they do. These guys get rid of everything. I mean everything." A vulpine smile lit Leo's face. Even in the red light, his face was too pale, almost clown white. Contrasted with his thick, raven black hair and eyebrows, the pallor of his skin became even more pronounced.

Bill was visibly upset. "I thought that was the whole point of this thing we're doing...not to have to eat like that anymore." His voice quivered slightly at the end of his sentence.

"Hey, big guy, calm down, okay? I was just kidding," Leo

attempted to reassure his companion. "We've done this before; you know everything will work out fine."

"It's just that, well...things are so much better now than they were before. Beth is thrilled with not having cellar duty three nights a month. I'm finally in control of this thing, you know. I'm in control of my life for the first time since my eighteenth birthday." Bill's voice trailed off. "We're even thinking of having kids. I've done some research, family tree online and all. This...this thing, this family curse only seems to hit the firstborn male every other generation. My kid could be normal. It would be safe."

"At least you got a family, buddy. The first thing I did was kill mine after I came out of the tomb. My bloodline tends to feed on family and loved ones first. I went through a wife, three kids, and a nosy neighbor in record time. It would have been nice if the old gal who turned me had schooled me a bit before she drained and buried me."

"The person who turned you into what you are...she didn't teach you about what she was...about what you would become?"

"Nope. And I wouldn't exactly call her a 'person,' if you catch my drift. I guess I must have been some kind of accident. When I came back looking for her, she went ballistic, trying to shove a table leg through my chest. I found out later that we tend to be a solitary race, with rules and borders and specific hunting zones. She considered me a rival predator in her territory. Bitch." Leo took a drink from his glass.

"Well, my Beth has been great. I don't think I could have managed without her."

"You got yourself one heck of a dame there."

Bill scowled. "Dame?"

"Hey, I got turned in the fifties; what do you want from me?"

"That poofy hairdo you have looks more late eighties than Eisenhower era."

Leo ran a long-nailed hand up through his styled, blow-dried mop. "I fell in with the heavy metal/power ballad crowd for a while there. I was trying to look like the lead singer from Whitesnake. Dames used to go for that stuff—not so much anymore. My problem is I'm always one or two decades behind time. I'm working on it, trust me. If I were you, I wouldn't be commenting on other people's hair. I've seen what happens to you on a full moon."

Bill grimaced and looked down at the table, his lips tight. Leo observed the big man's reaction and sought to redirect the conversation.

"Look, I'm sorry. I'm just a dumb walking corpse with no memory of what it's like to be human. I don't know what I look like because I can't see myself in a mirror. You're still human most of the time; things are different for you. You're cursed. I'm infected and dead. But you can lead an everyday life now. We've been through the hard part already. We know what works now," Leo said, looking directly at Bill over the table. "What works for both of us."

THE WOLFMAN STALKED OVER THE GRASSY PLAIN, MOONLIGHT *reflecting off his black pelt, the hot exhaust of his breath steaming rapidly out of his muzzle into the cold night. Although the beast stood over eight feet tall, he was hunched over, the sheer mass of his upper torso bending his spine so that his front paws apishly dragged on the grass. Patches of frayed clothing that had covered his human body still clung to his massive lupine form. His keen nose pointed into the*

air, sifting through the various scents of the plains. A stiff, icy breeze blew down from the mountains, ruffling the beast's thick hair coat.

The man deep inside the creature resented the hunt, as always. And, as usual, he had little say in the matter.

On the nights of the full moon, his will became subservient to the rage of the wolf demon within, a rage that boiled over and became physically manifest. The beast was in full predator mode, having caught fresh blood odor in the air when he vaulted the fence. The wolfman sprinted across the plain with unnatural speed, chasing the source of the blood trail on the wind, the reluctant man inside in tow.

The creature stopped near a copse of oak trees, his senses confused. He could still smell the spilled blood, even hear the heavy pumping of a deer's heart. But there was another more menacing odor masking the blood trail, a scent that reeked of old death, decay, and mold. The wolfman's brilliant yellow eyes found the deer splayed out in the grass adjacent to the marshlands. The animal was held in place by a pale human male in dark clothing; its neck bent back at an unnatural angle.

The man had planted his face in the deer's neck and appeared to be drinking from it. Bright blood trickled down the man's lips and onto the thick grass. The wolfman could sense an unnatural black aura surrounding the man, a miasmic cloud of necrotic magic laced with sulfur. He noted that the deer's attacker was not breathing.

The man inside the wolf was shocked and wanted to sprint away, but the beast recognized a challenge to his territory. The dead man had stolen his prey. The wolfman's liver-spotted lips pulled back, exposing rows of deadly teeth dripping saliva. The creature covered the distance to the deer within a heartbeat, a snarling tornado of unnatural rage and force, raising a clawed hand high to strike.

"I just don't want to return to the way things were before. I don't think either of us enjoyed those days," Bill said, taking another sip of beer.

"I've got to admit, Bill, sometimes I miss the old days. The hunt, the kill, the spike of delicious endorphins into the bloodstream. Some people need to go missing, if you know what I mean," Leo stated almost wistfully, his eyes scanning the other bar patrons, a slight smirk on his lips.

"Killing draws attention, remember? You told me all those stories about the old days, the torch-wielding mobs, the church people?"

"Oh, I remember them. I can't count the number of times I was this close to having a silver crucifix shoved up my...well, you can imagine. If you ask me, there are still too many church people around today."

"That's a matter of opinion. At least these church people aren't trying to kill you nowadays," said Bill.

"I'd like to see them try. And, technically, I can't be killed, only destroyed, you know—technically, I'm already dead."

"You catch my drift. We discovered together all those months ago on the plains that we're good for each other. I can lead an almost normal life now and have a family. You can exist without drawing attention to yourself. Things are better now. We can fit in."

The wolfman's claw descended but never reached its intended target. A pale hand of immense strength rose with serpentine speed and latched onto the beast's forearm, halting the blow.

The dead man rose from the still-breathing deer with fluid grace, his mouth a bloody maw. Twin fang teeth descended from his upper jaw, nearly as long as the wolfman's. The beast was momentarily bewildered as the man grasped him and raised his massive frame into the air without effort.

The confusion was short-lived as the dead man tossed the wolfman fifty feet across the plain. He landed hard on his head, a fall that would have killed a mortal. The wolfman shrugged it off and bounced to his feet, boundless fury filling his bestial heart. The man inside the beast screamed in protest, sensing an ancient evil emanating from the dead man. The beast ignored his more civilized half and roared a primal challenge.

The dead man accepted. His eyes flashed red in the night as he launched himself at the wolfman. The two collided with tremendous force over forty feet in the air and proceeded to tear into one another in an explosion of eldritch fury. They fell to the earth, a virtual hurricane of fangs and flying claws, blood spraying in all directions. It was an incredible display, a magnificent primordial battle. Wounds were inflicted, tissue torn, bones shattered, only to heal and reshape within seconds. Neither combatant appeared to tire.

It ended some twenty minutes later with the dead man on top, his fangs buried deep into the wolfman's neck. The beast raged as he felt his lifeblood vacuumed out, weakening as his foe became stronger. He frenzied and reached forward with his large snout, biting the meat around the dead man's shoulder. Icy ichor seeped into the beast's mouth, a taste both nauseating and exhilarating.

A strange power flowed through that dark blood, so much energy that the beast gagged and released his bite. The dead man withdrew his fangs and fell back into the grass, a shocked look on his face.

The beast inside the wolfman receded, and the man surfaced. He gained confidence as the beast retreated and used the opportunity to take control of their mutually inhabited body. Hair fell off in heaps, limbs shortened, the spine straightened, and fangs and claws receded. As he sat in the grass, the man realized that he had returned to his human form, despite the moon still being full and bright. He regarded the dead man, who was now sitting up just across from him.

He noted that his opponent's clothing was now as shredded as his own. The dead man's fang teeth had receded, and his hell-red eyes had softened to a calm blue. His skin, though still pale, bore the beginnings of a flush. The wolfman found his opponent's outdated eighties haircut amusing and had to suppress a snicker. The dead man had a confused look, similar to the one the wolfman imagined was stamped on his seconds before.

Not knowing what else to say, the wolfman said, "Hi, I'm Bill." He extended a now-human hand.

The dead man appeared hesitant at first but eventually offered his long-fingered right hand.

"Leo," the dark man said.

And so it began.

"You're lucky it ended where it did. I was just about to kick your furball ass," Leo said.

Bill swirled the beer in his mug, looking skeptical. "Oh really?"

"Yeah, man, don't you know about all my superpowers? I move like the wind; I've got the strength of twenty men and am practically impossible to kill."

Bill was unimpressed. "You're like Bela Lugosi. You've got the strength of a dozen heroin addicts."

"Smartass. I can see in the dark too. 'No small power at night,' like Van Helsing said in the book."

"Seeing in the dark makes it easier to play with yourself inside your coffin, I bet."

Leo's jaw dropped slightly. "How did you know...I mean, never mind... I'm glad you've never tried to pee on me when we wrestle. I know wolves are territorial too, but that would take things too far."

"I'm going to pee on you the next time for fun since you mentioned it. By the way, I've never had the guts to ask before, but I've just got to know—do you sparkle in the sun, oh immortal one?" Bill grinned mischievously.

"Oh, that's real funny, dogboy. No, I don't sparkle. I'm like a woman in heat...I glow. Bitch."

Bill chuckled and changed the subject.

"So how come this has never happened before? I mean, I've never heard of it or read about it. Werewolves and vampires drinking each other's blood? Surely it's been done before."

"Probably so, but remember, each race is secretive and somewhat isolated. Most wolves and vamps are just out for themselves and not interested in passing along helpful information. Who knows, maybe they all still enjoy eating people. It's funny. I get all high and moral and try substituting animals for humans in my diet, and what happens? I run smack dab into your dumb hillbilly ass. Who would have thought?" Leo said.

"Your black blood gives me the strength to control the change. I'm no longer subject to the whims of the full moon. If I need the beast, I can call him, but I make a choice, not him," Bill said.

"And your animal blood takes away the worst of the hunger, allows me not to have to hunt every night," Leo replied. "I could have used your blood that first night I crossed over. It would have saved me a lot of grief."

"That's why we get together every month now, on the first night of the full moon, and take out our aggressions on each other. With no wood or silver involved, nobody gets hurt. That's the game plan. We're good for each other, Leopold. We fill gaps."

"I told you not to call me by that name. It dates me. Nobody names their kids 'Leopold' anymore. My name is Leo, just Leo. And it is nice to see you lighten up a little for once."

As the two men spoke, a motley crew of tattooed bikers stormed into the bar and promptly began to harass the patrons. They poured beer onto people's heads, fondled women, punched out some rivals, and threw others out the front door.

When the bartender attempted to intervene, he was summarily smashed over the head with a bottle of vodka and left unconscious on the floor. The apparent leader of the crew— a huge bald man wearing a black leather jacket and sporting prison tattoos on his bull neck—stepped over the sprawled bodies and placed his fingers in his mouth, whistling to get attention. He addressed the bar patrons in a loud, confident voice.

"My pals and I just got out of prison and need a new place to settle, so this place is Berserker territory from now on. Anybody got any complaints?"

Leo looked over at Bill, a mischievous grin on his face.

"I don't know about you, buddy, but I don't plan on ever coming back here. The caliber of clientele is too low, even for me. I say we have a little fun while we're here. You know, live a little. It's not like anybody here will talk to the cops—they've all got arrest warrants. I'll call the owner and have him send the cleanup crew when it's over. Of course, first, I'll apologize for being in his territory without being invited."

Bill looked skeptical, frowning. Leo continued to prod.

"Did you ever hear the story of the fox and the scorpion?"

"No."

"Okay, well, I'm not going to bore you with it now, but basically, what it comes down to is a zebra can't change its spots. At heart, we're both still killers. We eat people. We can go cold turkey for a while and play the co-existence game, but sometimes you must let the beast out of its cage. If you don't, it will take over. I promise we'll have time for our little Ali-Frasier fest afterward. I just want to get a little warmed up."

Bill was still unconvinced. As he began to reply, a husky biker walked up behind Leo with an aerosol can and lighter. He addressed the bald leader, a smirk on his fat face.

"Hey, boss, look at this poser and his frilly hairdo. What say I see how loud he screams when I set it on fire?"

Bill threw up his hands and smiled.

Some people really are that stupid. He let the animal out, still attached to the tether of his human will. He was halfway transformed, ruining yet another set of clothes, when Leo ate the fat biker's face.

UNCHAINED: A TALE OF TATJANA AND LORENA

> *"Where there is love, there is life."*

> — *GANDHI*

The hot summer sun beat down relentlessly on Tatjana as she lay stretched out atop the stone rampart, sweat slick on her furrowed brow, her auburn hair hanging in wet clumps across her face. A Santa Ana wind kicked up the sand from the ground below her, clogging her nostrils with acrid dust that collected in the back of her throat, choking her. Her once-pale skin was now bronze from countless hours spent working outside, preparing for this moment. The dry air was pregnant with the harsh inevitability of battle and suffering.

She looked through the binoculars and saw a pack of at least twenty slavering ghouls assembled on the sandy crest of a ridge adjacent to the abandoned estate, an estate she had recently appropriated. Sunlight reflected off the fiends' slick

313

yellow fangs as they writhed and snarled, impatiently awaiting the commands of their leader.

Tatjana located Lord Liverbelch amongst the horde. He stood a foot taller than any other flesh-eaters, like a tree amongst ferns. Unlike his naked soldiers, the alpha ghoul wore tattered black trousers that cut off just below his knees and were slick with blood and decaying scraps of human entrails. Liverbelch's scarred upper torso was covered in thick, dispro-portionate slabs of muscle, reminding Tatjana of the Hulk comics she read as a child. The fiend's elongated arms ended in long-fingered, razor-sharp black claws capable of carving metal.

Unlike his hunched, apelike followers, the alpha ghoul stood straight and tall. His arms were crossed over his chest, affecting a lordly demeanor as he stared back knowingly at her, his yellow predator eyes wide and brimming with menace. Tatjana got the odd sensation that Liverbelch could somehow see her expression, even at this distance. He spoke, and though Tatjana could not hear his words, she could read his lips.

"I will eat your eyeballs, lackey," the fiend said, his black, mottled lips curling into a sadistic grin.

We'll see about that, asshole.

Liverbelch's words motivated her to the task at hand. Tatjana looked to the sky, attempting to gauge the hour. She missed the reassuring presence of a watch on her wrist, but watches and batteries were in short supply since the Ghoul Apocalypse had devastated the planet several years ago. In fact, practically everything worthwhile was in short supply, with supply chains and freedom of movement seemingly a thing of the past.

Misery and death, though—there's no short supply of either, that's for damn sure.

She estimated another hour before the sun set on the western horizon.

Tatjana sat the binoculars to the side and performed a quick weapons inventory. When satisfied, she looked one last time at the courtyard and the weathered mansion behind it. She recalled the day she first arrived here after long weeks on the road, the sense of relief it brought her gazing upon this relic of the American frontier. The sliding metal gate had fortunately been left open, allowing her to pull her dirt-covered SUV into the courtyard. The dry grass had been littered with the abused skeletons of the previous owners, the bones bearing the marks of the sharp ghoul teeth that had stripped the skin and flesh from them. It had been tedious work, long hours spent collecting all the bones and properly burying them, but she had felt compelled to do so, a symbolic gesture of sanctity and sanity in a wicked, insane world. And it gave her added resolve for what she was about to do.

She pulled her AR-15 from its camouflage bag. The weapon was immaculately clean and well-oiled, the black steel barrel reflecting in the sunlight as he leveled it at Liverbelch. The arrogance in the ghoul's eyes turned to fear as she drew a bead on him and fired a .223 round at his head.

Choke on that, fucker!

The flesh-eater dodged the round with inhuman agility as the sound of gunfire echoed in the late afternoon air. The hapless ghoul behind Liverbelch was not so lucky—the hollow-point round struck it in the forehead and exploded out the back of the apish skull in a hailstorm of blood, bone, and brain matter. Now nearly headless, the ghoul's corpse tottered like a kid's punching bag, then sagged to the ground, causing the other ghouls to scatter in panic.

Liverbelch roared angrily, turning to his horde and waving them forward with pale arms. The ghouls screamed in primal fury as they flooded down the embankment in a roiling sea of mottled, fish-white flesh.

Tatjana moved her focus to the front of the pack. A lithe male led the way, long, loping strides pushing it ahead of its flesh-eating compatriots. For all she knew, the flesh-eater might have been a good man once: a businessman who attended church and was part of a fantasy football group; a storekeeper who gave discounts to seniors and free ice cream to kids on Sundays; or, perhaps, a fireman, cherished by his community for his acts of daily heroism, someone who loved his family and was loved in return. That man was gone, his red blood turned black by the infectious ghoul venom saturating his veins. Now all that remained was a turbo-charged, cannibal killing machine intent on eating her viscera.

The ghoul was a dead man walking.

She aimed center mass and fired. Countless hours of range practice paid off. A massive hole erupted in its chest, a kill shot that shredded its heart. The corpse stiffened and fell, its gangly limbs tangling with those of nearby ghouls, causing them to careen off-course into a writhing pile. Tatjana skillfully dispatched three more flesh-eaters with headshots before they could right themselves.

The other ghouls crossed the intervening distance with incredible speed, all their attention focused on her. She was able to kill another with a shot through the neck, severing its spine, before they began scaling the wall. The creatures' claws scrabbled noisily on the stone and punched handholds in it. With hatred for these putrid cannibals and the devastation they had wrought upon her world flooding her frame, Tatjana aimed down and blew the closest ghoul's head into bloody ribbons. She adjusted her aim slightly and sent another round through the snarling mouth of an adjacent ghoul. The dead fiend fell and crushed the creature climbing beneath it. She picked off an older ghoul with long, stringy white hair that was close to breaching the parapet, and then she was fighting for control of the weapon as a slavering, black-lipped female wrapped its claw around the barrel.

Tatjana feared she would lose the rifle, the ghoul's strength far exceeding her own. Still, she had the advantage of the high ground, and the creature was off-balance. Tatjana could muscle the barrel end back toward the fiend's chest. She fired, and the ghoul fell as the round tore through its torso.

She pointed the barrel at another howling face, but the trigger clicked empty when she squeezed.

Fuck! Fuckfuckfuckfuck!

Tatjana felt unwelcome panic rear in her. She stifled it, regrouped, and used the stock as a club, smashing in the face of a ghoul that had surmounted the wall and sending it back over the edge in a spray of black blood. Other ghouls bellowed in triumph as they hoisted themselves onto the rampart. Grasping claws tore the empty rifle from her hands; Tatjana realized she needed to make a tactical retreat.

She lowered herself from the railing with practiced precision and remarkable dexterity, making a crunching sound when her feet hit the ground. Her thick-soled, heavy boots ignored the shattered glass she had scattered there, but the ghouls were not so lucky when they landed. The sharp, multi-colored fragments shredded their bare feet, causing them to howl in distress. Some fell and cut themselves further. In short order, however, they recovered and resumed pursuing the woman prey.

Tatjana dashed across a pre-selected pathway in the grassy courtyard. Water was hard to come by these days, and it had been difficult keeping the grass even relatively green, requiring endless trips to the still-functioning well. Fortunately, her efforts proved prescient as she neared the porch, pivoting sharply and triggering a hidden lever of stretched bamboo she had painstakingly constructed and concealed.

Two panels of punji sticks exploded from the ground, the camouflage of leaves and grass covering each scattering in the hot air. Four ghouls were immediately impaled, the small wooden stakes piercing lungs, hearts, mouths, and brains. Two died instantly; the other two clung tenuously to a pain-filled, immobile existence, mewling pathetically and spastically twitching as their brackish blood pooled on the thirsty ground.

Tatjana did not rest on her laurels and instead sought to press her advantage. Using the impaled ghouls as cover, she retrieved a semi-auto pistol from a hip harness and drew down on the forefront of the ghoul pack. The creatures had been caught off-guard by the appearance of the spiked trap and stood stunned, looking on in disbelief at their dead and dying colleagues. Tatjana took out three more creatures with headshots, the hollow point rounds shredding the ghouls' brains.

Then Lord Liverbelch appeared out of nowhere, moving almost too fast for Tatjana's eyes to follow as he ran between the panels of his impaled underlings, dodged the fallen bodies on the ground, and loomed large in front of her.

"Miss me?" he asked in a dry and raspy voice as he smashed his knobby fist into her chest. The blow would typically have killed a human, the inhuman force behind it shattering the sternum and sending bone into the heart. As it was, Tatjana was thrown back, her Kevlar vest absorbing much of the impact.

She hurtled across space and slammed through the heavy wooden front door of the mansion, coming to rest on her back. Tatjana coughed blood as she painfully pulled herself to a sitting position; she could feel at least one broken rib.

Liverbelch leaped onto the porch like a pouncing jaguar and

surged through the shattered front door, assuming a dramatic pose with his arms and hands flung wide.

"You and all your esteemed company are welcome, Lord Liverbelch. Enter freely and of your own will!" the ghoul lord proclaimed in a faux theatrical voice. In between wheezing breaths, Tatjana marveled at the fiend's audacity. Then again, perhaps such confidence was justified; his fiends had practically subjugated the planet in a short time.

Liverbelch dropped the dramatics and spoke in his familiar guttural voice, a tone akin to nails scratching on a chalkboard.

"Those words were meant to be somewhat ironic, Tatjana. I mean, given your unique personal history," he said.

More of the ghouls surged into the foyer. Tatjana pumped the remaining pistol rounds into the first creature, stitching its torso with black holes. The ghoul was tough, and Tatjana's bullets hadn't struck a vital organ. It snarled and ignored the pain.

As the creature lumbered toward her, claws outstretched, viscous black blood dripping from its stomach and chest wounds, Tatjana gained her feet. She deftly reached behind her right shoulder and grabbed the handle of the katana sword strapped to her back, a relic of her time with the Cadre. She retrieved the katana and slashed the ghoul across the neck, the keen edge of her steel blade slicing through the monster's bleached flesh and unleashing a geyser of dark blood. The ghoul futilely sought to stanch the wound with its claws; it staggered and finally collapsed, wheezing through its ruptured larynx as it died.

The next fiend used the fallen ghoul's body as a launching ramp, leaping high into the air, its claws raised above its hairless head to shred Tatjana's flesh. She pivoted and thrust the katana through the ghoul's chest, the blade smashing through the breast bone and impaling the black heart before erupting out the back. The ghoul's eyes widened in disbelief, pupils dilating as its autonomic nervous system failed. Tatjana slung the corpse aside as more fiends entered the house.

She parried their claw swipes with thrusts of edged steel, severing fingers and limbs. Still, she was gradually being forced back across the living room, relinquishing precious ground. She kicked a small wooden table in the path of a rampaging ghoul, but the fiend smashed it into kindling and surged toward her. She ducked a savage swipe of its claws, and the backslash of her sword opened up its stomach, its moldering entrails bursting forth like maggots from rotten sausage. A foul miasma of shit and sulfur filled the stale air, gagging her and nearly causing her to vomit. Tatjana's blade had sliced through the ghoul's intestines, revealing bits and pieces of human remains, the foul remnants of its last gluttonous meal. The fiend tried unsuccessfully to push its intestines back into its ruptured belly as its brethren continued attacking.

Outside, the sun had begun its steady descent on the horizon, nestling amongst a ridge of purple and amethyst clouds. Tatjana wondered briefly at the clouds' sudden appearance; the sky had been clear not long ago.

Lorena? No, that's impossible.

She pushed the thought aside. Through the haze of battle, she saw Liverbelch sniffing with his pointed nose near the massive grandfather clock on the wall, looking for something. Tatjana knew from bitter experience that ghouls possessed olfactory senses equal to bloodhounds. Apparently satisfied, he grasped the heavy heirloom by the base and tossed it aside as if it were a child's toy, revealing the hidden metal door that led to the basement. Liverbelch's eyes beamed in triumph.

"Well, well, what do we have here? Is this what you were so fervently defending?"

Panic gripped Tatjana's heart, and a bottomless pit opened

in her stomach. There was still too much time remaining until sunset. Time enough for Liverbelch to strip her of what was most precious, that without which her life became meaningless. Desperation lent her strength, and Tatjana redoubled her efforts. She hacked down with the katana, burying it like an ax in the nearest ghoul's neck. As the creature fell, she pulled the blood-slick blade out and thrust it through the skull of another, bone parting like butter beneath her finely honed steel. Black blood flew through the air, saturating her body.

The tide of the battle had seemingly turned; the cannon fodder ghouls realized they could not stand before the berserker whirlwind that Tatjana had become. A male flesh-eater fled for the door, only to be plucked from the ground by Liverbelch's outstretched claw. Malice burned bright in the ghoul lord's unforgiving eyes as he ignored the struggling fiend in his hand and focused his cruel gaze on his remaining underlings.

Liverbelch closed his claw, crushing the ghoul's throat and breaking his neck with an audible SNAP! The message was clear: the female hunter may be bad, but he was far worse. Stay, and die a noble death. Run, and suffer a miserable coward's death.

The ghouls followed their lord's implicit commands and marched toward their inevitable deaths beneath Tatjana's steel. While she massacred his ghouls, Liverbelch inspected the door's digital lock.

"Oh, this modern security is much too complex for an old gentleman like me to figure out. I'll just have to resort to other tried and true methods."

The ghoul dug his claws into the door frame, warping the metal. The huge muscles of his torso writhed and contracted as he strained. With a mighty roar, he tore the heavy door from its frame, rending metal with his enormous strength. The mansion shook when he dropped it to the floor.

"I wonder what's down here?" he asked facetiously.

Tatjana cut the last ghoul in two, its upper body sliding off its base in a gory spray of dark fluids and slimy intestines. Then she stared daggers at Liverbelch, her eyes twin balls of hate.

"You don't scare me, Liverfuck! You're already dead, you prissy little ponce; you're just too stupid to realize it!"

She hurtled across the room, the black blood of her victims dripping from her limbs, the katana held high with both hands over her head. She planned to chop his head down the middle and cut his devious tongue in half.

Liverbelch seized her by the throat as she descended, picking her from the air as he might fruit from a tree and holding her off the ground effortlessly with one clammy hand.

"Such language. I'm going to have to tear your tongue out for that!" he said, his fetid breath washing over her like a miasmic cloud.

Tatjana choked, her wind cut off. She fought the instinct to panic, recalling her Cadre training, and was still able to thrust the blade into Liverbelch. The angle was off, and the steel buried into his stomach rather than his heart.

The ghoul bellowed in anger and pain, thrusting Tatjana against the wall and bouncing her head off it, leaving a cracked imprint in the drywall. White-hot pain seared her, blinding her. She beat her fists against the iron grip that held her and battered her feet against the wall, but she lacked leverage and couldn't free herself. Her limbs felt leaden, exhaustion over-whelming her.

Liverbelch used his free claw to rip the sword from his belly and throw it across the living room, burying it to the hilt in the opposite wall. The alpha ghoul tore the Kevlar vest from her torso and slashed her across the upper chest, shredding her shirt and leaving bloody furrows in her skin.

Tatjana screamed in frustration, feeling the poison in Liverbelch's claws seep into her veins and arteries and begin to pump throughout her body. The claw venom was how the flesh-eaters procreated, gradually transforming the host into a damned creature neither dead nor alive. The disease would enter her brain within an hour, and she would be forever lost to an insatiable lust for flesh; she would become another cannon fodder ghoul in Liverbelch's army of the damned.

That was, if he didn't kill her first.

She brought her knee up into Liverbelch's stomach wound, doubling him over in pain and causing him to put her back on the ground.

"Fucking bitch!" he roared as he tossed her down the wooden cellar stairs like a doll. Tatjana could barely raise her hands in front of her face to cushion the impact as she tumbled down, breaking her left thumb as her forehead smashed into a stair. She went ass over teakettle more than once before coming to rest on the dirt ground. Stars flared in her head, and the room spun around her.

Memories flooded her battered brain, unbidden and unfiltered. She recalled the early days of the Uprising, or Ghoul Apocalypse, when Liverbelch rose from whatever dank tunnel or crypt he'd secreted himself in for the past few centuries. The ghoul had picked a most opportune moment: The pandemic had decimated the world, flooding hospitals with virus-infected patients and morgues with corpses, seeding distrust and panic amongst the living. Human turned on human in an escalating blame game as once-strong countries faltered and fell, consumed by dissension from within. World supply chains ground to a halt as countries hoarded their natural resources; famine, hysteria, and disease reigned.

And then the ghouls struck in force: powerful, efficient machines of mayhem, killing many, turning others with their foul venom, all at the behest of Lord Liverbelch. The fiend's timing could not have been better. The world governments quickly fell beneath the onslaught.

As a race, humans turned out to be relatively weak. It wasn't long before many joined up with the flesh-eaters, serving as vassals hoping to be converted into full-fledged flesh-eaters.

The East Coast went up in flame and riot, a slaughter subsequently dubbed The Night of Torn Throats. Tatjana remembered the chaos: New York streets were littered with torn corpses as the ghouls streamed up from the sewers and train tunnels and engaged in mass slaughter. They swarmed vehicles in the road, tearing open locked doors to get to the helpless meat bags inside, and ran down panicked pedestrians like lions culling zebra herds. Wild-eyed fiends crawled up buildings walls and swung from street lamps, leaping from structure to structure with uncanny agility. Blood flooded the gutters as the flesh-eaters fought over kills, then joined in decorating shops and apartments with wormy strings of entrails that hung like obscene Christmas ornaments. The ghouls ate until they could eat no more, lying comatose amongst piles of skin-stripped skeletons, their mouths besotted in blood and round bellies filled to bursting.

Tatjana packed everything she could take from the house and hit the road in an SUV, heading west. At the New Mexico border, she had tried to go down a side road, hoping to avoid detection. But, as night fell, she had been pinioned by a flood of lights and surrounded by armored vehicles. The vassals surrounded her car, rifles pointed at her face as they extracted her.

Her heart beat so rapidly that she feared it would burst from her chest. She tried to answer their questions as best she could: who she was, where she was going, which ghoul lord she served. Then they made the mistake of opening the rear hatch and pulling out the heavy black box lying within, a box that might be mistaken for a coffin by the casual eye.

She tried to warn them, telling the overcurious vassals that the box contained her recently dead mother, whom she was taking to New Mexico to bury in a family plot. She tried to save them, but they wouldn't listen. They kept pestering her with more inane questions.

She could see it in their eyes, an inquisitiveness she was incapable of satisfying, a need to prove to their masters that they were doing their job and were thus worthy of elevation.

The vassals made a fatal error, firing into the box, shredding it and the heavy metal lock. And then the screaming started as the box's occupant erupted out in a shower of shattered wood and clinging soil...

A grating noise brought her back to full consciousness. Liverbelch sauntered slowly down the stairs, his weight causing them to creak with each step. The ghoul dragged his long nails across the wood railing as he descended, gauging long rivulets into it and leaving curled slivers in his wake. He threw a switch at the bottom and turned on the weak overhead lights, revealing a stark basement with a dirt floor. Two concrete pillars spaced ten feet apart supported the roof.

"The lights are for you, hunter," he said sarcastically. "My night vision is perfect. I've got to hand it to you; you held out far longer than I imagined. Actually, I shouldn't be surprised—you were a monster hunter, a trained Cadre member, long before I changed the world. I've eaten my fair share of Cadre assassins over the years—most were middle-aged men, their flesh dry and bitter, better-suited for dog food than my refined palate. Yours will be different—young and sweet; it will scintillate my taste buds before tantalizingly sliding down my throat. You and your lover have killed so many of my brethren. You represent the final, fading flame of resistance to my authority. Now, I'm going to snuff you out, and I'm going to enjoy it. Immensely."

Something electric and weighty seemed to gather in the air. As her blood flowed remorselessly and pooled into the soil floor, Tatjana sensed a comfortable, familiar presence stir beneath her, giving her the strength and courage to continue fighting. If she could just hold out a little longer...

She pulled out the curved combat blade secreted in her boot

and sliced Liverbelch, catching him off-guard and reopening the wound in his stomach. As the ghoul doubled over in pain, she rammed the blade up under his throat and out his mouth, breaking his teeth. Black ichor flew in the stale air as Liverbelch tried to remove the knife from his throat, but the blade was buried deep, and his big claws could not grip the tiny handle.

The stench of his foul breath billowed over her as they grappled. Tatjana blasted the ghoul across the jaw with brutal elbow strikes, sending chipped fangs and saliva flying from Liverbelch's maw. She head-butted him and immediately regretted it, knowing she had caused more damage to herself than the thick-skulled flesh-eater. Reaching into a black leather belt case concealed by her shirt, Tatjana retrieved a wire garrote and expertly looped it over Liverbelch's head, twisting and pulling tight with the thumb handles. Planting her knee in the fiend's back, she exerted her full strength as the razor wire bit into the ghoul's throat, causing more of the flesh-eater's blood to flow.

The alpha ghoul gagged as the wire tore into his larynx but then did the unexpected: instead of panicking, he slipped his elongated fingernails under the wire, one on each side of his neck, slicing into his own flesh as he did so, and slashed the wire. Tatjana fell off as the garrote was destroyed but somehow landed on her feet. She used the last of her strength to deliver a front kick to the ghoul's stomach wound with her steel-toed boots, feeling Liverbelch's ribs break under the impact. The ghoul screamed in agony and frustration as he staggered back. Then he laughed hauntingly, reminding her of the eerie sound effects of the carnival spook shows she'd attended as a kid. The ghoul pulled the blade from his throat and crushed it in his claw, tossing it aside like garbage. Liverbelch was no common ghoul, she reminded herself; he was the oldest, the fountainhead of the disease ravishing the world, and infinitely more powerful and dangerous than the cannon fodder fiends he commanded. He stood straight and tall, acting as if none of her attacks had caused any lasting damage. Liverbelch delivered a left cross that blasted across Tatjana's jaw, breaking it, and sent her flying across the room. She hit the wall hard, indenting the drywall again, before sliding down in a beaten heap.

She sat against the wall, broken and bleeding internally, listening to the ghoul lord rant as his venom filled her veins like snake poison. The pain was so bad that her lungs seemed permanently stuck in the exhale position.

"You hurt me, woman," Liverbelch said. "More than any mortal ever has. Now, I'm going to hurt you. You'll watch as I destroy that creature you love so much, which you would sacrifice your very existence for."

Tatjana flinched as Liverbelch snapped off a wooden piece of stairway railing, creating an impromptu stake.

"I've dealt with her breed many times over the years. Such powerful beings, nigh demi-gods, are practically invincible at night. But during the day, as long as the sun remains in the sky, they are inert—helpless. That's why she needs you. Not because she loves you, but because she needs a protector when she is vulnerable. You are her Renfield, nothing more, on the same footing as the lowest of my vassals. And you have both outlived your usefulness. She's a relic of a bygone era when my people were nothing but slaves to her kind. Now, she's the last of her bloodline, making way for young and vibrant people. My people."

Tatjana's eyes flashed to the undisturbed soil in front of her. The ghoul noticed the slight movement.

"Dash all hopes of salvation, hunter. Though you delayed me longer than I had anticipated, there's still time for me to end this. The sun yet hangs stubbornly on the horizon, refusing to go down. Until it sets, she cannot stir."

Liverbelch bent to the ground and sniffed it like a blood-hound. After a few dust-raising whiffs, he seemed pleased.

"Soil from Styria, the land where she died and was resur-rected. She's right here," he said with a wicked grin, black blood staining his yellow fangs as he pointed a long-nailed finger at the ground in front of him and sank it into the knuckle. "Now, hunter, your little rebellion ends."

The alpha ghoul raised the stake above the ground. Tatjana closed her eyes, unable to watch.

Then, as the spike descended, the ground exploded in a shower of dirt and rock as a pale figure shot out in a grim parody of birth. The thing from the ground roared a primal scream that shook the house to its foundations. It tackled Liver-belch, and the two became engaged in furious supernatural combat. Their movements were too fast for the human eye to follow as they tumbled across the basement like a tornado, destroying anything in their path: blows were struck, bones were broken, and black blood flew in the semi-obscurity. At one point, they careened through one of the concrete pillars, exploding it into dust. Tatjana wondered if the roof would hold. It was a glorious battle, the likes of which would never be seen again.

Then the fight ended almost as quickly as it had begun, with the thing from the ground holding a bloody and broken Liverbelch aloft in one magnificent claw. Tatjana saw that the female creature was now a hybrid mix of a bat, wolf, and dragon, with dark leather wings that ran from its wrists and attached to its lower back. The head was canine and furry, with black lips pulled back from bloodless gums, exposing amaz-ingly long eye teeth. The she-creature's pointed ears twitched as it turned its vulpine face and gazed upon Tatjana with seething sapphire eyes, eyes the dying woman recognized and loved with all her being.

The she-creature cast no shadow on the ground.

"End it," Liverbelch croaked, his windpipe nearly closed off by the titanic force of the savage grip that encircled his throat. His dark blood streamed from the holes the monster's claws had torn in his neck.

The creature complied, thrusting the long, dagger-like fingernails into the open stomach wound and wrenching up. Intestines and organs flowed out as the claw dug into the ghoul, shattering his breastbone and shredding his heart. The sounds reminded Tatjana of her childhood when her father returned home from hunting in the nearby woods. She had cringed and covered her eyes as he gutted game on the kitchen table, the nauseating sounds of flesh ripping and bones breaking assaulting her young ears as a miasma of noxious gases flooded her sensitive nose.

The creature continued upward, slicing into the twitching ghoul's throat and ripping out the spine. Liverbelch stopped moving, and the light went out from his eyes. The monster let the ruptured, deflated body fall to the floor, the bulbous head lying at an unnatural angle, the black tongue lolling out the mouth.

Then, in a heartbeat, the feral creature was gone, replaced instantly by an attractive young woman in a bloody white blouse. Her ashen face was calm as she approached Tatjana, concern stitching her brow.

Tatjana reached out to the familiar angelic woman.

"Lorena," she gasped.

"My love, what have they done to you?" Lorena took the dying woman in her strong arms and held her close.

"You rose, despite the daylight. I didn't think that was possible. The lore..."

"To hell with the lore! That's why it's just lore, love—feckless, idle musings passed down from one generation of bored shut-in researchers to another. They could never understand what love can do, what we can do. I felt you, just above me, fighting and protecting me—I summoned clouds to dampen the daylight and let you know I was aware of your peril. I love you, my constant protector. My brave guardian."

"That's what spouses do," Tatjana said, blood dripping down her chin. Her shattered jaw was swollen. "That's how I roll." Her breath came in broken shudders as her eyes closed.

Lorena acted swiftly. She plunged her teeth into the wound created by Liverbelch's claws and sucked out the venom, spitting it across the room. Then she slashed her breast with her fingernails and held Tatjana to it like she might a child. She whispered in the dying woman's ear.

"I know this is not what you wanted, but I can't be without you. You can yell at me later—you always do."

She pushed Tatjana's slack mouth to the dark ichor that dribbled from the wound in her breast. After what seemed like an eternity, Tatjana sipped the blood, taking in half a dozen mouthfuls. Then she died, her heart ceasing its rhythm, but only a mortal death. Lorena held her in her arms, whispering comfort to her and holding onto her soul.

The vampire dug a hole for them to sleep the day in, anticipating the coming night. She would return her lover's soul to a now-immortal body. Night—when they would be reunited for all eternity.

ABOUT THE AUTHOR

The world was just a tad dull and unimaginative for a young Scott Harper growing up in 1970s' Southern California. He found a creative outlet in the world of Marvel Comics, following the monthly adventures of Iron Man, Hulk, and Captain America. One day he happened to watch a television showing of Dan Curtis' *Dracula* starring Jack Palance; Scott was bit by the vampire genre and never turned back. His taste in comics veered toward the Marvel monster titles, fervidly devouring each issue of *The Tomb of Dracula* and *Tales of the Zombie*. Influenced by these works and great authors such as Bram Stoker, John Steakley, and Marv Wolfman, Scott's unique writing style combines horror and fantasy elements with superhero action. His stories have been published in various speculative fiction markets, including *Space and Time*, *Weirdbook*, and *Best New Vampire Tales*. When not writing, Scott spends his time reading, working out at the gym, adding to his model collection, or walking his two dogs. He lives in California with his wife and son.

You can follow him at www.Scottharpermacabremaestro.com

CPSIA information can be obtained
at www.ICGtesting.com
Printed in the USA
BVHW042348130223
658470BV00005B/74

9 781953 112477